Dear Reader,

This has been a tumultuous time for me. Cousin Michael and I have ended our correspondence, after he grew angry at my repeated attempts to determine his true identity and said he would no longer write.

His silence has nearly destroyed me. I never realized how much I depended upon his advice until he withdrew it, along with his friendship. But how could he abandon me, especially with the school in need right now? You see, my next-door neighbor, Mr. Pritchard, is determined to sell his property to a man who will build a racecourse there, and I cannot have such a scandalous enterprise so close to my girls. I don't know where to turn. My cousin had helped me when it seemed that Mr. Montalvo had had a similar aim, but now that I am *truly* in trouble, he is nowhere to be found.

To make matters worse, someone else has come back into my life who has me quite flustered. You see, my friend, I was once in love with a young man, and it ended very badly. I did something unforgivable to him. Now I find, with his sudden renewed interest in me, that my feelings for him are as deep as they once were. But can I trust his reasons for pursuing me? He should hate me for what I did. So is he courting me because of some secret, belated need to revenge himself on me? Or is he telling the truth when he says that he has put our past behind him?

Oh, how I wish I could turn to Cousin Michael for advice on this matter. But I fear that is no longer a choice—even my most imploring letters go unanswered. I am on my own . . .

Or am I? I simply don't know what to think!

Desperate for answers,
Charlotte Harris,
Owner and headmistress of
Mrs. Harris's School for Young Ladies

"Anyone who loves romance must read Sabrina Jeffries!"
—*New York Times* bestselling author Lisa Kleypas

Praise for *New York Times* and *USA Today* bestselling author Sabrina Jeffries and her delightfully enticing series, THE SCHOOL FOR HEIRESSES

LET SLEEPING ROGUES LIE

"Consummate storyteller Jeffries pens another title in the School for Heiresses series that is destined to captivate readers with its sensuality and wonderfully enchanting plot."
—*Romantic Times* (4½ stars)

"Scandal, gossip, greed, and old enmities spice up the pot in this fast-paced sexy romp that bubbles over with Jeffries's trademark humor and spirit. . . . Sparkling dialogue, stirring sexual chemistry, and an engrossing story."
—*Library Journal*

BEWARE A SCOT'S REVENGE

"Irresistible. . . . Larger-than-life characters, sprightly dialogue, and a steamy romance will draw you into this delicious captive/captor tale."
—*Romantic Times* (Top Pick)

"Exceptionally entertaining and splendidly sexy."
—*Booklist*

The School for Heiresses titles are available as eBooks

ONLY A DUKE WILL DO

"Bringing together a bold heroine and a scarred hero while incorporating political scandal into a tightly woven romance, Jeffries once again proves her mettle as a first-rate Regency author."

—*Publishers Weekly*

"Marvelous, powerful, and sensual. . . . Jeffries fans will devour this treat."

—*Romantic Times*

"Politics and passion prove to be a particularly potent combination. . . . Expertly crafted and delectably sexy."

—*Booklist*

NEVER SEDUCE A SCOUNDREL

"Jeffries delivers lively lovers in an entertaining, sensual historical romance."

—*Booklist*

"Jeffries carries off this cat-and-mouse game of mutual seduction so cleverly that you'll be turning the pages at lightning speed. . . . Warm, wickedly witty, and brilliantly plotted, this is a must for anyone who just wants a fast, intelligent read."

—*Romantic Times*

Sabrina Jeffries

Wed Him Before You Bed Him

POCKET BOOKS

New York   London   Toronto   Sydney

Pocket Books
A Division of Simon & Schuster, Inc.
1230 Avenue of the Americas
New York, NY 10020

This book is a work of fiction. Names, characters, places, and incidents either are products of the author's imagination or are used fictitiously. Any resemblance to actual events or locales or persons, living or dead, is entirely coincidental.

First Pocket Books paperback edition July 2009

POCKET and colophon are registered trademarks of
Simon & Schuster, Inc.

For information about special discounts for bulk purchases, please contact Simon & Schuster Special Sales at 1-866-506-1949 or business@simonandschuster.com.

The Simon & Schuster Speakers Bureau can bring authors to your live event. For more information or to book an event contact the Simon & Schuster Speakers Bureau at 1-866-248-3049 or visit our website at www.simonspeakers.com.

Front cover and stepback illustration by Alan Ayers
Hand lettering by David Gatti

Manufactured in the United States of America

10 9 8 7 6 5 4 3 2 1

ISBN 978-1-4165-6082-1

To the English teachers who encouraged my writing:
Dr. Anita Tully, Dr. Rosanne Osborne, and Ms. Saluja

And to my son's wonderful teachers, too many to name,
who have made such a difference in our lives—
thank you for hanging in there.

Wed Him Before You Bed Him

Chapter One

Richmond, England
November 1824

*C*harlotte Harris, headmistress and owner of Mrs. Harris's School for Young Ladies, sat at her desk and reread—twice—the pleading letter she had composed to Cousin Michael, her anonymous benefactor.

Then she tore it up. What was the point of writing him, when every letter she sent to his solicitor was returned unopened?

She wiped her clammy hands on her skirt. He had to know what desperate straits the school was in—he knew everything. And until six months ago, he had always told her everything he knew. But after she had pressed him so hard about his identity, he had ended their correspondence. There had not been a word from him since.

The hollow fear that gripped her so often these days made her stomach clench. All right, so perhaps he had good reason to be angry at her. She *had* agreed not to press him about his anonymity.

Still, how could he abandon them after all this time? He had been part of the school's inception fourteen years ago. Indeed, without him there would *be* no school. She would probably still be languishing as a teacher at the school in

Chelsea, dreaming of the day when she could open her own institution governed by her own curriculum and her own rules.

Now their idiot neighbor, Mr. Pritchard, was about to sweep it all away. He was rumored to be on the verge of selling Rockhurst, the estate adjoining the school's property, to the owner of a racecourse in Yorkshire. She could just see it—rough men flocking to bet on the races, spilling onto the school's lawn and accosting her girls.

How could Cousin Michael stand by and let it happen? He owned this property. Did he not care if she was forced out?

She sucked in a breath. That was what hurt the most—the possibility that he was letting it happen so he could gain higher rents. From the beginning, her rent had been lower than that charged by other landlords in Richmond, and now, with property values in the area soaring, it was ridiculously low. In all these years, her mysterious cousin had never raised it. Why, she wasn't sure. Perhaps because he realized she could only afford a modest increase?

That was especially true now that enrollment had fallen off, fueled by the scandals dogging her pupils in the last year. If rumors about a possible sale of the property next door proved true, it would make matters even worse.

She would have to fight it. When she had thought that Rockhurst was about to be bought months ago, she and her friends had come up with several good ideas for thwarting Mr. Pritchard's plans. They could set up a petition to the licensing board again, or—

"Beg pardon, madam."

She looked up to see her personal footman in the doorway. "Yes, Terence?"

"Lord Kirkwood is here to see you."

A pounding began in her chest. David? *Here?* No, that could not be. What possible reason could he have now that his wife, a former pupil of the school, was dead?

She thrust her shaking hands under the desk to hide them from her too-perceptive servant. "Are you sure it's Lord Kirkwood?"

"The one who married Miss Sarah Linley, right?"

She nodded. "Did he say what his visit concerns?"

"I asked, but he told me it was private." Terence, always protective of her, crossed his arms over his meaty chest. "So I told him that men aren't entitled to privacy when they visit a girls' school."

"Terence!"

His lip twitched. "And he said *he* wasn't in the habit of giving up his privacy for the amusement of impudent footmen."

She gave a rueful laugh. "That does sound like something he would say."

Terence looked perplexed. "You know him, then? I didn't think he had ever been here, not even after he married Miss Linley."

"I know him socially through Lord Norcourt."

That was both an overstatement and a vast understatement of her association with David Masters, the Viscount Kirkwood.

She was fortunate he was even civil to her on the few occasions they met in society. Considering the great wrong she had committed against him and his family years ago, she would not fault him for giving her the cut direct.

Indeed, she had been afraid of his doing exactly that when she had attended poor Sarah's funeral months ago.

But despite knowing how uncomfortable her presence would make him, Charlotte had felt compelled to make an appearance.

She and David had exchanged the barest of greetings, though he had been surprisingly cordial for a man who must despise her. Why, just remembering the summer of the Great Debacle made her cringe.

So what on earth had brought him *here?* She could not imagine a more awkward situation. In all these years, she and David had never been alone together, never spoken of what she had done to him.

"Should I send him packing?" Terence asked.

For a second, she was tempted. But something important indeed must have brought him to visit the woman who had once wronged him so horribly. "No. Just show him in."

After Terence left, she checked her appearance in the mirror to make sure her auburn curls were not too badly askew and her face not too pale. Perhaps it was foolish, but she wanted to look her best before *him,* of all people. She scarcely had time to smooth her skirts and pinch her cheeks before he was ushered into her office, bringing her face-to-face with the man she had nearly married so long ago.

Pasting a smile on her lips, she walked forward with her hand extended. "Lord Kirkwood. How nice to see you again."

His eyes flashed with some hidden emotion. "Charlotte." He took her hand and pressed it briefly before releasing it.

Charlotte. Not *Mrs. Harris,* but *Charlotte,* spoken in the husky tone that had made her heart flip over when she was eighteen and he nearly twenty.

No, she must not think of that. Those days were gone forever, lost in the pages of their pasts. Time and her own mistakes, as well as his, had changed them both irrevocably.

Nothing proved that more than the dusting of gray at his temples, the lines of care worn into his brow. At thirty-seven, David was still uncommonly handsome, with the aggressively masculine features of a man who had always commanded attention, from the sharp blade of his nose to the cleft in his chin. His coloring reminded her of the forest—his eyes a leafy green and his thick, wavy hair the dark brown of walnuts and bark and rich tilled earth.

And his body . . .

She turned sharply and hurried behind her desk, afraid she might blush. At eighteen, she had noticed his body in the vague way of a virgin unfamiliar with sensual delights. But now, as a widow of some years, she noticed it with an awareness bordering on pain.

Since Sarah had been dead for six months now, he wore half-mourning, with some white blended in with his black. Ebony trousers encased the lean hips and muscular thighs of a man who kept himself fit, while his finely tailored morning coat of jet black saxony showed off his broad shoulders. And she could well imagine those large gloved hands, one of which gripped the handle of a leather satchel, playing over a woman's body with the surety of experience . . .

Heavens, she had to stop this. Terence was eyeing her from the door with rank curiosity, obviously hanging about to make sure David did not harm her.

She frowned at him. "Thank you, Terence. You may go."

With a grunt the man left.

"Rather a rough sort for a footman," David said dryly.

"He used to be a pugilist."

"Why on earth would you hire a boxer as a lady's footman?"

Bristling at the criticism, she said, "Because his skills are more useful to a woman going about town alone than any niceties of behavior." She forced a smile. "But I'm sure you didn't come here to discuss my servants, Lord Kirkwood."

Gesturing to the chair before the desk, she took her own seat, needing something massive between them to keep her mind from wandering to her unwelcome attraction to a man who surely loathed her.

Yet he did not *look* as if he loathed her. He watched her steadily as he sat down with the easy motion of a man very comfortable in his surroundings. "Actually, I've come bearing good news."

Good news? From *him*? "And what might that be?"

"In going through Sarah's things recently, I discovered a handwritten codicil to her will. In it, she left a substantial sum of money to your school."

Had she heard him right? "I don't understand."

"She bequeathed some of her fortune to the school."

"Your wife, Sarah. Bequeathed me money."

"Not you," he corrected with a lift of his eyebrow. "The school."

"Yes, of course, the school. But . . ." She thought of Sarah's snide remarks, the way the woman had behaved at the last tea she'd attended, the seeming contempt Sarah had always shown her fellow pupils. "But why?"

He shrugged. "She always admired you and thought fondly of her days here."

"Your *wife*, Sarah, thought fondly of her days here."

"I believe we've already established that the woman under discussion is my late wife, Sarah," he said dryly.

No doubt he found her response insulting. "Forgive me. It's just that . . . she never seemed to . . . that is . . ."

"I know Sarah could be . . . difficult. But I believe she secretly held you and the school in high esteem."

Charlotte muttered, "That was a secret buried so deep as to be invisible." Then she groaned. "I'm sorry. That was rude. It is just such a shock to think that Sarah had any particular regard for me *or* the school."

"Well, the truth of the matter lies in the size of her bequest." He leveled her with a gaze of dark intent. "It's thirty thousand pounds."

Charlotte sucked in a breath. "Oh my word. Are you sure?"

A faint smile touched his lips. "I wouldn't be here if I weren't." He removed a sheaf of papers from his satchel and placed them before her. "I took the liberty of having our family solicitor draw up a legal document that fully sets out the particulars she gave in her codicil. Feel free to have your own solicitor examine it."

Still unable to take in the news, Charlotte just gaped at the formal-looking papers with the name of some legal firm stamped at the top.

"Before you read it, however," David said, "I should warn you that there is one . . . er . . . string attached to the bequest."

Charlotte's gaze flew to his. Of course there was. This had begun to seem like a fairy tale, but life was never so tidy. Sarah had been a malicious little thing, much as Charlotte hated to admit it of any of her pupils. "What sort of string?"

"Sarah wanted the money to fund a new building to house the school. To be named after her, of course."

"Of course," she said mechanically, though her mind was elsewhere, trying to make sense of this. "Forgive me, sir, for I know this will sound insulting again, but . . . well, your wife didn't even give money to the charities we support. I can't imagine why she would bequeath a fortune to build a new school."

"She actually donated a great deal to charities anonymously," he said smoothly. "She was far more philanthropic than anyone knew."

The picture he painted of Sarah was so odd as to be suspicious. Charlotte hated to speak ill of the dead, but she had to know what was at the bottom of this. "Again I must beg your pardon, but I thought that Sarah's primary interest was cards, not charity." That was the nicest way she could put it.

Even so, he flushed. "Yes, well, that is true. But that was a function of her desire to rise in society. She gambled to be accepted among a select group of ladies. And their acceptance came at a high cost."

"Yet she still had enough money to leave the school a huge sum?"

He flashed her a thin smile. "Sarah's fortune was substantial. Why do you think she and I were forced to elope six years ago? Her father was none too happy to see so much money go to a 'titled wastrel.'"

The conversation was dancing very near to their own situation years ago, and that was the last thing she wanted.

Yet she could not ignore his opening. "Speaking of Sarah's family, how do *they* feel about this bequest?"

"They don't know of it, and I prefer to keep it that way

as long as possible. It would pain her brother in particular to learn that Sarah gave money to your school rather than to her siblings. She and Richard were quite close, and she left him only a token amount. I hope I can count on your discretion."

"Of course," she said.

He cleared his throat. "About the building . . . I understand that the school's situation is rather unsettled just now. That Samuel Pritchard means to sell Rockhurst to a fellow who runs a racing establishment."

"You know Mr. Pritchard?"

"We've met in society a time or two."

She leaned forward. "Do you know if the sale is certain? It will be the ruin of the school if they build a racecourse next door."

"I can see how it would create difficulties for you," David said. "But surely you could sell this house and property to build the school elsewhere. That would solve your difficulties, wouldn't it?"

"For heaven's sake, no. Aside from the fact that I prefer this location, I do not own the house *or* the property."

He did not seem surprised to hear it. "Then who does?"

Charlotte stared down at her hands, wondering what David would think of her strange relation. "To be truthful, I do not know my landlord's real name. When he offered the property for my use, it was with the condition that I allow him to remain anonymous. He . . . er . . . communicates with me using an alias. We go through a solicitor, a Mr. Joseph Baines."

"Norcourt's solicitor?" David asked.

"Yes, actually." Anthony Dalton, Lord Norcourt, was one of David's closest friends and had married Madeline, a former teacher from Charlotte's school. "Anthony and I had a good laugh about it when I learned that he and Cousin Michael have the same solicitor. Do you know Mr. Baines?"

"In passing." His eyes narrowed. "Cousin Michael. Sarah mentioned him once. *He's* your anonymous benefactor?"

"Yes, though he has been virtually nonexistent of late."

"A pity," he said, rather curtly. "Now, about your situation with Mr. Pritchard . . ."

But she did not hear anything else, caught by an astonishing thought. What if David was Cousin Michael? Might that explain the sudden supposed "bequest" from Sarah to build a new school?

No, it was impossible. Her "cousin" had approached her through Mr. Baines only four years after the summer of the Great Debacle and her hasty elopement with Jimmy Harris. He had said that her late husband had mentioned her interest in opening a girl's school and that he wanted to help her achieve her dream.

At that point, David's public humiliation at her hands would have been fresh in his mind. He would have hated her virulently. He would certainly not have helped her start a school.

Besides, she had seen the solicitor's name at the top of David's document, and it was not Joseph Baines.

"Charlotte?" David prodded. "What do you think?"

She blinked, then sighed. "I am afraid I must once again beg your pardon. I was so caught up in considering this bequest that I missed what you said about Mr. Pritchard, my lord."

"My lord?" His eyes darkened. "Surely we've known each other long enough to be less formal." His voice softened. "You used to call me David."

"That was before I destroyed your life." She cursed her quick tongue.

"It was a long time ago. We're different people now," he murmured, clearly unwilling to speak of it. He forced a smile. "Beside, thanks to my wife's unusual codicil, we'll have to learn to deal with each other. We're practically going to be in each other's pockets for the next few months."

She caught her breath. "I beg your pardon?"

"You really *weren't* listening to what I said." His tone turned wry. "I'll make it brief, so as to hold your attention. Sarah's bequest is contingent upon one thing—that I oversee the building of the new school. So you see, Charlotte, we'll have plenty of time to become reacquainted."

Chapter Two

⁓∞⁓

$\mathcal{D}$avid wished to God he'd never started his masquerade as Cousin Michael. His heart was thundering so loudly he was sure she would hear, and it took every ounce of his will not to tell her the truth.

But that wasn't possible. The only way he could set right the school's dicey situation was to reenter her life as himself, without her knowing of his alter ego.

Still, he could tell from the widening of her pretty blue eyes and the paling of her peach-tinged cheeks that he'd shocked her. Was that good? Or did it bode ill for his scheme?

Hard to tell. Charlotte had always had a knack for throwing him off balance, even as children, when she'd done such unorthodox things as climb trees in her pinafore and ride her pony bareback. Despite their years of correspondence, he never knew quite what to expect of her.

This was going to be so bloody difficult, even harder than the six months of mourning he'd endured so far, the six months of not writing to her, of not being sure of her situation. If he could have waited the full year to see her, he would have, but matters had become too dire with Pritchard for that. So he'd settled for waiting until he went into half-mourning, when society would find an association between him and a pretty widow less scandalous.

Now he had to pretend that he didn't know every difficulty she'd had with the school to date. That he had no clue about how she fretted over it. That he was completely unaware of how his wife's suicide had added to Charlotte's problems by rousing every scandal ever discussed about the school.

Because telling her he was Cousin Michael was out of the question. As illogical as Sarah's leaving money to the school must seem to Charlotte, the fact that he'd been playing a role with her all these years would seem even more so. She would demand to know why he'd set out fourteen years ago to help a woman he'd had every cause to hate. And then he would have to reveal the truth—that it had started out as a diabolical plan to revenge himself on her.

It didn't matter that his desire to destroy her and her little school was long gone, because the bones of his plan were still in place. Pritchard was determined to get his due, no matter who or what it destroyed. So David had to fix the abominable mess he'd created before she found out.

Unfortunately, the close call with that Spanish fellow Diego Montalvo, who had pretended to want to buy Rockhurst earlier in the year, had shown that David could no longer manipulate matters from afar as Cousin Michael. He needed more control, and that meant ending his masquerade.

Horrible as it had been, Sarah's death had given him the opportunity. He would step in as himself, inventing a legacy funded out of the money he'd made from investments through the years. No more "cousin," no more letters of advice.

No telling Charlotte the truth, either. It would devastate her to realize that her friend "Cousin Michael" had sowed the seeds of her destruction; then she would balk at letting him help her.

After losing his fight to save Sarah from herself, he refused to watch another woman drown because of his mistakes. He couldn't in good conscience let Charlotte lose her school, her only source of income, in a trap of *his* making. That meant persuading her to see sense. Knowing Charlotte, that would be bloody difficult.

Especially with her staring at him as if he'd just sprouted horns. "Why would Sarah want *you* to oversee the building of the new school?" she asked.

"Have you forgotten my interest in architecture?"

"It is one thing to have architecture as a hobby, sir. It is quite another to design an entire building."

Her dismissiveness made him bristle. "What Sarah knew—and you don't—is that my interest in architecture is more than a mere hobby. I worked very closely with architect John Nash in the building of my town house, and I was responsible for most of the renovation of Kirkwood Manor. You wouldn't recognize it now."

"I am sure I would not," she mumbled, with a fetching blush that staggered him.

As easily as that, he was catapulted back to the summer of his parents' house party and a handful of damned sweet kisses. Good God, if she continued blushing like a school-girl whenever he alluded to their past, he'd have trouble keeping his hands off her.

He stifled a curse. He would have trouble with that regardless. She was still a beauty and after all this time, his blood still raced at the sight of that softly bowed lower lip and that wealth of red curls. Even her mature face and figure only made him want to throw her down on her desk and ravish her.

But he was still in mourning for a wife he'd chosen badly, still drowning in the guilt of his own mistakes. An affair with Charlotte would only make that worse. He'd stupidly given her his heart once—he wasn't fool enough to do so again.

Not that he *had* much of one anymore. He'd survived these past few years by packing it away, and he wasn't about to pull it out so she could stomp the dry-rotted thing into dust.

"The point is moot, in any case," Charlotte went on, jerking him back to the matter at hand. "I can't build a new school on property that doesn't belong to me."

"Then buy property elsewhere and build the school there." He held his breath. He had advised that in letters, but she'd ignored him. So he'd refrained from writing, praying that once he reestablished their connection and convinced her to trust him, she would more easily turn to him instead of her "cousin."

He had to convince her to move the school before she was evicted. She didn't know how close that danger was. And he couldn't tell her, or his whole house of cards would come tumbling down.

"You assume I could afford such a thing," she said. "Even with the bequest—"

"Didn't you raise a nice sum at that charity event last spring, where that magician performed? If you couple that with a reasonable mortgage and Sarah's money, you can purchase property and have plenty left over to build a new place."

She arched one eyebrow. "Have you any idea how much it costs to build near London these days?"

"It doesn't have to be near London," he said irritably. "There are schools all over England."

"Yes, but none with this one's reputation. And I don't want to leave Richmond. My friends are nearby, and having the girls near town means better opportunities for education. Unless Mr. Pritchard's vile choice of a tenant puts me in a situation where I have to move, I intend to continue here."

She wouldn't continue here long, because the property didn't belong to Cousin Michael. It belonged to Pritchard. David had a secret lien on it that allowed him to collect the rents, but the lien ran out in eight months—scarcely enough time to build a new school.

Confound it all, why hadn't he invented a legacy big enough for her to buy property wherever she pleased?

Because he hadn't thought she would insist upon remaining close to town. And because he'd known she would be suspicious enough of the amount as it was.

"You're not thinking ahead, Charlotte. One day your cousin is sure to raise your rent beyond what you can pay, and then what will you do?"

A tiny frown wrinkled her brow. "Perhaps . . ." She brightened. "What if I were to buy the property from Cousin Michael?"

His gut twisted. "Are you sure he would sell it to you?"

"No." A smile touched her lips. "But I can be very persuasive when I want."

He knew that only too well. Unfortunately, she would be dealing with Pritchard, who couldn't sell the property because it was entailed. "You'd still have the problems with your neighbor's shenanigans at Rockhurst."

She sat back with a frown. "Yes. There is that. Though I might have some methods for mitigating that."

He knew her methods, and they wouldn't work. Pritchard wanted this property back the second the lien was up. "You really would be better off trying to buy and build elsewhere."

"But I can't afford—"

"What if I were to help you find a property close to town that you *could* afford? A place where you could build the school exactly how you want?" He could subsidize *that* without her knowing. He'd simply make a private arrangement with the seller.

"Why would you do that?" Charlotte asked, her eyes narrowing.

She was every bit as skittish as he'd expected. "Because I mean to honor my late wife's wishes." Considering how much damage his wife had done to the school's reputation, surely he could be forgiven for using her memory to counteract it. "Sarah clearly had some reason for giving you this money. The least I can do as her husband is try to finish the task she set for me."

Surely eighteen years had sharpened Charlotte's good sense. He'd just have to keep dangling that thirty thousand pounds in front of her. If he had to, Cousin Michael would raise her rents to force her out.

"I tell you what, Charlotte—why don't you write your cousin and see what he says about selling? In the meantime, I'll bring you a list tomorrow of local properties for sale. We could look at them, talk to the sellers—"

"I can't. Tomorrow is the meeting for the London Ladies Society."

"Ah yes, one of the charitable organizations Sarah mentioned you're involved in."

"She participated in precious few, and even when she did, she complained about our spending so much time with them." Charlotte's auburn eyebrows drew together in a frown. "Are you *sure* she left money to my school?"

He clamped down on his irritation. "It's in that document I gave you. Have your attorney look over it."

"I will, don't worry."

"If you don't have an attorney, I can suggest—"

"I have an attorney of my own, for heaven's sake," she said defensively. "What sort of fool do you take me for?"

"I was only pointing out—"

"Yes, you were always good at that, weren't you?" she snapped. "Pointing out. Suggesting. Bullying. Well, no one shall bully me into moving this school until I am absolutely certain it is necessary—not you, not Pritchard, not anyone. I am not the same fool I was at eighteen, David Masters, and I can handle my own affairs without the help of you or any other man!"

And just like that, the past crashed down between them, as palpable as a stone wall.

He fought for calm. Bad enough that the blow she'd administered to his heart and his pride half a lifetime ago still hurt, probably more so today, because she was here in front of him. But must she persist in thinking the worst of him *still*?

Not that it mattered, as long as he could fix his mistake. They might have killed whatever had been between them in those heady days, but he could still offer her his help, even his friendship. "I'm sure you're a very capable woman," he bit out, "and I have no desire to force you into anything that doesn't suit your purposes."

Mortification turned her cheeks a fetching pink. "Forgive me, I should not have spoken so bluntly." She rose. "I am grateful to you for bringing this matter to my attention, and honored that Sarah would offer me such a legacy. But before this goes any further, I will need to have my attorney examine the papers. When he is done, I will consider all the possibilities and ramifications and let you know my decision. That will take time."

"How much time?" he demanded.

"I cannot say. But I will keep you informed."

Anger boiled up in him. So she meant to stall him, did she? The hell she would.

She gestured to the door. "Now, if you will excuse me, my lord . . ."

Her deliberately formal "my lord" was the last straw. He shot to his feet. "By all means have your attorney examine the document." His eyes narrowed. "But I'll be here again tomorrow. And the next day. And the day after that, until you decide. I won't dishonor Sarah's memory by letting this matter drag on."

Setting her shoulders, Charlotte opened her mouth, but he had a trump card.

"Of course, you can always refuse the bequest, and I'll understand if you do. You never did like me much."

She flinched at his allusion to how she'd publicly humiliated him that blasted summer. Good. Now that he'd made it clear he would take her refusal as a repeat of what had happened years ago, her guilt might prevent her from heaping insult upon injury.

She sighed. "Give me two days to have my attorney look at it. I have my meeting tomorrow, but assuming everything is in order with the documents, you may come the day after, and we will discuss how to proceed."

"Thank you." Fighting to hide his relief, he bowed. "Until then."

As he strode from the room, he knew he'd only won a small skirmish. Time had firmed Charlotte's opinion of him, an opinion colored by their parents' machinations and events beyond their control. This would not be easy.

But regardless of their past, he meant to save her from herself. This time would *not* be like last time. Perhaps *then* he could finally put to rest his lingering obsession with Charlotte Page Harris.

Chapter Three

*B*y early afternoon of their trip to the Kirkwood estate, eighteen-year-old Charlotte Page wanted desperately to toss her father out of his coach. It just wasn't fair! If not for Papa, she'd be sitting across from Captain James Harris at Colonel Devlin's card party in Grosvenor Square. She might even have the chance to dance with him.

The handsome young officer danced awfully well, and he had a good mind, too. Best of all, he treated her as if *she* had a good mind. He was amiable and considerate and absolutely nothing like Papa.

She wished she could say the same for David Masters, the horrible son of Papa's horrible friend, the Viscount Kirkwood.

"You'll be civil to Mr. Masters, won't you?" her mother pleaded. Mama sat next to Charlotte in Papa's latest acquisition, a traveling coach so richly appointed that Charlotte was half-afraid of snagging her bracelet on the satin upholstery.

"She'll be civil, or I'll know the reason why," her father growled.

When Mama cringed, Charlotte nearly bit her tongue

through, trying not to say something that would get them both into trouble. "If Mr. Masters is civil to me, Papa, I'll certainly be civil to him. Though I doubt he'll bother. Why should he, when you've already guaranteed him my hand and my dowry?"

Papa's lips thinned. "You're lucky he'll even consider you, missy, dowry or no. His family has money enough— they don't need ours. Besides, 'tis not your place to worry about who gets your dowry. That is *my* concern."

"But I'll be the one who has to live with whomever I marry, Papa. And a man who wants me only for my money—"

"Like that Captain Harris?"

"Wh-what do you mean?" She'd tried to hide her interest in the cavalry officer, knowing what Papa would think about a man with no connections as a suitor.

"I'm not blind, girl. I've noticed you and the man talking and dancing together every time we go to Colonel Devlin's. Harris is the one who wants you for your money. You can be sure he's not sniffing round you for any other reason."

The cruel claim shot pain through her chest. "That's not true!" she cried, then caught herself before she could show how thoroughly he'd wounded her. Like a shark, Papa attacked when he smelled blood in the water. She modulated her tone. "Captain Harris is a fine, upstanding officer—he wouldn't court a woman only for her money. He hasn't made his fortune yet, but I daresay he will soon."

"You'll never have the chance to find out. I'll not have people laughing at us behind our backs because you married some nobody. You're marrying Masters, and that's an end to it."

Papa can't force you to marry, Papa can't force you to marry, she chanted to herself.

Now if only she could believe it. "I haven't laid eyes on Mr. Masters in ten years. Do you really expect me to wed a stranger?"

"Stranger! You know his family, and you played with him as a child. That's good enough."

It was more than good enough to make her *not* want to marry him. At eight years old, she and her family had lived close to the Kirkwood estate near Reading. She'd trooped adoringly after David Masters and his younger brother, Giles. A bit of a tomboy, she'd done whatever they did—run foot races, played cricket, scrambled over hedges. She'd even tolerated David's ordering her about.

Then one day when he'd tried to exclude her from their climbing game because of her skirts, she'd informed him in front of the neighborhood lads that she could out-climb him, even in her pinafore. Of course they'd had to put it to the test. And he'd been *so* furious when she'd beaten him to the top of their favorite oak.

That's when the trouble started. The beast claimed she only won because she had long monkey arms. The other boys laughed and danced about her making monkey noises, and he joined in. Thanks to her supposed monkey arms and the short curly hair she wore in pigtails that resembled a monkey's ears, she'd thereafter been dubbed Miss Monkey.

She'd had to live with the vile nickname long after David had gone off to school the following week. It only ended when Papa had moved them to London to further his political ambitions.

Lord only knew what David was like now, after years of

being coddled and catered to as a viscount's heir. She said, "Rumor has it that Mr. Masters and his friends are utterly debauched. Do you really wish me to marry an unrepentant libertine?" *Like you?*

Papa might make no attempt to hide his other life—the mistresses he paraded in front of Mama and the nights he spent drinking with his close friend Charles Fox, the foreign secretary—but he expected her and Mama to keep quiet about their outrage. That got harder for Charlotte to do as the years passed and Papa's drunken rampages at home became intolerable.

"Masters isn't a libertine," Papa said with a snort. "Like all young bucks, he sows his wild oats, but he's discreet. That is all you can expect from a man. And my inquiries into his character reveal that he's a diligent student and a well-respected gentleman who is perfectly aware of the obligations due his rank."

In other words, he used his father's influence to sway his instructors, knew how to put on a good show when it counted, and was "perfectly aware" of how far his rank could get him.

She'd dipped her toe into society enough to know how to interpret the usual lies about a titled gentleman. Papa was describing a man exactly like himself. And the last thing she wanted was a husband of Papa's ilk.

"Besides," Papa went on, "his friends include a young marquess, a brother to a viscount, and an heir to a duke. I could well use those connections, so if only for my sake, you'll smile and be demure and welcome his attentions like any eligible young lady. Because if not for me and my labors, you wouldn't even have a dowry to entice a young man."

"But Papa—"

"The king didn't give me a barony because I own coal mines, you know. He did it because I promoted His Majesty's concerns in the House of Commons. I've done *my* part to further the aims of this family. Now you must do yours."

She stifled a snort. Papa only furthered his *own* aims and ambitions, but there was no point in arguing. He'd just deny it.

"But why must it be David Masters? Surely some other man could further your aims just as well." A man who might want her for herself. "If you'd only wait until my coming out next spring—"

"I'm not wasting money on a come-out when a man like Masters is there for the taking. Besides, Masters's friend Simon Tremaine, heir to the Duke of Foxmoor, is destined to be the next prime minister. That's a connection I don't intend to lose the chance of."

"Then perhaps you should offer me to him instead," she said bitterly. "It would be a much better business transaction."

Her father's face darkened. "You watch your tongue, missy. I've had enough of your insolence. We've not yet passed Richmond—we can still leave the carriage at a livery and travel up the Thames by wherry."

The words thundered in the carriage, sucking out all her bravado. Up the Thames! Would he be so cruel?

Of course he would. Her breathing grew labored as she saw again the swirling waters closing over her head, the blackness blotting out her sight, the panic as she realized she could not hold her breath any longer . . .

"Rowland," her mother protested. "You shouldn't say such an awful thing. It upsets her."

"Hush your mouth, woman," Papa shot back. "Or you know what I will do to *you.*"

When her mother paled, Charlotte grabbed her hand. "You leave Mama be! She has naught to do with this!"

"She's the one who hired that bluestocking governess. God only knows what foul ideas that female crammed into you before I found her out and dismissed her."

"Foul ideas!" Charlotte protested. "She encouraged me to exercise my mind, read important books, learn science and history and Latin—"

"And look what it's done to you," he snapped. "You're insolent to your father. Well, I won't tolerate such rebellion, do you hear? It's time you recognize who runs this family, and it isn't you, missy."

She bit back a hot retort. As if she hadn't had that drilled into her since childhood.

"Now," her father said firmly, "will you comport yourself like a proper young lady this week, or shall we take a river jaunt to remind you of your duty?"

Every inch of her wanted to throw his threat back in his face. It would be so satisfying to deprive him of the weapon provided to him by her obsessive fear of drowning. But Papa never made idle threats, and the mere thought of sitting frozen in terror on a boat made her throat close up and her heart waver.

She must have shown her fear by a wince or shudder, for triumph leaped in her father's eyes. "I think we understand each other now, don't we?"

Numbly she nodded. She understood *him,* anyway. He wouldn't rest until she agreed to marry David Masters.

Turning her face to the window, she scowled out at the

forest lining the road. Somehow she would find a way out of this trap he'd built for her. Because she had no intention of being chained to a younger version of Papa for the rest of her life.

David sprinkled more whisky on his coat, then patted some on his cheeks for good measure.

"What the devil are you doing?" asked a voice behind him.

He jumped, then let out a breath. It was only Giles. "Preparing for the Pages' arrival."

His younger brother looked bewildered. "By dousing yourself in whisky?"

"Surely you've guessed why they're coming here after all these years. Why Father invited them, even though Mother detests them."

"To be honest, I hadn't thought much about it."

"That's because *you're* not the one Father hopes to marry off to Charlotte Page."

Giles burst into laughter.

"It's not funny," David gritted out as he donned his whisky-dampened coat. One sniff had him choking. Perhaps he'd done it up a bit too brown.

Still, he might as well let the chit think he bathed in the stuff. He might need the drastic measure to thwart her doe-eyed adoration and her father's scheming.

"I remember Charlotte," Giles said. "She thought you hung the moon. Until that 'monkey business.'"

David stared at him. "What are you talking about?"

"You don't remember? No, of course not. You left for Eton shortly after."

"After what?"

Giles chuckled. "Never mind. Why does Father want you to marry *her*?"

"Because Charlotte is an heiress. And knowing Father, he's figuring that Lord Page will be more willing to loan him money for his latest favorite venture if it's all in the family. Of course, I am the one who has to make it 'all in the family.' I'm the one who has to suffer by marrying some chit I barely know."

"I suppose since Father and Mother had an arranged marriage, they figure what's sauce for the goose is sauce for the gander."

"Well, this gander is not doing it."

"Seems to have worked for the Mater and Pater. They rub on fairly well." Giles plopped down on David's bed. "Or are you holding out for true love? Because you know what Father would say to that. 'Love is for fools and children, but money rules the world.'"

"I don't care *what* Father says," David muttered. "There's something cold-blooded about choosing a wife according to her station and wealth."

His friend Anthony said he was a romantic, which was nonsense. He simply didn't want to be treated like a bloody horse up for auction. He would pick his own bride, after he'd enjoyed a bit of the world, of course. And when he did get around to marrying, it would not be for money alone.

He scowled into the mirror. "Bad enough that I've been dealing with the steward and the tenants ever since I left Cambridge, because *he* is too busy chasing the next great investment. I draw the line at getting leg-shackled just to help Father cover his risky ventures."

"What does her family think of it? Why should they be

keen on the marriage?" When David eyed him askance, he added, "Ohh, right. The title. This is one time I don't envy your being the heir." He leaned back on his elbows. "Has Charlotte even had her come-out?"

"No." David pulled his cravat askew and mussed his hair.

Giles laughed again. "That's probably why Page wants to fob her off on you. She must have turned out ugly indeed, if he thinks that even her fortune won't buy her a decent husband."

"The thought did cross my mind," David said tersely. He had a vague memory of what Charlotte used to look like— carrot-red hair that stuck out everywhere, freckles, and long limbs that enabled her to run as fast as any boy. Now she was probably some gangly spinster with no breasts, a frightful face, and not a feminine bone in her body.

"I'm expecting you to help me, Giles. Tell her what a bad fellow I am, how I lose money at cards—"

"I can't say that with a straight face," Giles protested. "You mostly win. When you gamble, which isn't that often."

"Fine. Then tell her about my wild living and my women."

"I'm not going to talk about that in front of Father, for God's sake," Giles said. "He'll have my head for it. He's always raging about you and your friends spending so much time in the fleshpots."

"And I plan to spend a great deal more before I let myself be caught in the parson's mousetrap." He was too young to marry, damn it!

Though if he were honest with himself, the fleshpots were growing tedious. Although he still bedded his share of barmaids and whores, he found them rather boring lately. Outside of their obvious talents, they had nothing to offer in the way of interesting conversation.

Not that he would admit that to his friends, or his younger brother, who already fancied himself quite the ladies' man. David had a reputation to uphold, after all.

Besides, it really stuck in Father's craw to see his son gambling, drinking, and whoring his way through London. A grim smile touched David's lips. Father valued discretion, even while "discreetly" risking the family's assets with reckless investments. David didn't see how that was any different from gambling. At least *he* never risked more than he could afford.

"If you're that scared of Father," he told Giles, "just talk about my bad qualities when he's not around."

Giles thrust out his chin. "I didn't say I was scared of him. Besides, you're taking care of the problem yourself by using whisky as a cologne. Although I still don't understand why you're not just drinking the stuff."

"Because I'm not going to give our fathers a chance to coax me into doing something stupid while I'm drunk, like getting Charlotte alone. Then all she'd have to do is kiss me and wait for them to burst in upon us. Next thing you know, I'd come out of my stupor to find myself married." He rumpled his coat. "They're not going to catch me unawares, damn it."

At least sip some, so she can smell it on your breath."

"Good idea." He swigged a healthy gulp.

"I take it you're not worried about Father's reaction to your subterfuge."

"He's lucky I'm even showing up to greet them. Refusing to do so was my first plan . . . until I realized that he could twist that however he liked to his advantage. Let's see him try to smooth *this* over."

David checked his appearance in the mirror. He looked downright seedy. If that didn't scare the chit off, nothing would. He caught sight of Giles rummaging through his drawers. "What are you doing?"

"I was thinking about borrowing your dressing gown, since mine is a rag and we're expecting company." Being only a year apart, they were nearly the same size, though David was a couple of inches taller. "Then again, perhaps I shouldn't bother. No point in tempting Charlotte to look my way."

"I wouldn't loan it to you anyway. You always tear everything."

Giles grinned. "Can I help it if the ladies can't keep their hands off me long enough for me to undress?"

David rolled his eyes. Honestly, his brother was becoming as bad a rakehell as David's friend Anthony Dalton.

The sound of carriage wheels crushing gravel drifted in through the open windows. "Bloody hell," David growled. "That's probably them now."

Both men rushed to the window, watching as the carriage stopped. But a light rain had begun to fall, and the footmen hurried out with umbrellas. They couldn't even get a glimpse of her, for God's sake. Not that he couldn't already guess what she looked like.

"Come on," David headed for the door. "Time for our performance."

As they descended the stairs, the sounds of voices wafted up from the foyer. They neared the bottom, but the guests were too busy shedding their wraps to pay them any mind.

With a sly glance at his brother, David pretended to

stumble off the stairs. "Good day, Father," he said, deliberately slurring his words.

Father turned to stare at him just as David lurched forward.

"I see that our guests're come," David muttered. "Lovely." As Lady Page's eyes went round and Lord Page scowled, he reached for the only female with her back to him, who had to be Charlotte.

Leaning heavily on her shoulder to give her a good sniff of his whisky-soaked breath, he said, "And thish must be Miss Page herself. Welcome!"

Mother looked as amused as Father looked shocked, but David reserved his attention for his nemesis as she turned to thrust him back from her.

In that moment, David's "drunken" grin vanished.

Eyes bluer than the most brilliant sapphires met his slack-jawed gaze, and lips of lush sensuality curved up in a mocking smile. The carroty hair he remembered from childhood had darkened and was tamed into a profusion of auburn ringlets that danced about the flawless ivory skin of her perfect features.

Good God. Somewhere in the last ten years, Charlotte Page had turned into the most beautiful creature this side of the English Channel. And he'd just made an ass of himself in front of her.

Why that bothered him he couldn't say. It just did.

As he quickly straightened to his full height, Charlotte flashed her father an oddly triumphant smile. "I fear we've come at a bad time, Papa. It appears that Mr. Masters is out of sorts."

"David, you scoundrel!" David's own father snapped. "What is the meaning of this?"

David's mind went utterly blank. He could only stare at the woman who was nothing at all like he'd expected.

Unfortunately, Giles's mind was in full working order. "You know David, Father." Giles made a motion that signified drinking. "Started on the dinner entertainment early."

"Shut up," David muttered under his breath.

Giles cast him a gleeful look. "You told me—"

"Forget everything I said." Aware that Charlotte watched the interchange with peculiar amusement, David met his father's angry gaze and grabbed at the only explanation he could come up with. "It was just a joke, Father. Giles and I knocked over the decanter in your study, and it spilled whisky on me. Isn't that right, Giles?"

"If you say so," Giles remarked blithely.

Later David was going to knock him on his ass, but for now he had to get out of this predicament. "Since I'd already soaked myself . . . I . . . we thought it might be amusing if we—"

"Embarrassed me before my guests?" Father thundered.

David winced. "Clearly, not my best idea." When Father glared at him, he added hastily, "I'll dash upstairs and change my coat."

"Judging from your breath, you might wish to rinse out your mouth as well," Charlotte said helpfully, her beautiful eyes dancing. "Some of that whisky seems to have spilled right up into it."

He flushed. She was mocking him, damn her. Women never dared to do that to him. It was galling, to say the least.

"Charlotte, hold your tongue!" Lord Page growled behind her.

The teasing light left her features, and her manner

changed abruptly. "Forgive me, Mr. Masters," she told David as she dropped her eyes to the floor. "I don't always think before I speak."

David didn't like *that* reaction either. "And I don't always think before I act," he countered, wanting to put her more at ease, "so we're even."

Her gaze shot to his, and a fetching confusion spread over her face. Then she stiffened. "Not quite even," she murmured, low enough not to be heard by her father, "since actions generally speak louder than words."

The criticism stung. Yes, he'd behaved like an idiot, but she didn't have to rub his nose in it. And what the hell had happened to the doe-eyed adoration he'd been prepared to rebuff?

His mother stepped into the fray. "David, go change your coat. Giles, tell Cook that we'll be ready for dinner shortly. Lady Page and Miss Page, I shall show you to your rooms so you can freshen up while Lord Page and my husband retire to the study." She arched an eyebrow at David. "Assuming it doesn't still reek of whisky. You might wish to check that on your way to your room."

When Mother nodded toward the stairs, David stalked up them, conscious of Charlotte's eyes on him. At least she would see that he wasn't foxed after all. Though he wasn't sure why he cared what she thought.

Nothing had changed; he didn't want to marry her. For God's sake, he wasn't quite twenty, and he certainly wasn't about to tie himself to any wife of Father's choosing.

So why did it annoy him to have her think him either a drunkard or a clumsy fool or both? He could have his pick of women. He didn't need to impress some daughter of a pushy chap trying to claw his way to the top of society.

Let their fathers weave their web; David didn't mean to be caught in it.

Never mind that she was pretty as a picture. No, better than that, beautiful. Stunning, really.

He frowned. It didn't matter. He refused to marry some chit just to provide Father with new monies for his mad investments. And that was that.

Chapter Four

⁂

Dinner at Kirkwood Manor that evening was a grand affair, but Charlotte was aware only of the young man across the table from her.

She hadn't expected David to be so attractive. Granted, he'd been good-looking as a boy, but sometimes good-looking boys grew up to be ugly men.

Not David. When he turned to speak to her mother on his left, Charlotte sneaked another peek at him. Merciful heavens, he was handsome. As a boy, he'd kept his unruly hair in a queue like the other lads, but that fashion had passed. He now wore his hair cropped short enough to curb the worst of its curling. It looked quite good on him, too.

So did his clothing. She sighed. After the incident in the foyer, he'd changed into an emerald-hued coat that strained over his surprisingly broad shoulders and brought out the glorious green of his eyes. But it was his chin, set off by the folds of a snowy cravat, that she couldn't stop staring at. Had he always had that interesting dimple right in the middle?

As if he felt her studying him, he swung his gaze to her. Chiding herself for her ridiculous fascination with his looks, she dropped her gaze to her plate. It didn't matter that David was handsome. Or well built. It didn't matter that the piping tones of a boy had deepened to a husky voice that thrummed along her every nerve.

He was either a drunkard like Papa, or he'd pretended to be a drunkard as a joke. That didn't speak well for his character.

Or his brother's, for that matter. She glanced at Giles, who sat to her right. He was rather handsome himself, with the same hair color and build as David's. So why didn't *he* make her heart race?

She grimaced. David did not make her heart race. The very idea was absurd!

As the walnut pudding was brought around, Charlotte's mother flashed Lady Kirkwood a polite smile. "Where are your daughters this evening?"

Charlotte glanced up, startled that she'd completely forgotten about David's two sisters. If memory served her correctly, one of them was a year younger than her. As a child she had rarely played with either girl, preferring the rough-and-tumble games of the boys.

"Actually," David's mother said, "they're spending the summer with my sister in Essex. She's trying to prepare them for their come-outs, poor dear." She dipped her spoon into the pudding. "I wanted to send them to a school for that, but it's hard to find a good one. A girl of that age needs so much more than just lessons in dancing and deportment."

"I agree wholeheartedly," Charlotte chimed in, relieved to find as august a personage as the viscountess sharing her own views about education. "Young ladies should be taught history, mathematics, science . . ." She trailed off when she saw Lady Kirkwood's shocked expression. "Oh. You meant something else."

Papa glowered at Charlotte. "I keep telling my daughter that even if young ladies could comprehend such knowledge, they have no use for it. But she won't listen."

David, who'd been concentrating on eating his pudding, said quietly, "Amassing knowledge is good for everyone. We don't necessarily use poetry in our daily lives, but reading it enriches us, doesn't it? And what use is dancing, really, except for amusement and perhaps a little exercise? I don't see how it hurts either a man *or* a woman to learn something new."

Defense from such an unexpected quarter took Charlotte by surprise. When her gaze shot to him, David winked at her, setting off a quivering in her belly that was most alarming.

"Be that as it may, David," Lady Kirkwood said with a sniff, "I was speaking of a different sort of knowledge. About society. About men and their ways. There's entirely too little education on *that* score. Young ladies are taught everything but how to handle themselves while rogues like you and your brother are busily trying to corrupt them."

"Mother!" Giles complained laughingly beside her. "You'll have Miss Page thinking that David and I are untrustworthy blackguards. We don't want her hiding in her room for fear of losing her virtue."

"Somehow I can't imagine Miss Page hiding anywhere," David said with a faint smile. "She certainly wasn't any wilting violet as a girl." He drank some wine. "Do you remember, Giles? She threw herself into every fray. She could run and ride as well as any of us, not to mention outclimbing *me* the one time we put it to the test."

Charlotte tensed. Was he actually bringing up that horrible incident *now*?

"Climbed like a monkey," Giles drawled beside her,

apparently determined to make it worse. "Isn't that what you said?"

David frowned. "Did I? I don't recall."

What? The wretch had humiliated her before all the village boys, and he didn't even remember? She could hardly believe it!

"Well, I recall it perfectly," she snapped. "First, you made that hateful comment about—"

"One thing my daughter doesn't do very well," her father interrupted, "is swim. Isn't that right, Charlotte? You can't swim at all."

She glanced at Papa, whose warning expression said she'd better curb her tongue or he'd make sure she regretted it. Wiping her clammy hands on her skirts, she returned her gaze to her plate.

"Hateful comment about what?" David asked in clear bewilderment.

"Nothing." She didn't dare look at him . . . or Papa. "I just realized I was recalling the wrong thing. It was a long time ago."

After a moment of strained silence, David said, "Giles, that was the second time you mentioned monkeys. Was that supposed to mean something?"

Charlotte shot Giles a pleading glance.

The young man seemed to note her distress, for he glanced from her to his brother, then said, "No. Not in the least."

Forcing herself to meet David's gaze, she smiled weakly. "I somehow doubt I'd be able to match you in any athletic endeavor these days, Mr. Masters."

"But if you ever need to buy a horse, consult my daughter," Mama surprised her by saying. "Charlotte has quite a good eye for them, like her father. Rowland bought me the sweetest little mare—"

"They don't want to hear about your mare, Agatha," Papa cut in.

Stiffening, she murmured, "No, dear, of course not."

Charlotte's fingers tightened on the spoon. She remembered when Mama used to fight him, argue with him. But the years had worn her down, and Charlotte hated to see it.

"Well, I can testify to Page's excellent taste in horses," Lord Kirkwood put in, relieving the tension. "Whenever I go to Tattersall's, I take him along. Haven't ever regretted a purchase that he approved."

Fortunately, that kept the conversation going until it was time for the gentlemen to head for Lord Kirkwood's study while the ladies retired to the drawing room.

But Charlotte couldn't take one more minute of the tense conversations. The gentlemen probably wouldn't stay away from the ladies for long, and she couldn't bear any more of Papa's trying to control her every word and deed.

She told her mother she had a headache and was retiring to her room. Thankfully, Mama didn't press the matter. But halfway to her room, Charlotte realized she'd forgotten her shawl in the dining room. She went back to retrieve it and was passing some open French doors when she glanced outside and got a jolt. There stood the windowless garden hut the boys had claimed for themselves when they were all children. She couldn't believe it was still intact.

For a moment she simply stared at it, remembering what a forbidden place it had seemed to her as a girl. She'd never even seen the inside, for the boys had kept it padlocked when not in use.

A sudden mischievous impulse seized her. No one was around—this part of the house wasn't close to the drawing room or the study. Why not take a look?

Grabbing a candle, she ventured out and across the garden to the shed. No lock on the door. Probably it merely held hoes and such these days, but still . . .

She swung the door open, startled to find that the plain wooden structure was already inhabited. David sat in his shirtsleeves at an old desk, sketching madly by the light of a lantern.

As his surprised gaze shot to her, she blushed crimson, mortified that he might think she'd followed him there on purpose. "I-I beg your pardon." She started to close the door. "I didn't mean to invade your privacy."

He leaped from his chair. "Wait!"

She froze with the door half-open.

"Why don't you stay?" He hurried near enough that she could see his loosened cravat. "I could use the company."

"I'd have thought you came here to avoid company."

"Some company, yes." His expression was genuinely friendly, sending warmth spilling through her veins, despite her determination to stay immune to his charms. "Probably the same company *you* are attempting to hide from."

She thrust out her chin. "I thought you said I wasn't the sort of woman to hide."

A faint smile touched his lips as he gestured for her to enter. "Honestly, I think the devil himself would want to hide from that lot in there."

She laughed, relieving whatever tension remained between them.

One sort of tension, anyway. Now a new sort tightened

her nerves. She'd never been alone with a man. Even Captain Harris had always talked to her with other people about.

Feeling as jittery as a mare confronted with her first saddle, she reluctantly went inside. She would just stay a moment, long enough to determine his feelings about the marriage their parents wanted to force on them. And to make her own feelings clear.

David closed the door, then hurried behind the desk to hold out his chair. "There's only one decent seat, I'm afraid. We lads always preferred the floor." Amusement gleamed in his eyes. "More manly, you know."

Not nearly as manly as the sight of him without a coat, looking perfectly at home in this rustic spot. Setting her candle on his desk, she gazed about her at the bare plank walls, worn rug, and flattened cushions in faded fabrics. A faint scent of mold permeated the air, mingling with the smell of burning wax and lamp oil.

"When I used to picture what it looked like in here," she remarked, "this was not what I imagined. It's so . . . so . . . small."

He chuckled. "Go ahead, say it. It's filthy and wretched and lacking in any creature comforts. But we used to think it a castle."

"One devoid of women," she said archly.

"I hate to tell you, but no boy of nine or ten creates a secret inner sanctum that includes girls."

"Given that our fathers are presently ensconced in the study without their wives, secret inner sanctums must continue into adulthood."

"Ah, but the difference is that grown men don't mind having a woman invade the inner sanctum. Sometimes they rather enjoy it."

His sudden, wolfish smile sent her pulse into a wild dance. Heavens, she'd have to watch that. He did have a reputation, after all.

She gestured to the desk. "What exactly do you do in your inner sanctum?"

Noticing the direction of her gaze, he flushed, then hurried to shuffle the papers into a stack. "It's nothing. A hobby of mine, that's all."

"What sort of hobby?" she persisted.

"If you must know . . ." His expression turned belligerent, as if he dared her to make fun of him. "I have an interest in architecture. I realize it's not considered the thing for a—"

"I think it's wonderful," she blurted out. A blush warmed her cheeks. "I-I mean, it's good for a man to be industrious, no matter who he is."

His face lit up. "I've been working on a design for a hunting cottage." He spread out the papers again, his voice rising with enthusiasm. "My friend Stoneville says that if I come up with a decent one, he'll use it on his estate. After a real architect approves it, of course."

Edging closer to the desk, she gazed down at the plans David had meticulously inked. She couldn't help being impressed. She didn't know anything about architecture, but they *looked* like genuine plans for a building. And who'd have guessed that David had such a respectable hobby?

He shook the chair. "Come, stay awhile." His gaze burned into hers. "I promise not to tie you up or make you walk the plank or any of those other wretched things we boys did as children."

That reference reminded her of the last thing he'd done

to her, and her smile vanished. "I prefer to stand," she said with a lift of her chin.

He shot her a searching glance. "It's the monkeys, isn't it?"

Her heart dropped into her stomach. "You remember."

"No, I don't. But clearly you do. So would you *please* tell me what I did? Then I can beg your pardon, and we can be done with it."

His remark was so practical and matter-of-fact that it took the edge off her resentment. "You'll think it's ridiculous."

"Perhaps. But then, I think that much of what mattered to me at nine was ridiculous."

"I'm afraid I haven't been so sanguine about it." She related the tale as unemotionally as possible.

By the time she finished, he was wincing. "They kept calling you Miss Monkey after I left for school?"

His clear chagrin filed down her resentment even more. "Two years at least. Even after I took down my pigtails and grew a couple of inches."

"Good God, I'm sorry." His expression seemed to confirm that he meant it, too. "What a wretched thing to say to a girl. No wonder you called it hateful. I'm only surprised you agreed to come with your parents for this visit."

"My father didn't give me much choice."

His eyes locked with hers, suddenly somber. "Neither did mine." With an arch of his eyebrow, he shook the chair again. "Perhaps we should confer, because they're not going to leave us be. Might as well assess the situation together."

"True." This time she accepted his offer and took a seat on the lone chair. He sat on one of the moldy cushions, crossing his legs Indian-style like a foreign prince. A very handsome, dangerously appealing foreign prince.

"So," he said, "let me get this straight. Our fathers want us to marry. Does that about sum it up?"

She couldn't help it—a laugh sputtered out of her. The men she'd met at home were never so frank. "It does indeed."

He leaned forward to plant his elbows on his knees. "And you aren't terribly keen on the idea."

"Are you?" she asked, determined to be equally frank, though if Papa ever found out about this conversation, he'd cane her for certain.

"I wasn't." David's eyes darkened in a most mysterious and worldly manner as they made a slow circuit of her face and her breasts. "I'm not so sure now."

Though a blush flamed her cheeks, she cocked her head at him. "Are you flirting with me, David Masters?"

"Just stating facts . . . Charlotte."

She swallowed, unable to look away from the gaze that held her as surely as if he had his hands on her. He'd called her Charlotte when they were children. So why was it so disconcerting to have him do so now? "Well, I'm sure I don't want to marry *you*," she said, though she wasn't in the least sure.

"Why not?"

"For one thing, your own mother calls you a rogue," she told him loftily. "And I've spent too many years under the thumb of a rogue already. I don't intend to spend one minute more if I can avoid it."

"But if you want to break free of your father," David said quietly, "you'll have to marry *someone*."

Surprised by his quick perception, she rose to pace the room, wondering if she should tell him about Captain Harris.

"Then again," he went on in a voice tinged with disappointment, "perhaps you've already picked out your someone."

"Well, it's not as if he's made an offer yet," she admitted, "but I'm hoping he will soon."

"So there's still a chance for me."

She glanced over to find him wearing a cheeky grin. "I didn't say that."

"I'm here, and he's not." His expression was entirely too smug. "And I have your father's approval. Which, I'm guessing, he does not."

"How could you possibly know—"

"Because if he did, you'd already be married. No man in his right mind would take his time about securing *you*."

That sweet phrase softened her toward him further. Until she remembered who she was. Or rather, what she was. "You mean, because of my dowry and my inheritance," she said in a low voice.

His face darkened. "If I was only interested in that, I wouldn't have pretended to be drunk when you first arrived."

She caught her breath. So that *hadn't* been a joke. If she could believe him. "I smelled the liquor on your breath."

"I didn't say I hadn't had a drink. Just that I wasn't drunk." He leaned back to rest on his elbows. "Do I look drunk to you now?"

He didn't. And she had to admit he'd had very little

wine at dinner. Not to mention that he was here, instead of off with the other men drinking in the study.

But that wasn't the point. "So you pretended to be drunk until . . . what? You saw me? And *that* changed your mind?"

"Exactly." Then, as if realizing what he'd just said, he added, "No! I mean . . . that is . . ." When she continued to look at him with eyebrows raised, he said stoutly, "What about my being heir to a title? You have no interest in that, I suppose."

"None," she said, mildly amused by his consternation. "Papa is the one interested in that."

"And Father is the one interested in your dowry."

"Yes, you're only interested in my *face*," she said dryly.

A rueful chuckle escaped his lips. "You have to admit it's quite a nice face." His rakish gaze swept her body. "And the parts that go with it are rather nice, too."

She snorted. "Now I see why your mother calls you a rogue."

He made a dismissive gesture. "Mother is just trying to put you off because she doesn't want me marrying you." Then, as if realizing what he'd said, he sighed. "Sorry. It's nothing against you. She's hoping I'll find a grander wife. It's Father who's pushing the marriage."

"Papa, too."

"But not you," he said softly.

She stared him down. "I've heard all about you and your wild friends. I want a steady husband, not some randy rakehell."

His eyes gleamed at her. "Haven't you also heard that reformed rakes make the best husbands?"

"Are you reformed?"

"I could be." This time he was more leisurely in his perusal, lazily scouring her from face to foot, lingering over certain parts as if he could see right through her gown, even in the dim lantern light. "With the right incentive."

His pointed interest in her body had the most peculiar effect on her. She could actually feel heat rising from her belly to her breasts and up her neck to bloom in a blush. Which he could surely see.

"I swear," she chided him, attempting to sound stern, "you're every bit as bad as they say. And I don't believe that men of your sort up and 'reform' just for the sake of a woman, anyway."

"You wound me to the heart, fair lady!" Sitting up, he shot her a look that was half-serious, half-mocking. "Is there no way I can change your mind?"

"No," she said firmly, though a tiny, devilish part of her was tempted to let him try. Marriage to David would certainly make her present life easier.

But not her future one. The last thing she needed was to yoke herself to a man who did as he pleased while his wife sat at home and suffered. "And for all your outrageous flirting," she went on, "you aren't ready to marry yet, are you? Admit it."

"God, Charlotte, I don't know," he said uneasily. "To be honest, I hadn't thought about marriage at all until Father took me aside this morning."

"Exactly." She propped her hip on the edge of the desk. "So, what are we to do about our fathers? You know they'll plague us all week to spend time together."

A sudden mischief leaped in his gaze. "Perhaps we should give them what they want. We can pretend to court right up until the time you leave. If they believe we're seriously contemplating marriage, they'll stay out of our hair. Then, on your last day here, we'll announce that we've decided not to marry. If we both hold firm, they'll have to accept it."

"Why can't we just hold firm now, and tell them that we know we won't suit?"

"Do you really think they'd believe us, based on one day's acquaintance?" When she sighed, he added, "We have to convince them that we've sincerely tried. Otherwise, they'll just keep inventing reasons for throwing us together."

She had to admit his logic was sound. "All right. I suppose we could pretend to court." She flashed him a shaky smile. "Though I'm not sure what courtship involves. Since I haven't had my debut yet, I've never actually been courted."

"Not even by— What's his name, anyway? The man you've set your sights on back in London," he said, an edge to his voice.

"Captain James Harris." She picked at a loose thread on her sleeve, unable to look David in the face while talking about Captain Harris. "He's a cavalry officer."

"And he hasn't actually courted you?" he prodded. "What's wrong with the man?"

"He's a gentleman, that's all."

David rose, straightening to his full height. "No man is a gentleman with a woman he wants," he said in a husky voice.

The room, which was already small, suddenly felt like a closet. David was too near . . . too male. "I should probably go," she choked out, "before they discover us missing."

He stepped nearer. "They won't think to look here."

"Yes, but—"

"You wanted to know what courting involved." He moved close enough that she could hear his breathing quicken. "I can tell you one thing it involves."

Her heart clamored wildly in her chest. "Oh?" She couldn't believe how calm she sounded when she felt on the verge of shattering.

Then he laid his hand on her waist, and she nearly did shatter. Her stomach turned flip-flops, and she couldn't seem to find her breath.

"Courtship involves things like this." He bent his head to press his lips to hers.

She ought to be shocked. Appalled. Alarmed. Instead, she felt as if she'd been waiting all her life for him to kiss her.

And it proved well worth the wait. His mouth whispered over hers, teasing, caressing, as soft as a brush of silk, barely there. It tempted her to touch him, though she caught herself just as she reached for *his* waist.

"Mr. M-Masters, I d-don't think—" she stammered as she struggled to free herself of the sensual spell he wove.

"David," he corrected softly. "It's only a kiss, Charlotte."

It was so much more than that to her. It was her *first* kiss. And she'd expected to share it with Captain Harris, not with this roguish lordling who cared nothing for her beyond a flirtation to provide him with entertainment during a long week of unwanted guests.

She backed away. "If this is to be a pretend courtship, there's no need for kissing, is there?"

"What does it hurt?" he said irritably. "Unless you're bent on staying true to a man who hasn't even bothered to claim you for his own."

That stung. "I'm being true to myself." She crossed her arms over her chest. "At least I know what I want in this affair. You have no clue what you want."

"I want—I *wanted*—a kiss. That's all."

"Well then, you had your kiss. So now we're done with that."

She turned for the door, but he stepped into her path. Grabbing her head in his hands, he kissed her again, harder this time, with a boldness and thoroughness that drove the very breath from her. She was still reeling from the wild emotions he roused in her breast when he stopped abruptly and put her away from him.

"*Now* I've had my kiss," he said, his arrogance showing in every word.

For a moment, she didn't know what to say, what to do. His second kiss had left her in utter confusion.

Then she gathered her wits and stared him down. "You mustn't do that again, or we can't possibly have a pretend—"

"Fine. Whatever you wish." Eyes glittering with anger, he stepped to the door and opened it, giving an elaborate flourish with his hand to indicate that she could leave. "I'll see you in the morning, Miss Page."

She blinked, taken aback by his abrupt manner. But it was just as well that he knew where she stood. She gave a polite curtsy. "Good night, Mr. Masters." Then she swept through the door.

But long after she reached her room, she couldn't shake the feeling that she'd just entered into a disastrous conspiracy with a rather dangerous young man. If he ever kissed her like *that* again . . .

She wouldn't let him. They would spend a week of

polite conversation tempered by their knowledge that they were utterly unsuited for each other, and at the end she would go home to her hopes for a marriage to a noble soldier rather than a reckless young lord.

Now she would just have to pray that the soldier could kiss as well as the lord. Or her heart might be in serious trouble.

Chapter Five

Four days later, David was still kicking himself for putting Charlotte on her guard. Ever since their amazing kisses, she'd closed up like an oyster at low tide. Oh, she still smiled and talked to him, behaving as if she enjoyed his company when their fathers were around.

But she managed never to be alone with him. If he proposed a walk, she invited Giles or her mother along. If he lingered behind the others after dinner, she hurried to catch up to them. She even rose at an ungodly hour for breakfast, since she was always gone from the breakfast room by the time he entered.

Not today, however—not if he could help it. Throwing his striped silk dressing gown over his shirt, waistcoat, and riding breeches, he paced to the window. Dawn had just broken. Not even Charlotte rose so early. Besides, he'd paid the maid who was attending her and her mother to scratch on his door when Charlotte left her room. She wouldn't escape him this time, damn it.

Her persistent avoidance of him had begun to rankle, though he wasn't sure why. He still didn't consider himself old enough for marriage. Certainly he had no desire to have any close connection to that ass, Lord Page.

So why the bloody hell did he spend so much time thinking about the man's daughter?

Dropping into the nearest chair, he conjured up an

image of Charlotte as she'd looked after he'd kissed her. Then he undressed the image, piece by delectable piece. Unfortunately, his imagination had little to go on. She had curly red hair, but how long? Was her waist slender or full? Hard to tell beneath the shapeless tubes that constituted ladies' skirts these days.

Still, the parts he *could* see tormented him. There was that elegant neck, with its creamy skin that he ached to kiss. Then there was her shapely bosom, so nicely displayed in her dinner gowns. Just thinking of that bosom made him hard.

He squirmed in the chair. What sort of man thought of a respectable young woman with unbridled lust? Especially when he had no intention of marrying her? Though he wasn't even sure of *that* anymore.

Nonetheless, her avoiding him was going to stop. Today. Because how could he decide what to do if he only got to be around the coolly polite Charlotte? He needed more time with the sweetly passionate Charlotte who'd bewitched him in the garden shed. He had to know which one he'd be marrying, if he chose to do so.

The scratching at the door brought him up short. Already? But his valet hadn't even returned from pressing his riding coat! Very well, he'd join her in his dressing gown—he'd always thought he looked rather dashing in it.

When he arrived at the breakfast room, luck was with him—Charlotte was alone and had already taken a seat with her filled plate. He stepped into the room.

"Good morning, Miss Page."

She jumped and her eyes swung to him, wide with alarm. Then her expression changed, and she burst into laughter.

That was *not* the effect he'd been hoping for. "What's so funny?"

Struggling to withhold her mirth, she dropped her gaze to her plate. "Nothing. Nothing at all."

"Obviously not nothing," he grumbled as he strode to the sideboard.

Another peal of laughter escaped her when he turned to fill his plate. With a scowl, he faced her again. *"What?"*

"I'm sorry, it's just that . . ." She fought back another laugh, though her eyes remained suspiciously bright. "Don't you think your robe is rather . . . well . . . colorful?"

A flush warmed his cheeks. "This is the fashion, I'll have you know."

"Red, yellow, and orange stripes? That's the fashion?"

He stalked over to the table and set his plate down hard. "It's very expensive silk. Cost me half a month's allowance at one of the best tailors in London."

"Oh dear," she said in a tone that made it clear she thought he'd overpaid.

"You haven't even had your come-out yet." He dropped into the chair. "What do *you* know about men's attire?"

"Nothing, apparently. But I do have eyes."

And those eyes were laughing at him, which he didn't appreciate one bit.

"So what do *you* propose that I wear?" he snapped.

"Something less garish." Her lips twitched from the effort to contain her amusement. "Without orange in it. Or yellow. Or scarlet stripes, for that matter."

The little minx was clearly enjoying herself. And despite his irritation, he found himself responding to her infectious good humor. It was the first time she'd been relaxed around him since the garden shed. Perhaps he could turn this to his advantage.

Leaning back, he dropped his gaze to her mouth. "Already picking out my clothes, are you? Isn't that the task of a wife?"

She started; then her eyes narrowed. "Or a valet," she answered tartly.

"I don't think you'd make a very good valet," he quipped before she could retreat into her cool facade.

"I don't think you'd make a very good husband," she shot back.

He scowled. Leave it to Charlotte to get right to the point. "How can you tell when you barely even know me?"

"I know you well enough. 'For a man by nothing is so well bewrayed/As by his manners.'"

The archaic word *bewrayed* threw him off for a second. Then he grinned. "Edmund Spenser?"

She blinked. "You've read Spenser?"

Bloody hell, she must think him a complete twit. "Isn't he one of those fellows who writes—what are they called—books?" He couldn't hold back his sarcasm. "We have an entire room of the things upstairs. I even look inside them occasionally. I try not to notice what's on the pages, but once in a while even a debauched chap like myself can't help absorbing a word or two."

"Very amusing," she said dryly. "Do you ever take anything seriously?"

"Only when forced. But for you, dear Charlotte, I'll attempt to restrain my levity." He leaned forward. "If . . ."

She arched one brow. "If?"

"You agree to spend the day with me. Alone."

Her fetching blush made his blood roar through his veins. "I don't think that's wise," she said.

"Why not?" He fought for control over his wayward arousal. "We have much to discuss if you're to be my valet. There's the matter of your salary and my clothing budget, which will be much strained with all the new dressing gowns you mean for me to buy, not to mention—"

"Do be serious."

He leveled her with an intent gaze. "I am. Spend the day with me, Charlotte. We'll go for a long ride, have a picnic lunch . . ."

"Such a tête-à-tête would only give our fathers an excuse for forcing the marriage."

Bloody hell, she was as skittish as a yearling with its first halter. "Then we'll take a groom. Of course, if you're too much a coward to spend time with me alone . . ."

She bristled, as he'd known she would. "It has more to do with good sense than cowardice."

A new voice came from the doorway. "What does?"

David bit back a curse. If his little brother didn't watch it, he was going to find himself on the wrong side of a beating. "Nothing that concerns *you*, Giles."

Before Giles could answer, the maid entered with a pot of tea for Charlotte. Then she started. "Begging your pardon, sirs, I didn't realize the lady had company, or I would have brought more."

"It's fine, Molly," David bit out as the maid came round the table to him. Flashing him a coy smile, she bent close enough that her bosom brushed his shoulder as she poured him a cup. When Charlotte scowled at her, David ground his teeth in irritation. Molly had become quite the little flirt lately. He would have to have a talk with the housekeeper.

"Can I get you anything else, sir?" Molly said in a

voice that left no question as to what she really wanted to offer him.

"No thank you," he said. "That will be all."

"*I'd* like some tea," Charlotte said tersely.

"Of course, miss," Molly said as she walked behind David to pass in front of Giles.

When David saw Giles brush his hand over Molly's ass, he tensed. Thank God Charlotte couldn't see it from where she sat, or it would only reinforce her opinion of them as a family of profligates.

After Molly left, Charlotte flashed Giles a friendly smile that rubbed David raw. "Your brother has asked me to go out riding for a picnic," Charlotte said blithely. "Why don't you join us?"

"Certainly," said his imp of a brother.

"The bloody hell you will," David ground out.

"Tsk, tsk," Giles retorted. "Such language in front of a lady."

David shot to his feet. "I have to go put on my riding coat." He caught his brother by the arm as Giles attempted to pass. "And you're going with me. Now."

"But I haven't eaten," Giles protested as David dragged him toward the door.

"If you don't come with me," David growled in his brother's ear, "you'll be eating my fist."

Giles grimaced, then glanced at Charlotte. "Excuse me, Miss Page. It seems my brother needs help putting on his riding coat."

David ignored Giles's snide remark, but couldn't help noting the unease on Charlotte's face. He halted near the door to pin her with a dark glance. "Stay here. Don't you dare leave."

She shot to her feet, eyes flashing. "Or what?"

"Or I'll tell our fathers what we discussed in the garden shed."

He regretted the threat when the blood drained from her face. But at least she sat down again.

"I'll be right back," he added, then hauled Giles out the door, shoving him toward the stairs.

As soon as they were near it, Giles wrenched himself free. "What the devil was all *that* about?"

"I want to spend time alone with Charlotte." David hurried up the stairs as Giles struggled to keep up. "You are not going with us. Understood?"

"I thought you didn't want to marry her," Giles said peevishly.

"I haven't decided. But having you around isn't helping." David strode into his bedchamber.

Giles came in behind him and sank into a chair. "You'd better decide fast. They're leaving day after tomorrow. And judging from what she's said about that damned cavalry officer, if you don't secure her before they leave—"

An unaccountable jealousy seared him. "What has she said?"

"Enough to make it clear she's hoping for an offer. I think she was trying to discourage me." Giles chuckled. "As if I would settle for one chit's field when there's a whole world of females out there waiting to be plowed."

Frowning at his brother's crudeness, David peeled off his dressing gown. "Plow where you will, but I'm warning you now—don't dally with the maids. A gentleman shouldn't piss where he sleeps."

Giles waggled his eyebrows. "I'm not planning on doing any pissing."

"I mean it, Giles," David ground out. "If I have to, I'll go to Father about it."

Giles collapsed into a sulk. "You can be such a stuffed shirt sometimes."

How Charlotte would laugh to hear *that*. She thought he was a rogue through and through.

A rogue with no sense of fashion. David tossed his dressing gown at Giles. "Here, this ought to cheer you up. I don't want it anymore."

A laugh erupted from Giles. "I take it that Miss Page doesn't like it."

"She called it 'garish,'" David admitted, still annoyed by how she'd laughed at him.

"And pleasing her means so much to you that you'll get rid of your favorite dressing gown? Sounds to me as if you *have* decided about Miss Page."

David said nothing as he dragged on his freshly pressed riding coat.

"I'd be careful if I were you," Giles went on. "She's not the kind of female you can toy with. If you don't mean marriage, then—"

"Stay out of it, Giles. I know what I'm doing."

But that was a lie. All he knew was he had to be alone with her again, get to know her, see if he'd lost his bloody mind by considering marrying her.

Half an hour later, as he and Charlotte rode out with the groom, he realized that his plan might prove harder than he'd thought. She had come along with ill grace, and she sat the bay mare like a haughty queen, her aloof facade firmly in place.

He fell back a little, as if to speak to the groom trailing behind them, but really so he could watch her ride. While he'd been arranging for the horses, she'd changed into a riding habit, and by God, she was fetching in it. At least he had his answer to what one part of her looked like, for her habit was nipped in at her natural waist. Her nicely slender, natural waist.

She was a fine rider, too, with a good seat, her body moving in perfect time with the horse's gait. She looked as comfortable in the sidesaddle as on a settee.

"Now that you've bullied me into this," she called back to David, "where are we going?"

"I didn't bully you into anything." He spurred the horse forward to take the lead, then turned down a path that led to one of the more secluded roads. "You like to ride, and you know it."

"I still don't see why Giles couldn't come along," she complained.

"Because it's not a courtship if the two people never court."

She shot him a startled look. Then, nervously glancing back at the groom listening to every word, she urged her mare closer to David's black gelding. "It's only a pretend courtship," she said in a low voice.

Perhaps. Perhaps not. "That doesn't mean we can't have fun. It's a beautiful day, and we've got a whole estate to explore. Try to enjoy it, will you?"

They rode a few moments in an uncomfortable silence. Then David asked, "How do you find your mount?"

"Perfect," she muttered.

His hands tightened on the reins. "You don't *sound* pleased."

She sighed, then patted the mare's withers as if to reassure the creature. "Oh, but I am. She has enough spirit to be enjoyable, but a yielding temperament that makes for pleasant riding."

"So why the long face?"

Fixing her gaze on the path ahead, she squirmed in the saddle. "I'm just . . . annoyed that you knew precisely what sort of horse to pick for me."

"You hate not being the only one with a good eye for horses, don't you?" he teased, determined to lighten her mood.

A small smile curved her lips. "Exactly."

But that wasn't the real reason for her annoyance. The chit didn't want to approve of anything he did, yet she couldn't help herself sometimes. Thank God.

The path suddenly opened out into a long road between two fields of barley. At the end stood a forest they used to play in as children. David flashed her a challenging smile. "Want to race to the woods?"

She eyed the dirt road, then him. "Only if you promise not to call me a nasty name when I win."

"I promise." He grinned. "But you're not going to win." And with that, he goaded his mount into a run.

She followed him with surprising speed, impressing him with her skill. But she'd pricked his pride already once this morning. He meant to show her that he wasn't the lecherous twit she took him for, who dressed badly and spent his days lolling about in luxurious debauchery. He rode to win, putting every bit of his horsemanship to the test.

She nearly bested him anyway. But just as they neared the part of the road that bisected the forest, David pushed his gelding to his limits and thundered past the line of trees ahead of her. With a laugh of pure triumph, he pulled up and turned toward her in the saddle. "Good show," he said, trying not to gloat.

"I see you gave yourself the faster horse," she grumbled.

He laughed at her, not the least daunted by her ill humor. "Why, Charlotte Page, you're as bad a loser as I am."

Her irate gaze shot to him, and she opened her mouth as if to protest. Then she gave a weak laugh. "I suppose that's true. I despise losing."

"Good of you to admit it," he said as she continued down the road. He pulled his gelding into step beside her. "Feel free to call *me* a nasty name if that will make you feel better. I hear that Monkey is taken, but you could try, oh, Garish Goer. Or Mr. Fast and Loose. Or . . . Wait, I have the perfect one: the Debauched Devil."

"Perfect?" Her brows arched high. "You'd consider *that* one a compliment. You and your friends, strutting about, bragging of your wickedness."

"I never brag. Don't need to." He grinned over at her. "My wickedness is self-evident."

She laughed outright. "I swear, you're incorrigible, Mr. Masters."

Delighted that he'd made her laugh at last, he pushed his success further. "Come now, can't you call me David? Surely even your pretend fiancé deserves that."

"My pretend fiancé is stretching the rules of propriety," she chided, then gave him a pretty smile that took the sting off her refusal.

They rode awhile in companionable silence. He surreptitiously checked his pocket watch. Surely he'd given the servants enough time to do as he'd ordered last night. He couldn't wait to see how Charlotte liked his surprise.

When they reached a certain small clearing near the
road, he stopped and dismounted, motioning the groom
to come forward for the horses. "I have something to show
you," David told Charlotte as he helped her down.

"Oh?"

Now came the dicey part. He offered her his arm, which
she took. Then he nodded to the groom, who gathered the
reins of their two horses and started leading them back
down the road.

"Where is he going?" she asked.

"I told him we'd walk back." With her hand firmly
tucked in the crook of his arm, he headed for the woods.

"Mr. Masters—" she said, dragging her heels a bit.

"Charlotte, you're safe with me, I promise."

There was a moment when he was half-afraid she might
run after the groom to retrieve her horse, or even set off
alone on foot to the house.

When she didn't, he exulted. From here, everything
would be smooth sailing. Because he finally had Charlotte
to himself.

But as they crossed through the woods and the sounds
of rushing water began to trickle through to them, she
dragged her feet again. "Have I been here before?"

"Yes, as a matter of fact. We used to play here. Don't you
remember?"

They came close enough to the edge of the wood to
see the Thames beyond. He wondered if she remembered
Saddle Island in the middle, so called because of its unusual shape. It had been forbidden to them as children.
Now it boasted a gazebo. And a lavish picnic luncheon set
out earlier by the servants.

She dug her fingers into his arm. Apparently she did recall it. But when he glanced at her face, expecting surprise or pleasure, she was pale as a ghost.

"What are we doing here?" she asked, a strange note of panic in her voice.

He led them toward the boat moored at a little landing on the bank. "We're going over to the island for a picnic."

Abruptly, she dropped his arm. "We most certainly are not. I'm heading back."

Confound it all, why was she turning skittish again? He thought they'd put that behind them.

Gathering up her skirts, she rushed back to the woods at a near run.

"Don't be absurd," David cried as he hurried after her. "We're not coming out all this way just to return without even seeing Saddle Island." He grabbed her about the waist from behind, meaning only to stop her, but she struggled wildly against him.

Did she think he meant to ravish her out there? What sort of man did she believe him to be? "Calm down, it's merely a picnic, I swear. There's no need for this—"

"You can't make me get in that boat!" she cried. "I won't do it! Let me go!"

There was something more to this, something odd. "Charlotte, you're being—"

"He told you, didn't he?" She pried frantically at his arm.

"*Who* told me *what*? I don't know what you're talking about!"

When she twisted in his arms to face him, he saw, to his shock, the tears streaming down her face.

"Stop pretending! I know Papa must have told you. I know that's why you're doing this." She grabbed his lapels.

"Please don't make me go out on the river, I beg you! I-I'll do whatever you want, whatever *he* wants. Just don't—"

"Shh, sweeting, shh, I won't make you do anything, I promise," he murmured, gathering her close. "I swear your father told me nothing!"

He chanted it as he held her tight, trying to calm her. His heart ached to hear her sobbing. Too late he understood. Her fear had nothing to do with being alone with him. It had to do with the river.

"It's all right," he assured her over and over. "You're safe. We won't go anywhere near the water, I swear."

Oh, God, what had he done? He hadn't meant to hurt her. He certainly hadn't meant to reduce her to this.

Somewhere in the maelstrom of her fear, his words must have sunk in, for she stopped fighting his embrace. But now she was shaking violently, and that alarmed him. Dropping onto the grassy bank, he dragged her down with him so he could cradle her in his lap, soothe her with strokes of his hands, hold her close.

It took several moments to halt her tears, and several more to calm her enough so she stopped shaking.

When he was sure she was more her normal self, he drew back to cup her face in his hands. "Feel better?" he asked softly.

Her eyes were red and swollen. "Actually, I . . . feel a bit of a fool."

"No need." Pressing her head to his chest, he stroked her hair. "I'm sorry. I had no idea, or I would never have—"

"I know," she mumbled into his damp coat. "I see that now."

"It was just a stupid surprise. I thought you'd like going out to the island for a picnic."

She uttered a harsh laugh. "Little did you know you were setting out with a lunatic."

"Not a lunatic. But I *would* like to know why—"

"I go mad at the sight of a boat on the river?" she finished for him.

Ignoring her self-deprecating tone, he pressed a kiss into her hair. "You used to play in the water with the older children all the time. When did that change? *How* did it change?"

"If I tell you, you'll laugh at me," she whispered.

"No." He settled her more comfortably in his lap. "I promise I won't."

Turning a wary gaze up to him, she searched his face. "And you won't make me go out on the river?"

A lump caught in his throat. "No." He brushed the hair back from her tear-streaked face. "Not if you don't want."

"Don't want?" She tried for a laugh and failed. "I would rather chew needles."

He fished out his handkerchief and offered it to her. She blew her nose and wiped her eyes.

"It happened the winter I was nine, when we still lived near here. There'd been a storm, and the Thames was swollen and very swift. Mama and I were walking beside it when my favorite bonnet flew into it. Before she could react, I rushed in after my bonnet."

David could see the fear rising again in her face, though he felt helpless to banish it.

"The current swept me off. I-I struggled, but I didn't know how to swim, and the water was so powerful. Our footman dove in after me, but I'd already been carried quite a ways."

Her chest rose and fell with her quickening breaths.

"For a while it was a near thing. The water was churning, and I went under, dragged down by my wool skirts. The footman lost sight of me—I don't know for how long. All I remember is the horrible panic of not being able to breathe, of knowing I was about to die."

A shudder wracked her, and he rubbed her back, wishing he could do more.

"I must have lost consciousness. When I came to, I was lying on the bank, and my chest hurt from someone pressing against it, forcing the water from my lungs. Mama was bending over me, and the footman's teeth were chattering from his dunking in the icy waters."

Good God, she'd nearly died! His heart stopped just to think of it. "I hope your father rewarded him well for saving your life."

She flashed David a wan smile. "The footman retired from service on what Mama gave him alone. Opened a cook shop in Reading, I believe."

"And you've been afraid of the river ever since?"

"Lakes, rivers . . ." She swallowed. "The ocean gives me nightmares. I start . . . seeing it all again, feeling the panic, the searing pain of the water entering my lungs just before I passed out. I even tense up when I go over bridges." A ragged sigh escaped her. "I know it's irrational and silly—"

"Certainly not. A fear of drowning is perfectly rational. In you, the fear is a bit exaggerated, that's all. What was it Shakespeare said? 'Blind fear, that seeing reason leads, finds safer footing than blind reason stumbling without fear.' It's dangerous to be without fear entirely."

She gaped at him.

"What?" he asked.

"You read Spenser and quote Shakespeare?" She gave a shaky laugh. "I swear, you are not at all what I thought."

The words brought him up short, reminding him of what else she'd said in the throes of her fear. "Yes, I know what you thought," he said tightly. "That I'm the sort of man to use your terror against you."

She winced. "I'm sorry. I'm just so used to the way Father—"

When she caught herself and dropped her gaze from his, a knot of apprehension twisted in his belly. "The way your father does what?" he prodded.

"Nothing."

She'd said her father must have revealed her weakness to him, and David saw nothing sinister in that.

But . . . now he remembered their dinner conversation that first night, with her father saying something about her inability to swim. Charlotte had gone white. At the time he hadn't thought anything of it, but . . .

"Charlotte, does your father use your fear of drowning to threaten you?"

For a long moment, she merely twisted the handkerchief in her hands. When at last she answered, her voice held a tinge of bitterness, "He tries."

Anger boiled up inside him. No wonder she was skittish around men. "All this time, I thought your father was merely an ass. Now I see he's a bully, too."

She met his gaze steadily. "He is indeed."

The knot in his belly tightened. "And you thought he put me up to this?"

Remorse spread over her cheeks. "I wasn't thinking. You were acting as if you'd changed your mind about marrying me, and given the threats Papa made on the way here about what he would do if I wasn't . . . nice to you, I thought he might have . . . or you might have . . ." She swallowed. "I'm sorry, I shouldn't have assumed that the two of you had conferred on the matter. It was very wrong. You've been nothing but nice to me."

"When I'm not forcing you to go riding," he said acidly, remembering how she'd reacted. "You think I'm a bully like him, don't you?"

"No." She lifted an earnest gaze to him. "Not anymore, David."

He blinked. "You called me David."

A warm smile trembled on her lips. "I suppose I did."

It was the most beautiful thing he'd ever heard. It made him painfully aware that she was sitting on his lap, with her delicate hands pressed to his chest and a new softness in her eyes.

Fire erupted in his veins. He didn't stop to think or give her any warning. He just kissed her.

And she kissed him back. By God, how she kissed him back, with the tender innocence of an untried maid. It was heaven. And hell. Because it wasn't enough.

Heedless of anything but how wonderful it felt, he grabbed her head and took her lips with more boldness. Before he'd even realized it, he was sliding his tongue inside her mouth.

She jerked back, her eyes huge. "What are you doing?"

He came reluctantly to his senses. "I'm sorry, I shouldn't have been so forward," he blathered, wanting to kick himself for alarming her yet again. "I just wanted to give you a real kiss—"

"A real kiss?" Instead of looking shocked or alarmed, she looked intrigued. "All right."

His pulse jumped into triple-time. "All right, what?"

She curled her fingers into his lapels with a tremulous smile. "Show me what a real kiss is."

Heat roared through him. Bending his head again, he brushed her lips with his. "Open your mouth to me, sweeting," he murmured, "and I will."

She did. And he did.

God help him. Charlotte's mouth was a heady feast. She was warm and luscious and unbearably sweet. And when she looped her arms about his neck and gave herself up to his now ravenous kiss with a shy excitement that fired his blood, he realized he was in trouble.

No night with a barmaid compared to this, the luxurious pleasure of kissing a woman who wanted him for himself, not for the money he could pay or the title that would one day be his. He could grow very used to this.

Bloody, bloody hell.

Chapter Six

꧁꧂

*C*harlotte had never dreamed that a respectable woman could find so much enjoyment from a kiss. She'd assumed that only the shameless females Papa consorted with were capable of that.

Judging from the soaring pleasure David was giving her with his mouth, relations between men and women might be very different from what she'd thought.

"Oh, sweeting," he murmured against her lips, "you're driving me mad."

"Me, too," she whispered.

It was all she got out before he took her mouth again, his tongue toying with hers, then delving in and out in silken strokes that made her quiver in odd places. Real kisses were even better than the other sort, and the other sort had been quite nice indeed.

His hands began to roam, at first just down to her shoulders, then up and down her sides as if he were counting her ribs. He was breathing hard—so was she, for that matter—and a strange lump had pressed up against her bottom.

Abruptly, he broke the kiss. "We have to stop this."

"Why?" she asked, still dazed by the deliciousness of being kissed so thoroughly.

He gave a shaky laugh. "Because I don't wish to deflower you here on the bank in front of God and everybody."

"Oh." Heat crawled up her cheeks. She wasn't sure what

deflowering involved, but it had to be scandalous. "Did I do something wrong?"

"Hardly." He cupped her face tenderly. "But I don't think we should keep sitting here like this."

In an instant, she realized that she was perched on his lap like some . . . some doxy, with her arms about his neck. Merciful heavens, what he must think of her!

Scrambling out of his lap, she said, "I'm sorry. I-I didn't—"

"Don't you dare apologize." He got up, too, and dusted off his breeches. "I don't regret one minute of those kisses. I hope you don't either."

A cautious smile crept over her lips. "No." So *this* was what it was like to do something naughty with a rogue. She rather enjoyed it.

She mustn't do it ever again, of course, especially if there was a risk of "deflowering," but she could see why young women were tempted. Kissing was awfully exciting.

"But I do regret ruining your lovely picnic," she went on.

"Nonsense, it's not a bit ruined."

Her gaze flew to his. "I can't go out there."

"I know." He grinned. "Wait here. I'll be right back."

She watched in confusion as he leaped into the boat and released it from its moorings. When he took up the oars and began pulling toward Saddle Island, her heart jumped into her throat in fear for his life.

But as he navigated the coursing waters of the river with expert ease, her blood quickened for another reason entirely. David was the very picture of virile male, all flexing muscles and windblown hair. She hated to admit it, but he was even handsomer than Captain Harris.

Captain Harris! Lord, she'd forgotten all about him.

What did that say for her character? She must be quite a wicked girl.

Now that she had the captain in mind, however, she couldn't help comparing the two men. In some ways they were similar—both attractive, both gentlemen, both strong and virile. Certainly, both of them made her laugh, which she considered very important, since Papa only made her angry.

But David was a thoroughbred stallion next to a gelding like Captain Harris. The captain had none of David's heat or restless energy—he was amiable, but not serious, the way David sometimes could be. Of course, David also had a roguish side, which, while entertaining, didn't speak well for his character.

David disappeared into the gazebo, emerging moments later with a big bundle that he placed in the bottom of the boat.

A smile touched her lips as he rowed back. He must have arranged this picnic ahead of time with his servants. Imagine that! For *her*. No wonder he'd been so determined to go out to Saddle Island.

Yet he'd changed his plans at her request. Any man who would do that for a woman couldn't be too lacking in character, could he? He liked the same books she did, and he dabbled in architecture. Surely that spoke well for him, too.

He reached the dock and moored the boat, then tramped up the bank with the bundle, which made clinking noises as he walked. "We can still have our picnic," he said. "And we needn't even have it here, if you don't want."

"Here is fine," she said gamely. It was the least she could do. "I can bear to *look* at the river, as long as it stays a healthy distance away from me."

For the next hour they had a pleasant time. He'd had the servants prepare a veritable feast—cold ham and cheese, bread and butter, peaches with cream, and some delicious little lemon cakes, washed down with wine from a silver flask. They talked about all sorts of things—his school, her governess, his hopes for the estate after he inherited.

She told him something she'd never revealed to anyone, that she secretly dreamed of opening a school for girls to teach them science and history and mathematics, the same things that men learned. He didn't mock her as another man might. He even seemed to understand why she was so passionate about the idea.

Once they were sated and the sun had slid down alarmingly, he reached into his coat and removed a snuff box. She'd seen him with it before and wondered if he took snuff. But he opened it to reveal a number of what smelled like lemon drops.

He offered her the box. "A sweet for the lady?"

"Is that what you always keep in there?" She took one and popped it into her mouth.

"Lemon drops. Peppermint drops. Bergamot drops." He grinned at her. "I have a bit of a sweet tooth."

"I did notice your liking for desserts," she teased as she took another and held it out to him.

With eyes gleaming, he caught her hand and brought it to his mouth, taking the sweet from her fingers.

As her breathing grew labored, he turned her hand over to kiss the palm, then kept hold of it. "I need to ask you something."

"That sounds serious," she said, struggling for nonchalance.

"It is." He threaded his fingers through hers. "I know

this is too soon, and you'll probably think me quite mad, but I want you to at least consider what I'm about to say."

For the first time since she'd met him, he looked uncomfortable. It was rather endearing.

"I want to marry you, Charlotte," he said bluntly.

Her breath caught in her throat. She didn't know whether to shout for joy or flee in alarm. "David . . ."

"Don't say anything yet." His eyes bore into hers with an intensity that made her shiver delightfully. "All I'm asking for right now is that you give me a chance. We have three more days before your family leaves. Just spend time with me, get to know me. Don't set your mind against me."

She flashed him a shy smile. "I'm not the least set against you, David."

Relief flooded his features. "Thank God."

"But . . ." She chewed on her lower lip. "I do have a few concerns."

"Why does that not surprise me?" he quipped, then added more soberly, "What sort of concerns?"

"I don't want a rogue for a husband," she told him, thinking of the flirtatious maid at breakfast. How many such maids vied for his attention every day? And how many did he kiss in the passionate way that he'd just kissed her?

His look of offended dignity reassured her a little. "I'm not such a rogue as all that," he growled. "I wouldn't marry a woman if I couldn't be faithful to her."

She wanted to believe him. "I have other concerns, too, like your gambling."

"I play the occasional game of cards, but no more. I hardly think it's enough to worry you."

"And your drinking?"

"Charlotte," he said firmly, "all I can promise is to be moderate in my habits. But I'm not going to turn into a monk, if that's what you want."

"No, it isn't," she hastened to say. Thinking of his fever-ish kisses, she added, "I'm not sure I'd like you as a monk. I just—"

"You're worried, I know. I understand that. And I prom-ise not to force you into anything. For the time being, I only ask that you let me court you, so you can get to know me as I really am. All right?"

She squeezed his hand. "I can do that."

"Good," he said in a husky voice. "That's good."

In the days that followed, David proved true to his word. He never again raised the subject of marriage, but he courted her with a vengeance. He brought her violets and wrote her a very bad sonnet. He rose before everyone else to take her riding. They spent hours talking, spinning wild dreams of a school for girls that he would build and that she would run.

It was all nonsense, of course. They had their prescribed roles. He was to be a great lord, and she was to marry one. Yet she enjoyed their fanciful talks—too much. She was afraid of falling in love with him, of being in love while he was only interested in making a good match.

Or in placating their parents. Their fathers were inordi-nately pleased to see them together, as was Mama. David's mother, however, didn't seem too happy about it. After their picnic, Lady Kirkwood ensured that they were always chaperoned.

Yet being with David, even with others around, was heady stuff. Although occasionally Charlotte felt guilty for having shifted her affections so quickly from the captain to David, she tried not to think about it.

The only dark spot on their courtship was when she came down on her last full day at Kirkwood Manor to find David in deep conversation with the maid, after which Molly hurried off, blushing furiously. When Charlotte asked him what they'd been talking about, he said it was a matter of household business and changed the subject.

Though the incident nagged at her all morning, she told herself she was seeing problems where there were none. In every other instance, David was showing himself to be a man of character. *That* was what she focused on.

That night, while the ladies were still in the drawing room and the gentlemen in the study, she slipped out to go to the retiring room at the same time as David left the men to retrieve another bottle of port from the cellar. Seeing her alone, he dragged her into an alcove and proceeded to kiss her senseless.

He met no resistance—she'd spent two days dreaming of being alone with him again, of kissing him again. To have this private interlude foisted upon her unexpectedly was like stumbling upon a well in a desert. All she could do was drink and drink and drink some more.

When at last they broke apart, he rasped, "Must you leave tomorrow?" He gripped her waist fiercely, his gaze raw and hot. "Surely if you asked your father, he'd prolong your stay another week."

"David," she said, having given that very matter some thought, "I need time apart from you to be sure about what we're doing."

His fingers dug into her waist. "You mean, time to compare me to your Captain Harris."

She laughed. "I assure you that Captain Harris is the furthest thing from my mind." But she didn't want to leap into marriage with a man she barely knew, especially while he was fogging her brain with his presence. She needed to consider the matter in the cold, rational light of her home, far away from David and his drugging kisses.

"Besides," she went on, "your father said you'll be going to town in a week. You can call on me then."

"All right. But in the meantime . . ." He kissed her again, so long and hard and deep that he left her half-swooning. When he drew back, his eyes were alight with a passion that sent shivers to her very toes. "*That* is to keep me fresh in your mind. Especially when you're consorting with that damned cavalry officer."

"Consorting! I do believe you're jealous, David Masters."

His mouth was set in a belligerent line. "So what if I am? I have some right to feel proprietary about you, don't I?"

She caught her breath. It was the first time he'd hinted at marriage since that day at the river. She knew what he was really asking, too—for a sign that they had, at the very least, an understanding.

"Yes," she said softly. "You do have some right."

The tension left his face. He was bending toward her once more when his mother appeared behind them.

They sprang apart, and he mumbled something about going to fetch the wine.

As soon as he'd left, Lady Kirkwood frowned at Charlotte. "If I were you, Miss Page, I'd be careful."

Fighting a blush, Charlotte tipped up her chin. "About what?"

"What you do with my son. The wrong sort of woman can easily tempt him into behaving badly."

The warning stung. "Then it's a good thing I'm not the wrong sort of woman, isn't it?"

The viscountess gave a thin smile. "What makes you think I was speaking of you? I merely thought you should know that my son came by his reputation honestly." She held out her arm. "Now come, your mother needs you."

Charlotte pushed past her to walk back into the drawing room with her head held high, but inside, she was a wreck. She had done everything to make her ladyship like her, but the woman seemed bound and determined not to. That was the only reason she would say such horrid things about her son. Wasn't it?

Lady Kirkwood's words kept Charlotte up that night, dry-mouthed and anxious. Charlotte had only known the adult David for less than a week. How could she be certain she was seeing the real him and not some version of him he took out for company?

Worse yet, Papa had chosen David as a husband for her—that in itself ought to put her on her guard. Except that David didn't like Papa, which showed David's discernment. Besides, she could judge a man as well as Papa, and her instincts told her that David was exactly what she thought—a sometimes roguish fellow with a good heart and a fine character. It was merely a trick of fate that Papa wanted them to marry. Letting that influence her either way would be foolish. Wouldn't it?

The night dragged on while she vacillated between worry about David's motives for marrying her, and dreams of what marriage to him might be like. After 3:00 A.M., she gave up on sleep and wandered down the hall to the library. She was just choosing a book when she heard a sound coming from outside.

When she went to look out the window, she smiled. Apparently she wasn't the only one who couldn't sleep. David stood below on the terrace—though his back was to her, she knew him from his atrocious dressing gown. Even in the dimness of moonlight, the stripes showed up well.

She was just wondering if she dared to go downstairs and slip out to join him when someone else appeared. It was that flirtatious maid, Molly. The girl sidled up next to him, then slid between him and the rail to loop her arms about his neck.

Tensing, Charlotte waited for David to put the girl aside. But he didn't. Instead, he began to kiss her with the same ardent passion he'd shown Charlotte.

Only he didn't stop with kissing. As Charlotte watched in horror, he pulled up Molly's skirts and lifted her legs on either side of his in the same vulgar position Charlotte recognized from when she'd once caught Papa with a whore. Then David began to move in a similarly vulgar fashion.

Charlotte's heart shattered.

Blanching, she jerked back from the window, struggling to choke down the bile rising in her throat. How could it be? How could he do this to her? She'd thought that he might actually be falling in love with her.

Oh Lord, how utterly wrong she'd been about him! And to think she'd been in his arms just hours ago! How dared he? They might not be betrothed yet, but they had an understanding. How could he kiss Charlotte with such passion and then the same night do . . . do *that* to some kitchen maid? It was unconscionable! Appalling!

Unforgivable. This wasn't acceptable—not before they

married, not ever. If he could flit so easily from one woman's arms to another, he wasn't the man she'd thought.

This was what she could look forward to if she married him. How long would it be before he was parading his women in front of her? How long before her life ended up exactly like Mama's? It was no wonder Papa approved of him—wolves always ran in packs.

Her stomach roiled, and she rushed back to her bedchamber just in time to lose the contents of her belly in the chamber pot. She stood over it, trembling, her skin clammy as she hugged her stomach. What was she to do?

She had to break it off, that was all, as quickly and discreetly as possible.

But how? If she didn't give him a reason for changing her mind, he'd just kiss her and talk sweetly to her until she relented. And if she berated him for what she'd seen, he would dismiss it or deny it. Worse yet, he might bully her into marrying him anyway. Thanks to her, he now knew exactly how to do it, too—just go to Papa and let Papa do the bullying for him.

He wouldn't do that, her heart said. *He's not that sort of man.*

Tears stung her eyes. Her heart hadn't thought he was the sort of man to dally with one woman while engaging himself to another, either. Her heart was a blind fool, ignoring all the evidence of his character. Even now, her heart protested the very evidence of her eyes, telling her that she must have seen a servant or Giles.

She caught her breath. *Might* it have been Giles? Might she have jumped to the wrong conclusion?

For a second, she clung to that hope. Then she remembered how that girl had always flirted with David. Not

Giles, but David. Molly had even blushed at something he'd said this morning. For all Charlotte knew, he'd been arranging tonight's assignation. He'd certainly acted as if he had something to hide. If he hadn't, then why had he changed the subject when Charlotte asked him about it?

There was that hideous robe, too. On their very first day, Giles had come down to breakfast in his own dressing robe, a faded blue silk thing.

Her heart twisted in her chest. No, only David was so confident of his appeal that he felt safe wearing the ugliest stripes. And she'd fallen for that confidence, too! How could she have been such an idiot? How could she not have realized that David's tender solicitations were false? Clearly he'd been acting a part the whole time, determined to gain her money.

He said he didn't care about your money.

He'd said he didn't want to marry either, but that had certainly changed once he saw that she was pretty! Apparently he could stomach marrying for money if his wife was handsome enough to tolerate.

Tears now streamed down her cheeks. How could she have let herself be so deceived about him? What was wrong with her?

She spent the next hour sobbing into her pillow. Even after she was cried out, choking desolation filled her. She lay in bed, clutching the damp pillow to her chest. If she could just keep herself together for another few hours, they would be leaving this place. She would be safe.

Safe? A chill struck her. Perhaps from David and his two-faced lying and cheating, but not from Papa. He wouldn't care that David had dallied with a maid. If she told him of it, he would just give her some nonsense about looking the other way, since that was precisely what he expected from Mama. And if she said she meant to refuse David . . .

Her mouth went dry. She dared not tell Papa yet. Remembering his threats, she rubbed her arms feverishly in a vain attempt to banish the icy fear stealing over her. Papa wouldn't accept her refusal. He would take her onto a boat and sail the seas until she begged him to stop, until she agreed to whatever he demanded.

Oh, what was she to do? She could wait until they reached London to tell Papa, but that would only delay the worst. Eventually David would make a formal offer, and Papa would demand that she accept it. And if she didn't . . .

Icy tendrils of fear curled round her heart. The only way Papa would leave her alone was if David never made an offer at all. Papa would blame *her* for it, of course, but he wouldn't be able to do anything about it.

Her breath quickened. Yes, that would work!

But how to manage it? Leaving the bed, she paced the bedchamber. She had to make David give her up. She would dearly love to throw his dalliance with the maid back in his face, but he would just deny it. So she had to convince him that she had simply changed her mind, but in such a way that he was glad of it. She had to provoke him into despising her.

Spotting the writing table, she walked toward it. She would write him a letter detailing exactly why she was a bad choice for a wife, fortune or no. She would promise to make his life a misery if he married her. And since he hated having his pride pricked, she would do that, too. She would infuriate him to the point that he washed his hands of her and her whole family.

Giving him a piece of her mind wouldn't prove difficult; right now, it was all she could do not to throttle him for how he'd betrayed her. Her blood teeming with righteous indignation, she sat down and picked up her pen.

It took two hours to perfect her missive. When it was done, she sat back, drained but feeling decidedly more in control. If he didn't decide against marrying her within moments of reading this, then he was a fool. He might be a heartless, smooth-tongued cad, but David was no fool.

Now she must manage her good-byes without showing her unhappiness, so neither David nor Papa suspected anything. And the letter had to be left for David without Papa learning of it and demanding to see what she'd written. After all, young ladies weren't allowed to write to young gentlemen on their own.

She hid the letter in her writing case, then stretched out on the bed while she decided how to deliver it. A servant? No, she couldn't trust them not to tell Papa or David's parents of it.

Could she sneak it into David's room? Hardly. He had probably returned to his bedchamber by now, and if she were caught with him there, she'd *have* to marry him or be disgraced.

Perhaps she could wait until she reached home . . .

It seemed like only moments later that Papa's shouting made her start up in confusion. Lord, she'd fallen asleep! Papa was ordering the footmen about, trying to hurry them along with taking down the packed trunks.

The door edged open and her mother's head appeared. "Oh, good, you're awake. Your father is eager to be off. He's worried about the weather. Are you packed?"

Papa pushed into the room. "Never mind that." He planted his hands on his hips. "How do you stand with young Masters?"

A pity she couldn't speak the truth: *I detest and despise him, and I will never marry him!*

She sat up in bed. "I believe he intends to call on me in London, Papa."

Papa frowned. "So he hasn't offered marriage?"

"Not formally, no."

"But you think that he will."

She steeled herself for the lie. "Probably. It's only been a few days."

"True. A young man like that—he has to be cautious."

She clenched her hands into fists behind her back. "Yes."

"Well then, missy, get dressed. We have to be off."

Thankfully, Papa was in such a hurry that she only had to see David briefly, and his mother kept them from having a private moment. Still, the way he looked at her made her blood boil. How *dare* he give her that smoldering glance after what he'd done?

She fumed about it all the way back to London. By the time they reached home, several hours later, she'd figured out how to send her letter. She couldn't use one of the servants, since they all spied for Papa, and she couldn't mail it without Papa franking it. He would want to read it first.

But David would be in London in a few days, and there was a lad who sold cross buns in front of the house every morning. She would pay him to deliver it. She'd just have to make sure that while David knew exactly whom it came from, there was nothing to tie it to her in case it fell into the wrong hands.

She'd be careful, very careful. But one way or the other, she would get David Masters out of her life forever.

Tom Dempsey couldn't believe it. The young miss at 15 St. James's Square had entrusted him with a letter to deliver. And she was paying him handsomely, too. It almost made him forget the rain as he hurried along the streets, the prized letter carefully tucked inside his breast pocket.

Unfortunately, he was so busy congratulating himself on his good fortune that he didn't see the older lad with a bag stuffed full of envelopes until he ran smack into him. It exploded to scatter mail around him like gigantic confetti.

"You ass!" the other lad snapped as Tom stood gaping at the disaster. "What the devil do you think you're doing?" He boxed Tom's ears. "Well, come on then, help me pick these up! Mr. Bowmar will have my head if I lose all these letters on account of you!"

The two boys scrambled to gather them up as the rain beat down on their backs and the ink on the envelopes began to run. When the last one was in the bag, the other lad ran off without even so much as a thank-you.

"Bloody sot," Tom grumbled, now soaked to the skin as he hurried on.

But when he got to the proper address, he reached inside his pocket to find that his letter was gone. Frantically, he patted all his pockets, then retraced his steps, hoping perhaps he'd dropped it on the path. After reaching the corner where he'd encountered the other fellow and still not finding it, he had to acknowledge the truth. Somehow it had fallen out and been mixed in with those other letters.

He groaned. That scurvy fellow was gone, and Tom's good fortune with him.

The miss had said she would give him one of her ear bobs when he delivered the letter and the other when he brought back a note from the butler of the house saying he'd done so. Now he had nothing to bring her. And what was he to do with one ear bob?

Blast, blast, blast.

Meanwhile, in the offices of the *Morning Tattler,* Charles Godwin, a young reporter, was called into his editor's office.

"Listen to this letter that just came in," Bowmar said, brandishing a sheet of paper. It sat atop a pile of woeful-looking missives with running ink. Bowmar read aloud a few lines of a rather sharp litany of some poor fellow's sins. "I want you to use it in one of those editorial pieces that you're so good at, the ones about the evils of society. It's juicy stuff."

Bowmar tossed it to him, and Charles read it. It was witty, in a flay-a-body-alive sort of way, but he would swear it had *not* been meant for the paper. "You can't publish this. It's clearly personal."

Bowmar flashed his usual smarmy smile. "It came with the rest of the mail. And there's no return address."

Charles turned the sheet over to see nothing but blurred ink. He thought he could make out an *M,* but that was it. "It doesn't matter. You still can't print it in good conscience. It's obviously private, and someone will come after you for libel." He handed the letter back to Bowmar, pointing to one particular line. "Why, it even mentions that the man is a viscount's son."

"It hints at it, that's all. Besides, there are any number of viscounts' sons. And no one can come after the paper for libel unless what's said in here is false. Even if they do, you simply point out that the letter begins with 'Dear Garish

Goer' and is signed 'Miss Monkey.' No one could blame you for thinking it was meant for publication."

Bowmar's blithe unconcern angered Charles. The two parties would surely recognize who was meant, even if no one else did. The letter was intensely private, clearly the result of a love affair gone terribly wrong. Somewhere a young lady's heart was breaking because a scoundrel had misused her. It seemed wicked to profit from her misery.

The fact that Bowmar didn't care about that and expected him to do the dirty work roused his hot temper, something Charles was famous for. "Only a cad with no heart would print this letter."

Bowmar sat back and sneered. "Heart? A heart has no place in the newspaper business, sir. Material as juicy as this will sell papers by the hundreds."

"I won't do it. It's wrong."

Narrowing his eyes to slits, Bowmar said, "You'll do as I say if you want to keep your position."

Since coming to work for Bowmar two years ago, Charles had suffered several moral dilemmas. He'd gritted his teeth and weathered every one without losing his job. But this one really stuck in his craw. And he'd had enough.

"I don't give a damn about my position, if this is what I have to do for it." He turned toward the door. "I quit."

Charles walked out without a backward glance.

Chapter Seven

❧

Five days after the Pages had left Berkshire for town, David rode toward home after his early morning gallop. Riding had been his salvation ever since Charlotte had left, though it didn't keep his mind off her.

A smile curved his lips. He was in love. No question about that. He could hardly sleep without thinking of her. And in only two days he would see her again in London. This time he would make her give him an answer. He might be young, and he might sometimes be a fool, but he was not going to let her get away.

Of course, Father would be delighted. He sighed. He hated that he was playing right into Father's hands, but it couldn't be helped. If practicality and love just happened to coincide, well, who was he to question it?

As soon as David entered the manor, the servant told him his father was calling for him most urgently. David hurried to his father's study, surprised to find the man pacing and drinking whisky, never a good sign at this hour.

"You wanted me, Father?"

His father whirled to fix him with a look that would have frozen steam, then slapped a newspaper down on the desk. "Do you want to explain how this happened?"

"How *what* happened?" David asked, utterly bewildered.

"There is an article here that says scathing things about a gentleman who sounds an awful lot like you."

A chill coursed down David's spine. Scathing things about *him*? In the bloody *Morning Tattler*?

Grabbing up the paper, he began to read. It was an editorial full of pompous attacks against "wayward" gentlemen. As an example, the editor had produced a letter from a young female whose dignity had been trampled by such a man:

Dear Garish Goer,

Recently I have come to understand that honor and good character are costumes of convenience to you—something you don when you wish to dine on a particularly juicy female. But we both know that beneath the costly striped dressing gown you're so vain about lies a heart as fickle and deadly as the waters of the Thames.

So while you are gambling and wenching with your debauched friends from Cambridge, busily counting the days until you become a viscount and can live a wild life with impunity, remember this: There was once a lady who saw you for what you really are. She saw the vanity behind your every remark and the falseness behind your every kiss. You lulled her good sense for a brief time with a rakehell's sensuous spell, but in the end she recognized you for an unrepentant libertine who gains amusement from deceiving a feeling young lady, and pleasure from destroying female lives.

If you should happen to ask for her hand, be clear on one thing. She might marry you if forced, but she

*will never look the other way for your dissipation,
never countenance your bullying, and never give
you what a man expects from his wife—loyalty and
support. So you might want to think twice before
taking an asp into your bed.*

> *Yours with contempt,
> Miss Monkey*

He couldn't breathe, his blood roaring so loudly in his ears he thought he might faint like some stupid girl. Miss Monkey. It was by Charlotte? How could she have written this . . . this vile thing?

Every word was a knife to his heart. He barely registered the rest of the editorial, in which the editor raged about the behavior of young gentlemen toward respectable women in the vicinity of Cambridge. He didn't hear his father's questions or even notice the room around them. He just stood there, impaled on her words.

Why had she written this? What had he done? They'd had an understanding. He'd been sure that she cared for him. The last time he'd kissed her, she'd seemed as happy and eager to be married as he.

"Well?" his father repeated. "I can see from your face that it's about you."

He nodded, only half-conscious of doing so.

"Am I to guess from the timing of it that it was written by Charlotte Page?"

"Most assuredly," he said dully.

"So what have you to say for yourself? What did you do to that girl?"

Heat rose in his cheeks. "I did nothing except ask her to be my wife." And act like a besotted fool. And bare his heart for her dagger, which even now twisted in his breast. "She must have heard gossip about me after she returned to London."

But why had she believed it? That's what sent the knife digging deep—the fact that she had learned some nastiness about his wenching, and instead of coming to him about it, had done *this*. She hadn't even waited until she saw him again to accuse him. She had sent it to the bloody paper to be published! How could she?

He'd known she was a bit high in the instep, that she had wild notions about him and his reputation, but he'd never expected something so inexplicably cruel. What sort of woman did such a thing?

His only consolation was that no one would guess it was he who . . .

The blood chilled to ice in his veins. He read it again, a glacier creeping over his body, freezing everything it touched. "Everyone will know it's me."

"Ridiculous," his father said. "She at least had the good sense not to use any names. The only reason *I* guessed it was the bit about your dressing gown."

David glanced up at his father. "Exactly. I wore that dressing gown at Cambridge many a time. I was known for it." He let out a foul curse. "It won't take long for word to get round that it's me."

The color drained from Father's face. "Where is it now?"

"I gave it to Giles."

Father called for Giles. As soon as the young man entered, Father asked, "Where is the dressing gown your brother gave you?"

Giles glanced uncertainly at David. "Why?"

"Do you have it?" Father barked.

"It's in my dresser."

"Have you worn it publicly yet?"

Giles swallowed, clearly afraid he was being accused of something. "No, sir."

"Good. Then burn it."

"What? Why?"

David tossed him the paper, then turned to his father. "Burning it will do no good. Hundreds of chaps at Cambridge saw me in it."

As Giles read the story, David stalked the room, unable to get warm, unable to stop the ice stealing over him.

"We'll sue the *Tattler* for libel," Father said.

David whirled on his heel. "Thus confirming for everyone that it's me? Are you mad?"

"According to you, they'll know that already," Father bit out. "Besides, if the little bitch wants to ruin you publicly, she should suffer ruin as well."

For some reason, an image of a terrified Charlotte balking at going on the river swam into David's mind. But of course it was a false image. If she truly feared her father, why send this letter to a newspaper? Surely she was clever enough to realize that Lord Page would recognize her hand in it. The man had seen David in the dressing gown one morning. He would put together the rest.

David bit back a foul oath. Perhaps that was why she'd done it—to punish her father. That at least made sense. She wasn't brave enough to identify herself, but she was brave enough to drag the son of her father's friend through a scandal in order to destroy Lord Page's scheme of marriage.

Whatever her reasons, they were insupportable. He would never forget what she'd done. Or forgive it.

The glacier stealing over his body now crept toward his heart. "As appealing as ruining Miss Page sounds to me at the moment," David ground out, "that is the surest way to fuel the fire. She'll be touted as a martyr while I am vilified in the press for my attempt to vilify *her*. Give the press even a morsel of the truth, and they will pounce on us like ravening dogs. They'll unearth the fact that you wanted me to marry her for her fortune and that her father had hopes for political gain. We'll be publicly humiliated as scheming scoundrels, which is probably exactly what she wants."

The arctic fury sliding over him was vastly preferable to that first white-hot lance of pain in his heart. He welcomed the frost, embraced it, letting it freeze his soul to a solid block of ice. "Silence is our best recourse. Silence, and a hope that no one connects me to this bloody letter."

His father glanced over at Giles. "What are you doing standing there like a slack-jawed fool? Go burn that dressing gown. That's one thing we can do."

"Yes, sir," he mumbled and fled the room.

David stared after him, now numb to the very soles of his feet.

"I'm sorry, son," his father said in a low voice. "This is my fault, for bringing them here. For asking you to consider the chit as a wife. I had no idea she was such a madwoman."

No, but David had known. Somewhere in the part of him that treated all people with caution, he'd known that she and her parents were an unpredictable lot. He should have listened to that instinct, instead of letting his cock lead him into trouble as usual.

Much as he hated to admit it, Father had been right. Love *was* for fools and children. David should never have conflated the practical advantages of marrying Charlotte with some dubious and foolish emotion. Then he wouldn't be standing here with his heart in shreds.

Fine. He would weather this as best he could, but he would learn from his mistakes. There would be no more debauchery, no more whining about Father's investments, no more drunken orgies with his friends. There would certainly be no more attempts at love matches. He was done with that. He would set the course of his life with the same ruthless efficiency as she.

And after the gossip had died down, and he'd had time to develop a plan, he would make Charlotte Page pay for making a public laughingstock out of him. Just see if he didn't.

Charlotte was about to enter the breakfast room when her father's raised voice wafted out to her in the hall.

"I tell you, this time she's gone too far!" Papa shouted.

Her heart racing, Charlotte slid up next to the door to listen.

"You don't know that it was her," came her mother's timid voice. "Truly, Rowland—"

"What? You can defend her after this travesty?" There was a rustle of paper. "She sent it to the *Morning Tattler,* of all things! I saw young Masters in that dressing gown one morning—I know he's the one who is meant in the letter."

Charlotte's heart nearly stopped. A letter? They'd got hold of *her* letter? No, that wasn't possible. It wouldn't be in the newspaper.

"It does sound like him," Mama said, "but I'm sure it

was some other girl who wrote to the paper. He does have a reputation, you know."

"What about this line here: 'as fickle and deadly as the waters of the Thames'? It's something she would say. And she actually called him an 'unrepentant libertine' before we arrived in Berkshire. Don't you remember her terming his friends 'debauched'?"

Fear crawled up from Charlotte's belly, clawing at her, making her sway on her feet as she recognized phrases from her letter. Oh god oh god oh god, how had it ended up in the *Morning Tattler*?

"I don't think our Charlotte would—"

A smack sounded, then a sharp cry from Mama. Charlotte stilled, panic gripping her. Papa had never hit Mama that she knew of. If he were to start now, because of Charlotte's stupid, *stupid* letter . . .

"Rowland, please," her mother said in a low voice, "hitting the furniture will accomplish nothing. The servants will hear. Besides, you can't be sure that it *was* her."

Relief coursed through Charlotte, but it was only temporary. Papa's temper was sure to be ungovernable after this. And what would he do to her? He would never forgive her for this, never!

"I've asked her three times since we returned how it went with him," he cried, "and she got close-mouthed about it every time." The paper rattled again. "That's because she was plotting *this*, damn her! I won't stand for it, do you hear? She will apologize to him in person. I'll see her grovel before him and all his family if that's what it takes to make this right! Because if she doesn't, I'll suspend her by her damned feet from the London Bridge until she does!"

The very idea sent horror slicing through Charlotte.

Papa continued to curse as he tramped about the room. "I swear to you I'm never letting her leave this house again. She will stay locked up in her room until hell freezes over! I've had enough of her impudence!"

She was done for. Fearing he would burst into the hall any minute and find her skulking there, she crept toward the back entrance to the house. Once she got outside, she ran for the furthermost corner of their little garden.

She paced beneath her favorite willow, frantic to figure out what had happened and what she should do. How could her letter have gone to a newspaper? Oh, if she ever saw that Tom Dempsey again, she would box his ears! She'd known something was wrong when he never returned for the other ear bob.

"Miss Page!" hissed a voice from behind her, making her start.

Turning toward the iron bars of the fence, she was shocked to find Captain Harris sitting astride his charger in the alley. Color crept up her cheeks. She'd scarcely thought of him in these past few days, too caught up in her pain over David's betrayal.

"What are you doing here?" she whispered, hurrying toward the fence.

Before she could stop him, he'd vaulted off his horse and over the sharp-tipped bars to land on his feet before her.

"I came to pay a call on you," Captain Harris said, "but the butler told me you weren't home to visitors. So I rode back to the alley, hoping for a glimpse of you."

Under the circumstances, she didn't know whether to be flattered or alarmed. "I-I suppose you read the letter in the paper."

His eyes narrowed. "So I was right. It *was* you who wrote it."

She dropped her head in shame. "I didn't mean for it to go to the papers, I swear. It was supposed to be private." A thought occurred to her that chilled her blood. "How did you know it was mine?" If *he* had known, others might know, too.

She had kept David's name out of it, so no one would guess about him, but they might figure out that it was she who'd written it. She would never be able to marry! Who would marry the woman who wrote such a letter, no matter how justified?

Catching her by the chin, Captain Harris lifted her head until her gaze met his. "I was so utterly miserable after you'd gone that I paid one of the servants to tell me where you were, and they said your family was in Berkshire visiting the Masters family. And word is already spreading around town that young Masters is the man who was meant in the letter. But I have not told a soul about your connection to this, I swear."

His expression growing even more solemn, he seized her hand. "Indeed, I have come to save you. I won't let your father marry you off to such a cad. I won't!"

She caught her breath. "What do you mean to do?"

"To marry you myself, dear girl." Dropping to one knee, he pressed a fervent kiss to her hand. "I adore you. Could you not tell?"

Come to think of it, no. In light of her explosive kisses with David, her brief flirtation with Captain Harris now seemed more like a courtly minuet than the prelude to a love affair.

She frowned. Of course it did. For all his easy manner, Captain Harris wasn't a rakehell and a scoundrel. He hadn't practiced for years at breaking young ladies' hearts, nor was he capable of insulting a woman with fiery but decidedly improper kisses. If that made him a tad less interesting, it was only because villainy could be awfully enticing. But villainy was villainy, and the captain's appearance here despite her disgrace showed that he was not a villain.

"We will leave for Scotland this very hour," he went on, staring up into her face with a look that did seem rather adoring. "Even now, a friend awaits us with a post chaise that will outrun anything your father can send after you. We can be in Gretna Green in a matter of days, and you will be safe once and for all from the cruel marriage your father seeks to arrange."

It was a bold plan of action, a decidedly romantic plan that would have had her throwing herself into his arms two weeks ago. But David's betrayal had made her cautious. Even as she thrilled to the captain's offer, her father's cold words about the man's intentions trickled into her mind, insidious in their poison.

"This is rather sudden," she said.

His face darkened. "Perhaps you still have feelings for this scoundrel."

"No!" She squeezed his hand. "No, never."

With an earnest glance, he pressed her hand to his chest. "If you're worried about your past with him, I swear you need not. I will never reproach you for anything that you and he might have done in the heat of the moment."

"My past? Done?" When it dawned on her what he was saying, she blushed violently and attempted to pull her hand free. "I assure you, sir, that I am still chaste. I would never allow—"

"Of course not, dearest Charlotte, I didn't mean to imply otherwise." Refusing to relinquish her hand, he scattered frantic kisses over it. "You *will* let me call you Charlotte, won't you?" His eyes raked her with a tenderness that soothed the insult she'd thought he was offering her.

"You know that Papa isn't likely to give you my dowry," she cautioned him. "He's very angry over what I wrote."

"I don't care," he said, with a lofty air that sounded sincere. "It is you I want. We will live on love."

The idyllic promise made her wince. She wasn't sure what love was anymore, but she was fairly certain she didn't feel it for Captain Harris. Still, if he felt it for her, that was more than she could expect now that she'd destroyed her life. Indeed, he was risking everything to have her. If anyone ever learned that she'd written the letters, he would be publicly mocked. For a man to take such a chance on her behalf surely showed deep feeling.

And what choice did she have, anyway? If she didn't marry Captain Harris, Papa would make her life hell. He would force her to apologize to David, which was unthinkable. As mortified as she was that the letter had ended up in the papers, she saw no reason she should apologize when David was the one who'd wronged her.

Besides, if the press discovered that she had written the letter, everything would turn even uglier. It would mean a huge scandal, and Papa would make sure she suffered for it.

But if she ran off with Captain Harris, Papa could never hurt her again. She would have her own household and a dashing husband who cared about her. In time she would surely come to love him.

When she smiled faintly at the thought, Captain Harris clutched her hand to his heart. "Is that a yes, dear Charlotte?" he asked, his eyes almost as lovely as David's.

Thrusting the traitorous comparison from her mind, she covered his hand with hers. "Indeed it is, sir. I accept your proposal."

Chapter Eight

❦

Richmond, England
November 1824

Shaken by her encounter with the ghosts of her past, Charlotte stood at her office window watching David ride off in his carriage. He had not changed. He was still as aggressive and bold as ever.

She rather liked that about him.

In recent years, she had grown used to making men dance to her tune. From the moment she had established this school, she had sworn that no man would ever bully her as Papa had done. No man would ever use her for his own purposes as her late husband had done. In her little domain, *she* was in control.

Even Cousin Michael had respected her boundaries. It had been wonderful to have a friendship with a man who knew the difference between dictating and advising, whose very anonymity made it easy for her to talk honestly with him. And to keep at a distance.

David had never kept her at a distance—until she'd mailed that stupid letter that had cut them off forever.

She still couldn't believe no one else had ever learned who had written the thing, but within days the world had figured out for certain that David was its subject. That cursed dressing gown had said it all. Who could have known he was the only viscount's son from Cambridge who'd ever worn a striped dressing gown?

By then, Charlotte had been newly married to Jimmy, and in no position to do anything about it. So she'd had to watch in abject mortification as David was vilified in the press. Even though she had still hated him for his betrayal, she had not wanted him to suffer public humiliation.

There had been mocking caricatures printed for the shops, irate letters to the paper. He had been given the cut direct by half the ladies in good society. After all, it was one thing for a well-born buck to live a dissolute life—it was quite another to do it so indiscreetly that young ladies wrote letters to the newspaper about him.

Although his friends had rallied around to protect him as best they could, every barmaid he had ever drunkenly bussed had told her story for the press, and every sin he had ever committed was trotted out for the public's amusement.

Through it all, David had remained utterly silent, never revealing her name. At the time, she had assumed it was because he had not wanted her to tell her side of the story, making him look even worse than he already did.

Now she knew better. Years later, she had learned that Giles, not David, had been the one wearing the robe on that awful night. And her shame had been complete.

It still filled her with horror to think of what she had done so impetuously. Granted, her fear of her father had been very real, and she had truly believed that David was toying with her affections. Still, she should have taken proper care to make sure the letter never fell into the wrong hands. Her pique and cowardice had ruined David's reputation for a long time.

What might her life have been like if she had gone to him in person instead of writing that stupid letter? Or what if he had guessed his brother's part in the matter and came after her to reveal her mistaken assumptions?

A sigh escaped her. She probably would not have believed him. She had been so certain of his bad character, so convinced of her own good judgment. Then she had compounded her mistake by running off with Jimmy. At the memory of Jimmy's proposal, she shook her head. Foolish, silly girl. Live on love, indeed. What a joke that had proved to be.

She turned away from the window. Not that Jimmy hadn't cared for her. Sometimes she thought he really had. Certainly they'd had some enjoyable times together. But in the end, the money had clouded everything.

Her elopement and the ensuing scandal had sent Papa over the edge. He'd had a stroke, dying before he could change his will and disinherit her. Her mother had followed shortly after. As a result, Charlotte had received a very handsome inheritance. All of which merely compounded her guilt and shame. She couldn't help blaming herself for her parents' deaths.

Jimmy had told her not to. But then, Jimmy had been eager to spend her money, so he had hardly cared how it had come to them. Unfortunately, spending her inheritance had been his right as her husband. It had taken him a mere two years to work through the entirety by living extravagantly and investing badly.

By the time he had made the mistake of insulting a fellow officer and dying on the dueling field for it, there had been only enough money left to pay for his funeral. And even then, she'd had to borrow against his small pension.

Thank heaven she had been able to find a position with a girls' school in Chelsea, or who knows how she would have lived?

"Good morning, Charlotte," boomed a robust male voice behind her.

She jumped, then spun around to find her closest male friend standing in the doorway. "For heaven's sake, Charles, don't startle me like that!"

Charles Godwin quirked up one blond brow. "Actually, since I'm ten minutes late, I expected you to be out front tapping your foot, ready to remind me how busy you are when school's in session."

Late? For what?

Suddenly it hit her. He had promised to take her into town to view the Angerstein Collection today, so she could make sure that the paintings would be acceptable viewing for her girls. "Oh Lord, I completely forgot. I am so sorry."

With a smile that looked forced, he entered the room. "Does your sudden lapse of memory have anything to do with the fact that I just saw Kirkwood's carriage leaving here?"

Merciful heaven, this was awkward. Unable to meet his eyes, she went to sit behind her desk. "As a matter of fact, yes. He came here to discuss a matter of business."

"Business?" Suspicion darkened his handsome features.

Charles was the only person alive, other than David's family, who knew about her and David. She hadn't even told Cousin Michael, unable to bear letting him know the worst about her.

But Charles knew it. Indeed, that was how she and the newspaperman had become friends. If anyone could advise her, it was he. Like Cousin Michael, he never pressed her beyond what she would accept.

Gesturing to a chair, she waited until Charles dropped into it before explaining about David's visit and Sarah's bequest.

When she mentioned the amount, Charles's blue gaze narrowed. "That doesn't sound like Sarah."

"No," she agreed. "But Lord Kirkwood insists that she was always a supporter of the school."

"It must really stick in his craw that the woman who once destroyed his reputation will now receive a hefty portion of his wife's money."

"If it did, I saw no sign of it. He said that what happened between him and me is all in the past. And he acted as if it truly were."

"Ah, I see."

But Charles did not *look* as if he saw anything. He looked shaken. And she feared she knew why. Although Charles had been devastated by the death of his wife, Judith, a couple of years ago, in the past few months he had made it clear that he was ready to move on with his life. Judging from his recent behavior, which was more like a suitor's than a friend's, his readiness to move on included Charlotte.

She did not know what to do about it. She had always liked him a great deal, but had never thought of him as a man she could marry. She had been quite close to Judith, and it seemed disloyal to contemplate him as anything but her old friend's husband. She suspected that the only reason he had not yet asked her to marry was that he realized how awkward things would become between them if she refused him.

Sometimes she wondered if *he* might be Cousin Michael. After all, Charles had come into a fortune through an uncle around the time of Jimmy's death—it was what he had used to purchase the failing *Morning Tattler* and transform it from a gossipy rag into the *London Monitor,* a radical paper advocating government reform. Being married, he would have wanted to keep his involvement with her school very private.

Still, she had read his editorials—which bore no resemblance to Cousin Michael's style. And if indeed Charles had been masquerading as her cousin all those years, why continue to do so now that he did not have Judith's feelings and reputation to protect?

"May I see the document Kirkwood brought you?" Charles asked.

"Of course." She handed it to him.

He took his time, reading it more carefully than she'd had a chance to. "Only an attorney could say for certain, but it seems legitimate."

"Why wouldn't it be legitimate?"

"Because it makes no sense. Sarah was certainly vain enough to want a building named after her, but this nonsense about having Kirkwood oversee the design seems blatantly intended to throw you and her husband together. That isn't something she would do, even from the grave."

Heat rose in Charlotte's cheeks. "Sarah did not know about my previous association with her husband."

"You can't be sure of that. Husbands say a great many things in the privacy of the marital bed."

She sucked in a breath. That had not even occurred to her, though it would explain why Sarah had always been so nasty toward her. "So what are you saying? That Lord

Kirkwood *invented* this legacy? Why? What would it accomplish?"

He shrugged. "Perhaps he wants to begin where the two of you left off. This gives him an excuse for doing so."

A wild laugh escaped her. "You must be joking. What I did to him was unforgivable."

Charles gazed steadily at her. "You're a beautiful and successful woman, Charlotte. Perhaps after marriage to Silly Sarah, Kirkwood wants a wife with more character."

There was no mistaking the jealousy in Charles's voice. She rose, uncomfortable with the direction the conversation had taken.

"If even I," Charles went on, "who didn't know you at the time, recognized how you were hurting when you wrote that letter, then perhaps he did, too."

"Do not be a fool." She went to stand at the window. "According to Anthony, who told me about it without knowing of my involvement, David Masters only spoke of me once to his friends. Although he would not reveal my identity even with them, he called me a vile name and thanked God that he had not ended up 'leg-shackled to a woman who was half-mad.' Does that sound to you like a man who could tell I was 'hurting'?"

"It sounds like a man in the heat of anger," Charles said. "But eighteen years gives a person time to cool down. And you said yourself that he didn't act today as if he were angry."

"No, but neither did he act as if he were eager to court me. David always was able to put a good face on things when necessary."

"*David?*" Charles echoed, always the observant man of the press. "After all these years, you still think of him by his Christian name?" As she cursed her quick tongue, he added, "You must still have feelings for him."

She whirled around, startled. "Do not be absurd. That is well in the past."

He studied her for a long moment. "If you say so."

She managed a smile. "This is nonsense. Sarah undoubtedly did this out of vanity, and thought it would be great fun to force her husband into being part of it." Walking to her desk, she picked up the notebook she was taking to the Angerstein exhibit in Pall Mall. "Let's go. If we do not leave soon, we will not have time to view the paintings before you have to be back at the paper."

"I can spare a day." He rose, his gaze still on her. "Besides, after we're done at the exhibit, we should pay a visit to my friend Robert Jackson. He may be able to shed more light on this interesting document of Kirkwood's."

"I already intend to bring it to *my* attorney."

"Do not take this wrong, my dear, but while your attorney is perfectly acceptable for dealing with parent contracts and vendor agreements, you need someone with a specialized knowledge of estate law. Jackson has that."

A sigh escaped her. She hated it when he was right. "Very well." She set her shoulders. "But I will pay the attorney's fee."

"For God's sake, Charlotte, let me—"

"I mean it. Either I pay the fee or I do not use him."

With an exasperated look, he offered his arm. "As you wish, madam. Though I don't understand why you must always be so willful."

Cautious, more like. Though she took his arm and let him lead her out, she had learned the hard way that a woman was responsible for saving herself. Relying on a man was dicey business. She had relied on Jimmy to save her, and instead he had left her destitute. Then she had been forced to rely on Cousin Michael for help, and even the man she'd come to regard as a friend had abandoned her.

Men were not the solution to her problems, and Charles most certainly was not. He would expect nothing less than love from her, and she did not feel that for him. She had married once without love, so she saw no point in doing it again, even if Charles *was* twice the man that Jimmy had been. She wasn't even sure love was wise anyway. She had fancied herself in love with David, and it had only brought them heartache.

Besides, she was thirty-six, for heaven's sake. A marriage at this age would be absurd.

Though a love affair would not be unwelcome.

The thought came out of thin air, as shocking as it was tantalizing. She had considered it before, of course, but she had always dismissed it because of the school and the necessity of upholding her reputation. But with the school in trouble and the now unattached David coming back into her life . . .

She stifled a curse. What was she thinking? That would be the height of madness.

"You know, Charlotte, there might be yet another reason that Kirkwood came to you with this bequest," Charles said, startling her.

"What is that?" she breathed, praying that he did not guess the reason for the sudden tension in her.

"Perhaps Sarah *did* leave you the money out of vanity. But if it were in a codicil, Kirkwood might have influenced the attorney to write the contract he gave you in such a way as to involve himself in the process."

"To what purpose?"

"So he could control how the funds were spent. So he could have you where he wanted you."

"And where would that be?" she snapped, growing inexplicably annoyed with her friend's determination to view this in the worst possible light.

"He might have seen this as the perfect chance to get back at you for what you did to him that summer. He might be using this to gain revenge."

The possibility of that rose up to smite her where it most hurt—in the part of her that still found David far too appealing. "That is ridiculous," she said in a hollow voice. "It has been eighteen years. No one holds a grudge that long, not even Da- . . . Lord Kirkwood."

"We'll see what the attorney says. But heed me well, Charlotte. There's more to this than meets the eye. I'm sure of it."

Sadly enough, so was she.

Chapter Nine

❧

The night before David was to return to the school, he sat at a table in the Eel and Drake awaiting Joseph Baines, attorney-at-law, trying not to think about what Charlotte would say tomorrow.

He honestly couldn't blame her for her suspicions. She had to find it odd that he was stepping back into her life after she'd treated him as she had. He found it a bit odd himself, even after all these years of corresponding with her.

God knows he'd been furious that summer, especially after hearing that she'd eloped. In his eyes, she'd not only toyed with his affections and publicly humiliated him, but she'd also thumbed her nose at him by marrying his rival for her hand. Even to this day *that* rubbed him raw.

He'd spent the next two years buried at the estate, preparing for when he came of age. But he couldn't remain in hiding forever. Eventually he'd ventured out into society. Still shunned by people whom he'd once considered friends, he'd decided to show them that he didn't care. Though he'd spent his days in fairly sober pursuits, letting his clever friend Anthony direct his investing, he spent his nights in wild carousing, trying to forget Charlotte.

It was during his second year in London, the fourth year after that blasted letter had been published, that news of

Charlotte had trickled through the grapevine to him. He'd already known that she and her husband had inherited her family's money, but it was the first time he'd heard that she had been a widow for some time and working as a teacher at a very prestigious school in nearby Chelsea.

For reasons he only half-understood now, it had infuriated him. *She'd* been doing precisely what she'd always dreamed of; *she'd* come out of their encounter smelling like a rose, while he'd still had matrons giving him the cut direct at social affairs. She'd embarked on a new life, while he'd been unable even to find a suitable wife with that albatross of a scandal hanging over his head. How he had resented that!

A week after hearing the news, drunk to the gills and stewing over Charlotte, David had wagered a huge sum on whist against Samuel Pritchard. Winning had given him little satisfaction—the nearly broke Pritchard had been in such dire financial straits that he'd risked more than he could afford, always a nasty situation.

That was when David had hit upon a way to gain his money from Pritchard and revenge himself on Charlotte at the same time. First, he'd convinced Pritchard to agree to a lien on the property where the school now resided. Since it was entailed, Pritchard hadn't been able to sell it to pay his debt, but he'd agreed to give David the rents for fifteen years. Back then, Pritchard and his family had lived in Rockhurst next door, so the man had been grateful for a chance to save his honor without bankrupting his family or having to sell his own home at a loss.

Remembering Charlotte's passion for opening a school, David had then approached Charlotte through Mr. Baines, pretending to be Captain Harris's distant cousin so he could coax her into setting up her school on Pritchard's land. She'd been so eager to pursue her dream that she'd taken him up on his offer. He'd even thrown in a bit of his own money to sweeten the deal, never dreaming that one day he'd need that money to drag his family out of debt.

His plan had been to offer her a very cheap rent until she'd had her school fully staffed and functioning, until she'd been lulled into complacency. Then he'd intended to raise the rents dramatically and demand repayment of the loan, watching with glee as she floundered.

A wicked plan to be sure. And one he had soon come to regret.

"I hope you haven't been waiting long, my lord."

Blinking, David glanced up to see that Mr. Baines had arrived at last. David brandished his tankard of ale. "Not long enough to get foxed."

The solicitor laughed. "A pity, that." Tossing his hat onto the bench opposite David, he folded his skinny frame into the seat and slid a document across the table. "I brought your original agreement with Pritchard as you asked, but you'll find it unhelpful. I read it over again. My professional opinion is that there is nothing you can do to keep him from evicting the widow."

With a grimace, David slid the agreement into his satchel. "I know you're right, but I still want to look it over."

Baines called for a tankard. "Did the 'codicil' pass muster?"

"Frankly, I'm not sure. Charlotte is too clever to swallow such a tale on my word alone. She wouldn't even discuss it until she could have it examined by her own attorney. Will that be a problem?"

"My lord!" Baines exclaimed, his pasty face stiff with the insult. "That document is unshakable. Your family solicitor and I made sure of it."

"Forgive me, Mr. Baines. This matter has me out of sorts."

"I imagine so, what with Pritchard on the verge of selling Rockhurst to that Watson fellow from Yorkshire."

David swallowed some ale. "Actually, that might help me. It will signal to Mrs. Harris that it's time to move the school."

"You do realize the irony of this situation." Baines eyed him closely. "If you were to let matters take their natural course with Pritchard, you'd have Mrs. Harris exactly where you'd wanted her when you started this."

"I know that only too well. I just pray that *she* never discovers it."

"You had good cause to be angry."

"Yes. But as I recall, you cautioned me against demanding that lien from Pritchard."

"It wasn't the lien I cautioned you against. That was clever. At least you had the forethought to realize that rents for properties in Richmond would soar."

"You give me too much credit." David knocked back the rest of his ale. "I didn't give a bloody damn about soaring rents; revenge was my only aim."

"Yes, well, *that* was what I cautioned you against. Fortunately for Mrs. Harris, you changed your mind."

David snorted. "*She* changed my mind."

"Got to you with her letters, didn't she?"

A rueful laugh escaped him. "The woman can write, I'll give her that. Here I was, relishing the moment when I could throw off the mask and demand what she couldn't pay. Then she starts sending me all those missives, thanking me for my 'kindness and generosity,' asking advice about how to save her 'dear girls' from making the same mistakes she'd made." He shook his head. "I swear, only a man with a heart of stone could have stood up to that for long."

"Aye."

"I should have told her the truth then. But after Father . . ."

He trailed off, still unable to speak easily of his father's suicide, which had occurred six years after Charlotte opened the school. Two suicides—his father's and later, his wife's. The first was not his fault, but the second . . .

Baines glanced up, then frowned. "Sir, there is a man approaching."

David scarcely had time to turn before a stranger reached the table, hat in hand. "Good evening, my lord. My name is Ned Timms, and I am—"

"I know who you are," David growled as he recognized the name of a moneylender notorious for shady dealings. He rose to tower over the man. "You have the audacity to corner me in this public place?"

Timms wore the placid expression of a man used to being rebuffed but not deterred. "You leave me no choice, my lord. Your servants refuse to admit me at your home."

"Because you can have nothing to say to me. My wife has been dead for some time. Try as you might, you can't get blood from a corpse."

"She left behind many debts."

"Yes. And I paid off every legitimate one."

"Her debt with me was legitimate, I assure you." Reaching into his frock coat pocket, he pulled out a jewel case and opened it to reveal the Kirkwood sapphires, which

David had been unable to locate since Sarah's death. "She used these to secure it."

With his stomach roiling, David stared down at the glittering parure—a matched set of ear bobs, necklace, bracelet, and ring. It was part of the collection of jewels that had been in his family for generations. Even Father, in his darkest hour, had never attempted to sell or pawn any part of those.

How could Sarah have done it? Had she hated him so much that she would pawn something precious to his family rather than come to him for money?

He knew the answer to that. Their arguments had always been over her gambling. "If my wife owed you, then you have the means right there to cover it. The sapphires are surely worth more than any debt she could possibly have contracted. That's how your kind operates, after all, by preying on those willing to take a pittance for their valuables."

That garnered a reaction from the bastard. His gaze turned deadly cold. "Ah, but sir, such a lovely heirloom. I should think you would want to keep it in the family. I'll be happy to return it to you for a reasonable price—"

"Go to hell," David snapped, knowing full well that the man's reasonable price would be more than the jewels were worth. "You'll never get a penny from me. Between you and your kind, you killed my wife. I have no use for you and your blood money."

The man's eyes narrowed to slits. "You would do well to rethink your position, sir. I'm sure the papers would love a tantalizing little tidbit about what your wife was willing to do to gain money for her . . . pleasures."

It was the wrong thing to say to him, of all people. He

marched forward, forcing Timms back with every step. "Are you threatening me, you little worm? I would advise against that. Because I'm very friendly with the local magistrates, and I daresay a hard look at your affairs would turn up certain illegalities. Are you willing to chance it?"

Timms was forced to halt when he came up against a nearby table. "Forgive me, my lord," he said, an edge of resentment in his tone. "I thought to do you a favor. I see that I was mistaken."

"Quite mistaken. But now that you've been set straight, I expect no repetition of this discussion. Have I made myself clear?"

Bobbing his head, Timms slid from between David and the table. "I shall not trouble you again, sir." Then he scurried off.

David was still trembling with rage when he returned to take his seat at the table with Baines. "You heard, I suppose."

"I did. Are you sure you don't want them back?"

"Absolutely certain." How could he ever look at them again without thinking of where they had been and why? Wondering what had possessed his fool of a wife to give over something of such sentimental value to his family?

Wondering again how he had managed to go so wrong with her.

He called for more ale. "I should never have married Sarah."

"You did what you had to."

"That's little comfort now."

He should have married Charlotte. Indeed, he'd been on the verge of approaching her to reveal his foolish deception, when his father had sent the family finances crashing.

That and Father's suicide had changed everything, putting the burden of supporting his family on David's shoulders. Faced with crippling debts, he'd known there was only one way to save them—by marrying an heiress.

So he'd married Sarah, and the masquerade had continued. After all, he couldn't let his wife know that he was supporting another woman's school.

A chilling thought occurred to him. Had that been the key to Sarah's pain? Had she somehow found out about his connection to Charlotte?

It was hard to believe that she would even have cared. Their marriage had lapsed into a formal one shortly after their elopement, though that had been her choice as much as his. Indeed, that's why her suicide left him reeling. He would never have guessed that his petty and frivolous wife would have felt *any* pain so deeply that she would kill herself over it.

And her brief note had been distinctly uninformative: *Forgive me, David, but I can no longer endure this intolerable life.* He'd told people she'd killed herself over her gambling debts. What else could he say? That his wife had been living in utter misery, and he'd been too much of a bastard to realize it?

Clearly, he had no talent for reading women. First Charlotte, then Sarah . . .

He ran his fingers through his hair. How he wished he could go back and do everything differently. Not take up with Pritchard. Not marry Sarah.

Not lose Charlotte.

The rumble of long-ignored pain settled in his chest. What if he had gone to her the day her letter hit the papers? What if he'd demanded to know why she'd written it? Why she'd actually been so angry as to let the papers publish it? Now that he knew her better, he realized how strange that had been.

But back then he'd been too bent on salvaging his pride to do something as silly as talking to her. And what good had pride done him? While he'd been posturing and cursing her name and plotting a stupid revenge, James Harris had swept in to marry her.

Her turning to Harris for comfort still gnawed at him. Even knowing that Harris had proved a disappointment as a husband didn't assuage his jealousy.

Jealousy? Nonsense. He refused to be jealous of Charlotte's husband, suitors, or male friends. He would not let her mean that much to him. Confound it all, he'd put that behind him!

Muttering a curse under his breath, David thrust his empty tankard at a passing taproom maid and barked, "Another!" He would not let Charlotte get under his skin this time. This was just . . . tying up loose ends. Correcting a disastrous mistake. Nothing more.

Right. And the Taj Mahal was just a building.

"Keeping the truth from Charlotte was the worst mistake I ever made," he growled. "But I honestly thought matters would resolve themselves before they came to this pass. I expected her to have remarried by now and closed the school for good. She's a beautiful woman, after all."

"She certainly is *that*," Baines agreed, with more enthusiasm than warranted. When David glared at him, he said hastily, "Merely an observation, my lord."

David bit back a hot retort. What in the bloody hell was he doing provoking Baines, the only man with whom he could discuss any of this? David dared not bare his soul to his friends—they would be appalled by his wicked behavior to a woman who'd done well by them. And the only way he could explain was to reveal *her* past actions, which he didn't wish to do.

The taproom maid set another tankard in front of David, who stared blindly into its foam. "Pritchard will evict her without a thought in eight months. I have no doubt of that. I have to get her out of there before that happens." He drank deeply. "I *will* get her out of there, damn it!"

Baines eyed him over the tankard. "Why not just tell her the truth?"

"That Cousin Michael, a man she's trusted for years, was setting her up for failure? That I hated her that much? It would devastate her. And then she won't trust me to help her. She doesn't have the money to save the school without me; nor will she take the money from me outright. She's too proud for that."

He stared down into his ale. "It's better this way. All I have to do is keep shoving that thirty thousand pounds in her face and giving Sarah the credit until Charlotte sees the writing on the wall and moves the school. Hopefully she'll do it before Pritchard can evict her."

"I wish you luck," Baines said. "You're going to need it."

A frown creased David's brow. "Don't I know it."

He would also need time with her to break down the barriers of their past. Would she give it to him?

The next day, as he approached the school, he grew nervous. Two days of thinking things over might have convinced her to refuse the legacy. Then what would he do?

Expecting to be shown into her office, he was surprised

to be taken down a dim hall and ushered into a small sitting room instead. As he waited for the butler to fetch her, he popped a peppermint in his mouth, then strolled about the room. He noted with curiosity the books on racing, the carafe of wine, the needlepoint cushions stitched with such odd sentiments as "Bread and jam warm the heart" and "The truth always shines in a clean face." He was just tipping a cushion over to read it better when Charlotte entered.

"Good morning, Lord Kirkwood," she said, her voice brisk and businesslike. "I see you are admiring my students' work."

He turned to face her. "It's . . . er . . . not the usual sayings embroidered on cushions, is it?"

She laughed as she closed the door behind her. "No. The usual material is rather dull. I let the girls invent their own. Then I display the most interesting ones in my sitting room. I find it inspires them to work harder and be more creative."

"A novel idea."

"Too novel for my fussier parents, I'm afraid."

"Yet they keep enrolling their daughters here."

Her amusement faded. "Not lately." Taking a seat on the edge of a Windsor chair, she gestured to a settee opposite. "I hope you do not mind meeting in my sitting room. People are always darting in and out of my office. Here, we will have more privacy. I do not want any of my staff or servants hearing us discuss this delicate matter until it is . . . more firmly resolved."

Though she clearly wanted privacy for perfectly respectable reasons, his blood rose into a wild heat at the idea of them alone together. He sat down abruptly, fighting to quell his inappropriate reaction.

It didn't help that she looked so bloody fetching today, in a simple blue gown that led the eye inexorably down to the breasts that strained against her bodice. He rose again and began to pace to keep his traitorous body under strict control.

"I received your mother's invitation to the dinner for Amelia and Major Winter that she's throwing at your town house," Charlotte said, to break the uncomfortable silence.

Winter was David's cousin, who had married Amelia, one of Charlotte's former pupils, while in Charlotte's care.

"I confess I was rather surprised that she invited me," Charlotte went on. "Under the circumstances, I assumed it would be a small family affair."

"It is. I think it's a little soon, but Mother is languishing under the restrictions of mourning, so she has convinced herself that a private dinner won't offend sensibilities too much. And when she wrote to my cousin's wife about it, Amelia insisted upon your being included. I take it that Amelia doesn't know about our past together?"

"No," she said in a small voice.

He wondered if Charlotte knew that he'd offered for Amelia and had been refused before he'd turned his attentions to Sarah.

"Do you plan to attend tonight?" he asked, wishing he didn't care so much about her answer.

"Of course. It will be my first chance to see Amelia and Major Winter since they arrived in England. I wanted to go to Devon to visit with them as soon as they reached her parents, but matters at the school . . ."

She trailed off, not needing to finish the sentence. He

knew better than anyone that it wasn't a good time for her to leave.

"Have you had the chance to show the agreement to your attorney?"

"Actually, yes. He said it is all in order."

He let out a breath. "So you mean to accept the legacy."

"I have a few questions first."

Gritting his teeth, he halted to face her. "What sort of questions?"

"Why would you want to give up your valuable time to oversee the building of my school?"

"It's a condition of the bequest. Assuming you accept the money, I am bound by the terms of it as surely as you." That was sort of the truth, wasn't it?

"Let me put it another way. You did not have to pursue the matter. Assuming you were alone when you found the codicil, you could have burned it and no one would have been the wiser. But you did not. I want to know why."

The woman had a maddening ability to ask pertinent questions. Perhaps it was time to make her as uncomfortable as she was making him. "Because no matter what you think of me, Charlotte, I do have a conscience." *That* was definitely the truth.

She colored. "Still, it probably would not have pricked your conscience too much to make it so that the money came to me without your having to be involved. So why didn't you?"

"Perhaps because I thought helping you build your school would be a challenge. And there are few enough challenges in my life these days." He stalked up to loom over her. "Are we done with the questions?"

Neatly slipping out from between him and her chair,

she rose and went to stand beside the fireplace. "Just one more." She paused as she stared into the flames. "Did Sarah know about . . . did you ever tell her that you and I—"

"No," he said curtly. "And since I gather that you never told her, I doubt she would have found it out on her own. My mother wouldn't have mentioned it, and neither would Giles. As you might imagine, I myself never spoke of it to anyone."

"Except Anthony, Foxmoor, and Lord Stoneville," she murmured. "Though I suppose that does not count since you left out my name. Indeed, I am grateful that they did not know who the 'vindictive bitch' really was."

He groaned as his past sins rose up to taunt him. "Confound it all to hell."

"I'm sorry. I-I did not mean to throw that in your face. I understand why you said it. Honestly, I do. When Anthony casually mentioned it to explain why you hate the press—"

"Anthony ought to know better," he snapped.

She faced him with a tight smile. "My point is, I am well aware that you have no reason to be fond of me."

He couldn't address that without blatantly lying. "I don't see what that has to do with anything."

"Actually, a great deal." She steadied her shoulders. "You see, I didn't only show the document to my attorney. I also showed it to Charles Godwin."

He fought to keep his temper in check. "You showed it to a bloody newspaperman?"

Alarm sparked in her eyes. "No! I mean, yes, I did, but not because of his affiliation with the press. I consulted him because he is my friend."

Though he knew that, it still provoked an unwelcome

burst of jealousy. "Just how close a friend *is* Godwin to you, anyway?"

Her expression went cold. "My friendship with Charles is none of your concern, my lord."

David bit back an oath. She called Godwin "Charles," but he was still "my lord." "And the legacy is none of his concern. The last time I checked, Charles Godwin had no experience in legal matters."

"True, but he does know quite a bit about the parties involved. And like me, he found it curious that Sarah would have bequeathed anything to the school."

"Tell Godwin he can keep his opinions about my late wife to himself."

Charlotte stared him down. "Charles did have an interesting suggestion for how this 'bequest' came about."

David's heart began to pound. "Oh?"

"He pointed out that while Sarah might indeed have left money to the school out of some vain impulse to have her name plastered on a building, the part about *your* involvement seems suspect. He is of the opinion that you might have turned the situation to your own use."

Damn Godwin. The man was too bloody clever by half. "Why would I have done that?"

"First, I need to explain how Charles and I met."

"I already know—he served in the same regiment as your late husband."

A strange look passed over her face. "Where did you hear that?"

You told me in one of your letters.

Confound it all. "Sarah must have mentioned it," he hedged.

Her expression cleared. "Oh. Of course."

"But I don't see what that has to do with anything."

"You will." She drew in a steadying breath. "Shortly after Charles joined the regiment, Jimmy and I and Charles and his late wife were invited to an officer's dinner where the talk turned to scandal."

Folding her hands at her waist, she began to pace. "When the men began saying what a shame it was that poor Mr. Masters had been savaged by a cruel female in the papers, Charles jumped in to defend the woman."

Her breathing grew labored, her tone agitated. David's breathing was none too steady, either.

"As it turned out," she said, "Charles had been working for the *Morning Tattler* when her letter arrived there. He told his editor that the letter was clearly personal and not meant for publication. When his editor published it anyway, he was so disgusted that he quit the paper and joined the army."

While David was still reeling from that piece of information, she turned to fix him with a tormented gaze. "That is how Charles and I became friends. In time, I revealed my part in the matter. And that my letter had never been meant to be anything but private." Her voice dropped to a whisper. "I swear it is the truth. It was supposed to go to your town house. The boy who took it brought it to the papers. I never knew why or how."

David could only stare at her, words failing him. That piece of the puzzle had never made sense—how she could be so vicious as to smear his name publicly. And to hear that it was an accident only increased the knot of guilt in the pit of his stomach.

"So you see," she went on, "Charles knows *everything* about us."

"Apparently so," David choked out.

"And he suggested that perhaps you . . . insinuated your-self into this situation because you wish to gain control of it. Because you wish to destroy everything I have worked for." She dropped her gaze. "He had a notion that, well, this legacy is your revenge for what I did to you."

"Revenge?" he echoed hollowly. She was a little late to accuse him; the irony of it was too painful for words.

Except *she* hadn't dreamed up this "notion"; Godwin had. That ignited his already simmering temper to a roaring flame.

He strode toward her. "You think I would wait eighteen years until my wife happened to commit suicide, and then concoct an elaborate scheme using my late wife's money to *revenge* myself on you?"

"I-I didn't say I agreed with him," she retorted, nervously backing away.

"You didn't say you didn't, either." He grabbed her arms, drawing her close to stare down into her face. "Trust me, Charlotte, if I'd wanted revenge against you, I would have taken it years ago." As he very nearly had.

"That is exactly what I told Charles," she said evenly.

He blinked at her. "So why bring it up?"

Her eyes met his, as blue as a thousand summer skies. "To see what you would say to it."

Her breath was uneven, her face alight with an expression that was painfully familiar. And suddenly he was tired of the dancing around, the parsing of their past, the evasions that seemed to fill Charlotte's life these days.

It was time to cut through the nonsense. Especially when he had her this close to being in his arms again. "If I'd wanted revenge," he rasped, letting his gaze drop to her mouth, "I would have done something more direct. More personal."

She swallowed hard. "Like what?" she whispered.

He caught her head in his hands. "Like this," he growled. Then he covered her mouth with his.

For a moment she froze, her lips trembling beneath his. Then, to his shock, she parted them ever so slightly. And he knew she wouldn't resist him.

It was like going home. Only he was older, so the home-coming was sweeter.

Fire erupted between them, so intense he thought it might singe them. His hands were instantly in her hair to hold her still for a kiss that was too hard and hungry to be cautious, and she was meeting his mouth with an eagerness that matched his own.

He thrust his tongue deep inside her welcoming warmth, and she thrust back, tangling hers with his as if she could not get enough.

God knows he couldn't. For eighteen years he'd imagined kissing her again, and the pent-up need was more than he could control. He hadn't intended this, but by God, he would take it.

Chapter Ten

❧⦅❧

*C*harlotte was incapable of thought or breath. She knew only one thing—David was kissing her as if they had never been apart.

Somewhere in the back of her mind, she knew this was unwise for so many reasons. But right now all the defenses against men that she had nurtured so carefully for over a decade had gone into hiding. She was too lost in the excitement of being held by him again to think of caution.

It was both a feast and a torment to have him kissing and touching her. He tasted of peppermint drops and smelled of the same spicy cologne he used to wear—a blend of rosemary and wine. It was all so enticingly familiar.

"Ah, Charlotte," he whispered against her lips before dragging his mouth down her jaw to her neck, "it's been too long."

Far too long. "This isn't much . . . of a revenge . . . if you ask me," she choked out. His lips found the hollow of her throat and played there briefly before heading lower.

"I'm only getting started."

His husky words sent an errant thrill through her, especially when he dropped onto the nearby settee and tugged her astride his lap.

Shocked, she reared back to press her hands against his chest. "My word, David!"

"Shh, sweeting," he breathed as he gripped her thighs through her rucked-up skirts. Bending forward, he branded her neck with warm kisses. "Let me finish my revenge."

Her hands stilled on his chest. *Sweeting.* No one else ever called her that. It swept her back to the heady kisses of her youth, to the way he used to make her feel every time he entered a room, to the last time he had kissed her so fiercely.

Only half-conscious of what she was doing, she slipped her arms about his neck, making no protest as he yanked her fichu free.

While his mouth did hot, devilish things to her throat, his hands lowered her bodice and loosened her chemise. She clung to his neck, heedless of anything but a mindless need to have his wicked mouth on her breast. And when at last it was there, she let out a moan that had him lifting his other hand to tease her other breast.

How could she have forgotten what it was like to have a man touch her, fondle her? And for it to be *David* . . . it seemed too incredible to fathom. He sucked hard on one nipple while he thumbed the other, his free hand slipping under her skirts to caress the stretch of bare thigh above her garters.

She felt his arousal swell against her privates, even through the kerseymere of his trousers. "You know," she gasped, "Charles had . . . another theory about you and your part in this . . . legacy."

"Do tell," he growled, then lightly scraped her nipple with his teeth, sending a white-hot surge of heat down her spine.

"He said you might . . . have manipulated it so you could take up . . . where we left off eighteen . . . years ago."

David's hand hesitated in its journey up her thigh. "And what did you say to that?"

"That he was mad."

He lifted his head, his heated gaze locking with hers. "Clearly not as mad as you thought."

Before she could react to that astonishing statement, he was kissing her again, one hand fondling her breast as the other edged beneath her skirts toward the part of her that burned to be touched by him.

A knock came at the door.

They both froze. As she drew back, the awareness of where she was and what she was doing crashed into her mind, uprooting her from her pleasure.

David stared at her with a darkening gaze. "Ignore it," he breathed. "They'll go away."

Unfortunately, she knew better. Pushing free of his hands, she stood and began frantically to repair her clothing. "Yes?" she called out. "What is it?"

Everyone in the school knew not to intrude upon her private sitting room without being invited, but this was still madness. The door was not even locked!

"The new applicants for dancing master are arriving, madam," Terence said.

She walked close to the door. "Tell them I will be with them shortly," she ordered, praying that her voice did not betray her agitated state.

"Very good, madam."

As Terence's footsteps faded she fought for calm, beating down the arousal that still inflamed her senses. Then with a shuddering breath, she turned to David, who was already rising from the settee, his gaze intent on her.

"Forgive me," she said shakily, not ready to even think

about what they had been doing, much less talk about it. "We lost our dancing master a week ago, and I have to attend to the matter."

"Of course," he said smoothly. "I understand completely."

She blinked. That was not the response she had expected. "You do?"

"Certainly." He drew out his pocket watch. "That should take, what? Two hours? Three? I'll use the opportunity to get a good look at the school, so I'll know what sort of property you might consider adequate."

"But you should not . . . you must not . . ." she sputtered.

"Don't worry about me," he said with a wave of his hand. "I'm sure I can find my way around perfectly well until you're done."

A decidedly feminine panic seized her. "You do not mean to hang about while I am occupied elsewhere!"

His eyes locked with hers. "Why not?"

"Because you cannot wander my girls' school on your own," she said firmly.

"So let that fierce footman of yours accompany me."

She thrust out her chin. "I cannot spare Terence just now."

One of his eyebrows arched upward. "Then it looks as if I'll be wandering on my own, doesn't it?"

"That is not acceptable."

"Don't you trust me around your girls, Charlotte?" he asked softly.

It was not her girls she was worried about. "It has nothing to do with them."

"Then what?"

As if he didn't know. Whenever he got near her, funny things happened to her insides, and she feared that if he stayed around until they could be alone again, the two of them might progress beyond kissing and touching.

She was not ready for that. It had taken her years to repair her damaged life, years to feel secure and settled. And if those years had sometimes been lonely, it had not mattered because she was safe. For the first time ever, she had felt safe.

Until Pritchard had begun trying to make his property commercially viable in a way that was sure to damage her school. And now David had marched back into her life, stirring up old feelings, making her want to toss everything aside just to be in his arms again.

It was not to be borne!

"I am concerned about how other people will see your presence here."

"Probably the same way they see Godwin's. They'll think I'm a friend to the school." A sudden devilish glint lit his gaze. "Or they'll assume that I'm waiting around for Mrs. Harris to let me make wild, passionate love to her on her settee."

Alarm swelled in her chest. "Now see here, you cannot—"

"I'm teasing you." His eyes searched her face. "Does no one ever tease you?"

The question brought her up short. Godwin was too serious for such, and the teachers were too cognizant of her role as their employer. Cousin Michael had teased her, but then he had abandoned her. The way David would abandon her when times grew hard.

"Actually . . . most people are too circumspect for that."

"Have you grown so formidable, then?"

She forced a smile. "I hope not."

"Because you look as if you could use amusement these days."

"And I suppose you mean to give it to me?" she said sharply, the words leaving her mouth before she could stop them.

His brow lowered in a frown. "I'll tell you what I don't mean to do. I don't mean to ignore the fact that we were wrapped in each other's arms a few minutes ago." He approached her with determined steps. "I won't act as if there's nothing between us, when I know you enjoyed every kiss and caress as much as I did." He halted within easy reach of her. "And I sure as hell don't mean to leave here without resolving a few matters."

"Such as?" She stared him down, determined not to let his height and sheer masculine energy cow her.

"Do you intend to accept the legacy?"

"Do you intend to seduce me?" If he could be direct, so could she.

A strange wariness came over his face. "Seduction implies an unequal division of power. I have no desire to play that game with you." He came close enough that she could smell the peppermint on his breath. "If we share a bed, sweeting, it will be because of a mutual desire. *That* I can promise you."

"I cannot share your bed."

He lowered his voice to that erotic thrum that had always sent her senses aflame. "Afraid of getting too close to me again?"

"Afraid of losing all I have worked for," she countered.

A muscle flicked in his jaw. "Despite what Godwin claims, I have no intention of destroying your school."

"That is not what I meant," she said hastily. She stepped away, needing to compose herself, which was impossible with him looming over her. "But you do not have the same stake in it that I do. You have not spent years developing its reputation, coaxing students here, placating parents."

She thrust out her chin. "I am proud of what I have done, and I do not mean to throw it away on a fleeting pleasure." When his eyes glittered at that, she added, "The reputation of this institution lies on my shoulders, and with matters so shaky just now, I dare not do anything to ruin it. It would be scandalous if people thought that you and I were . . . well . . ."

"Yes," he bit out, "I suppose it would." He was silent a long moment. "But since I have made it clear that I have no intention of forcing any 'fleeting pleasure' on you, you have naught to fear from me. So you have no reason to refuse the legacy."

She could scarcely suppress a laugh. Naught to fear? Only the constant temptation he offered to touch him, to confide in him, to lean on him. She was not even sure she could *trust* him, for God's sake! How could she be sure she wasn't making a huge mistake by letting him this close?

But what choice did she have? "If I accept the legacy, that does not mean I accept the necessity for moving the school."

"I understand," he said blandly. "You still wish to write your benefactor about buying this property."

"Actually, I already have. I hope to hear from him shortly."

"In the meantime, why not look at other properties?" He removed a paper from his coat pocket. "I have a list of available ones right here. Once you've finished your interviews, we can go look at them. While awaiting your leisure, I'll tour the school."

She faced him with an arch glance. "That should be a unique experience for you, awaiting a woman's leisure."

"Dangerous perhaps, but not unique. I did it once before." His eyes bore into hers. "It proved the biggest mistake of my life."

She sucked in a breath, remembering the last time they had been together in their youth, when she had asked him to wait for her answer to his proposal.

Deliberately she pretended not to know what he meant. "Then perhaps you should *not* await my leisure. I would hate to disappoint you. You could always return this afternoon."

"And risk finding the place barred to me? Not a chance."

A thin smile touched her lips. "I would never do anything so silly."

"Good. Because it won't keep me away."

When he followed those words with a look of raw hunger that set her every nerve afire, she knew his persistence had nothing to do with the legacy and everything to do with her.

And she couldn't decide how she felt about that. "I really must go," she murmured. "I do have to conduct these interviews."

"Of course." He bowed. "Until later."

Just as she opened the door, he said, "There's one thing you should be aware of. It was not me you saw kissing Molly that last night of your visit."

Pausing in the doorway, she cast him a long look over her shoulder. "I know," she said simply.

Then she left.

Chapter Eleven

❦

$\mathcal{D}$avid stared, frozen in disbelief, as Charlotte waltzed out the door. She *knew*? How had she found out? *When* had she found out, for God's sake? He'd learned of it himself only eight years ago, after Father's suicide.

Faced with the stark knowledge of why their father had killed himself, he and Giles had drunk an inordinate amount of whisky one night. Somehow their talk had turned to women, to the fact that marrying an heiress would solve David's problem of how to cover the massive debts Father had left behind. Mention of heiresses had led to a discussion of Charlotte, and Giles had admitted that he'd often wondered if Charlotte had seen him with Molly, wearing David's robe.

When it had dawned on David that it was very likely, he'd taken out his anger on his brother. The two of them had engaged in a drunken brawl, and for a while they'd stopped speaking entirely.

But in time he'd had to acknowledge that it was himself he was angry at, for not examining the situation more, for not forcing her to tell him what had happened. By then he'd already been corresponding with Charlotte as Cousin Michael for a few years, and had realized the value of what he'd thrown away too easily.

What if he had gone to her after Giles had told him the truth? What if he had said to hell with the world and married her instead of Sarah?

He ran his fingers through his hair. His family would have lost most of their property. His sisters would not now be in good marriages; Giles would not be a respected barrister. And Charlotte would have been forced to support *him* with the income from her school. It would have been intolerable.

But he would not now be regretting so many things. Like the fact that he wanted Charlotte and she didn't want him. Or was afraid to want him.

He swore under his breath. It had been heaven to hold her and kiss her, but hell to watch her put him aside. He was sure she had felt the same pull as he. They'd been halfway to doing the deed when they'd been interrupted.

Still aroused, he paced the room. What was he to do about this . . . this unwise attraction between them, this palpable yearning that clogged his throat even now? He couldn't be near her without wanting to make her his. And she clearly had no intention of letting him.

"Beg pardon, my lord," said a voice from the door, "but Mrs. Harris has asked me to give you a tour of the school. I understand you have a friend who wants to enroll his daughter?"

Apparently she'd been able to spare her pugilist servant after all. And how clever of Charlotte to drum up a scandal-proof excuse for David's presence.

"I have quite a number of friends who would be honored to enroll their daughters here," he evaded.

"Good," said the burly servant. "We could use more young ladies these days."

Trying not to dwell on why that was, David followed the man out. "It's Terence, isn't it?" David asked.

"Yes, sir," he clipped out.

The man must not be too keen on this duty. That wasn't

surprising, given that his talents would be better used else-where. He was a few inches taller than David, and his arms were big as oak limbs. He looked as if he probably ate a heifer for breakfast every day.

"Are you the same Terence who fought Jack Higgins about twelve years ago at Salcey Green?"

Terence Sullivan had killed Higgins, a bare-knuckle boxer of great renown, in the ring that day. He would be about this man's age and size now, too.

"Do you want to see the school or not?" Terence said belligerently.

Apparently he'd struck a nerve. "Only if you want to show it to me. I don't mind striking out on my own if you have more pressing duties."

Terence shot him a veiled glance. "Forgive me, my lord. I prefer not to speak of those days."

"As you wish. Though I *am* curious about how the great Terence Sullivan came to be hired as a footman."

"I started out as one. I only got into fighting later. After the bout with Higgins, I went back into service." He clenched his fists at his sides. "Except nobody would hire me. Until Mrs. Harris took a chance on me."

"Ah." No wonder he was so protective of Charlotte.

"Now here is what we call the 'great hall,' " Terence began, clearly eager to leave the subject.

For the next hour, the fighter took David through every room. David found it fascinating to see the place for him-self after years of seeing it only through Charlotte's eyes in letters. He'd been to the Elizabethan-era building when he and Pritchard had signed the lien, and remembered it as chilly and cavernous, with a hodgepodge of questionable improvements made by Pritchard's grandfather.

He didn't recognize it now. "I gathered from things my late wife said that Mrs. Harris made a number of renovations when she first moved in."

"Indeed she did," Terence answered. "Got permission from her cousin to do so."

David bit back a smile, since *he'd* been the one forced to ask Pritchard's approval on every improvement. In those days, Pritchard had been glad to have someone else improve his property, since it had been naught but a burden to him.

What a difference a little paint and carefully placed furnishings made to a stately old pile like this. The mahogany furniture and the draperies of dark green velvet lent it a courtly grandeur that would inspire any young girl. This was no cramped brick box where girls were packed in like biscuits in a barrel, but a place to roam and discover, a place that kept a person ever mindful of England's past.

No wonder she was reluctant to leave it.

David well understood the attachment one could have to a building. He'd fought hard to keep his family's manor from sinking under the detritus of time. And the enormity of what he'd done to Charlotte by encouraging her to fall in love with this place sent a blow to his chest.

"It's a shame her cousin doesn't ever come here," Terence added, "or he'd know how much she's put into it."

"I understand that he helps her only under condition of anonymity," David said, curious to hear her footman's perspective on the odd arrangement.

"Aye." Terence took him down a hall past several classrooms where girls were being taught arithmetic and natural history and Latin, an unusual curriculum for young ladies.

"Has she never attempted to learn his real identity?" David prodded.

"It isn't allowed. She had to sign a paper saying that she understood she would lose the low rent on the property if she ever tried to discover it."

David feigned a look of male camaraderie. "Yes, but surely she lets *you* do some digging around."

"Not if it means breaking the agreement. She told me to keep my nose out of it, and I always do as I'm told."

"Ah." Thank God for loyal servants.

"Though I think I know what sort of man he is," Terence went on as he led them into a large room that was clearly used for dancing.

This should be interesting. "Oh?"

Terence stopped in the center. "The mistress says he's probably some philanthropist who doesn't want people looking too closely at his private affairs." His eyes narrowed. "But I figure he's a rich and ugly old codger who took a liking to her, but knew he hadn't a chance in hell of winning her. So he set matters up to make her beholden to him."

"You mean, by his cunning donation of money to the school and his wicked provision of low rents," David said sarcastically, more than a little annoyed that Terence was so close to the truth. Or what used to be the truth, anyway.

"Nobody ever gives something for nothing."

"Interesting theory." David fought the urge to defend himself. "And what exactly do you think he wants for his 'something'?"

"The same thing most gentlemen want from a beautiful young widow." A dark frown crossed his brow. "One day he'll pounce, and there will be hell to pay."

"He's certainly taking his time about pouncing," David said irritably. "Hasn't he been helping the school for years?"

The footman shrugged. "I didn't say his plan was clever. It doesn't take brains to be a randy bastard."

"Just a great deal of money, apparently."

Terence fixed him with a level gaze. "As my old da used to tell me, 'never trust a rich man.'"

No mistaking *that* warning. "Good thing I'm only moderately rich," David said dryly.

"Which is why I only moderately distrust you," Terence shot back.

David blinked, then burst into laughter. "You are the most unusual footman I've ever met."

Crossing his arms over his chest, Terence shrugged. "I'll take that as a compliment."

"I didn't mean it as one."

For the first time, the man smiled. "I know."

Oddly enough, that defused some of the tension between them. As they continued around the school, David said, "It sounds as if you spend plenty of time protecting your employer from unwanted attentions."

"Plenty enough."

"What if the attention is not so unwanted?"

"That doesn't happen," the footman said decidedly.

"Not even with Charles Godwin?" he bit out.

Terence shot him a curious glance. "Why do you want to know?"

He opted for honesty. "I find it's always useful to gauge one's competition before one enters the ring."

Terence bristled. "If I were you, my lord, I'd first be worried about leaving here with all your teeth."

David chuckled. "Believe me, that concern is high on my list as well. You forget—I've seen you fight."

When the footman let out a reluctant laugh, he knew he'd scored a point, even if he was no closer to learning the nature of Charlotte's association with Godwin.

By now they'd finished with the interior. They were already strolling toward the front entrance so they could go out to see the gardens when Charlotte appeared at the top of the stairs.

"Terence, could you come here for a moment, please?"

"Certainly, madam."

"I'll go walk about the gardens," David said.

It didn't take him long to tour the gardens in front of the house. He'd finished there and was admiring the cherry orchard on the edge of Rockhurst when an unwelcome figure emerged from the trees.

Pritchard. Confound the bastard.

Samuel Pritchard was the firstborn scion of a wealthy London merchant. Though he was now nearing sixty, he'd been quite the reckless blade most of his life, as his ravaged features and look of dissipation attested. Indeed, Pritchard's penchant for debauchery was how the man had come to be at David's mercy during their fateful card game years ago.

David had been drunk, as he'd often been in the early days of his disgrace. When Pritchard had made a nasty comment about the Garish Goer, David had set out to fleece him. And he'd succeeded beyond his wildest expectations, something he was still paying for.

"Well, well, if it isn't Cousin Michael," Pritchard remarked.

"You'd better pray no one heard you, Pritchard," David

snapped. "Or have you forgotten that revealing my identity voids our agreement? You can be sure I'll be happy to demand the full fifty thousand pounds on the spot. Since you can't pay it now any better than you could pay it then, I suggest you hold your tongue."

Though the man paled, his nasty smile didn't dim. "So the poor widow still doesn't know who you really are, does she? Well, it won't be long before she learns of it, in eight months, when she's thrown out on her pretty arse. Then nothing you can do or say will keep me from telling her who's the real culprit behind her troubles."

David clenched his hands to keep from throttling the bastard. "Why don't you sell Rockhurst to me and be done with it? You know I'll pay you more than it's worth."

Pritchard thrust his thumbs in the waistband of his trousers, which only accentuated the gut he was rapidly acquiring. "Why, so you can move the good widow and her school over onto it? No thank you. Since the entailment prevents me from selling the school's property, I mean to make good use of it. And I won't have Mrs. Holier-than-Thou hanging around causing trouble for me. I want her gone from both parcels of land, her and her pack of girls."

"A smart businessman would see the abundant advantages to having a girls' school as a tenant. They're not hard on the property, and they're willing to pay for the improvements themselves."

"But they're not willing to pay much of a rent, are they?"

"I'll subsidize the rent if necessary," David said. Pritchard would be a fool to refuse such an offer. "And I might point out that your kindness to the school might help you repair your poor reputation in society."

Pritchard's eyes narrowed. "I've begun to see that a poor reputation can gain a man more than a good one." He jerked his head toward where a thin fellow was wandering the orchard some distance behind him, appearing to measure it out. "Watson there is fairly serious about buying Rockhurst and turning it into a racing establishment. And do you know why?"

David merely stared coldly at him.

"Because I've promised him that as soon as the lien is discharged, I'll be turning the school building into an impressive hotel, with a restaurant and a taproom that will tempt any young blade. I'll have half the racing community here every week, paying good money for their gin and ale while my friend there gets their money on the races next door."

Sheer glee showed on the ass's face. "So you can see why I don't want the good widow hanging about. And why I have better prospects than whatever extra money you can offer for her rent."

David's stomach sank. A hotel. The building would be perfect for that. How clever of Pritchard to have thought of combining a racecourse with a hotel, especially with Richmond being so close to London, and right on the river besides.

"The town will never allow it," David said.

"No? They've already agreed to approve licenses for both me and Watson." He smiled. "Very hush-hush, of course. They know I have a financial obligation to someone else that prevents me from taking possession of this property until next year. But I've assured them that it will occur."

So *that* was what the bastard had been planning. "And

they are willing to see the school go under for your benefit?"

Pritchard gave a condescending laugh. "They don't care about that. When I pointed out that her girls don't spend nearly as much money in town as would be brought in by a racecourse, they were fairly salivating over the prospect. The town fathers are not fools—they know a sure success when they see one."

"She has done nothing to you!" he snapped. "I understand your anger at me, but if you're using her to punish me—"

"Don't be a besotted fool, Kirkwood. This is strictly business. It has nothing to do with you or her. Indeed, you ought to be thanking me." He sneered at David. "Your presence here indicates that she's found a better way to save herself." He thrust with his hips in a vulgar motion that left no question as to what he meant. "Giving you some . . . extra services, is she? In exchange for the new fortune you inherited from your poor wife?"

David saw red. Before he could think, he had his hands around Pritchard's throat and had slammed him into the nearest tree. "Listen to me, you bloody ass, and listen well. If you ever insinuate anything so vile to her or anyone else, I will hunt you down, cut off your ballocks, and shove them down your throat! Do you understand me?"

Pritchard's eyes were wide with fear as he struggled for breath. He nodded in agreement, his fingers clawing futilely at David's hands.

Abruptly, David released him, watching as he slid down the tree gasping. "Do whatever you feel you have to with Rockhurst. But I still have a lien on the school's property, and a great deal can happen in eight months."

With his temper still raging, he turned on his heel and marched off before he beat the bastard to a bloody pulp.

But he hadn't yet passed out of earshot when he heard Pritchard mumble, "You'd think the damned woman was your wife or something . . . Christ!"

The words echoed in his brain as he stalked back to the school. His wife.

He let the idea sink into him, calming his murderous rage. What if he were to marry Charlotte? Then she wouldn't even need the school. After all, he could afford to support her. And if he made her his wife before the eight months were out, he'd never have to reveal the double game he'd played with her all these years. She'd simply close the school, and that would be that.

Yes, it was the perfect solution. Simple, practical.

Well, not entirely practical. There were difficult issues . . . like the fact that he was still in mourning. He wasn't even supposed to think about remarrying for another six months, but the longer he waited to secure her, the more chance she would find out about what Pritchard was up to and why.

Fortunately, society tended to be more lax with regard to men and mourning. He had no heirs, so people expected him to look for a wife to bear one as soon as possible. Though Charlotte would balk at marrying before the mourning period was up, he could surely change her mind.

He frowned. That was assuming he could persuade her to marry him in the first place. She still barely trusted him. He couldn't even think about proposing marriage until he had softened her toward him.

Very well, he'd go on as before, trying to convince her

to move the school, offering her Sarah's legacy. And in the process he'd play on the attraction that still burned between them. That shouldn't be too difficult. She was a vibrant, sensual widow who'd spent the last sixteen years celibate. Surely she was eager to change that.

Unless she hadn't spent it celibate. After all, there was a reason society called widows "merry." And she hadn't answered his question about her relationship with Godwin.

He scowled. If the man *had* been sharing Charlotte's bed, that would end right now. So would any courtship between them. Because David didn't mean to let that damned newspaperman have Charlotte.

Take care, man. Such an obsessive desire was what got you into trouble with her last time.

But that was different. He'd been young and foolish. He'd believed in love, confusing a perfectly normal and healthy lust for a pretty woman with some ridiculous emotion. This was merely a practical decision. And if, in the process of gaining Charlotte as his wife, he also got to have her in his bed, all the better. Why shouldn't he have a wife he desired?

Absorbed in his thoughts, David didn't see Terence approach until the man was nearly upon him. "Having a few words with our neighbor, I see," Terence said bluntly.

Confound it all. The footman must have seen his encounter with Pritchard. David considered rebuking him for not minding his own affairs, but it might be better to engage the man as an ally. "He insulted your mistress. I merely warned him not to do so again."

Something like admiration gleamed in the man's eyes. "And very handily, too. Mayhap you'll leave here with your teeth after all."

David acknowledged the veiled compliment with a nod. "I must ask you not to mention my . . . er . . . loss of temper to Mrs. Harris. I wouldn't want to have to reveal what that bastard said about her." And if Charlotte ever did go digging and discovered that Pritchard owned the property, David didn't want her wondering about their connection.

"As you wish." Terence fell into step beside him. "Incidentally, she ordered me to tell you that she regrets she'll be busy with interviewing for the remainder of the afternoon. She said that if you'll leave the list that you showed her, she will look it over."

"The hell she will," he growled.

The footman blinked.

David restrained his temper with some difficulty. Clearly, she feared that if he stayed around until she was free, he would tempt her into bed. And she was right to be afraid, too. Because he wasn't giving her up this time.

Nor would he let her dictate the terms of their new association. "You may tell your mistress that I'll be happy to hand over the list tonight when she comes to my town house for my mother's dinner. If she can't attend, then I'll be here in the morning to give it to her personally. Understood?"

"Perfectly, my lord."

"Good." With that, David turned and strode toward the stables. He'd tried to be patient. He'd given Charlotte every chance to refuse the legacy and his part in it.

No more. It was time he took control of this situation. Because one way or the other, he meant to have Charlotte as his wife. And neither the school nor her skittishness would stand in his way.

Chapter Twelve

❦

*C*harlotte sat in her coach, staring up at the Kirkwood town house with trepidation.

"Is everything all right, madam?" Terence asked as he opened the door.

"It's just . . . I haven't been here since I chaperoned Lady Amelia at the Kirkwood spring ball six years ago." The ball designed to find an heiress wife for David.

At the time, Charlotte had been painfully aware of the significance of the invitation—Lady Kirkwood had meant to rub it in Charlotte's face that David had moved on with his life despite Charlotte's apparent attempt to ruin him.

"Surely you're not nervous about seeing the young lady again," Terence said.

"Of course not." Amelia was the only reason she was here.

It had nothing to do with David's sly tactics, taunting her with a list of properties and threatening to show up on her doorstep again tomorrow if she did not come tonight. It had nothing to do with her being desperate to see him again.

She groaned. All right, so perhaps she *had* spent the entire journey into town reliving their delicious kisses and caresses and wondering if she dared repeat them. But she was no simpering girl, with her insides all aflutter at the prospect of meeting her beau. She was a grown woman of good reputation, whose school was widely acclaimed for its education of young ladies.

She was also a widow who hadn't been touched intimately in sixteen years. Until today. Why was it that all the fine lessons she taught her girls flew out the window whenever she saw David Masters?

"Shall I knock then, madam?" Terence asked.

"Of course."

As soon as he announced her to the butler and came down to hand her out, she squared her shoulders and marched up the steps. She would not let the prospect of seeing some *man* turn her into mush. The very idea was absurd.

After entering the house, however, her confidence faltered. While the butler went off to announce her, the first footman cast her furtive glances. No doubt her arrival at such a time to such a party would be remarked upon in the servants' quarters for the next week.

Fortunately, Amelia chose that moment to burst into the foyer, greeting her with hugs and kisses.

"You look wonderful!" Amelia cried as she pulled back to look Charlotte over. "I daresay you haven't aged a day in six years!"

"Nor you." Delighted to see her friend again, Charlotte surveyed her from the top of her elegant coiffure to the hem of her pretty dinner gown of dark green silk. "No one would guess you'd already borne two children, and in a foreign country, too!"

"Yes, what a surprise that one can actually have children outside the blessed isle of England," Major Winter said dryly, as he came to stand beside his wife.

"Do not start that again," Amelia chided him with a

laugh. She bent toward Charlotte. "He still thinks we English are rather too full of ourselves."

The American slid his arm about his wife's waist and gazed at her with a smile of pure love. "I suppose some of you have cause to feel superior. But as for the rest—"

"And which category do I fall into, sir?" Charlotte asked.

"The superior category, of course." Smiling genially, he thrust out his hand. "Truly, it's good to see you, ma'am. I hope you've forgiven me for carrying off your star pupil years ago."

"And if I had not forgiven you, what could you possibly do about it now?" she teased as she gave him her hand.

"Get my wife to soften you up. She's very good at it."

"I do believe she is," Charlotte agreed. Amelia had certainly softened up Major Winter. There was no denying the difference in his manner since the last time he had been here. Despite his comments about the English, he seemed happier. More relaxed.

Funny how being in love did that to a person.

Just as envy seized her painfully by the throat, another voice broke in. "Come now, what's all this?" Giles Masters entered the hall, looking as much a rascal as ever. "Why are you lot standing out here when everyone is waiting upstairs?"

With a laugh, Amelia looped her arm through Charlotte's, and they headed off chattering, leaving the gentlemen to follow behind.

The minute they entered the drawing room, Charlotte's uneasiness returned. Everyone else was a relation of David's. In addition to his brother and Major Winter, his two sisters were there with their husbands.

And of course, at the center was David's mother.
Since the prescribed time for mourning Sarah had
elapsed for the rest of the family, leaving only David and
Lady Kirkwood in half-mourning, she'd dressed quite
splendidly in a gray silk gown with an overlay of black
gauze, trim of black bugle beads, and a striking necklace
of jet. Clearly she did not plan to let something so minor
as the death of her daughter-in-law cast a pall over her
fashionable attire.

Nor did she mean to welcome with open arms the
woman who had once injured her beloved son. Charlotte
did not blame her for that, and tried not to take offense at
the viscountess's cool nod of acknowledgment.

Then Charlotte spotted David at the back of the room,
and everything else, everyone else, disappeared. She didn't
hear a word of Amelia's chatter or notice Giles crossing to
speak to one of his sisters. She only had eyes for David.
And when he turned to notice her there, her breath lodged
in her throat.

He scoured her from across the room, taking in every
inch of her dinner gown. She'd had a devil of a time choosing it. Her favorite ruby gown had seemed too brazen for a
family in mourning, and her yellow one too cheery. At last
she had settled for a gown of dark periwinkle, since it was
the most subdued.

Unfortunately it was also the most provocative she
owned, a fact that did not escape David's notice, for he
stripped her bare with his eyes. He paused very deliberately at her breasts and the juncture of her thighs, reminding her pointedly that only this afternoon he'd had his
mouth and his hands on her most intimately.

Beneath the onslaught of that heated gaze, her nipples

tightened and warmth gathered low in her belly. And when his eyes swept back up to lock with hers, the heat flaring in his face made her want to leap into his arms.

Or turn tail and run.

Then he headed toward them, and it was too late for running. Ignoring his mother's disapproving frown, he approached with purposeful steps that launched Charlotte's pulse into a mad dance. Though he bore the requisite black armband and wore the most somber clothing of anyone in the room, he looked more alive, more robust than the other men in their flashy blue coats and gold buttons. Even Major Winter, with his rough good looks, could not hold a candle to David.

"You came," he said in a husky voice as he reached her. "After you sent me packing this afternoon, I wasn't sure if you would."

"Sent you packing!" she said with a forced laugh to remind him that they were not alone. "I did no such thing. The timing of your visit was inconvenient, that's all."

Amelia was watching them closely. "You paid Mrs. Harris a visit today?" she asked David, curiosity implicit in every syllable.

"We had a matter of business to discuss regarding the school," he said, apparently not the least concerned about what anyone would think of *that*.

"His lordship has been advising me on how to handle Mr. Pritchard and his shenanigans," Charlotte explained hastily. She glanced at Amelia. "You know, the horrible man next door whom I've mentioned in my letters?"

Her friend's eyebrows arched high. "Yes, I remember those letters. I don't remember any mention of Lord Kirkwood's help, however." She turned to her husband. "What about you, dearest? Did you have any idea that your cousin was helping my friend so kindly?"

"None," Major Winter said, his lips twitching. "But Kirkwood always was quite the gentleman."

Except for when he was dragging Charlotte onto his lap and baring her breasts for his lascivious mouth. Though that was probably not evidence she should offer in countering Major Winter's claim.

"Advising Mrs. Harris was the least I could do," David said smoothly. "After all, she was the one who brought me and my late wife together."

That was stretching it a bit, since all Charlotte had done was give Sarah lessons in how to avoid fortune hunters, thus ensuring that the recalcitrant girl went right out and married the first one who approached her.

Apparently Major Winter thought it was stretching the truth as well, for he eyed his cousin oddly. "I thought Amelia brought you and Sarah together." Ignoring David's scowl and Amelia's chiding glance, he added, "Wasn't Amelia the one who delivered Sarah's letter to you? After conveniently rebuffing your overtures herself, I might add."

"Lucas!" Amelia exclaimed as David glowered at his cousin.

"What?" Major Winter asked. "It's true."

"Yes, but it's not the sort of thing to bring up at a time like this. Really, sometimes I think you were raised in a barn."

"Nonsense," Charlotte put in lightly, "I am sure you mentioned it to me at some point."

But they both knew she had not. And hearing of it shook Charlotte to her toes. David had once pursued Amelia? Had he . . . been in love with her? How had Charlotte not known about the two of them?

"Lucas, dear," Amelia said swiftly, "why don't you and Lord Kirkwood go fetch us some wine? I'm sure Mrs. Harris is quite thirsty after her long ride from Richmond."

"Certainly," Major Winter answered, knowing when he was being dismissed. Though David glanced uneasily from Charlotte to Amelia, he nonetheless headed off with his cousin.

As soon as they were gone, Amelia asked, "Are you all right?"

Why must people keep asking her that? "Of course. Why wouldn't I be?"

"You look as if you've seen a ghost." Her eyes narrowed. "Is something going on between you and Lord Kirkwood?"

"I cannot imagine why you would think such a thing," Charlotte said hastily, her heart pounding in her throat.

"Perhaps because he looks at you the same way Lucas does me. Or perhaps because you went white as a sheet when my idiotic husband mentioned that Lord Kirkwood once made overtures to me."

"I do not care about that in the least."

"Then why are you so fidgety and nervous all of a sudden?"

"What do you mean?"

Amelia cast a meaningful glance to where Charlotte was running the strap of her reticule through her fingers over and over. With a grimace, Charlotte willed her fretful hands to stop.

"You must understand," Amelia said, "Lord Kirkwood's pursuit of me was not remotely romantic. He spoke of how we would suit and how he found me amiable. No words of love, no attempts to kiss me. I knew it was prompted only by his need for my fortune. Why do you think I rebuffed him before he could even make a formal offer?"

Relief coursed through Charlotte. "I assure you, whatever lay between you and Lord Kirkwood means nothing to me."

What a bald-faced lie. It reminded her that much had happened to him in eighteen years, things she could not possibly know about. Something had transformed David from the teasing suitor of her youth into a man of such fierce intensity that he sometimes frightened her.

What had done it? His ill-fated marriage? His father's suicide? The humiliation she had forced him to suffer? Or perhaps all three together?

Because beneath the cordial surface he showed to the world lay a man of hidden depths. He was clearly keeping secrets, from her and from everyone else. She just could not figure out what they were.

"See here," Amelia went on, "it's clear that you care for Lord Kirkwood. And if he cares for you, too—"

"Do not be silly. He is in mourning."

"He won't be in mourning forever. Six more months, and he's free to remarry. And since he hasn't yet sired an heir . . ."

The words sent another shock down her spine. She had not even considered that. In her two years married to Jimmy, she had not once conceived a child, despite their spending plenty of time in the bedchamber. She had always assumed she was barren, which meant that she could not bear David the heir he needed.

As a shaft of pain went through her, she fought to ignore it. It did not matter whether she could or no—she was being ridiculous to even consider marriage to David.

He had not mentioned such a thing, and he could have any woman he wanted. Why should he pick one who was getting too old to have children? One who had wronged him in a most public fashion?

"Speaking of children," Charlotte said, desperate to stop this mad talk about her and David, "how are your little angels?"

The doting mother was only too happy to wax on about her girls and their accomplishments.

Just as they were arranging a day for Charlotte to see the children, the gentlemen returned empty-handed. The wine had been taken away, since dinner was about to be served.

Telling the Winters that he wanted to show Charlotte a new painting he had acquired, David pulled her rather forcefully into the hall. Once they were well away, he growled, "You ran me off so quickly this afternoon that I didn't have the chance to—"

"I did not run you off!" she protested, trying to keep up with him as he half-led, half-carried her down the hallway to where a series of paintings hung. When they reached the first and he halted to face her, she added, "I could not help that I had people to interview. Or that it took me longer than expected."

"Through no fault of your own, I'm sure," he said dryly.

She thrust out her chin. "If you cannot accept that I have responsibilities—"

"I accept that perfectly well," he said in a low voice. "What I can't accept is your willingness to let your precious school be destroyed by your negligence."

"Negligence! How dare you!"

"Sarah's legacy is the only thing standing between the

school and certain ruin. If you hadn't had Terence send me away this afternoon, I would have told you what I learned from Pritchard and his potential buyer when I encountered them near your grounds."

Her blood began to pound. "You . . . you spoke to Mr. Pritchard?"

"I did indeed. And he informed me that the town has already approved Mr. Watson's license for a racecourse. Now all that's left is for him and Pritchard to come to terms on price. Pritchard expects that to happen soon." He cast her a somber glance. "You can't have a racecourse next door, Charlotte."

"Certainly not."

"So you must resign yourself to moving the school elsewhere."

She glared at him. "Not until I hear from my cousin."

"Damn it, Charlotte, your cousin can do nothing about Pritchard!"

"You do not know that!"

"If he could have, don't you think he would have by now?"

She swallowed. Cousin Michael's abandonment was the cruelest stroke of all. "He did try, when Señor Montalvo seemed bent on building a pleasure garden. He intervened on our behalf."

"And from what I understand, that ended up with one of your pupils eloping and causing another scandal for the school. How good of him to help."

His sarcasm sent her over the edge. "Stay out of things you do not understand, David."

"Oh, I understand very well," he snapped. "You would rather trust some anonymous fellow who writes you letters and who, for all you know, is a complete bastard in the flesh, than a man who has known you for years and has your best interests at heart."

"Why should I believe you have my best interests at heart? After what I did to you, you have no reason to want to help me."

He stepped very near, lowering his gaze to her mouth. "You know better than anyone what reason I have. It's the same reason you came here tonight, despite your fears."

There was no mistaking the look in his eyes. All of a sudden, she was having a great deal of trouble breathing. "I came here to get that list you promised me."

"The hell you did."

"I came to see Amelia."

He bent toward her mouth. "Liar," he whispered.

The sound of footsteps on the stairs made him curse under his breath. He backed away and turned to face the painting just as the butler cleared the top and went to announce that dinner was served.

As the others came out into the hall, Lady Kirkwood called, "Come, David. You're taking me in to dinner, are you not?"

When David hesitated, Charlotte gazed at him with abject panic. Of course he was. It was the only proper thing. If he didn't, it would be a clear signal to the rest of the family that there was something more between them.

Yet for half a moment she thought that he would actually flout propriety. He cast Charlotte a glance of such frustration that it made her blood quicken.

She mouthed the words, "Please don't." The last thing she needed was to have his family set against her for tempting him into breaking the rules of mourning.

A muscle ticked in his jaw as he glanced to his mother. "Certainly, Mother."

"And Giles will take in Mrs. Harris."

Giles obligingly strode down the hall toward her.

David paused only long enough to murmur, "We're not done, sweeting," before stalking off to join his mother.

The words had her fighting a shiver as she and Giles waited for the others to descend the stairs. *We're not done.* That held a promise as well as a warning. She was not sure which alarmed her more.

"Shall we?" Giles said with a smile, offering her his arm as the last couple went down ahead of them.

At least *he* could be congenial. Indeed, he seemed far more relaxed with her than he had been the last time they had spoken, a few years ago at a party they had both attended.

Casting him a furtive glance as they walked toward the stairs, she was reminded of how much he resembled David. No wonder she had mistaken them for each other on that fateful night. In the dark, with their hair the same color and their build so similar, anyone might have done so. Ah, but how different her life might have been if she hadn't!

As they reached the stairs, Giles dragged his steps to put them out of earshot of the others. "You look ravishing tonight," he murmured.

She smothered a laugh. "I see that you never change, Mr. Masters."

"Allow me to have *some* enjoyment, if you please. The life of a barrister is very dull."

"I have trouble believing that. No one is good at what they do without having some passion for it, and I understand that you are quite good."

He shrugged off the compliment. "I understand that you and my brother have been keeping company of late."

"He is helping me with a matter at the school," she said, not sure how much David had revealed to his brother about the legacy.

"Are you taking up with him again?" Giles asked bluntly.

She blinked.

"Forgive me. That was rude. And none of my business, I suppose."

"So why do you ask?" Charlotte eyed him suspiciously. "Did your mother send you to enquire?"

Giles laughed. "Hardly." He covered her hand with his. "Perhaps I'm just trying to figure out if *I* have a chance with you."

Shaking her head, she removed his hand. "You forget—I now know what a rascal you are."

He released an exaggerated sigh. "I see I shouldn't have told you my little secret when last we met."

That was when she'd discovered that it was Giles she'd seen outside the window, and not David.

"Why *did* you tell me?" she asked.

His teasing smile faltered. "Because I had to know for sure if it was your seeing me with Molly that had ruined everything between you and David." His gaze searched her face. "Why didn't you tell *me* that you never meant to send that letter to the paper?"

Apparently Giles had heard from David about her revelation earlier. "What would have been the point? By then he was married. Your telling him about the letter might have given him regrets, and I did not want old ghosts to damage his union with Sarah. I had already damaged his life enough. I thought it easier for him to continue believing that I was a 'vindictive bitch.'"

They cleared the bottom of the stairs and headed for the dining room, but Giles stopped her short of the dining room door. "He certainly doesn't think that now." When she did not answer, he added, "So, *are* you taking up with him?"

She met his gaze steadily. "I honestly do not know."

Sometimes the idea of being with David again was so tantalizing she could hardly bear it. And how lovely it would be to have a partner in her dealings at the school, to have someone else to share her burdens for a change.

But that meant marriage, and she doubted that he wanted that with her. Even if he did, David could not possibly feel the same attachment to the school as she. Would he expect her to close it? Sell it? To give up everything she had worked for, so she could play the doting wife?

She had played the doting wife once, and it had cost her everything. She did not mean to go through that again. Ever.

"Be careful with my brother, Charlotte," Giles said softly. "Sarah's death hit him harder than any of us expected, and I wouldn't want—"

"Do not worry," she said through a throat thick with emotion, "I have no desire to hurt him."

"I am more worried that he will hurt *you*. He has not been himself in a long time, and I don't think he knows what he wants anymore."

She had already sensed that. Marriage to Sarah had changed him—and a wise woman would be careful with a man who had lost his wife only months ago. "Do not worry about me either. I know how to handle men."

"For my sake, I hope that's true." A sudden grin split his face. "I could use some handling from a woman like you."

A laugh sputtered out of her. "I swear, Mr. Masters," she said, matching his light tone, "you are as incorrigible as your brother used to be. The difference is—he grew up. Apparently, you did not."

"Growing up is vastly overrated," Giles said blithely. "I avoid it whenever possible."

She was still chuckling when they entered the dining room to find everyone awaiting them. Lady Kirkwood looked positively frigid, and David looked fit to be tied.

Clearly, it was going to be a very long night.

Chapter Thirteen

❦

$\mathcal{D}$avid couldn't remember the last time he'd been so frustrated. Charlotte might as well be miles away; Mother had placed him as far from her at the dinner table as was possible.

At least she was nowhere near his rascal of a brother. Instead, she spent dinner between Amelia and Lucas, being entertained by stories of life in Morocco.

He should thank his damned cousin for letting it slip that David had once offered for Amelia. Otherwise, he wouldn't have been so certain of Charlotte's feelings for him. But there was no mistaking the way that bit of news had upset her.

Good. It was about bloody time she had a taste of the jealousy he'd been swamped in for the last few days.

When they left the table at last, the men adjourned to the study for port and the women headed for the drawing room. Fortunately, since it was a family party, the men rejoined the women after only a couple of drinks. Unfortunately, when they entered the drawing room, one of his sisters accosted them with the proposal that they do some dancing.

David scowled at her. "That would be highly improper."

"Well, *you* can't dance, as you're still in mourning," she said petulantly, "but the rest of us can."

"Of course you can," Mother said, always willing to

indulge her daughters. "David will watch, and I shall play the music."

"Mother, this is not remotely—" he began.

"Oh, don't be such a stuffed shirt," she said as she removed her gloves and headed for their pianoforte. "It's just family; no one will know. It's not as if we're throwing a ball or anything."

It might as well have been. The minute they decided there was to be dancing, the others rushed about, pushing back chairs, rolling up the rug, and settling on music. Charlotte alone looked uncomfortable with the scheme, though David noticed that she didn't let it stop her from accepting Giles's invitation to dance.

Wonderful. Now he had to stand by and watch as his damned brother swept her around the room. The same man whose inability to keep his prick in his trousers had been responsible for tearing Charlotte from David in the first place. Confound the bastard to hell.

As the pair glided through step after step, it occurred to him that never in all these years had he seen Charlotte dance. There'd been no dancing during their week at Berkshire. The few occasions David had seen her in society since then, she had been too busy guiding her young ladies to do any dancing herself.

What a pity. Because she danced splendidly. Her grace on the floor outshone any other woman's. Her fringe of auburn curls bounced with every step, and her blue gown swirled about her hips to give her the look of a blossom floating on the breeze.

A blossom that his brother seemed determined to pluck. Every other turn, he shot her provocatively displayed bosom a furtive glance.

David clenched his hands together behind his back to keep from marching over and dragging her away from Giles. He would deal with his little brother later. For now, he would content himself with imagining what it would be like to be in the man's place, resting his hand on that slender waist, smiling down into those shining eyes . . . making her laugh as Giles was now doing.

She and Giles had just finished their final circuit and the music of the pianoforte was dying when a commotion in the hall drew their attention.

"I'm not going to wait, damn you!" shouted a voice that he recognized only too well. "I want to know what's going on in there!"

David had only seconds to compose himself before a disheveled young man burst into the room, his face flushed with anger. Everyone in the party froze except for Winter, who was feverishly whispering to his wife, probably trying to determine who the man was.

The rest of them knew only too well. It was Richard Linley, Sarah's brother. And he was clearly drunk.

Bloody hell.

"Good evening, Richard." David strode forward to meet his brother-in-law. "What brings you here tonight?"

"I can't believe it!" Richard cried, always a firebrand when he was in his cups. "You're having a party? Here?"

Mother rose from behind the pianoforte. "Not a party, dear, just a little family affair."

"With dancing?" Swaying a bit on his feet, he shot David an accusing glance. "Might as well be dancing on her grave!"

Guilt stabbed David's conscience.

"Don't be silly, Richard," Mother began. "We only—"

"Quiet, Mother!" David ordered. Catching the young man by the arm, he urged him toward the door. "Let's continue this discussion elsewhere, shall we?"

"Right, don't cause trouble in front of your friends, eh? She always said you cared for naught but appearances!"

Hearing his late wife's favorite accusation through the voice of his brother-in-law was unnerving. He didn't try to deny it, just dragged Richard out into the hall.

The young man wriggled free to face him down with a belligerent air. "You never cared a whit about her. Not one whit!"

"And you did?" David snapped. "Coaxing her into playing cards with you and your fast friends, introducing her to moneylenders. You might as well have handed her the knife she cut herself with."

The minute Richard paled, he cursed himself for letting the young man's drunken nonsense goad him into speaking so cruelly.

He lowered his voice. "Forgive me, Richard. I didn't mean that. Blaming each other does us no good. She's gone, and there's naught we can do about that."

When Richard straightened his clothes and dropped his gaze to the floor, David relaxed a fraction. Once the man's temper was spent, he could usually be reasoned with. Especially if he could be sobered up.

"Now," David went on, "why are you here? It's not usual for you to pay me a visit at night."

Glancing nervously back to where various members of David's family were peeking out to see what was happening, Richard said, "Could we go somewhere more private?"

"Of course." Telling a servant to bring coffee to the

study, David led his brother-in-law there. He was fairly certain what Richard wanted to discuss, and he needed the man sober for that.

As soon as they entered, Richard dropped into a chair and buried his head in his hands. The gesture reminded David of how very young he was.

At twenty-three, Richard was the eldest of Sarah's siblings and heir to her wealthy banker father. When David had first met him, he'd been indulging regularly in the usual bad habits of a rich youth—drinking, gambling, and wenching. Once he'd come of age, however, he'd seemed to start maturing. Then Sarah had died. Now his father was at his wit's end with him again.

Although initially Linley senior had assumed that David was merely another fortune-hunting wastrel, the man had eventually changed his opinion. After David had turned his own family's fortunes around with the help of shrewd investments and Sarah's money, Linley senior had begun to consult him on business matters. They'd been on such good terms in the past few years that he'd also recently turned to David for more personal advice . . . on how to handle his reckless son.

David feared he'd been little help. Sarah's death had sent the young man spiraling downward. As Sarah's darling, Richard had always been the only person to garner her affection. Without her to spoil and pet him, he seemed lost these days, and neither David nor Linley senior knew what to do about it.

"What can I do for you this evening?" David asked, never certain whether to take a tone of sternness or indulgence with the fellow. Sternness hadn't worked on Giles, but neither had indulgence. Some men had to thrash their way through to adulthood on their own. David suspected that Richard was one of them.

Richard lifted his head and reached for a cup of the coffee that the servant had brought in. He clasped it between his hands, staring into its dark depths. "I need a thousand pounds. Father won't give it to me, and I thought—"

"We went over this last week," David said gently. "I didn't mind covering your debts at first, but now your father has requested that I not do so. He says you'll only keep gambling, and he doesn't want to feed your vice."

The requests for money had begun after Sarah's death. Before that, Richard had never asked for so much as a penny from David. According to his father, until then he'd had only minor gambling debts. But these days he seemed determined to follow in Sarah's footsteps. It alarmed David as much as it did Linley senior.

Richard drank shakily from the cup. "It's not for gambling, I swear. It's . . . I . . . well, there's a girl I sort of . . . got with child, and she says she'll tell Father if I don't give her money."

"So she wants blackmail, is that it?" David said, unable to keep the disapproval from his tone.

A flush spread over the young man's cheeks as he set his cup down on the desk. "I can't have her telling Father. He'll skin me alive!"

"Very well. Send the girl to me, and I'll take care of it."

The panicked expression crossing Richard's face told the whole tale. The chap was lying.

David scowled. "Surely you didn't think me such a fool that I would just hand a thousand pounds over to you to give some girl."

Richard shot to his feet, his fists clenching. "You're as

bad as Father! The two of you, so pompous and sure of yourselves. The money isn't even yours! It's Sarah's, damn it! And she would want you to help me. You know she would!"

"But I'm not Sarah. I know it sometimes takes a firm hand to guide a young man." The firm hand his own father had wielded. "Go to your father. Tell him the truth. Promise him whatever he requires, and then hold to your promise. That's the only way to end this madness."

"Perhaps I don't wish to end it," Richard said with a sneer. "Perhaps I don't want to end up like you and him, old and settled and boring."

"That's your choice. But speaking from experience, gambling, wenching, and drinking can deprive you of much that you'll come to regret losing."

Of course the words fell on deaf ears. They generally did.

As soon as Richard stormed out, David dropped wearily into the chair behind his desk. Bloody hell, sometimes he *felt* old and boring. But it was better than suffering agonies of regret for mistakes one made in one's youth.

All right, so he hadn't saved himself from that. But he refused to stand by and do nothing while Richard made the same errors. He would force the man to see sense . . . even if he had to cut him off completely to do it.

From their vantage point near the drawing room door, Charlotte and Giles saw Richard storm past, headed for the stairs. "Poor thing," she whispered.

"Poor thing, my ass," Giles growled, then realizing whom he was speaking to, added, "Forgive my language, but he's driving David mad."

"You have to expect that. The young man is grieving."

And finding his in-laws engaged in rank frivolity couldn't have helped. Charlotte probably shouldn't have allowed Giles to talk her into a dance, but it had been so long since she'd had the chance to kick up her heels, and Lady Kirkwood had made it sound perfectly harmless.

She winced. The minute David had frowned on it, she should have taken *his* stance. "Will your brother be all right?"

Giles was still staring at the doorway with a distracted expression.

"Giles?" she prodded.

"Hmm?" He jerked his gaze back to her. "Sorry, I was . . . woolgathering. You have no idea how awful it's been for David since he married that spoiled chit. Even with only eleven years between them, he was more of a father than a husband to her, since she didn't have the sense God gave her. I'm sure that's why Richard is casting him in the same role." He raked his fingers through his hair. "But I suppose I shouldn't speak ill of the dead."

"No need to apologize," she demurred, though the virulence in his tone had shocked her. "We all knew how . . . difficult Sarah could be sometimes. I only wish I had been better able to impress upon her the dangers of gambling."

"It wasn't just the gambling. Sarah had other problems."

Charlotte stared at him. "What do you mean?"

"She had a dark side. One she didn't even show David."

A chill ran down Charlotte's spine. "But she showed *you*?"

He glanced at her, suddenly wary. "It doesn't matter anymore. She's gone now."

She was about to press him about Sarah's "dark side" when David appeared in the doorway. The minute she spotted him, Charlotte's throat tightened with a mix of concern and pity. He bore the look of a man who'd fought demons and ended up skewered on a pitchfork for his trouble.

She wanted to comfort him, but this was not the time or place. He needed his family about him now.

Purposefully, she headed for him. "I think I had better leave," she murmured. "I do not wish to be in the way."

"You're not in the way." He cast a glance to where his sisters and his mother were conferring. "But if you want to go, I'll take you home. Just give me a moment to speak to Mother."

"I came in my own carriage. I do not need an escort."

His brow lowered. "London is dangerous this time of night, Charlotte."

"And it has been just as dangerous for years, yet I continue to come and go as I please." When he cast her a bleak look, she added more gently, "Terence has not failed me yet. Besides, if you accompany me home, how will you return?"

He released a sigh. "At least let me see you out."

"Very well." In truth, she welcomed the chance to speak to him privately and make sure he was all right.

It took her a few minutes to thank her hostess and say her good-byes to her friends. After she and the Winters settled upon a day and time for Amelia to visit the school with her girls, she rejoined David.

He certainly seemed impatient for her to be gone, given how he hurried her down the stairs. But when they reached the bottom of the staircase, she realized his impatience was not for that. Before they could head for the entrance or attract the notice of his footmen at the far end of the passage, he pulled her into the nearby library. Then closing the door, he hauled her into his arms.

"David—"

"Not one word, Charlotte," he murmured. "Not now. Just let me have this."

Then he kissed her with such fierce intent that her toes curled in her slippers. Oh, heavens, what the man could do with his mouth. It was tender and bold all at once, and so needy it made her heart ache for him.

When at last he drew back, she dropped her reticule to grab his lapels and tug him down to her again, not ready to end their interlude.

That was all the encouragement he needed. With a guttural moan, he shoved her against the door, his mouth savaging hers, his tongue thrusting deep as his lean body slid against her in a motion that was unmistakably intimate. Already she felt the ridge of his flesh pressing insistently against her belly. His hands roamed up and down her sides, over her hips and up to her breasts.

But when he filled his hands with them, she pushed him back. "No," she said softly. "Not here."

A dark knowing flared in his face. Oh Lord, she'd as much as said that elsewhere would be fine.

But it was true. She wanted him. She had always wanted him. And would it be so very bad to have an affair? She was a grown woman; she could do as she pleased. And he was not married anymore.

He bent his head to her cheek, dragging his open mouth along her jaw to her ear. "Then where?" he murmured. "When?"

She could hardly think with him still cupping her breasts, thumbing her nipples through the fabric. "We ought to wait until you are done with mourning."

"No, damn it." He tongued her ear, nipping the lobe with his teeth. "I won't. And you don't want to either."

A pox on him for being right. "Well . . . then . . . we must be discreet."

"Discreet, yes," he breathed in agreement against her ear, though he rocked into the cradle of her thighs, his erection arousing her, marking her as already destined for his bed.

Her mind was swimming, her body alive to the feel of him. "I just know it cannot be here."

"Right." Yet he reached for her leg and pulled it up, pushing into her, mimicking the act he wanted to perform. "Not here."

She must be mad, both to be considering this, and to be letting him touch her now. They could be discovered at any moment. "We have to stop."

"Yes." Still, he tried to take her mouth again.

This time she shoved him hard enough to make him fall back. His gaze burned into her like a brand, sparking a fever in her chest.

"*Not here*," she said firmly. "Not tonight." She had to escape him. To *think* about what she was doing, before she fell into something she regretted. "I have to go. We can talk about this later."

"Tomorrow." His eyes glittered in the firelight. "We'll discuss it tomorrow when I take you to see those properties."

"Properties?" she said blankly.

"The ones for the new school building? Remember? So you don't have to deal with a racecourse next door?"

"Oh. Right." She had completely forgotten about that. At the moment she could hardly think.

Still trying to catch her breath, she bent to retrieve her reticule, then remembered something else. "Didn't you tell Terence that you would give me a list of those properties tonight so I could look it over?"

"Of course." Delving inside his coat pocket, he drew out a folded sheet of paper, but when she seized it, he grabbed her by the wrist. "You must promise you won't go tour them without me."

"Why?"

"Because it's dangerous for a woman to do that sort of thing alone. Some sellers are unscrupulous, and some of the vacant properties could have vagrants—"

"I have Terence."

With a scowl, he tightened his grip on her wrist. "I'm not giving you the list unless you promise."

"Oh, very well. I promise." As he released the list, she tucked it into her reticule and opened the door to peek out into the hall. Fortunately, David's footmen were involved in a heated discussion, leaving the two of them free to slip out and head for the entrance as if they'd just descended the stairs.

While waiting for her carriage to be brought, they said very little, but she was painfully aware of his body beside hers, of its heat and strength, which could be hers whenever she wanted. The knowledge was as exhilarating as it was terrifying. Merciful heavens, when had she turned into such a wanton?

Then she caught that same footman she'd noticed earlier staring at her, and the color rose in her cheeks. What an impertinent servant he was. Why, the look he shot his master was positively malevolent.

David didn't seem to notice, for he led her out and down the steps when the carriage arrived, as if it were his right.

Perhaps it was. But only because he had made it so. "You never really answered my question this afternoon, you know," she said as they approached her barouche.

"What question?"

"About why you decided to pursue Sarah's legacy to the school, even though you would have been perfectly within your rights not to. Thirty thousand pounds is a lot of money. No one would have been the wiser if you'd kept that piece of information to yourself. So why didn't you?"

He cast her a long, smoldering glance. "You already know the answer, sweeting."

Her blood soared at the words, and she stumbled. He slung his arm about her waist to right her, then let it linger just long enough to make her breathless.

By the time they reached the carriage, she was tempted to invite him to go home with her and throw caution to the winds. But then she saw Terence's carefully impassive features when he lowered the step for her, and she thought better of it.

As Terence took his place at the back of the coach, David handed her in. "You never answered *my* question this afternoon either."

"Which one?" she asked as she settled herself on the seat.

He leaned into the open door, his jaw taut. "Exactly how close a friend is Godwin to you?"

She laughed. It was too horrible of her, but it thrilled her to see David behaving like a jealous lover. Should she tell him the truth? Or torment him a little?

She opted for truth. "Let me put it this way—he has not been nearly as close a friend to me as you have already been."

Some of the tension left his face. "Good." His gaze drifted down her body in a heated glance that made her squirm. "Because I intend to be a great deal closer still."

As unwise as it might be, she was glad of it. "Good night, David," she said softly, secretly delighting in the look of frustrated hunger upon his face. It mirrored her own feelings.

"Until tomorrow, sweeting." Then closing the door, he called up to her coachman. "Drive on!"

As the coach pulled away, neither Charlotte nor David noticed Richard Linley skulking in the shadows on the steps that led down to the basement. He was watching the entire scene.

And the only look on *his* face was rage.

Chapter Fourteen

～⧼⧽～

$\mathcal{D}$avid spent the long cold night in dreams of Charlotte lying in his bed, all porcelain skin and wild blushes, while he and she did every wicked and lascivious thing he had ever imagined. He awakened hard and restless, his hand already doing what his body urged.

After he gained his release, he lay there staring at the ceiling, willing his heart to settle into normalcy.

What was wrong with him? Why was he back where he'd started eighteen years ago, as obsessed with Charlotte as ever?

He'd thought himself successful in putting her from his mind once he was married. Determined to make a clean start with Sarah, he had set aside the dream of him and Charlotte. And even after the hope of a decent marriage with Sarah had died, he'd managed to find his enjoyment in friends, in designing buildings, in investments.

He'd actually convinced himself that he'd conquered his mad passion for Charlotte, that writing to her as a perfectly disinterested friend had dulled the heat of youthful desire to the mere warmth of affection.

What a fool he was. His desire burned as fiercely as ever. And judging from what she'd done and said last night, it did for her as well. He'd given her plenty of chances to protest, and she'd spoken only of the logistics of it.

He swung his legs over the bed. As long as she was willing, he could bloody well handle the logistics.

To that end, he dressed and set off for the outskirts of London. He had a couple of stops to make before he reached Richmond to take Charlotte around to those properties. Fortunately, the sunny day meant he could drive his phaeton, and there'd be no room for anyone but him and her and his tiger. Her fighter footman would have to stay home; at last they would have a chance to be alone. Thank God.

He arrived at the school midmorning to find Terence racing out the door, with Charlotte speaking in a raised voice to someone inside.

"What's happened?" David asked as he met the footman halfway up the steps.

"Mrs. Harris accosted that Mr. Watson as he was walking the property next door, and he told her some dreadful thing about the sale. So now I'm off to the solicitor's office to see if her cousin has answered her letter yet."

She'd talked to Pritchard's prospective buyer? Confound the woman to hell! The last thing David needed was her meddling in *that* situation. He wasn't sure what Watson might know of David's arrangement with Pritchard, or what the bloody fellow might have told her about it.

"She's in a fine temper, sir," Terence went on. "This might not be the best time to visit."

"I'll be sure to tread lightly." At least until he could get her away and question her privately.

As he continued up the steps, he could hear her storming about in the foyer, complaining to the butler. "That little worm of a man ought to be shot! How dare he speak to me that way? He is as bad as Mr. Pritchard, I swear."

David entered the school, but she was too angry to notice.

In high dudgeon, Charlotte was a rare sight indeed, with her curls shaking beneath her bonnet and her gloved hands flitting about. "And what did he mean by his hints about Cousin Michael?" she spat.

As a chill coursed down David's spine, the butler noticed him.

"Madam," he said in a low voice.

She ignored him. "That wretch made it sound as if he actually expects to be doing business with my cousin in the future!"

"Madam, you have a visitor!" the butler interrupted.

That brought her up short. When she whirled to find David standing there, her mouth dropped open. "David!"

"Good morning, Charlotte," he said warily. "Have I come at a bad time?"

"No . . . I . . . um . . . It's good to see you."

Given how her expression softened, it didn't look as if she'd learned anything of the truth.

Thank God. Because just the sight of her in that red silk gown made his heart race. It had a line of little bows stretching from neckline to hem, and he found himself wondering if they actually untied and how long it would take him to manage that . . . with his teeth.

He *had* to stop thinking about getting her out of her clothes. Right now there were more important matters. "Ready to go look at those properties?"

She glanced nervously out the door to where his phaeton stood waiting. "Now?"

"We did agree to do it this morning, and it's a fine day. I thought we might as well take full advantage of it." David thrust out his arm. "Shall we?"

"But I've barely had a chance to look over the list!"

"No excuses, Charlotte." He lowered his voice. "Besides, it will give us the chance to finish our . . . discussion from last night in the library."

She colored deeply. It made his blood run high. But just when he feared he'd said the one thing sure to make her balk, she steadied her shoulders. "Very well. Let me just go put one of the teachers in charge while I'm gone."

"I can take care of that, madam, if you wish," the butler put in with a gleam in his eye. At least David had one servant on his side.

"Oh," she murmured. "Thank you."

Moments later they were off. As David tooled his phaeton down the drive, he could tell she was still agitated. He waited until they were well on the road before broaching the subject. "So, I hear you had words with Watson."

She muttered a distinctly unladylike oath under her breath.

He couldn't help but laugh. "Your vocabulary has changed substantially in the past few years."

"That is not funny."

"Personally, I find it quite amusing. One rarely gets the chance to hear such a prim and proper schoolmistress curse."

"Then you should have been there when I spoke to Mr. Watson," she said ruefully. "I am afraid I . . . lost my temper somewhat."

"Somewhat?"

She thrust out her chin. "Very well. I admit to having raged at him. You cannot blame me; that man is the devil incarnate."

"What did Watson say?" David held his breath, praying she would confide in him. Feeling her gaze on his face, he willed himself to appear only mildly interested as he concentrated on guiding his matched pair along the rutted country road.

He knew when she'd decided to trust him by the way she leaned against his arm and let out a heartfelt sigh. "He confirmed what you said about the license. And when I . . . lost my temper, he hinted that Cousin Michael is playing me false."

Fear churned in his belly like a poison. "In what way?"

"Mr. Watson seemed to think my property was also about to be sold."

She must have misunderstood. That made no sense; Pritchard couldn't sell.

"Does he know your cousin?" David asked, wondering again how much Watson knew of his situation with Pritchard.

"I didn't dare ask, given the terms of my agreement with Cousin Michael. If it got back to him . . ."

"I know, you'd lose your low rents. So what exactly did Watson say?"

"He was very mysterious. Said that the owner of the school's property had a mind to do something profitable with it very soon, and that I had best be thinking about clearing out before I found myself on the street."

Ah, *that* made more sense. And he ought to thank Watson for giving her such a warning. "The man has a point. One day your cousin is bound to tire of subsidizing you."

"Even if he did, he would never put me on the street without giving me a chance to make other arrangements," she said firmly. "Mr. Watson was making idle threats to run me off. He does not want to deal with having us next door, complaining about his racecourse."

David gritted his teeth. "Are you sure that's all it is? Your cousin is still a stranger to you, as are his motives. You have no idea why he's giving you low rents."

She grabbed at her bonnet as they hit a rut. "You do not know the man."

"Neither do you."

"I know his character."

David muttered a curse under his breath. What she didn't know about "his character" could fill a wheelbarrow.

"You cannot possibly understand, David. When I began my school, I was barely twenty-two. Until then it had only been a dream, and I had assumed it would take years of working as a teacher before I could even consider applying to be a headmistress somewhere."

A ragged breath escaped her. "Then I received his letter saying that he felt bad about Jimmy leaving me so destitute. That he felt honor-bound to make it right." She stared out over the fields they drove past. "You know better than anyone how little I deserved such kind consideration."

God, how could he bear to listen to this? "Charlotte—"

"No, let me finish." Her fingers twisted her reticule strap. "I know now that he is probably not my husband's cousin. Perhaps he is one of my husband's compatriots who came into some money or a rich man whose child I taught."

She steadied her shoulders. "I do not care who he is. He helped me turn the shambles I had made of my life into something wonderful. He saw the value of what I was then; he believed in me as no one ever had. Without him, I could never have realized my dream at so young an age."

Her *dream*? Good God. What if Charlotte couldn't be

persuaded to close the school, even after marrying him? What if it were more than just a source of income to her?

He hadn't even considered that.

But she wasn't fool enough to think she could be wife to a viscount and also run a girl's school. She would have responsibilities, social and otherwise. Charlotte would recognize that. Surely she would.

"So you see," she said softly, "I will not tolerate anyone saying anything ill of my cousin. I owe that man everything. Whoever he is."

He squirmed to hear the adoration in her voice. He couldn't believe it—he was jealous of himself! And what made it worse was knowing that the fellow he was jealous of did not deserve her thanks. Had never deserved it.

Perhaps I should tell her.

Yes, and then she would hate both him *and* Michael. She would wash her hands of him forever. There would be no going back from that revelation.

He had to stay the course. It was the only way.

"So," she said lightly, clearly done with the topic of her cousin, "where are we going?"

"To a property in Hampstead Heath. And then to a couple in Acton that are right up the road from each other."

"Why, those are good areas."

"Don't sound so surprised."

"I just assumed, given the small amount I can afford . . ."

"Believe me, none of them are in peak condition. The advantage is, they have buildings already. That way you have a choice—if you decide to build, you can raze them to the ground and start over. If you can save money by renovating, you can do that, too."

"Does Sarah's will allow for that?" she asked.

"Sarah's will allows for whatever the executor says." Literally. "As long as whatever building you end up with is named after her, you'll have followed the letter of the law." He flicked the reins. "I haven't seen the first two yet myself. The buildings may not be in any condition to renovate, or they may not be large enough to suit your needs. But after today, I should have a better sense of what your needs actually are."

They were approaching Kew Bridge over the Thames. Suddenly he felt her stiffen beside him. That's when he remembered her aversion to water.

"Are you all right?" he asked as he slowed the horses.

"Yes." She flashed him a game smile. "I cannot believe you remembered my silly . . . peculiarity."

"It isn't silly. And I generally remember whenever a woman goes to pieces in my arms. I don't relish having it happen again. Not out of fear, anyway," he teased.

She smiled gamely. "It is not a problem. I cross this bridge every time I go in to town. I am quite accustomed to it."

Noting her pallor, he cast her a skeptical glance. "You don't look accustomed."

"I will be fine, I promise. Just get it over with."

"All right." Taking her hand, he tucked it in the crook of his elbow and then urged the horses to a quicker speed. "I won't let anything harm you, you know."

"I know."

But she gripped his arm so tightly as they drove over the Thames, that he wondered if she'd leave bruises.

As soon as they were across, she relaxed, though she kept her hand on his arm. "Have I thanked you yet for taking me to see these properties?"

He snorted. "Until now, you've acted as if I'm mounting an attack on your life."

A laugh escaped her. "Can I help it if I hate the idea of uprooting the entire school?" She squeezed his arm. "But I believe in keeping an open mind. And I am glad you are the one carrying me around. You see? I *can* be reasonable."

"Right." *Reasonable* would be her letting him handle this from now on. Which would only happen if he could convince her to marry him.

One thing at a time. Bed her first. Then marriage will naturally follow.

And once they were married, surely the problems with the school wouldn't matter.

He hoped not, anyway. Because after they reached the first property and the land agent brought them around, David realized that convincing her to move the school might prove difficult. After years in a beautiful old Elizabethan manor, she had unrealistically high expectations.

Before they could even make it inside, Charlotte objected to the small size of the lot, to the poor condition of the drive, to the lack of adequate trees.

"You can plant trees," he pointed out.

"Yes, but it would be years before we could have trees the size of those on our present property."

She'd be out on her ear long before then. "How about if I trim those hedges over there to *look* like trees?" he snapped.

"Very amusing. Trees are important, you know. They provide shade."

"Shade is certainly something every young lady needs for a proper education. Next you'll be telling me that sunshine warps the mind."

She laughed. "I just prefer trees."

"Fine. The next property has plenty of trees."

So off they went to Acton. Unfortunately, though the first property there had a virtual forest, it also had overgrown gardens and a soulless Palladian building that would take a great deal of work. Inside, the moldings were crumbling, every wall needed repainting, and the ceilings were black with half a century's worth of coal and candle smoke. Worse yet, the staircase was in bad need of repair. Still, a little effort might bring it up to snuff.

But not according to Charlotte. "It's too dark," she announced after the agent had taken them through the entire place. "Not enough windows."

"I see," David said dryly. "The outside of the last property had too much sun, and the inside of this one has too little. Perhaps I should explain the concept of sunshine to you. It generally stays on the outside. That is why we have candles for the inside."

She arched her eyebrows at him. "Are you done mocking me?"

"I'm not sure. Are you planning to say anything else mockworthy?"

"I'm planning to leave you here and go on to the next property alone if you don't behave," she chided.

"You don't know where it is."

"Then I will steal your phaeton and drive myself home."

"Ah, but you don't want to miss the next property."

"Why?"

"Because it has a stable twice the size of the school's present one."

She sighed. "You do know the way to a woman's heart."

God, he hoped so. Traipsing about the countryside with her was making him hungry. Very, very hungry. Only the presence of the land agent kept him from sweeping her up in his arms on the way back to his phaeton and kissing her into the same state of mindless lust he had been stewing in for the past couple of hours.

Fortunately, the next property would have no land agent waiting for them. He smiled.

"I don't suppose we could pick up again tomorrow," she said as he handed her up into his rig. "That way I could go back to the school and see if there's a letter from my cousin."

There was no letter. David had waited to have a better sense of what to say after today's jaunt.

"I promise you'll love this property up the road." He climbed into the driver's seat and took the reins. "Besides, it seems clear to me that your cousin has decided on a tactic of benign neglect. He figures if he keeps ignoring your letters, you'll give up and go away."

"I don't want to hear any more complaints about my cousin," she grumbled as they set off. "You sound just like Terence. He doesn't trust Cousin Michael either."

He slanted a glance at her. "Your bodyguard doesn't trust any man where you're concerned."

"Bodyguard? He's a lady's footman."

"You may have hired him as such, but you use him like a bodyguard."

She fiddled with her reticule strap. "What makes you say that?"

"Women don't generally hire boxers as footmen." He returned his gaze to the road. "Did you know he killed a man in the ring?"

"Yes."

"That he was put on trial for it?"

"And was acquitted. As well he should have been. If boxing weren't illegal, there wouldn't even have been a trial. He deserved better, after the way he trounced Jim Belcher at the Salisbury."

David gaped at her. "Don't tell me you follow boxing."

She shrugged. "I used to, when Jimmy was alive. He was an enthusiast, and I always made him bring me along so I could keep him from betting excessively. I didn't watch, though. It was a bit too bloody for my taste." Her voice dropped a fraction. "Especially when the women fought."

The truth suddenly hit him, so painful it made his chest hurt. "Did your father used to hit your mother?"

Her gaze shot to him. "What? No!"

"No?" he prodded, not believing her.

She sighed. "No. But he . . . came very near to it a number of times. Mostly, he preferred more subtle punishments."

Since the bastard hadn't balked at threatening his daughter with what terrified her the most years ago, David could well imagine what sorts of punishments he'd inflicted on the mother.

They traveled some way in silence before she spoke again.

"When I was a girl, I used to pray that someone would step in to defend us, especially when Papa was saying cruel things to Mama," she said softly. "I thought that if a man could just lay Papa out once on our behalf, he would stop his bullying. Of course, there was no one."

David wished again that he could have been that man for her.

"And anyway," she went on, "it probably wouldn't have worked. It would just have enraged him more."

So once she was grown, she'd hired a footman who could lay anyone out at her command. But first . . . "Is that why you married Harris?"

"What do you mean?"

"Did you marry him so he could protect you from your father after that letter came out in the papers?" Belatedly, it had dawned on him that if she hadn't sent the letter to the paper, then she hadn't anticipated how her father might punish her for it. "That is, assuming your father had guessed who'd written it."

"Oh, he guessed," she said in a hollow voice. "He knew at once it was me."

A chill passed over him. "So that's why you ran away with Harris."

"Yes," she admitted. "That very day. While Papa was still ranting to Mama about it, Jimmy came to the house and found me alone in the garden, fretting over what was going to happen. He offered to take me away. I knew Papa would lock me up forever if I didn't seize the chance to leave then, so I did."

David gripped the reins as if they were a lifeline. Harris had offered marriage because *he* had not. Because he had been too much of a coward, too intent upon protecting himself and his pride to explore why Charlotte had changed from his sweetheart into his enemy overnight.

"Clever fellow, your Jimmy," he said hoarsely. They'd reached the next property. He drove up in front of the building, then turned to her. "He knew to strike when you were at your most vulnerable."

"It wasn't like that."

"No? Did he not get the benefit of your dowry and inheritance?"

"Yes, but he didn't do it for that reason."

"Really? So Harris is not the reason you drill into your students the lesson that fortune hunters are to be avoided at all costs?"

"No."

Before he could respond to that astonishing remark, she climbed down from the phaeton and headed up the steps of the building.

Handing the reins over to his tiger, he hurried after her with a building feeling of dread. "Then who *is* the reason?"

She stopped short on the top step. "Where's the land agent?"

That momentarily distracted him. "There isn't one. The owner gave me the key. He didn't want to come all the way out here just to show the property. Told me to look around to my heart's content."

As the ramifications of that hit her, she sucked in a harsh breath. "So we . . . have the place to ourselves?"

He unlocked the door. "Exactly." Holding the door open, he met her startled gaze with one of challenge. "Shall we go in?"

She glanced to where his tiger was driving the phaeton off to the nearby stables, and a hint of panic touched her face.

But it was gone in a flash, replaced by a tentative smile. "Why not?"

His blood thundered in his ears. He led her inside, then closed and locked the door behind them.

But he was not so far gone that he'd forgotten their previous conversation. Backing her against the door, he planted his hands on either side of her shoulders. "Answer the question, Charlotte. If Harris didn't inspire your heiress lessons, then who did?"

"I'm sorry, David," she said, her eyes not meeting his. "*You* did."

Chapter Fifteen

Charlotte winced to see anger flaring in David's face.

"The hell I did," he ground out.

"Please, you have to understand—"

"I did *not* court you for your money, damn it!"

"I know," she said softly. "I know it now, in any case."

His eyes looked haunted. She couldn't bear to see it, knowing how sorely she had misjudged him years ago.

Slipping under his arm, she wandered down the marble-floored hall. "But back then I thought you had only pretended to care about me to gain my fortune. I believed it for years. And it didn't help that you married Sarah for her money."

"Because I had no choice!" he ground out as he followed hard on her heels.

"I realize that now. Giles explained it very well."

"Yes, he told me last night about encountering you at some social affair a few years ago. You believed *him* when he told you I never bedded Molly, yet you didn't give me the chance to argue it for myself!"

"Don't you think I have tortured myself over that ever since?" She halted, her stomach knotting to remember the effect of Giles's revelation on her that night. "Bad enough that I wrote that horrible letter and that it ended up published, but to realize that I had done it so foolishly . . ."

A sob caught in her throat. He slid up behind her.

Catching her about the waist, he pulled her back into his arms. "Why didn't you come to me? Why didn't you ask me about Molly?"

"Because I was stupid and young and terrified of my father. I thought that you and he . . . that you would tell him, and he would make me . . ."

"My God, sweeting," he said hoarsely. "I would never have done that to you."

"I realize that now." Her voice dropped low. "When I sent the letter, part of me prayed that you would come after me when you read it. I so wanted to be proved wrong, yet I didn't dare believe it . . ."

"Instead it went to the paper, and I was too proud, too horrified to attempt to get you back. What a fool I was." The anguish in his tone was unmistakable. "Did my chatty little brother happen to tell you what I did to him after he revealed how he'd acted with Molly that night?"

She wrapped her arms over the arm that manacled her waist. "No," she breathed.

"I beat him within an inch of his life." The scent of his spicy cologne intoxicated her, and when he kissed a path to her ear, her blood roared in her veins. "We didn't speak for a long time because I was so angry. Because he'd lost me the only woman I'd ever cared for."

The tender words made a wild alarm rise in her breast. She had convinced herself that this could work, that they could have an affair as long as she did not let her heart become engaged. She had to keep herself safe. There were so many reasons not to hope for more from him.

But when he spoke of how he felt, it roused her hopes dangerously. She did not dare believe in it. Instead, she turned in his arms to press a finger to his lips. "Shh, no more talking." Then she replaced her finger with her mouth.

He hesitated a fraction, then gave in with a groan, kissing her ravenously, drawing her up against the length of his hard body as their tongues warred. Still kissing her, he tore at the bows on her gown, untying them one by one.

She made no protest, looping her arms about his neck as he opened her bodice clear down to her waist. Reaching inside, he jerked down her corset cups so he could fondle her breast through her chemise, thumbing her nipple into a hard point beneath his hand.

But when she tried to push his coat off, he drew back to growl, "Not here."

Her heart nearly stopped. "But I thought we . . . I thought you wanted—"

"I do," he clarified hastily. "Just not in the hall. I've waited half a lifetime to have you, and I'm not going to take you on the bare floor." Clasping her by the waist, he tugged her toward an open door. "Come on, sweeting. This way."

Seconds later, he led her into a small sitting room. Charlotte stared around her in a daze of frustrated desire. There was one spindly chair and a rickety table bearing a picnic basket. But most telling was the pallet laid before the hearth.

"You . . . you *planned* this?" she accused, then realized how stupid that sounded. The house with the key . . . his comment back at the school. Of course he had arranged it ahead of time.

With a devilish smile, David released her to go light an impressive stack of wood in the fireplace. "I always plan." He struck the flint until it sparked and caught on the kindling. "You ought to know that about me by now."

A laugh bubbled out of her as she remembered their picnic across from Saddle Island years ago. "And here I was thinking how wicked we are to be doing this in some stranger's house. Should I be flattered or insulted that you felt so sure of me?"

"Sure!" Shaking his head, he nursed the tiny fire into a roaring flame. "No man has ever been less sure of a woman in his life." He rose to fix her with an unreadable gaze. "I believe in being prepared. But I said this had to be mutual, and I meant it. If you want to leave—"

"No," she cut in.

His eyes glittered darkly as he came toward her, shucking his coat and tossing it onto the lone chair. "I've done nothing since yesterday but think of making love to you."

Truth be told, neither had she. "Aren't you worried that someone will come along—"

"No," he said as he reached her. "We're alone here. I swear it."

"In that case . . ." She began to untie the rest of the bows on her pelisse-robe, but he halted her with one hand.

"Let me," he murmured. "I can't tell you how often I've imagined undressing you."

Her breath seemed lodged way down in her throat as he undid bow after bow, his hands fumbling a little. She was glad he was as nervous as she was.

Perversely, that emboldened her. She unbuttoned his waistcoat, her blood heating at the idea of seeing him naked for the first time. "I assume that the owner of this fine house doesn't know you are appropriating his property for an illicit affair."

He shed his waistcoat. "Certainly not. But I don't think he'd care. In my place, he'd do the same."

That perplexed her. "Who is it?" she asked as she slipped off her gown and petticoat, then threw them onto the chair with his coat.

"Stoneville." He circled behind her to unlace her, his breath hot upon her neck.

"Stoneville!" Lord Stoneville was not only David's friend, but a friend to the school, along with Anthony and Simon Tremaine, the Duke of Foxmoor. "But why—"

"He's strapped for funds and has decided to rid himself of this place. I told him I'd take a look at it." With her corset off, he rounded her again. "I neglected to mention that you'd be with me, of course, but fortunately he was having too much fun in town to come show us around."

"That was fortunate indeed," she said shakily, feeling very exposed in only her chemise.

Before he could strip her of her last vestige of modesty, she went on undressing *him,* needing to keep her hands busy and her thoughts off her sudden nervousness. It had been years since she had lain with her husband. What if she could not please David? He had always been more worldly than she.

She got his cravat off and his shirt unbuttoned, exposing part of his chest. When she turned to unfastening his trousers, he hardened to iron beneath her hand.

Lifting his hands to her hair, he tugged it free of its pins. "Do you realize I've never seen your hair down?" As it tumbled to her waist, he lifted a lock and twined it about his fist, rubbing it against his face, kissing it. "I've always wondered what it would be like to have you standing before me wearing only your hair, a Lady Godiva come to life."

The image brought such fevered fancies to her mind

that she undid the buttons of his drawers with renewed haste, no small feat when he was so thoroughly aroused. Who would ever have guessed that David could be such a romantic? Every word tumbled another brick from the wall of her defenses, and she couldn't even make herself care.

He was here, with her. That was all she cared about.

Meanwhile, he had untied her chemise and pulled it up, forcing her to stop long enough for him to get it off. Once he had her naked, he stepped back. "Let me see you, Charlotte. Before I lose my mind."

She had not stood this way before a man in years, and she was painfully conscious that she was not as young as she once had been. David was used to having a younger woman in his bed, for Sarah had been only twenty-six at her death. Would he care that Charlotte's breasts were not as high and firm? That her belly was slightly fuller?

His gaze raked her appreciatively. "My God, sweeting, you're a vision," he said hoarsely.

"A vision?" she said with a giddy laugh. "I do not feel like a vision these days."

"Then you clearly haven't paid attention to your long list of male admirers." Jealousy lent his tone an edge. "I assure you it's not merely your prowess in the schoolroom that enchants them."

The compliment delighted her, exaggerated though it was. A long list of admirers, indeed. She had noticed no such thing. "And do you consider yourself one of my admirers, my lord?" she asked coyly.

"I hope soon to consider myself far more," he rasped as he reached for her.

She held him off with a teasing smile. "Oh no, not yet. It's my turn to look."

After dragging his shirt up over his head, she ran her hands slowly down his broad chest to shove his trousers and his drawers off in one fell swoop. Then she stepped back to gaze upon the man she'd desired for what seemed like years.

She was not surprised to find him exquisitely formed, his muscles finely defined, his waist amazingly taut for a man of his age. But the size of his shaft did take her aback. Either Jimmy had been more moderately equipped than she had realized, or David was what was commonly termed "well hung."

He had more hair than her fair-skinned husband, too, which made him seem intensely masculine. And dangerous. Especially when he caught her to him with undeniable hunger, taking her mouth in a kiss that was a heady tumult of passion and excess.

Caressing her breasts shamelessly, he fired her blood to dizzying heights, while she skimmed her hands over every part of the body she'd always wondered about. His thighs and buttocks were well muscled, the mark of a man who spent a great deal of time in the saddle.

One moment they were feverishly touching and kissing; the next, he was lowering her to the pallet before the fire and she was parting her legs to accommodate him as he knelt.

He stroked his long, hard shaft against her privates, rousing her desire most furiously. But when he did no more than that, making her grab at his hips to try to make him take her, she whispered, "David . . . please . . . I want you . . . inside me . . ."

A strained smile touched his lips. "I intend to torment you a while, sweeting, to pay you back for the tortures I've suffered wanting you the past few days."

"Don't you dare," she breathed, though the idea of how he might choose to torture her was tantalizing.

"This," he murmured, ignoring her protest, "is for last night." He dipped his head to suck her breasts, first one, then the other, blowing on the wet nipples until she thought she might scream.

"What did I do last night?"

His breathing was already labored. "Paraded your pretty breasts before me and never even let me kiss them."

"You know why," she said, a little petulantly. He was still rubbing her with his rigid flesh, and she was about to go out of her mind.

"Next time you have dinner at my house, sweeting, I'll make sure none of my relations are there." His eyes gleamed down at her. "And *you* will be dessert."

Bracing himself over her on one forearm, he reached down to tease her flesh so exquisitely she nearly came right there. "And this," he managed, as he fondled her into a mindless fever, "is for stopping me yesterday afternoon before I could have my wicked way with you on the settee."

He slid two fingers inside her, his thumb deftly tormenting her little bud of flesh until he had her writhing and gasping beneath him, already teetering on the edge of release.

"You wicked, wicked man," she choked out. "Two can play your game, you know." Sliding her hand down to seize his thick member, she tugged it in a long, slow stroke. "This, my lord, is for rubbing yourself against me last night when you knew we could do nothing about it."

He groaned and thrust into her hand. "Don't do that."

"Why? Are you the only one allowed to play this game?"

With a growl, he caught her hand. "All right. You win."

She arched up against him with a sensual smile. "Then give me my prize."

That's all it took to have him sliding his cock inside her in a slow, delicious motion that had her squirming beneath him. "Ah, God, Charlotte, you're so tight . . . so hot . . ."

She nearly came just at the exquisite pleasure of being filled by his flesh, of seeing the stark hunger on his face as he pressed forward until they were joined so intimately, she thought she could feel his heart beating inside her.

"Are you all right?" he rasped, pausing to let her adjust to him.

She tongued his throat, undulating against him. "Take me," she whispered, "please . . . now . . . please . . ."

With a guttural moan he began to move, slowly at first, then quickening rapidly until he was pounding into her so hard it made the floor vibrate.

"Yes . . . that's it." Her fingernails dug into his arms. "You're very . . . good at that."

He let out a choked laugh. "And you are quite the little wanton, Mrs. Harris," he teased as he brushed kisses to her forehead, her hair, her shoulder. "I never guessed . . . I had no idea . . ."

"Neither did I."

Jimmy had been a good lover, considering her own inexperience. But even when he had made her cry out in bed, she had always been conscious of holding a little part of herself aside, never giving herself wholly.

Now she knew why. That part of her had belonged to David.

And he seemed bent on taking it with thorough efficiency. He was making her insane, and the endearments he whispered only heightened her pleasure. He pulled her legs up more until he was strumming her sweet spot with every thrust, rousing her to greater and greater heights as he thundered over her, around her, inside her.

"Heavens, David," she gasped, straining against him as she felt her release stealing over her like a thief bent on wresting away her soul. "Yes . . . oh yes . . . oh my word . . ."

"Charlotte . . . my own . . . wonderful . . . Charlotte," he rasped, and then drove into her so deeply she climaxed. As her flesh tightened on his in waves, he pumped his seed into her with a hoarse cry.

It was ecstasy beyond any she'd ever known. She could feel her heart pounding to the same tempo as his, and finally understood what the marriage vows meant by the two becoming one.

He had thoroughly crashed through her wall. And it would be nearly impossible to pile the bricks up against him this time.

Chapter Sixteen

❧

Drunk with contentment, David lay on the pallet with Charlotte in his arms. After all these years, she was his at last. He would never let her go now. He wouldn't even let Cousin Michael come between them.

He wished he'd never invented the fellow. But then, he would never have had this with Charlotte if he hadn't.

"What is that frown for?" she asked lightly.

She had raised her head up from his shoulder with a minxish look that set his pulse racing anew. One of her surprisingly long legs was draped over his knee, and her soft breasts were pillowed against his chest.

She had such pretty breasts, too—full and dimpled, with pink, pouty nipples. Just the thought of tasting them roused his cock from slumber.

"I was merely wondering how long it would be before we could do this again," he said, caressing one of those lovely breasts.

"*We?*" she teased. "I am ready again now."

"I know," he said dryly. "Women have all the luck. But as it happens, this was my second performance today, so it will take me a while longer to recover."

When the light faded from her eyes, he cursed his clumsy tongue and quickly held up his hand. "Meet your competition. A man has to do *something* to take the edge off his lust when a certain female is driving him out of his mind."

As comprehension dawned, she let out a shaky laugh. "If you mean what I think, Lord Kirkwood, then you are very naughty indeed."

He chuckled. "I know I shouldn't say such outrageous things to a proper schoolmistress, but you bring out the devil in me."

"You just enjoy shocking me, that's all." She snuggled close to kiss his neck, her gorgeous hair catching the light like golden threads in red damask.

He ran his fingers along her downy shoulder, marveling at the creamy perfection of her skin. "You don't look very shocked."

"That is only because a schoolmistress always has to affect an expression of serenity. Otherwise, her pupils misbehave just to see her reaction." Her hand played over his chest. "But inside, I assure you I am rapping your knuckles with a ruler."

The very idea roused his mischievous bent even more. "Shall I tell you what I was thinking about while I was boxing the Jesuit this morning?"

"B-Boxing the Jesuit?" she sputtered.

He grinned. "It means—"

"I can guess what it means!" she said, half-laughing. "But bringing religion into it makes it sound even more wicked."

"That's the point, isn't it?" He smoothed her hair over her shoulder, his smile fading. "Anyway, as I lay in my lonely bed, I was imagining you lying in it, too." Seizing the moment, he added, "All the time. As my wife."

She caught her breath and her amusement vanished, replaced by a wary expression. "You mustn't say that." She pushed away from him.

His joy plunging, he grabbed her before she could leave him. "Why not? I want to marry you, Charlotte."

"You're still in mourning," she pointed out as she knelt beside him, on the verge of bolting.

"Only for six more months."

Her solemn gaze met his. "And then what?

"What do you mean?" He sat up and crossed his legs, suddenly finding it hard to breathe.

"I mean, what role would I play in your life?"

"What *role*?" Her reaction to his proposal twisted his gut into knots. He should have realized it was too soon to propose marriage. What was wrong with him? Yet he blundered on. "I think you know what sort of role a wife plays."

"Yes, I do. You forget, I have played it before, and I did not particularly like it."

He couldn't believe she was saying this. "It would be different with me."

"Would it?" She shifted her position, clutching her knees to her chest and folding her naked body in such a way that she looked as modest as a nun. Or as modest as a nun *could* look, if she'd just come fresh from a man's bed. "What about the school?" she asked, her eyes solemn.

"What about it?"

"Does the wife of the Viscount Kirkwood get to run a girl's school? Or is she expected to be a viscountess and nothing more?"

That threw him off balance. "You would want to keep running the school," he said inanely. He'd feared as much, but still . . . "You do realize I can afford to keep a wife."

"Of course," she said softly. "That is not what I asked."

He was in dangerous territory now, and he honestly

didn't know how to navigate. "Given your present financial difficulties with the place, I thought you might prefer to—"

"Close it? Let you absorb me into your life so the only thing I have left is you?"

"No!" Only Charlotte could make an offer of marriage sound like an insult. "I don't care about the school. It has nothing to do with this."

She flinched as if struck. "It has *everything* to do with this, for me."

"Why? You started it so you could support yourself."

"I started it because I believe that women should receive a proper education. That means a great deal to me. I thought you understood that."

He did, especially given the many letters that had passed between them. Yet part of him had hoped she'd be eager to share his life without her bloody institution intruding. "Fine. Then keep it open. I don't care." It meant convincing her to move the school, but he could handle that better if he were her husband. "I'm sure you could find a suitable headmistress to replace—"

"So your answer is that the wife of the Viscount Kirkwood *cannot* run a girl's school." Not meeting his gaze, she rose and found her chemise, then slid it over her head. She kept her back to him, closing him out again, which made him insane.

"Why is it so damned important for you to be the one to run it?" he asked as he too rose and slipped on his drawers. Walking up behind her, he pulled her into his embrace. At least she allowed him that.

"When I was a little girl," she whispered, folding her arms over his, "my father knew exactly what were my favorite toys. And do you know why?"

Given what he knew of her father, he wasn't sure he could bear to hear.

"Because he used them to control me. When I made too much noise one day with my toy harp, he made me watch while he cut the strings from it one by one. Once, when I came tromping down the stairs too loudly, he took my doll. 'This is what happens to little girls who don't walk softly,' he said, and broke her legs."

"Oh God, Charlotte," he said hoarsely, clutching her close and wishing her father were alive so David could break both of *his* legs.

"When I was thirteen, Mama gave me a brooch. It was only blue glass, but it had little gold specks in it and I thought it very pretty. I was careful not to let him see how much I loved it. I only wore it when he wasn't around. But as children will, I forgot one night and had it on at dinner." Her voice grew steely. "He was drunk, as he often was at his cruelest. He said some horrible thing to Mama, and I defended her. So he took my brooch and crushed it under his heel."

She stiffened in his arms. "That was when I learned it did not matter what I had. He would find it, and he would destroy it. So I taught myself *not* to care—about anything. Because if the choice was defying him or giving up everything I treasured in the world, I knew I would defy him to my dying breath."

Turning in his arms, she stared up at him. "But after Jimmy died and I found myself alone and miserable, I had to have a purpose beyond survival. The school became my reason for living, my salvation. It was the first thing that belonged to me, and me alone. Even my inheritance was essentially taken from me by Jimmy. He did not do it to be cruel—he just lacked any sense of how to handle money, and he thought we should have a jolly good time while it lasted."

With his heart in his throat, David reached up to rub away the tears falling down her cheeks.

"I built my School for Young Ladies from nothing," she said hoarsely. "I put my soul into it. And now you think I should just . . . toss it aside?"

"Of course not," he bit out. "Contrary to what you seem to think, I'm not your father. I'm not Harris. I don't want to destroy your toys or your school. I certainly don't want to make light of your accomplishment."

Staring down into her tormented face, he softened his tone. "But you know as well as I do that a viscountess has responsibilities. When I go to my estate in Berkshire, what do you propose to do? Stay in Richmond?" He caressed her cheek. "And what about our children? How will you be a mother to them if you're spending all your time elsewhere?"

The blood drained from her face as she pushed free of his arms. "I do not even know if I can *have* children."

That sent a chill to his very soul. "Of course you can have children."

"I never did while married to Jimmy. I did not even miscarry." Her eyes were sorrowful. "What if I am barren?"

Trying not to show how much that possibility shook him, he paced to the fire. "You're just assuming that. There's no reason for you to be barren."

"Even if I were not, thirty-six is old to be having a first child. You know that. Anything could go wrong."

He turned to fix her with a fierce look. "Then Giles can be the heir. Let him inherit the title and carry on the family name. As long as we're together, it doesn't matter."

"You say that now, but—"

"Damn it, I won't let you do this!" He strode up to grab her by the arms. "We finally have a chance to be together, and you want to ruin it!"

"I don't, I swear." She cupped his face in her hands, a tear trickling down her cheek. "But neither do I want us jumping into something without giving a thought to these things. You came back into my life only three days ago. Why can't we just go on as we are? As lovers?"

"Because I want you as a wife, not a mistress." He covered her hands with his. "I don't want us having to go sneaking around," he said, hunting for something, anything, that would keep her from shutting him out. "I don't want to be constantly worrying about your reputation and your position, afraid to show people that we belong to each other."

"Tell me something, David." Her eyes shone up at him, awash with tears. "Do you love me?"

The question rocked him. How could he tell her that he'd given up on love the day she'd sent that letter?

At his hesitation, she murmured, "I thought so," and tried to pull away.

He caught her before she could. "Surely you don't believe in love anymore, either. Love is for the young. They have the stamina to endure the wild fury of such nonsensical emotions. Mature people like us, with years of experience—"

"We are not that old, David."

"You're the one who said thirty-six was old to be having children." He glared at her. "I would say it's definitely too old to be countenancing a foolish idea like romantic love. People our age don't marry for love."

She gazed solemnly at him. "Then what do they marry for?"

"For companionship. For . . . mutual respect, admiration, affection." He kissed her hands. "And desire. Surely that is all any marriage needs."

"I married without love once," she said gently. "I have no need to do so again. If I am to consider giving up everything I have worked for, it will have to be for something more than conversation and companionship."

"Are you saying that you're in love with *me*?" he asked bluntly.

Drawing away from him, she folded her arms about her waist. "I . . . I honestly do not know. I am not sure I am even capable of the sort of love a woman should have for a husband."

For some reason, that thought disturbed him. He didn't want to examine too closely why that was. "Then love is not a consideration at all."

"It is if you are still in love with your wife."

"Sarah?" he said, incredulous. "She and I were never in love. Our marriage was barely more than a business transaction. You *know* that. She never pretended to love me, never said she wanted my love. As long as I agreed to bring her into the social sphere she aspired to join, she was content."

"Are you sure about that?"

He caught his breath, remembering Sarah's suicide note. Anger surged in him, the same anger that had clawed at him since the day she'd died. "If she wasn't content, it wasn't my fault."

"I did not say it was," Charlotte told him softly.

But he saw only the words of that damned note: *I can no longer endure this intolerable life.*

"I did everything I could to make her happy." He knew they sounded like empty excuses, yet he felt compelled to defend himself. "*She* was the one who refused to accompany me anywhere that didn't improve her status, and *she* was the one who showed no interest in making our marriage anything but a cold and formal union. *She* was the one who denied me her bed."

"You didn't . . . the two of you didn't . . ."

He winced. He hadn't meant to reveal such a personal thing, but it was probably best that she know how empty his marriage had been. "Not in the last few years. After she miscarried twice, she said she wasn't going through that 'nonsense' again, even though the physician told us there was no reason to believe she couldn't bear a child."

Spearing his fingers through his hair, he stared past her into the fire. "It wasn't like it is with you and me. I couldn't even *talk* to her, for God's sake. If I'd realized when I courted her that she had so little to commend her beyond her pretty face, I never would have—" He broke off, guilt swamping him anew. "But then, as you once remarked, I always was inordinately fond of a pretty face."

"Shh," she said, touching a finger to his lips. "I never meant to rouse your guilt over marrying Sarah. I should not have said what I did earlier. I know you were caught between a rock and a hard place." She gave him a shaky smile. "Amelia would undoubtedly have suited you better. It was not your fault that she had another sort of man in mind."

Catching her hand, he pressed a kiss into the palm. "But it *was* my fault that I let the one woman I should have married slip away. I should have come after you instead of nursing my hurt pride." He stared at her, frustration well-ing up in him again. "So now you mean to make me pay for that by refusing to marry me."

"No! If I made you pay, I would have to make myself pay, as well. I was ten times more guilty for what happened than you." She cupped his cheek. "I'm refusing to marry you because you do not know what you want right now. You are still in mourning, and being alone frightens you."

Tugging free of him, she headed to where her gown lay on the floor. "I understand that—I went through it myself. But after you have been alone for a while, the world becomes clearer. You start to figure out what really matters to you. Only then is it safe for you to make important decisions about your life and future."

She picked up her gown and cast him a pitying smile that grated on him. "Why do you think the mourning period is so long? Because it takes that much time to sort through everything."

He stalked toward her. Jerking the gown from her fingers, he tossed it aside. "I don't need to sort through anything, damn it. I know what I want. I want *you*."

"Fine. In six months, if you still feel—"

"Six more months won't change what I want," he growled.

"We shall see," she said, with another of those gentle smiles, and turned away.

He caught her shoulders in his hands, forcing her to face him. "So a lover is all you desire, is that it?"

She fixed her gaze somewhere in the vicinity of his neck. "For now."

She might think she had her life in order, that she knew exactly what she wanted—but the way she'd shattered when he'd made love to her showed she wasn't nearly as settled as she pretended. She was just afraid to trust him, to trust *this*.

And perhaps with good reason, given their past. So he would have to beat down her wall of uncertainty and fear. And he could think of only one way to do that.

"Very well," he said tightly. "Then *for now,* your lover is asking you to spend the rest of the day with him. We haven't even eaten yet." He nodded toward the picnic basket.

"I . . . I really should get back."

"I don't see why," he said, emboldened by her skittishness. She knew exactly how susceptible she was to him, and Charlotte was very good at running away from what she feared.

"My servants will wonder where I—"

He cut her off with a kiss, reveling when she not only responded but let him deepen it. Skimming his hands down to her sweet behind, he dragged her against his burgeoning erection, rubbing against her.

Only when she slipped her arms about his waist did he tear his mouth from hers to press it against her ear. "I want you again, sweeting."

She gave a dazed laugh. "I can tell."

"So," he murmured, "do you really have to go . . . just yet?" He sucked at the tender skin of her neck as he fondled one of her breasts.

Her breathing grew uneven. "Mmm . . . perhaps . . . I *could* stay . . . awhile . . . longer."

"Good." He tugged her toward the pallet. "You haven't even seen the house, after all."

"That's true," she choked out, her hands now locked on *his* behind so that they were sliding against each other in a fever. "It would be a shame to . . . come all this way . . . and not . . . see it."

"Quite a shame," he rasped, then tumbled her down onto the pallet.

But as he shed his drawers and drew up her chemise, he knew that this was only a reprieve. He could not keep her in bed indefinitely. Soon he would have to press the issue of marriage again.

And if she thought he would wait six months to make her his wife, she was mad.

Chapter Seventeen

◦◦◦

As they drove away from Lord Stoneville's house, Charlotte noted how low the sun was in the sky. The only one who knew exactly where they had been all day was David's tiger, and David had assured her that the lad could be trusted to keep quiet.

But she would still have a hard time explaining why she had been gone so long without revealing that she and David had been looking at properties. She did not want her staff to know about the possible move just yet.

On the other hand, she did not want them guessing what she and David had spent most of the day doing.

A delicious shiver ran down her spine. She had certainly chosen her lover well. Their second time had been even better than the first. He had taken his time, kissing every inch of her body and bringing her to the edge again and again, before finally joining her in a release so explosive it had hardly seemed real.

Then they had eaten the lavish picnic lunch he had brought, all of it food fit for a queen. She smiled to herself. David certainly knew how to spoil a woman.

When they were done eating, they had toured the property, but she scarcely remembered it. Between their sweet kisses and caresses, it was hard to pay attention. And though the stables had been as impressive as he had promised, all she remembered of them was David's taking her again, hard and fast in the hay.

"So what did you think?" David asked in a husky voice.

She blinked at him. "I cannot believe you are asking that. Do you really need to know?"

"Well, yes."

Trying not to blush, she stared at the road and kept her voice low so his tiger wouldn't hear. "Surely you are well aware of how masterful a lover you are. I think the number of times I . . . you know . . . ought to have shown you that."

He burst into laughter. "I meant, what did you think of the *house*?"

"Oh." Heat rose in her cheeks. "This is certainly embarrassing."

"Not for me," he said, chuckling, then bent close. "You were rather magnificent yourself. In fact, I believe I shall tell Stoneville that I'll need to visit his property again." His gaze drifted down to her bosom. "That I did not have a chance to view its beauties to my full satisfaction."

"You would deceive your friend just so you and I . . . so we . . ."

"Absolutely. Stoneville goes to Tattersall's on Tuesdays. Is Tuesday good for you?"

She eyed him askance. "You are very wicked, Lord Kirkwood."

"I certainly hope to be on Tuesday," he said in that seductive tone that thrummed along her senses.

They rode awhile in silence. Then he leaned over to whisper, "So I'm a masterful lover, am I?"

With a glance back at the tiger, she hissed, "Behave yourself."

"Too late for that." He pressed his mouth against her

ear. "Tell me, sweeting, how do I compare to your other lovers?"

She rolled her eyes. Men could be so ridiculously competitive. "What other lovers?" she said in an undertone. "Aside from my husband, there have been no others. Now will you please pay attention to the road, before we end up in the ditch?"

Grinning, he moved back. "I'm the only one since Harris, eh? Interesting."

She would dearly love to know why he found that so interesting. But she wasn't about to ask with a young lad sitting a mere foot behind them, even if he probably couldn't hear a word over the wind and the horses' hooves.

"So what *did* you think of Stoneville's property?" David asked after a moment.

She tried to recall what she'd seen of the building, but all she could think was that it was an excellent place for lovemaking. "It is certainly large enough. Though I did notice an odd chemical smell in one room . . ."

"Probably the one where he used to have his nitrous oxide parties."

Lord Stoneville was known for his wild affairs where his friends imbibed the intoxicating gas for pleasure. "*That* was the house? Good Lord, I never would have guessed." She slanted a glance at him. "Did you ever go?"

"To his parties? Once or twice. Why?"

A sudden chill snaked down her spine. Last year, Cousin Michael had written to warn her about one of her teacher's scandalous participation in a nitrous oxide party at Stoneville's. "Were you at the affair that Anthony and Madeline attended together?"

Flicking the reins to send the horses into a trot, he

frowned. "They went to one of Stoneville's parties? Really? I can see Anthony doing that, but it doesn't seem like something his wife would do."

His surprise seemed genuine. She released a breath. What was she thinking? She had already decided that David could not be Cousin Michael. And surely if he were, he would have told her by now. "I know. It was very odd. It was before they were married, too."

"Ah."

They fell silent. There was something so comfortable about sitting here beside him, watching him tool his phaeton expertly. She still could not believe he had proposed marriage. If anything convinced her that he had put the past behind them, it was that.

Was she being silly to refuse him? To insist that she be allowed to continue with the school?

Perhaps. Yet the thought of becoming nothing more than an ornament in his life, of having no place of her own and no destiny beyond that of fulfilling societal obligations, terrified her. Mama had let such obligations drain the life from her in her efforts to please her cruel husband. And though David was as different from Papa as a man could be, he was still a man, still used to being in control of everything and everyone in his domain.

Charlotte couldn't help remembering Sarah's complaints about his fierce control over her money. Granted, he'd had good reason with Sarah, but still . . . Did Charlotte really want to give up her independence to him? Even a benevolent dictator was still a dictator, after all.

And the problem of children was insurmountable. He'd said he did not care if she bore him an heir, but he'd lied. She was fairly certain of that.

"Blast!" David said out of the blue.

"What is it?"

"I took the more direct route from Acton to Richmond. I wasn't thinking. Now we'll have to cross the Thames by ferry."

"By ferry," she repeated in a hollow voice. She'd be in a boat, with horses and a carriage. Lord save her.

"I'll turn around. We'll go back the way we came. It's a little longer, but—"

"No, it is far too late in the day as it is. We can go by ferry. I will be fine."

"Are you sure?"

She nodded and forced a smile.

But as they approached the Thames and she began hearing the rushing waters, her heart's pace trebled. She had seen the river ferries. They were none too secure. What if the horses panicked? Or God forbid, what if the ferry capsized, and she was trapped beneath it? It could happen. Stories of that sort of accident appeared in the papers all the time . . .

"We'll go the other way." David wheeled the phaeton around.

"What? Why?"

He grabbed her hand and squeezed it. "Your skin is like ice, you're shaking violently, and you've lost all color. I'm not putting you through that when it will only take us another thirty minutes to go to Kew Bridge."

She tried futilely to hide her sigh of relief. "Do you mind very much?"

"Not a bit." He twined his fingers with hers. "How can I mind spending more time with you?"

A lump stuck in her throat. When he was being like

this, the idea of marriage to him did not seem quite so daunting.

Those who knew of her fear of water generally ignored it or tried to jolly her out of it. Not David. He accommodated her, treated her with care. How many men would do that?

By the time they reached the school, she was beginning to wonder if she had been too hasty in refusing his offer of marriage. She had treated him with cruelty years ago, yet instead of seeking to hurt her for it, he had come back to her. That was unfathomable. What man behaved in such a manner?

The sun was sinking low when they pulled up in front to find a carriage waiting in the drive. She recognized it even before a man came down the steps to meet them.

Mr. Pritchard. And he was scowling. That could not be good.

"Been for a little drive, have you, Mrs. Harris?" he said with a vulgar leer as David helped her alight.

David's hand squeezed hers before he released it, probably warning her to watch her tongue.

She didn't need the warning when it came to Pritchard. "What do you want?" she asked bluntly.

Mr. Pritchard's gaze narrowed. "I want you to stay out of my business. As a result of your meddling with Watson this morning, he began reconsidering his decision to purchase Rockhurst from me."

"Good." The pressure on her chest from the past few days eased a bit.

"Oh, don't worry—I convinced him that he would be a fool to pass up this chance. But if I ever hear again that you're interfering in my business affairs . . ." He paused to look pointedly at David. "You will both come to regret it."

"How dare you!" she cried. "Lord Kirkwood has nothing to do with this. If you have a problem with how I run my affairs, you talk to *me*."

"Charlotte," David bit out, "why don't you go inside, so I can speak to Mr. Pritchard alone?"

"Absolutely not! This is *my* school, and I will handle its problems."

Mr. Pritchard ignored her to focus on David. "You'll keep her away from my business partner, if you know what's good for you."

To her shock, David said, "I'll do my best. As long as *you* stay away from *her*."

"Gladly." As Mr. Pritchard strode off and got into his carriage, Charlotte gaped at David, appalled. "You presume too much, sir," she hissed as Mr. Pritchard's carriage pulled off.

"You leave me no choice." Glancing up to where the servants stood watching the confrontation, David grabbed her by the arm, then propelled her down the drive and into the garden as if she were some child to be reasoned with.

Though that incensed her, she waited until they were out of sight and earshot of the servants before she rounded on him and let him have it full bore. "You have no right to intrude in my affairs!"

"I don't want to intrude." The dying sun illuminated the harsh planes of his face. "But antagonizing Pritchard is not in your best interests."

"Why not?" She crossed her arms over her chest. "It worked, didn't it?"

"Were you even listening? It didn't work at all. He convinced Watson to go on with the sale."

"Yes, but now the man is thinking twice about it. We shall see if he continues to be so accommodating once I complain to the licensing board. And get my friends to write a petition."

"Confound it to hell, Charlotte," he said as he grabbed her shoulders, "I will not let you take on Pritchard!"

She stared at him, a chill coursing down her spine. "You will not *what*?"

As if realizing what he'd said, he dropped his hands from her. "I didn't mean that how it sounds."

"I hope not. Because it sounded as if you are trying to force me into giving up on saving the school." Her stomach lurched. "Indeed, it sounded a few minutes ago as if you made some sort of pact with him. About me. A pact you had no right to make."

A dark flush spread over his face. "I'm thinking only of your safety, damn it. He's not a good man, do you understand? He can't be trusted."

His concern for her softened her anger only a fraction. "Be that as it may, this is not your concern. Sarah's legacy does not give you the right to dictate how I run my affairs."

"I realize that—"

"And neither does sharing my bed." She forced a calm into her voice that she did not feel. "I suggest you remember that the next time you consider stepping between me and the affairs of my school."

His gaze flared hot with temper. "I care about you, so I'm going to voice my opinions. You'll have to get used to that."

"Just do not overstep your authority, and everything will be fine." She jutted out her chin. "Now if you will excuse me, I have been away far too long today, and no doubt have a number of matters awaiting my attention."

Turning on her heel, she started to leave him, but he grabbed her by the arm and swung her around.

Before she could even react, he hauled her into his arms and caught her chin in an iron grip. Then he kissed her hard, his mouth demanding entrance to hers so fervently that she soon found herself weakening under the assault, until with a groan she let him in.

His devouring kiss stirred the smoldering embers of their earlier lovemaking into a roaring fire, and within moments he had her pulse racing and her blood pounding in her ears.

Only then did he draw back to fix her with a brooding glance. "Take care, sweeting. I'm not a lapdog you can pat on the head and send trotting off whenever you don't like what I have to say. You made me part of your life today, and I intend to stay squarely in the middle of it. Is that clear?"

"Perfectly." He started to release her, but she caught his cravat to pull him back to her. "But do not come between me and my school. Is *that* clear?"

Though his eyes glittered, he gave a terse nod.

This time when she turned to leave, he let her go, though he followed close on her heels.

As they reached his phaeton, he murmured, "I'll come for you Tuesday at ten." Without even giving her a chance to protest, he leaped up onto the seat, took the reins, and sent the phaeton plunging forward.

She had half a mind to run after him and tell him he could forget any more private interludes at Stoneville's estate. But given the state of arousal he had left her in after just one kiss, that would be rather like cutting off her nose to spite her face.

Very well. Perhaps she would indulge this mad urge to continue as his lover. She had set the rules of their association, and she would see if he could follow them.

If he could not, woe be unto him. She was fully in charge of her own life, so if he tried to get in her way, she would leave him in the dust.

Chapter Eighteen

❧

*D*avid rode back to town in a fury. He hoped to catch up to Pritchard on the way, but apparently the man had turned off the road somewhere.

No matter. David would find him tomorrow and warn him away from Charlotte. Because warning *Charlotte* away wasn't working—and he had only himself to blame for that. Since she didn't know the truth, she had no reason to suspect that Pritchard had designs on the school's property as well.

David gritted his teeth as he navigated the crowded roads. Didn't that idiot see that provoking her was unwise? It made her dig in and fight, instead of accepting the inevitable. David could understand why, after she'd told him about her father's cruelties, but it didn't change the fact that her opposition could be disastrous. If she continued to fight Pritchard, he'd have no choice but to tell her the truth.

A groan escaped him. He could well imagine how *that* would go. Years of lies would have to be explained. His whole sordid scheme for revenge would come out. She would despise him. What he'd done smacked too much of the cruel manipulations her father had practiced. How could she ever trust him again?

By the time he reached his town house, he was in a foul mood. It was bad enough that she'd refused his offer, but he'd managed to put her back up as well. Charlotte was proving every bit as difficult to handle as he'd feared.

He climbed the steps to his front door, but it didn't open at his approach as usual. Using his key to get in, he stalked inside and caught George, the first footman, napping in a chair. Though the man had been shirking his duty quite a bit of late, David normally wouldn't give a damn—but tonight it reminded him of a far more egregious lapse, one he'd meant to discuss with George for two days.

Slamming the door, he watched as George shot awake, then leaped to his feet in alarm. "My lord! I did not . . . that is . . ."

"I wish to have a word with you in my study, George."

The man paled. "Yes, sir."

David marched up the stairs to his study as George followed. When they entered and David said to close the door, the footman looked as if he might faint.

"My lord," he began, "I know I shouldn't have fallen asleep, but—"

"That isn't why I called you in here." David went to stand behind his desk. "Two nights ago, I was accosted by Ned Timms. Do you know who he is?"

George paled even more. "No, sir."

The bloody hell he didn't. "He's a moneylender. And it seems that he acquired the Kirkwood sapphires sometime before my wife died, when she apparently gave them to him as a surety for gambling funds."

"I-I wouldn't know anything about that, my lord."

"Are you certain? *Someone* accompanied her to Spital-fields, where the man does his business. As first footman, you would have been the one to do it."

The footman was already shaking his head. "No, sir,

I would never have let her ladyship go to such a part of town, I swear." He swallowed. "Perhaps her brother took her. They often went out alone together."

It was plausible, but David didn't believe the man. Something about George had struck him wrong for a long time. He wasn't sure why.

"Very well. I'll ask my brother-in-law about the matter." He leaned forward to plant his hands on the desk. "But if I find out that you were the one to take her there, that you hid such a thing from me and that you're lying about it now, I'll turn you off without any references. Do you understand?"

"Yes, sir," he squeaked. He'd begun to sweat profusely.

David narrowed his gaze. "You're better served telling me the truth. I can be lenient, especially since I know how persuasive my wife could be when she wanted something from a man."

George sucked in a harsh breath, but his gaze didn't waver from his master's. "That's true, sir. But I didn't take her there. I swear it."

David's gut told him the man was lying, but he needed proof before he acted. He didn't believe in turning off servants without reason. "All right. You may go."

After the man left, David dropped into the chair behind his desk. Once again, he was reminded of how little he'd known his wife. He stared about at what had been his sanctuary during his marriage. Perhaps he shouldn't have spent so much time in it. Perhaps he should have made more of an effort with Sarah.

But after their first year of marriage, he'd found it harder and harder to endure her company. Instead, he'd come here to sketch designs and pore over his investments.

That was the only thing that had given him a purpose beyond the mindless drinking and gambling his friends engaged in. It had been his salvation.

The school became my reason for living, my salvation.

He winced, remembering Charlotte's words. He was beginning to understand her determination to protect her academy. Sometimes one had to guard the only corner of one's life where sanity reigned.

Still, the place teetered on the brink of disaster and he could only save it if she would heed his advice.

Yet why should she? In her eyes he was an intruder, someone who'd popped back into her life and could pop out just as easily. Even the fact that he wanted her as his wife only made her wary. He was asking her to give up a great deal, after all, and in exchange he could offer her nothing but the security of marriage. Since Charlotte's marriage had ended in disaster and so had his, why should she trust in that?

It began to appear that the only way he could gain her was to make concessions he wasn't sure he was ready to make.

Over the next few days, that possibility plagued him continually. What if she really couldn't have children? What if she refused to give the running of the school over to a subordinate? Could he endure a marriage where he had to share her with her damned school?

Even as the questions ran around and around in his head, he had to fight the urge to ride over and see her. It didn't matter that he knew Charlotte needed space to breathe right now. He didn't want to give her space. He wanted to drag her to the altar and make her his forever.

His obsession with her should have slackened after he'd

slaked his thirst for her body. But if anything, it consumed him even more. Only answering the letter she'd sent to Cousin Michael about purchasing the school gave him a small measure of relief. That damned fool Watson had given him an idea of how to break her reliance on her cousin once and for all.

What he was writing would make her hate the man, while prodding her into trusting David more. And the more she trusted him to help her, the more chance he'd have to change her mind about marrying him.

Once that was done, he buried himself in other matters to take his mind off her. Spending half a week on the business of Charlotte and the school, he'd neglected his own affairs, and those needed to be handled. He also had to pay visits to Pritchard and his brother-in-law.

To his annoyance, he discovered that Pritchard had gone off to Bath, probably to celebrate the impending sale of Rockhurst. And according to Linley senior, Richard had disappeared into the bowels of bachelor hell—drinking and gambling and whoring with his friends.

At least Stoneville was around to give him permission to look over the property again. To his surprise, the marquess, generally a nosy sort, didn't seem remotely interested in why David wanted to revisit it. Apparently he was having problems of his own that occupied his attention. He told David to keep the key, and then ushered him rather summarily out of his town house.

Odd, that. But not nearly as odd as the terse message that arrived from Baines on the morning before David was supposed to see Charlotte.

It is urgent that I speak with you.

They'd been communicating only through notes, since

David hadn't wanted the solicitor to risk encountering Charlotte at the Kirkwood town house. No point in making her wonder why David was friendly with Cousin Michael's solicitor.

Baines generally reserved the word *urgent* for dire matters, and David was wondering what that might be when his brother strode into the breakfast room and headed straight for the pot of coffee on the sideboard.

"What are you doing here?" David asked, buttering his scone liberally. "Don't tell me you lost your bachelor lodgings again."

"No, this was just closer, and I have to be in court early today. Didn't want to ride all the way out to Chelsea, then ride all the way back this morning." Taking the entire pot to a spot at the table, he filled a cup with shaky hands, then drank deeply from it. "I've got to stop spending my nights in the stews. I'm getting too old for this."

"I've heard that before," David said dryly. "Quite often."

"I mean it this time. No more carousing."

"My lord," came the butler's voice from the doorway, so loud that it made David wince. "There is a Mr. Jackson Pinter from the Great Marlborough Street Magistrate's Office to see you. He says he's a Bow Street runner."

Before David could even react, Giles's head shot up. "What does he want?"

"Send him in," David told the butler. As the servant hurried off, David glanced at his brother. "It might have to do with Richard." Or Timms.

"All the same, you'd best let me handle it," Giles said. "I question these people in court all the time. I know how they work."

"Very well." His brother did have a point.

Jackson Pinter proved to be a tall, wolfish-looking fellow with thick black brows and an angular jaw. He seemed too young to be a Bow Street runner . . . until he began to speak in a world-weary voice that had an odd rasp to it.

They started to rise, but he said quickly, "Please, do not trouble yourself. In truth, I am sorry to disturb your lordship at breakfast."

His words were obsequious. His tone was not. It held an arrogance David found peculiar for a man of such low station.

Pinter glanced to Giles, then back to David. "If I may speak to your lordship alone—"

"I'm his brother," Giles cut in. "I'm also his barrister. What's this about?"

Pinter's manner underwent a subtle change, becoming more guarded. His expression turned as bland as the white linen cloth on the table. "I've come to clear up one small matter concerning the death of his lordship's wife."

"Sarah?" David said, a frisson of foreboding coursing down his spine. "I'm happy to help however I can, but I'm not sure what there is to discuss." He gestured to one of the chairs. "May I offer you some coffee, sir? Toast and jam?"

"No, thank you, my lord," Pinter said, declining to sit. Instead, he set a large satchel on the table near David, opened it, and removed a sheet of foolscap, which he slid in front of David. It was a draper's bill, with Sarah's signature at the bottom.

"To your knowledge," Pinter asked, "is this your late wife's signature?"

To his *knowledge*? David gave it a cursory glance. "It appears to be, yes."

The man pulled out another sheet of paper. As David recognized it, his heart began to pound.

"And this," Pinter said as he laid out Sarah's suicide note, which the authorities had kept after the inquest. "Is this also your wife's signature?"

"Of course." David fought the bile that rose up in him at the sight.

For a moment, he flashed on Sarah's lifeless face, drawn in her eerie repose, her robed body floating in the blood-stained water like a leaf on a stream. With an effort, he shook off the horrific memory.

"Are you sure it's her signature?" the man prodded. "Think carefully before you answer, my lord."

"What is the purpose of these questions, sir?" Giles put in.

Pinter cast Giles a frown. "Two days ago we received a communication from a gentleman claiming that the suicide note is forged. That it does not bear her ladyship's true signature."

The air left David's lungs in a great rush. Feeling as if Sarah had reached from beyond the grave to close her grasping hands about his throat, he fought for calm.

"Who's the 'gentleman' making this claim?" Giles snapped.

"I am not at liberty to say, sir."

David stared down at the two notes. "The handwriting looks identical."

"At first glance, yes. But we've had an expert in forgery examine the two documents, and he assures us that they differ in marked respects. Since the draper saw your wife sign the bill with his own eyes, the suicide note has to be the forgery. After all, no one saw her write *that,* did they?"

David struggled for breath, spots forming before his eyes as he tried to examine the notes. If the suicide note was a forgery . . .

"So what are you saying?" Giles demanded.

"I would suspect that his lordship knows what I am saying."

David's gaze shot to Pinter. "You think she didn't commit suicide at all."

"Exactly, my lord." His gaze sharpened on David. "We are now of the opinion that she was murdered."

David's heart hammered in his chest. Who would want to murder Sarah? "Do you have any suspects?"

"A few," the man said blandly. "So I must ask you to answer me truthfully, my lord. Are you *sure* that the signature is your wife's? Perhaps you found her in her condition and thought to save a messy investigation by, shall we say, tying things up more neatly?"

David gaped at the man. "Bloody hell, I didn't write that note, if that's what you're insinuating, sir. I would never tamper with the truth in such a foul manner."

When Pinter pulled out a notebook to write something down, David struggled to contain his temper. This was no time to explode.

"Until this very moment," David went on, "I believed the document to be written by my wife. Indeed, until I hear otherwise from someone besides you and your 'expert,' I'll continue to assume that it was."

Drawing the notes across the table, Giles examined them himself. "There was an inquest into her death, and as I recall, nothing untoward was found."

"You may also recall that the coroner was in Scotland at the time," Pinter said, "and we couldn't wait for his return to perform the autopsy. Unfortunately, although his apprentice took excellent notes, he made conclusions about the death that the coroner now says were probably spurious."

Giles's head shot up. "What sort of conclusions?"

"There were lavender petals from her bath in her stomach and her lungs. The young apprentice said that she must have slipped down beneath the surface once she died, thus taking in some of the bathwater."

Pinter cast David a veiled glance. "But recent experiments into drowning have proved that water will not enter a person's stomach or lungs without being swallowed or sucked in by a living person. The coroner suspects she was drowned, and then her wrists were cut to make it look like a suicide."

The deliberateness of such a thing made David's throat close up. "Good God," he said hoarsely.

Opening his little book again, Pinter said casually, "According to the inquest, you stated you had gone for a walk that night. Is that correct, my lord?"

Jumping to his feet, Giles stared the man down. "I do hope you're not implying that *my brother* murdered his wife," Giles growled. "He's a respected member of the community and a peer of the realm. So if you think he'd be fool enough—"

"Sit down, Giles," David said. "The man is only doing his duty." He met Pinter's gaze squarely. "I was here until shortly before ten o'clock." He'd been waiting for Sarah to return from a ball so he could confront her about rumors that she was still playing faro, even though he'd forbidden it. "Then yes, I went for a walk. I didn't return until midnight. Ask my servants, and you'll learn that I often go for walks late at night. It clears my head."

Pinter scribbled some notes. "Did anyone see you while you were out?"

He hesitated only a moment before saying, "No." Mr. Keel, the night clerk at Baines's office, had seen him, because that's where David had gone—to give the man a letter for Charlotte. But revealing that little piece of information would open his entire life before them, not to mention dragging Charlotte into this affair.

That was intolerable. If it proved necessary to reveal his whereabouts that night, he would do so, but he wasn't going to mention it until he had no other choice. Charlotte must be kept out of this.

"When I returned home," David went on, "I learned that my wife had also returned. So I summoned the housekeeper to let me into my wife's locked room. Since we found my wife together at midnight, I hardly see how I can be regarded a suspect."

"There was an adjoining door that led to your bedchamber as well, was there not?"

"Yes, and it was locked from the inside, too."

"But surely you have *that* key."

David clenched his fists under the table. "She requested the only key from me some years ago, and I gave it to her." The day she'd banished him from her bed. "Why do you think I had to fetch the housekeeper to open the other door?"

With a frown, the man wrote something else in his little book. "What prompted you to go into her room when it was locked?"

"There was a matter I wished to discuss with her, and she hadn't been home earlier. When I knocked, she didn't answer."

"What exactly was that matter?"

Giles shot to his feet again. "This conversation is over, Mr. Pinter. Until you have something more substantial than supposition and conflicting coroners' accounts, I suggest you leave my grieving brother alone."

"I don't mind answering his questions," David said in as calm a voice as he could muster. "I've done nothing wrong."

Pinter tucked his notebook into his pocket. "I've learned all I wish to know for now, anyway." He reached for the letters to put them back in his satchel.

"Wait!" David said. "Let me look at them again."

He'd seen the suicide note only once, on the night of Sarah's death. By the time he'd read it, he'd been half out of his mind from seeing her lying in the bloody water. He certainly hadn't paid attention to the niceties of her signature.

But he paid attention now, gazing hard at the first one, comparing it to the other. And he could see why questions had arisen. The *r*'s were slightly different, and the loops of the *k*'s markedly so.

"She had to have been in an anxious state when she wrote this," he said, shoving the note away. "That might account for any anomalies."

"We've considered that." Pinter slid the two documents into his satchel. "But according to our source, your wife made plans with a friend for the next day. That doesn't sound like a person on the verge of committing suicide."

"And her friend confirms your source's claim?"

"Yes."

For the first time, he allowed himself to believe that it

was possible. Though the thought of Sarah's being murdered in cold blood sent a chill through David's bones, it also relieved a measure of the guilt that had weighed heavily on him for months. It wasn't his fault. He hadn't driven her to the act.

But he'd also not been here to protect her from it. So either way he was guilty. And who in God's name would have been up in Sarah's room while she was wearing only her robe and preparing for a bath? It made no sense.

Mr. Pinter headed for the door, then paused and faced them again. "I did have one other question, sir. Why did you tell your friends that she killed herself over gambling debts when the note mentions no such thing?"

When Giles shot the man a shocked glance, David winced. He'd kept that from everyone, even his brother. "Given the choice between telling your friends that your wife's weakness for gaming led to her death or that she was simply unhappy in a marriage to *you*, which one would you choose?"

Pinter's gaze softened the merest fraction. "I see your point."

"If I had forged the note, don't you think I'd have chosen words that painted myself in a more favorable light?"

"Perhaps. Or perhaps you considered that and are merely more clever than most."

David fixed the Bow Street runner with a dark glance. "You're entitled to your opinion, sir. But I hope that when you make a decision regarding this matter, it's the evidence and not opinion that sways you."

"I assure you, sir. I don't form an opinion until I have evidence to support it." He bowed deeply. "I will take my leave of you now. But it would be most appreciated if you remain in town until this matter is settled."

David gritted his teeth. "Is that a request or a command?"

"A suggestion, if you will." Pinter nodded to Giles. "Good day, gentlemen."

As he marched out the door, satchel in hand, David could only stare after him. Good day? It wasn't going to be a good day in the least.

Worse, David began to fear it would never be a good day again. All his sins were rising up to haunt him. And there didn't seem to be a damned thing he could do about it.

That afternoon Charlotte sat in her office, rereading Cousin Michael's letter:

> *Dear Mrs. Harris,*
>
> *Your offer to buy the property on which the school sits was fortuitous. As it happens, my finances have been strained of late, so I have decided to look for a buyer for the property. Much as I wish I could afford to sell the place to <u>you</u>, I cannot. The land is quite valuable, and the amount you suggested is not even half of what it is worth. Since I will require a large influx of money quite soon, I will have to pursue other buyers.*
>
> *I can allow you to stay on at a reduced rent for three months more—as long as you continue to hold to our conditions, of course. That should give you plenty of time to find property elsewhere to rent.*

But at the end of three months, I shall have to sell.
I suggest you begin hunting for a better location for
the school.

> *Your cousin,*
> *Michael*

She stared at the letter, feeling a hollow sinking in her stomach. It was so cold, so aloof. Not like her Cousin Michael at all.

Why was he doing this to her? Was it the gossip? Had he lost faith in her ability to run the school? She had not believed matters between them to be this bad. He sounded like the usual landlord.

It was enough to make her consider breaking their agreement and sending Terence hunting for his real identity. Except that then she would have to deal with an increase in rent while also looking for a new place for the school. That would not do.

At least she had Sarah's legacy. And there were more properties on David's list to look at, though the prospect of spending the next few weeks traipsing about the country with him was rather daunting. It would be very hard to think rationally about his offer of marriage when every time she saw him, she wanted to throw herself upon him like some passion-starved wanton.

Closing her eyes, she rubbed her aching temples. How in heaven's name was she to extricate herself from this mess?

"Mrs. Harris," came a voice from the door, "there's a Bow Street runner here to see you."

She glanced over to find her butler standing there. Oh no, what now? Didn't she have enough to worry her these days? "What does he want?"

"He won't say. But he seems determined not to leave until you speak with him."

"All right," she said wearily. "Send him up."

Moments later, when the butler announced the man as Mr. Pinter, she rose to meet the attractive young fellow who entered her office.

"I am Mrs. Harris," she told him, "the owner of this school. How may I help you?"

The gentleman cast her an assessing glance as he waited for her to take her seat again before he took the one in front of her desk. "I've come on behalf of the Great Marlborough Street Magistrate's Office to ask you some questions concerning the late Lady Kirkwood."

That put her instantly on her guard. "What sort of questions?"

"I understand that Lady Kirkwood was once a student at your school."

"She was."

"Would you say that Lady Kirkwood had a melancholy disposition?"

"Melancholy? Sarah?" An incredulous laugh escaped her lips, but Mr. Pinter's disapproving look sobered her. "Not to speak ill of the dead, but she was more vain than melancholy. Why? Is this about her death?"

"Do you know how her ladyship died?"

His nonanswers began to alarm her. "She committed suicide."

"Yes, but do you know how?"

That threw her into confusion. What in heaven's name

was going on? "No. The papers only said that she had taken her own life."

Flipping out a notebook, Mr. Pinter jotted something in it with a pencil. "So you were not told anything by the family. Or by his lordship."

The mention of David put her further on her guard. "See here, I am not going to answer one more question until you answer mine. Why are you asking about Sarah six months after her death?"

Mr. Pinter's lips thinned into a line. "We are investigating Lady Kirkwood's murder," he said baldly.

"Murder! So it was *not* suicide?"

"She was found in her robe in the bath with her wrists cut. At the time, suicide seemed the obvious choice, since a note was found as well. But recent events have led us to believe that the note was forged, probably by her killer."

She sat back in her chair, feeling suddenly weak in the knees. A *killer?* They actually suspected someone of having murdered Sarah? How could that be? "Does his lordship know of your suspicions?"

"We informed him this morning, yes."

"The poor man," she said, careful to show only a fraction of the sympathy she felt for David. "How he must be suffering."

"I doubt he's suffering much," Mr. Pinter said coldly. "It was my understanding that his marriage wasn't a happy one."

Her gaze shot to the Bow Street runner. He was scrutinizing her most carefully, and the truth suddenly dawned on her. The authorities thought that David had killed Sarah!

How could they even think such a thing? It was ludicrous. "I cannot speak to whether his marriage was happy or not," she said hoarsely, choosing her words with care. "But as a widow, I assure you that no matter the situation, he suffered over her death. She was his wife, after all. And he *is* a man of good character."

"So I am told," the gentleman said.

Yet clearly he was skeptical. Righteous indignation swelled within her. "If you are harboring some suspicion that his lordship might have done this, you are vastly mistaken. He has too much honor and pride to stoop so low. And surely you do not have any evidence to suggest that he—"

"I understand that his lordship has been spending a great deal of time in your company of late."

The swift change of subject, combined with Mr. Pinter's sharp scrutiny, sent alarm bells clanging in her head. "Who told you that?"

"Is it true?" Mr. Pinter prodded.

His questions frightened her. Surely he did not think that she and David . . . that together they might have conspired . . . "It depends on how you define 'great deal of time.' He has paid me a couple of visits, yes."

"And you attended a dinner at his house three nights ago. Even though he is still in mourning."

"Now look here," she said, bristling at his insinuation, "I was only there to visit with another former pupil of mine, who happens to be married to his lordship's cousin. Not that it is any of your concern."

"I see." He scribbled something in his notebook. "And his lordship never said anything to you about the state of his marriage. Or explained how his wife died."

She stiffened. "Why should he? His lordship and I have a professional relationship. He does not tell me such things."

"Professional relationship?" For the first time since his arrival, Mr. Pinter's carefully emotionless face registered surprise. "What sort of 'professional relationship'?"

Oh, dear. Perhaps she should not have mentioned that. But honestly, would it not be better that the police know of the legacy than that they assume something scandalous was going on between her and David?

"Lady Kirkwood left a great deal of money to the school. And his lordship was appointed to oversee how it is spent."

That seemed to flummox the Bow Street runner. "I don't understand."

"Her will bequeathed thirty thousand pounds to my school for the construction of a new building to be named after her."

"That's impossible," Mr. Pinter said, his gray eyes deepening to slate. "Her ladyship didn't have a will."

Chapter Nineteen

❧

For six months David had fought to shove the night of his wife's death out of his mind. So it was wrenching to force himself to relive every moment, hoping for a clue to what had really happened. While Giles headed off to Lincoln's Inn to see if he could learn anything about the investigation from his many sources, David replayed the sequence of events, dredging up every visitor to the town house that day. But none of it unlocked the mystery.

Then he turned to remembering how she had been the day of her death. Her final words to him were emblazoned on his mind, since he'd examined those ruthlessly in the weeks after her death, trying to make sense of why she might have killed herself. None of their terse, angry conversations about her gambling had told him a thing. They still didn't.

Not even a search of her room revealed anything more than what he already knew—Sarah had been fond of cards, clothes, and gems, in that order. If she'd had a secret life beyond spending money, he didn't uncover it.

Meanwhile, another message came from Baines. This time, he sent the messenger back with a note that said, "Thank you for inquiring, sir, but I am afraid I cannot indulge your request for a meeting at this time."

David had already noticed the two Bow Street runners lounging outside his house—one in the mews and one in front. Clearly he was being watched, so Baines could wait.

Still, by the time Giles entered the town house, David was fit to be tied.

He pounced on Giles and dragged him into the nearby library. "Did you learn anything?" he prodded as he shut the door. "Like who their mysterious 'source' might be?"

"It has to be Richard," Giles said as he headed for the brandy decanter. "He's making trouble because you won't give him any money. He roused their suspicions, hoping they'd start going over your life with a fine-tooth comb. He's just doing it to strike back at you."

David grimaced. "So you *didn't* learn anything."

After pouring himself a generous amount of the amber liquid, Giles dropped into a chair and stared morosely into his glass. "No."

If it was just someone making trouble for him, it could be Pritchard as easily as Richard. That ass might think it a good way to repay David for not keeping better control over Charlotte. Except that Pritchard wouldn't have any knowledge of Sarah's handwriting.

He supposed that the source could be that bastard moneylender Timms, who would know Sarah's handwriting and had ample reason to cause him trouble. But why would the authorities have let him see the suicide note?

Yes, Richard seemed the most likely cause. He of all people would have noticed any difference in handwriting, and his anger at David might have prompted him to go to the authorities and ask to see the suicide note.

Unless the troublemaker had just shot in the dark, trying to stir up suspicion. The authorities might then have looked at the note and uncovered a murder they hadn't bargained for.

A chill passed through him. "Beyond the suicide note

and the questionable coroners' reports," David asked, "do they have anything to confirm that it's murder?"

"It doesn't appear so. But both of those are damning if we can't shake the various experts' testimony. Especially since you have no alibi and possess ample motive."

"What motive?" David snapped. "I already had control over her money—why should I risk it to kill her?"

"Because she was gambling it away faster than you could invest it."

"Oh, for God's sake, I wouldn't kill my wife over gambling debts. The very idea is absurd."

"They won't think so. They always suspect the husband first, you know. Their suspicions will prompt them to start asking questions of the servants and your friends and digging into your life. Even if it never goes to trial, it's going to be a messy business."

Exactly what he was afraid of.

A knock at the door proved to be their butler. "Mrs. Harris's personal footman is here, my lord," he said when David let him in. "He insists upon delivering his message to you in person."

David's blood began to pound. Charlotte had sent Terence over here? Confound it all—the runners had probably seen him, too.

Still, she wouldn't have done such a thing unless it were urgent. "Send him in."

Giles shot David a searching glance. "Either the good widow has heard about the investigation, or she just can't stay away from you. You'd best tread carefully. It won't do to have the authorities thinking there is something between you."

David groaned. If the police connected him to Charlotte, what assumptions might they make? Though he was innocent of killing his wife, it would arouse even more sticky questions.

"*Is* there anything between you?" Giles asked. "As your barrister, I need to know."

Should he tell Giles about Cousin Michael, about the fact that Baines's clerk was his alibi for the night of the murder? If he did, Giles would immediately go to Pinter with it, and David would no longer be a suspect.

But then his careful courtship of Charlotte would be shot to hell.

No, he wouldn't risk that until he had to. Still, he'd better let Giles know about his intentions toward Charlotte. "I've asked her to marry me," David said bluntly. "She hasn't yet given me an answer."

Giles toyed with his glass. "I thought perhaps the wind blew that way." His gaze met David's. "I suggest that you keep that bit of information very quiet until this is all over."

"Don't worry—that has already occurred to me." David paced to the fire. "Nothing will come of this nonsense, you know. I didn't kill Sarah, and there's nothing to say that I did. I searched every inch of her rooms, and I've gone over that night a hundred times in my head. Frankly, I can't think of why anyone would kill her. It will probably prove nothing more than an error on the part of their 'experts.'"

"I hope you're right."

Just at that moment, Terence appeared in the doorway. He started to walk in, then halted when he saw Giles. He turned to David. "My lord, I wish to speak to you privately."

Taking the hint, Giles rose and said, "I'll be upstairs in the study if you need me."

As soon as he was gone, David closed the door again. "What's going on, Terence?"

Terence handed him a note. David read it swiftly:

> A Mr. Pinter from the magistrate's office was here today. It is <u>extremely urgent</u> that I speak to you. If you can meet me at ten o'clock tonight at the school's boathouse, send word by Terence. If not, tell him when and where.

A chill ran through David as he lifted his gaze to Terence. "What did Pinter want with her?"

"I wasn't present for the interview, sir, but she told me that the magistrate's office seems to suspect you of killing your wife."

David crumpled the note in his hand, feeling the room sway about him.

"She said that their supposition is, and I quote, 'utterly ridiculous.'"

The room righted itself. "At least I have one friend left in the world."

"I'll wager you have more than that, my lord. Not everyone leaps to judge a man by what the magistrate's office says." When David arched an eyebrow at him, Terence added, "I find it difficult to believe that any man whose servants sing his praises so highly could be a murderer."

"Thank you," David said, oddly moved by the man's faith in him. "But if she doesn't believe that I killed my wife, why does she wish to meet with me?"

"She didn't tell me that, but I gather that it's——"

"Extremely urgent," he said irritably. "Yes, I know." He began to feel like a character in a gothic novel. "Did she say what she told the Bow Street runner about my . . . er . . . friendship with her?"

Terence stiffened. "No, sir. But if I know my mistress, she was discreet. She has always been so with her pupils." Although clearly that wasn't a part of his mistress's life he wanted to know too much about.

Something else occurred to David. "And were *you* discreet coming here from Richmond?"

Terence shot him an offended glance. "I should hope I know how to avoid Bow Street runners, my lord. We had to evade them whenever we arranged a prizefight."

David had forgotten about that. Fights were illegal and sometimes had to be moved several times to thwart the constables' attempts to close them down.

"So don't trouble yourself about that, sir," Terence went on. "No one was watching the school, and when I spotted the Bow Street runner in front of your town house and the one in the back, I was careful to slip in through the servants' entrance when neither was watching. No one saw me, I assure you."

Relief swamped him. "Thank you for your trouble."

"What about you, sir?" Terence asked. "Will you be able to leave here tonight without being noticed?"

"I'll manage it." He mustered a smile. "I may not be as familiar with constables as you are, but I've had to avoid a newspaperman or two in my time."

"If you go by the river no one will see you, even if for some reason the magistrate's office does set a man to watching the school. Any steam packet can bring you right up to the school's river landing."

"I appreciate the advice . . . and your help in this. Tell your mistress I'll meet her where and when she specified."

"Very good, my lord."

When the servant didn't leave, David arched one eyebrow. "Is there something else, Terence?"

Looking suddenly uneasy, the boxer rubbed the back of his neck. "After my mistress told me what you are suspected of, it occurred to me . . . that is, I may have information that could help you uncover who really murdered your wife."

David instantly went on the alert. "Oh?"

"I don't make a habit of gossiping with other servants, you understand, but—"

"Anything you can tell me will be much appreciated," David said firmly.

Terence nodded. "When I was here with my mistress a few nights ago for your dinner, I overheard some servants talking about her ladyship's activities. But I don't know if you . . . I'm afraid what they said about her was a bit unpalatable for a man to hear about his wife."

"At this point, nothing I hear about my wife would surprise me in the least," David said wearily. "Go on."

"I gathered that it was believed among the servants that her ladyship had been . . . showing special favor to the first footman." Terence actually blushed. "Of a personal nature. If you take my meaning."

David's jaw dropped. He'd suspected Sarah of a number of things, but not *that*. "You mean she was cuckolding me with George?"

Terence's blush deepened, though he stared stoically past David at the wall. "Yes, sir. That was the rumor. I would never have spoken of it except that under the circumstances—"

"Yes, yes, you were quite right to tell me." David went to the brandy decanter and poured himself a liberal amount. He took a large gulp, then stood staring into the glass, feeling as if he'd just been punched in the gut.

Sarah had taken a lover? Under his own roof? When she wouldn't even share *his* bed? Oh God, he was going to be sick.

Not because he cared whom she had slept with or why. It just showed him yet again how blind he'd been about what was going on in his own household.

But a footman, of all things. Christ!

"It could be idle servant gossip," Terence remarked.

"No," David said shakily. "It makes sense." It explained why George had been shirking his duties since her death. And why the man had always given David an uneasy feeling.

After Terence left, he couldn't get the boxer's revelation out of his mind. How long had the affair been going on? Is that why she'd stopped sharing David's bed in the first place? It was possible, but he wouldn't know for certain until he spoke to George. Which he wasn't ready to do yet.

First, he would have George followed to see if the man might be the mysterious "source" the magistrate's office was relying upon. Then he would have the footman's quarters searched.

Because there was now no doubt in his mind that George had been the one to take Sarah to Spitalfields to sell her sapphires. Worse yet, if that had somehow blown up in the man's face, he might just have been capable of murder, too. And *he* would certainly have had easy access to Sarah's bedchamber, key or no key, if they had been lovers.

Of course, others would have, too. Richard had a habit of sneaking in to speak to Sarah without anyone seeing him.

But Richard would never have killed her. Sarah had been his champion, and he had been her pet. She'd loaned him money and stood up for him to their father. No, Richard would not have killed the goose that laid the golden egg.

But he might have decided that David had done it and set out to make sure he was hanged for it.

David clenched his jaw. No matter who was at the bottom of this, he would learn the truth. About who was trying to get him hanged, *and* who had killed Sarah, if she had indeed been killed.

First, however, he had to learn what that bastard Pinter had told Charlotte to upset her. And the meeting must be secret, for the magistrate's office was sure to draw the wrong conclusions. But how to manage it?

Fortunately, Giles provided the perfect solution to his problem. Later that evening, he and Giles went out. Giles wore mourning and rode inside the carriage, while David, dressed as a footman, rode on the back with another footman. For once, having a brother that looked a great deal like him worked in his favor.

As they drove off, David noted that one of the Bow Street runners mounted his horse and followed the coach at a discreet distance. When the coach stopped to let Giles out at a popular tavern, the runner settled outside the place to wait—exactly as David had counted on. As the coach drove on to where the other carriages awaited the summons of their masters, David slipped off into the night.

It took him a couple of hours to reach the school by way of the river, yet even so he arrived a good half hour before the appointed time. He was able to enter the boathouse without being seen, since the door was unlocked. Thankfully, someone had left a lamp burning low on a hook near the door, so he wasn't forced to stumble about in the dark.

But "boathouse" proved a misnomer, which explained why she'd chosen to meet in such a spot despite her fear of the river. Though built near the Thames, which could be heard lapping on the bank a short distance away, the structure was self-contained, with a solid wood floor and four good walls. Only the grappling hooks overhead remained to show that it had once been used for boats.

Now the building was filled with archery bows, quivers of arrows, old furniture, steamer trunks, and lawn-cutting tools. He smiled. Leave it to Charlotte to turn a perfectly good boathouse into a storage and garden shed. Clearly she would never let her charges venture out on the river.

Unearthing a settee losing its stuffing, he stretched out on it, weary to the bone. He was tired of surprises. Right now he wanted only a chance to see and hold Charlotte, to forget the drama playing out in London. He had to make sure that this hadn't driven her even farther out of his reach.

Perhaps he should tell her everything, about Cousin Michael and the rest of it.

No. If he did, he would have to reveal the ugly secret at the core of his masquerade. Given that he wasn't even sure how she felt about this mess with Sarah, he couldn't take the chance of her hating him for it.

And if Charlotte stopped believing in him . . .

The very idea ripped his soul. He was not going to risk losing her by raising the specter of Cousin Michael! With his world crashing down about his ears, he needed her too desperately now. Let them take his dignity, drag his name through the mud—but he was *not* going to let them take Charlotte from him. Never again.

Chapter Twenty

❧

Charlotte hurried to the boathouse, wondering if David had arrived. She had spent the afternoon and evening fretting over Mr. Pinter's revelations, and she wanted answers. Now.

When she slipped inside the boathouse, she didn't see anyone at first. Then she spotted the servant dressed in Kirkwood livery sleeping on a settee. Disappointment coursed through her . . . until she went over and realized it was David.

The anger that had been simmering in her all afternoon flared high. Bow Street runners were investigating his entire life, and he could sleep? Oh, that was *so* like a man.

She picked up a brick and dropped it on the floor.

David shot up and glanced about in confusion, then met her gaze. "Charlotte, you're here. I must have fallen asleep."

"Perhaps dressing as a servant addled your senses," she said as she plucked the powdered wig from his head and tossed it aside.

At her clipped tone, he narrowed his gaze. He lunged forward and hauled her onto his lap. "Perhaps dressing as a schoolmistress has addled yours," he countered, bending his head to kiss her.

"Stop that," she protested. "We need to talk."

"We can talk later," he growled and took her mouth with his.

For a moment she forgot her anger. She forgot he had probably lied to her for reasons she didn't yet understand. Because *this* she understood, this fire between them. When he was kissing her, he was hers and it was glorious.

Until he turned to working loose the buttons on her gown. Then she remembered her anger and shoved away to scramble off his lap.

Closing her arms about her waist, she said, "We have to talk. It's important."

A wary expression crossed his face. "You're upset."

"*Upset* is a rather mild word for what I am feeling now, I assure you."

He rose from the settee and straightened to his full height. "Terence said that you don't believe I killed Sarah. Was he wrong?"

"Of course not. I know you would never do such a thing." Her voice hardened. "But in the course of questioning me about my pupil and my association with you, Mr. Pinter told me an interesting little piece of information that sounds exactly like something you *would* do."

He raked his fingers through hair that had been flattened by the wig, causing it to stand up in odd tufts. "Information about what? Sarah?"

"About the codicil to her will."

When he froze, a look of alarm spreading over his face, she knew the truth. She had desperately been hoping that Pinter was mistaken.

"And what did Pinter say, exactly?" David choked out.

She scowled at him. "You know what he said. He said Sarah did not have a will. So it would have been difficult for the thing to have a codicil."

"You saw the document." David's bland reply was a clear

evasion. "Your attorney checked it and said it was legal."

That *really* sparked her temper. She marched up to him with her hands fisting at her sides. "Yes, he did. Unfortunately, when I showed it to Mr. Pinter, he had an entirely different response."

"Oh God," he said under his breath. "You showed it to Pinter?"

The alarm in his face gave her a twinge of guilt that was swiftly banished by her reminder of what David had done. "What else was I supposed to do? After all, I assumed that my *lover* would never lie to me about such a thing."

Ignoring the look of remorse on David's face, she went on relentlessly. "Even after Pinter told me that Sarah's family claimed she had no will, I believed in you. I told him that the Linleys must be confused. I had that blasted document to prove it, after all." She dragged in a breath, fighting to keep from crying in front of him. "But it got hard to deny the truth when Pinter said that *your* attorney, the one who wrote up the agreement, also stated there was no will."

David groaned.

"So when Pinter asked if he could have the 'legacy' document," she continued, "I did not know how to answer. He is an officer of the law. I did not think I could refuse. And I figured he would take it and discover that he was mistaken about the will." She stared him down. "But he wasn't, was he? It *is* a fabrication. The whole legacy is just one big lie."

He did not even bother to deny it. How could he? Instead, he grabbed her by the shoulders. "Listen to me, Charlotte. I can explain everything."

"Explain? How can you possibly explain such a lie?" She wriggled free, her feelings of betrayal stampeding over her already wounded heart. "I must have been mad to believe you." A self-deprecating laugh boiled out of her. "What was I thinking? Sarah would never have given the school money."

Hugging her waist, she whispered, "But I wanted to have you back in my life so badly, I was willing to overlook the idiocy of what you were telling me." That was the worst of it. "Because believing it was a lie would have meant you hated me so much that you would deliberately make a fool of me just to pay me back—"

"No!" he cried, clearly horrified. "Damn it, you know it had nothing to do with paying you back for anything!"

"Do I?" It was the only explanation that made any sense. "Why else would you pretend—"

"Not for revenge, for God's sake! Do you really believe I could make love to you, ask you to *marry* me, out of revenge for something you did eighteen years ago? Especially when by then I knew why you'd done it?"

There was logic in that. But it did not answer her question. "So what other reason is there? Are you in league with Pritchard? You did seem to know him awfully well. Did he convince you to help him by lulling me into thinking I should move the school, just so he could get me out of the way?"

"Now you're not even making sense," he bit out. "The only way you could move away from here is if the money is genuine, and it is. Every penny is yours. Legally. It was always yours. If you want it."

Charlotte gaped at him. She couldn't believe what he was saying. She couldn't believe any of this. "How can it be mine legally if the will is not?"

"It's my own money. Out of my own investments." His gaze was black in the lamplight. "I knew you would never take it from me, so I made up a legacy." He reached out to stroke her cheek, but when she jerked back, his voice hardened. "If you don't believe me, ask my solicitor."

"He's the one who said Sarah didn't have a will," she choked out.

"He was uneasy with the situation from the beginning, so I'm sure he thought it in my best interests when speaking to the authorities not to mention the fake codicil."

"A pity that no one thought to include *me* in the little subterfuge."

David blanched. "If you ask him about it, he'll tell you why I did it. He knows everything. He knows I was doing it for you."

How she wanted to believe that. But it was a mad idea. "Why would you help me and the school with your own money? After all these years . . ."

"After all these years," he said hoarsely, "I wanted to regain the woman I so foolishly had thrown away." His voice caught. "I wanted you, and I couldn't figure out a way to cut through your defenses to have you."

"But thirty thousand pounds—"

"I would have made it more if I'd dared." His gaze played over her face, tender and tormented. "I knew the school was in trouble. If you'll recall, Sarah and I attended that charity to raise money for it. And after her death, I knew I wanted you back."

This time when he lifted a hand to her cheek, she did not stop him. "But I also knew you'd be suspicious if I offered you the money outright, and you would never have let me court you while I was in mourning. You needed the funds sooner than that, what with Pritchard starting all his nonsense. So I decided upon a different plan."

Everything he had said that first day came back to her—his insistence upon rebuilding the school elsewhere, about being involved. Surely if he had wanted revenge, he would not have wanted to spend so much time with her. And could she really think that David could make love to her while hating her?

Still, given what she had done to him, given how things had stood between them at that point, it was incredible. Why, he still hadn't even known that her foolish letter had only been published by accident. "How can I believe you?" she whispered.

He drew her stiff body into his arms. "I never stopped thinking about you, Charlotte. Never. Every time I saw you in society after I married, I had to force myself not to care, not to wonder whom you turned to in your lonely nights."

When he kissed her hair, she didn't resist him, though she hated herself for her weakness. It frightened her, how much she wanted to believe that he cared. How could she want him in her life so badly that she would throw away everything for him?

"But once Sarah died," he murmured, "there was no reason to fight my feelings. I had a chance to gain the wife I'd always wanted. So I did something stupid. I just didn't know what else to do."

"You could have told me the truth," she said against his shoulder. "You could have said you knew why I'd written the letter. You could have said all of it was in the past, and you wanted to start over."

"And would you have believed me?"

"I don't know." She lifted her gaze to him, her feelings still confused. "But you never even gave me the chance to believe you."

"I was afraid you'd dismiss the idea outright. I didn't know how you felt about me, if you even cared for me anymore. I needed a bridge to get to you. The legacy was the bridge."

Godwin had said as much the first time she'd talked to him about it, but she'd thought him mad. And now . . .

Now everything was so much more difficult. David had *made* it more difficult. "I cannot take your money. You realize that."

His eyes blazed down at her. "Yes, you can."

"I cannot. How would it look?"

"If you marry me, it will look like your husband helping your school."

She pushed free of his arms. "Surely you realize I cannot marry you *now,* not with Sarah's death hanging over your head. They will think that we . . . that you and I . . ."

"Oh. Right. I keep forgetting about this madness with Sarah. I can hardly even believe they think she was murdered. It makes no sense."

"So you understand why we cannot marry right now."

Uttering a groan of pure frustration, he stared down into her face. "Of course. I certainly don't want them coming after you. But this won't go on forever. They'll find whoever killed her. We just have to wait to marry until they do. In the meantime, let me loan you the money—"

"Oh, yes," she said with heavy sarcasm, "that would not look suspicious in the least, you loaning a widow thirty thousand pounds."

A look of uncertainty crossed his face. "Perhaps if we are careful in how it's done . . ."

"Have you gone mad? That man Pinter wants your head! And I will not be the cause of your being hanged."

He snorted. "They're not going to hang me. I have an alibi for that night."

"Then why did Mr. Pinter not mention it?"

His expression grew more guarded. "It's . . . complicated."

A cold chill seeped through her. She could think of only one reason he would have an alibi for that night that he did not want to tell *her* about. "Were you . . . with another woman, is that it?"

"God, no!" The shock on his face looked genuine. "I never broke my marriage vows. Not once."

The fierceness with which she wanted to believe him frightened her. "I would not blame you, you know. You said that you and she had not shared a bed in some time."

"That doesn't mean I felt free to take a mistress. I told you years ago, I believe in fidelity. And I always hoped Sarah and I could find some way through to repairing our marriage. I thought if I could wean her from the gambling . . ."

Pity rose up in her, despite her attempts to squelch it. "Then what is your alibi? And why did you not tell Pinter of it?"

He closed up, as he always did. "The secret is someone else's. And it has nothing to do with us, anyway."

"Your secrets never seem to involve us—until they blow up in my face, as they did this afternoon," she snapped.

She turned for the door, tired of trying to sort through his evasions, wishing to escape the emotional maelstrom he stirred up inside her whenever he was near. She did not need this agony in her life.

"Where are you going?" he demanded.

"You do as you please, David. I want none of it."

"What the bloody hell does *that* mean?" he growled as he followed her.

"That means this is not a good time for us to be . . . involved. We need some time apart."

"Look here, Charlotte, I know we cannot see each other until they've found Sarah's killer. It's too risky, not only for me, but for you. I can't have them thinking anything wrong of you." A note of desperation sounded in his voice. "But surely once this matter is settled, and things go back to normal—"

"You don't understand." She could not bear even to face him as she spoke the words. "It's not just about the danger or any of that. I . . . I just don't think that you and I are . . . a good idea right now. Not until I've settled the school's problems and made up my mind about how I feel about marriage. Until then, it is better if we do not—"

"No, damn it!" he hurried up behind her just as she reached the door. "You can't be saying what I think you're saying!" He grabbed her from behind, his fingers digging into her arms. "I won't let you do this. I need you too much."

Not love, but *need*. It was not enough. Not anymore. "You clearly do not need me enough to let me know your secrets."

"So you're just going to give up on us? Again? The way you did eighteen years ago? Is that what you're telling me? Because you know damned well that the school's problems are never going to be solved entirely, and you've made it perfectly clear that you're afraid to try marrying again."

She whirled on him. "That is not fair! I will not let you blame me for this. Every time I turn around I uncover another untruth or evasion. *You* are the one who keeps secrets and protects your heart at every turn!"

"And *you're* not protecting yours?" He stalked toward her, determination on his face. "You use your bloody school as an excuse for not taking risks in your private life, for not letting any man close enough to gain your heart. And do you want to know why?"

She stared at him sullenly.

"Because you're a coward, Charlotte Harris," he growled. "And we both know it."

Chapter Twenty-one

⊱⊰

*D*avid felt as if he were drowning. Everything was slipping away from him—Charlotte and his hopes for the two of them. Why was this happening to them? Why did she have to make it so hard?

If she used this thing with Sarah to cut him out of her life until she "settled the school's problems" and decided how she felt about marriage, it would be the end of them. She always ran away, always found an excuse to ignore what lay between them.

Well, by God, he would not let her. If it took making her angry to make her listen, then that was what he'd do.

And she *was* angry, oh yes. She hated being accused of any weakness, but especially cowardice. She prided herself on her strength and independence, and those were the qualities in her that he found so intoxicating.

But he'd be damned if he let her hide behind her independence right now.

"How dare you!" she bit out. "*You* are the one who lied to *me*. You are the one who is keeping secrets and asking the impossible."

"The impossible?" He walked up to loom over her. "You mean, by asking you to share my life?"

"Right now it is not wise—"

"Yes, right now. But you said that you mean it to go on beyond right now. That even after they find Sarah's killer, you mean to stay away. So you can *think*." His voice hard-ened. "Talk yourself out of marrying me, more like. And there's only one reason for that." He braced his hands on either side of her shoulders. "Your cowardice."

"Stop saying that! I am not a coward!"

"No? You're afraid to give up even a tenth of your pre-cious independence in order to marry me."

She met his gaze squarely. "Oh, but you do not want only a tenth. You want everything I have. In exchange, you offer me nothing."

"Except my name. And my money."

"That is not what I mean, and you know it. You offer me nothing of yourself."

"I offer you *this*," he murmured, bending his head to kiss her.

She shoved him hard enough to make him stumble back. "That is only your reckless desire, nothing more."

He glared at her. "Don't you dare play the offended schoolmistress with *me,* sweeting. I am not the only one feeling a reckless desire, and you know it."

"Yes. I desire you." Her eyes were glittering now, her face alight with her anger. "And you use that desire to control me." To his shock, she shoved him again, forcing him back another step. "You want to make me swoon so I don't no-tice you slowly taking over *everything* in my life: my school, my future, my heart."

She shoved him so hard that he fell back onto the set-tee.

His own temper rising, he grabbed her and pulled her down on top of him. "If it's control in our lovemaking that you seek, sweeting, I am perfectly willing to give you that." As she struggled off his lap, he stretched his arms out along the back of the settee. "Go ahead, take control." He let his thighs fall open just enough to show his rampant arousal. "Ravish me. I won't stop you."

Standing in front of him, her hands on her hips and her dander up, she was as fine a sight as he'd ever seen. "I do not see what *that* would prove," she snapped, though her gaze dropped to the painfully obvious bulge in his breeches.

"It would prove that I'm not the only one who can use desire to control." When a fetching blush spread over her cheeks, it aroused him even more.

"That's not the sort of control I meant," she shot back.

"No? That's what you said—that I use desire to control you," he goaded her. Right now, goading her into letting down her guard seemed the only way to stop her mad urge to be free of him. "But if you want to deny it because you're all talk and no action, as most women are—"

Her hands knotted up into fists. "You are the most infuriating, insufferable, arrogant—"

"As I said, all talk and no action." He taunted her with a smile. "Or perhaps you're merely afraid that you *can't* take control. What does a stiff-necked schoolmistress like you know about controlling a man by using his desire?"

"Oh, believe me," she hissed as she marched up to him, "if I wanted to, I could have you wrapped around my little finger. But I do not want a man who lies to me, who will not let me into his life."

"A likely excuse," he said. Considering how she was reacting to the news about the fake codicil, he could only imagine how she'd cut him out of her life if she learned the rest of truth. "You're just afraid to try. Deep down, you know you can't handle me."

He let his gaze trail down over her delicious body. "The idea of you using desire to control a man with my experience and sophistication is ludicrous." If that didn't provoke a response out of her, nothing would.

"Ludicrous, is it?" She climbed onto his lap and grabbed his head in her hands. "I can have you begging in moments, you insolent devil."

He held her gaze. "I never beg. Not for you, not for any woman."

"We'll just see about that," she bit out.

When she then took his mouth in a deep, soul-searching kiss, it was all he could do not to wrap his arms about her, lay her out on the settee, and take her like a savage.

But he wanted her to see that desire went both ways, that she had a certain amount of control over him, too. That marriage would *not* mean giving up her entire life to him the way she seemed to think.

So although he responded to the kiss, he deliberately let her control it, though it was pure torture to do so. It had been three long days since he'd made love to her, and all he could think of as she settled herself across his lap was how badly he wanted to be inside her.

Dragging her mouth from his, she said, "Take off that silly footman's coat. I feel as if I'm seducing a servant."

He was more than happy to comply, removing the cravat, waistcoat, and shirt as well. "Don't I get to see *you* naked?" he rasped as she ran her hands over his bare chest, thumbing his nipples until he groaned.

She bent close and pressed her fully clothed bosom against him, only to whisper in his ear, "Perhaps later. After you beg."

That's when he realized how badly he'd miscalculated. Still angry, she was determined to make her point by tormenting him.

"Afraid?" she whispered.

Her body squirming atop his bulging cock was driving him slowly mad. "Of you?" he managed to choke out. "Never."

"You should be." She moved her hands down between them to stroke his thighs, rousing the ache in his cock to such intensity that he thought he would die if she didn't touch him there.

"Oh God, Charlotte . . ." he said before he could stop himself.

"Did you want something, Lord Kirkwood?" She rubbed her lower body against him just enough to arouse him even more. "All you have to do is beg."

Though he had started this with the idea of letting her have control, now that she did, he was having trouble enduring it. The idea of begging her for his pleasure really galled him.

He reached between them to stroke her, hoping to inflame *her,* but she slid off his lap.

"Ah, ah, ah, my lord," she said, taking down her hair and shaking it out. Damn her if she wasn't enjoying this. "I didn't say you could touch me, did I?"

He watched hungrily as she reached up beneath her skirts and removed her drawers without showing him a damned thing of what lay under them.

"This is *not* what I meant by control," he growled.

"No? That's what you said," she mimicked his earlier words with perfect accuracy. "You said I should use desire to control you." She drew her skirts up above her knees, revealing the long, stocking-clad legs that he wanted to kiss and stroke. That he wanted to be between. Right *now*.

She swished her skirts over her thighs like some Drury Lane whore teasing a client. "But you're all talk and no action, as most men are."

Her deliberate echoing of his words earlier was starting to irk him. "If you want action—" he bit out, lunging forward to grab her hips.

But she resisted his attempt to pull her astride him. Instead, she lifted her leg and planted it on the settee next to his hip, exposing her lovely honeypot. "Actually, I would like a different sort of action. I want you to pleasure me with your mouth."

He looked up at her in shock. He'd done that with barmaids and the occasional mistress in his salad days, but never with a respectable woman. Sarah would have been appalled at the very idea. He hadn't even been able to coax her into removing her nightdress most of the time. "You . . . you know about *that*?"

"Looks like I'm not such a stiff-necked schoolmistress after all, am I?"

"Apparently not." *And thank God for it.*

More than eager to comply, he leaned forward to bury his face in her flesh. But within moments, he realized how well she had chosen her pleasure. Tasting her, smelling her pungent female flesh, aroused him while not even beginning to satisfy his rigid cock. The more he licked and sucked and delved with his tongue, the more he thought his breeches might actually burst before he got to be inside her.

Her hands closed on his head to hold him to her. "Yes . . . David . . . oh . . . dear heaven . . . like that . . ."

If he had any sense, he would withhold the ultimate

pleasure from her until she gave him what *he* wanted. But then he'd be doing exactly what she'd accused him of—using her desire to gain control.

Besides, he reveled in the mews and groans coming from her, in the quickening of her breath as she neared her release. And when he felt her explode beneath his mouth, he felt like a conqueror.

She stood there trembling, her head fallen back and her bosom shaking, the loveliest creature he had ever seen. "That was . . . wonderful," she sighed.

He nuzzled her thigh. "Do you mean to torment me all night to prove your point?" he asked hoarsely. "Or do I finally get a reward for performing to madam's expectations?"

With a taunting smile, she straddled his legs. "Only if you beg." She reached down and unbuttoned his breeches, then his drawers.

Before she could pull her hand away, he grabbed it and forced it down to his raging cock. "I'm not going to beg, so you can forget that."

She stroked him a few times, just enough to restoke the fires, then drew her hand back. "Then, my dear Lord Kirkwood, you will suffer."

When she started to rise, he gripped her by the thighs and wouldn't let her go. "The hell I will." He tried to kiss her, but she turned her head aside, so he nipped her ear. "You made your point, sweeting. Be happy with that. Because I want to be inside you, and you know damned well that you want that, too."

She drew back to stare at him, her eyes solemn. "All right. But only if you agree to tell me the truth about your alibi the night of Sarah's murder."

He froze. Confound it all, in his fog of desire, he'd forgotten that part of their discussion. But she hadn't. And clearly, this was what *she* meant by using desire to control.

"Why do you want to know?" he said bitterly. "So you can be sure that I didn't kill my wife?"

"So I can know that you want me in every part of your life, not just the ones you allow." A worried frown creased her brow. "And so I can be sure that you aren't going to hang."

Her concern warmed him to his very soul. Surely he could tell her something that would satisfy her without giving away too much. "Very well. I promise."

"Tell me now."

"No. After." He thrust his aching cock up against her belly. "Put me out of my misery first." He kissed the line of her jaw. "Please, sweeting, I can't bear any more."

She drew back, eyes alight with triumph. "You begged!"

He blinked. "I did *not.*"

"You said 'please.' That's close enough for me." With that, she rose up and slid down on his cock.

A hiss of pure pleasure escaped him. "Yes, Charlotte . . . oh God, yes. You are . . . heaven."

With a fierce glance, she began to move, undulating on top of him, wringing him with her body, making him fear he might spend himself inside her before she even came close to finding her release. It felt so good, so right to be inside her, moving with her, being part of her.

Dragging down her gown and corset cups, he filled his hands with her breasts. This was bliss. They belonged together, whether she could see it or not. Somehow he would make sure she did.

"So am I . . . enough for the . . . sophisticated . . . experienced Lord Kirkwood, after all?" she rasped as she rode him like some glorious Diana of the hunt.

"You . . . always . . . were," he admitted, before he lost the fight to hold back his climax and came deep inside her.

As she clenched around him and found her own release with a triumphant cry, he thought, *Mine! Accept it, sweeting. You're mine, now and forever. You just don't know it yet.*

Chapter Twenty-two

❧

*C*harlotte could not believe she had done it again. She had let David seduce her into forgetting her reservations.

They lay entwined on the old settee, with him holding her and her enjoying it far too much. Was he right? Was she a coward, afraid to take the next step? Afraid to promise all of herself to him—heart, body, and soul?

If she was, she was not alone. He was holding something back from her; she was almost certain of it. And how could they become man and wife if he would not share every part of his life with her?

She lifted her head from his chest to rest it on her hands and stare up into the features that had become painfully dear to her. "So tell me about this alibi," she said, determined to get *that* much out of him at least.

He let out a long sigh. "I can't tell you all of it. As I said, it's not my secret to tell." Glancing away, he said, "The night of Sarah's death, I had gone to help a friend. He was in trouble, the sort of trouble he wouldn't want anyone to know about. The sort of trouble he wouldn't want me to tell you about, either."

"Is that why Pinter didn't mention it? Because you didn't tell him?"

"Yes. I don't want to say anything unless I absolutely have to."

"Is it a friend I know?" She hoped it wasn't Anthony or

Foxmoor. Secret trouble generally meant women, and she couldn't bear to think of either of those men cheating on their wives.

"It's not one of your circle, if that's what worries you. But you do know the man." His voice sounded strained. "I left at ten to go see him, and I returned at midnight to find Sarah dead."

Her heart lurched with pity. "You were the one to find her?"

Pain flashed over his face. "Yes. The housekeeper and I found her together." His voice lowered to an aching rasp. "Her wrists were cut, and it stained the water pink. Now that I think about it, there probably wasn't enough blood, but at the time it seemed . . . like a great deal. Especially after I read the note."

She softly kissed his chest. "I am so sorry you had to endure such a thing."

"The note made no sense, but it has tortured me for months—'I can no longer bear this intolerable life,' it said. And I . . . I was sure it was because I had made her more miserable than I'd realized."

She could see how he had suffered over that. It made her angry at whoever really *had* written the note. "But it was not genuine. Right?"

A shudder passed through him. "That's what they say. Yet I can still hardly believe someone would murder Sarah."

"Do they have any suspects?"

His harsh laugh jarred her. "Aside from me? I don't know. *I* have a number of suspects. There's the little weasel of a moneylender who tried to extort money from me for her jewels a few nights ago, and made vague threats about going to the papers concerning my wife's activities. There's her brother, Richard, who certainly would have known how to forge her handwriting."

"Surely he would not have killed her!"

"No, probably not. They were quite close." He sighed. "But he would certainly try to frame *me* for her murder, out of spite." His voice hardened. "And then there's the footman she was apparently sharing a bed with, according to Terence, who was good enough to pass on the servant gossip from my own household."

"Merciful heavens. Sarah? And a footman? Surely she would not be so shameless."

"I certainly never dreamed that she would." He cast her a bitter glance. "But then, I had no idea she'd used my family's jewels as surety for a gambling loan. Apparently I drove my wife to all manner of deceptions in her thirst for entertainment away from me."

Charlotte pressed a finger to his lips, her heart breaking. "Don't blame yourself, my darling. Sarah was a devious little creature even when she was a student here. She was the sort of woman who would do anything to get what she wanted—flirt, lie, tease."

She caressed his cheek, desperate to banish his haunted look. "I did my best to guide her into better habits, but she was stubborn. Her father spoiled her shamelessly when she was a girl, and she always expected to get her own way in everything."

"I wish I'd known that before I married her."

"If you'll recall, she sneaked around behind her parents' backs to see you. So she was in true form even then."

"And I was blind."

"Honestly, plenty of young girls have poor habits, but

marriage generally straightens them out. The responsibilities, the guidance of a kind husband . . . I really thought she might come out all right in the end with you."

"Apparently my 'guidance' was faulty."

"She made her own choices, David. You cannot blame yourself for that." She stroked her hand over his shoulder. "Though I still find it incredible that she would be so wicked as to have an affair with a footman. Why stoop to eat mutton when you have a juicy steak at hand?"

Just as she hoped, that made him smile. "Thank you for that. But I rather imagine it wasn't the . . . er . . . eating part that interested her. She wanted something from him, and that was probably his price."

"That does sound more like Sarah."

"I won't know for sure until I question him. Which I intend to do as soon as I've satisfied myself that he isn't the one who went to the authorities to try to blame me for this."

A vague memory swam into her head that gained new significance in light of his revelations. "I don't know if I should mention this, but . . ."

"What? Please tell me anything you might know."

"It may not be significant, but the other night at dinner, Giles told me . . . that is, he said something odd. That Sarah had a dark side."

When David frowned, she added, "It might mean nothing—he could have been talking about the gambling, although he said he meant more than just that. I pressed him on it, but he changed the subject." The ashen look on David's face made her regret mentioning it. "I'm sorry, it was probably nothing."

"Doesn't sound like nothing. It seems I need to talk to my brother as well."

"Surely you do not think Giles is involved."

David sighed. "I don't know what to think. But I intend to find out the truth behind her death. Sarah deserved that much from me at least."

"Is there anything I can do to help?"

His gaze swung to her, full of alarm. "No," he said firmly. "The best thing you can do is not let on to Pinter that we have a personal connection. They may find out anyway, but it's better if they don't know." He cupped her cheek. "I'd never forgive myself if you got dragged into this swarm of suspicion."

The concern in his eyes warmed her, despite her reservations about their relationship. "Believe me," she said softly, "I have no desire to have any more dealings with Mr. Pinter."

David smoothed his thumb over her cheek. "Speaking of him, I should probably go, before either of us is discovered missing."

She nodded.

"But before I do, promise me one thing."

"What is that?"

"That you will seriously consider marrying me when this is over."

She swallowed. But really, it was an easy promise to make. She was already seriously considering it. "All right."

He let out a heartfelt sigh. "Thank God. I need some hope to keep me going right now."

So did she. Because from the sound of it, it might be a long while before they got to see each other again.

When David awakened late the next morning, Giles was ensconced in the armchair across from his bed wearing a grim expression. Rubbing his bleary eyes, David pushed into a sitting position. "What are you doing here? Thinking about moving back into the house?"

"No. I rode over here from my quarters. Because of this." Giles tossed a newspaper into his lap. "Sorry, old boy."

David glanced down at the headline, which screamed, "Viscountess Murdered."

Feeling a familiar punch to the gut, David read the article. He was spawning ugly news stories yet again. "At least they only hint that I could be a suspect. I suppose that's something."

"Right now they're afraid to do more because there's no official statement. This was probably leaked by some clerk in the magistrate's office. But mark my words, it won't be long before the whole sordid story comes out." Giles cast him a hard look. "So if there's anything you're keeping from me that might help me nip this in the bud, I advise you to reveal it now."

Giles's tone angered him, especially in light of his discussion with Charlotte last night. "I could say the same to you, *brother*."

Giles blinked. "What's that supposed to mean?"

The nasty suspicion that had tormented his sleep last night spilled out. "Were you sleeping with my wife before she died?"

"What?" Giles shot up from the chair. "Where the devil did you get such an idea?"

His outrage seemed genuine, yet David pressed on. He *had* to know. "Because *someone* was able to get into her room late at night without being noticed. Someone she trusted, someone she knew well enough to allow him to see her in her robe."

"It bloody well wasn't me! I was drinking in a tavern halfway across town." Giles crossed his arms over his chest, the very picture of belligerence. "If you don't believe me, I'm sure I can provide a witness or two."

David slumped, running his fingers through his hair. "I'm sorry, Giles. I just don't know what to think anymore. I found out yesterday that Sarah was having an affair with her footman." When Giles winced and dropped into the chair again, a cold chill skated along David's spine. "You knew."

"I wasn't sure, but . . . I suspected as much."

"Why didn't you say something?"

"Tell my brother that his wife might be a slut who would stoop to sleeping with a servant? How could I say such a thing? Especially when I had no proof. I saw them kiss once in the hall. That was all."

With a groan, David left the bed and went to the fire in a vain attempt to warm the ice freezing his blood. "I never guessed she was so unhappy in the marriage—"

Giles snorted. "The marriage had nothing to do with it. Sarah wanted the man under her thumb, and that was the way to manage it. As I said, I'm not even sure it ever progressed beyond a tender word and a kiss or two." His voice hardened. "Sarah liked to flirt. Especially if she thought it might gain her something."

Charlotte had said much the same. Turning from the fire, David gave his brother a hard stare. "I take it that she flirted with you?"

A sigh escaped Giles. "Once or twice. She started . . . insinuating that if I would convince you to loosen the purse strings, she might be willing to . . ." His gaze shot to David. "I told her she ought to consider herself lucky that you allowed her as much free rein as you did. And that pretty much put an end to any designs she had on me, thank God."

Wearily David shook his head. "You must think me a complete ass, to have been so oblivious to my wife's infidelities."

"No," Giles said softly. "She was very careful to hide the maliciousness of her character from you. And to be honest, neither of you ever made any pretense of caring what the other did."

"That's what got her killed," David said as he put on his dressing robe.

"She got herself killed." Giles mused a moment. "Now that you know about George, I suppose you've considered the possibility that he killed her."

"I have. In fact, I plan to have him followed to see if he might be the one who's making wild accusations to the authorities and trying to get me hanged."

Giles frowned. "It may be too late for that."

"What? Why?"

"George wasn't at his post when I arrived this morning. I didn't think anything of it at the time, but—"

"Damn it all to hell!" David hurried into the hall and called for his butler. As soon as the man mounted the stairs, David said, "Call George here at once."

The butler paled. "Forgive me, my lord, but no one has seen him since last night."

David fought for calm. "Is it possible he was sent on an errand without your knowledge?"

"No, sir. And . . . er . . . when we went to look for him this morning, we found his room empty of any personal belongings."

David scowled. "You're saying that he ran off in the night."

"It appears that way, my lord."

"Well, *that* certainly looks suspicious," Giles said dryly. "We'd better tell Pinter."

"Confound the man." After calling for his valet, David went back to his room and began to dress. "Let's just hope Pinter doesn't decide to accuse me of killing my footman as well."

"He and his men will question the servants—I'm sure someone saw the man leave. But George is a clear suspect in Sarah's murder, with no alibi. This should shift suspicion to where it belongs."

After David finished dressing they headed down the stairs, but the noise from the street stopped them in the foyer. The press—of course. Once the truth about Sarah's death had hit one paper, they'd all come to pick over her bones. And get his opinion of the matter.

David turned to the butler. "Send a footman out the back door without livery to fetch that runner who's been watching the house, will you?"

"Yes, my lord."

But before the butler could even leave, a knock came at the door.

"It's probably some bold newspaperman," Giles said. "Best to ignore him."

The butler went to look out one of the windows. "It looks like Mr. Pinter himself."

"Excellent," David said. "Let him in."

When the runner entered, he blinked to find them standing there in the foyer.

"We were just trying to figure out how to get to the

magistrate's office to see you," David explained. "We have new information about a possible suspect—"

"Actually, my lord," Pinter interrupted, "I came to ask if you would come with me."

"Why?" Giles demanded.

Pinter's usual stoic expression gave nothing away. "Some new evidence has come to light, and we require his lordship's help in evaluating it."

"My *help*?" David said, trying to ignore the apprehension stealing through his veins. "That's all?"

"Yes. If you will accompany me, sir—"

"What about the press?" Giles demanded.

"I brought men to restrain the crowds. My carriage is directly in front." When David called for both their coats, Pinter added, "I believe that Mr. Masters will want to remain here."

David narrowed his eyes on the runner. "Why?"

"Because if you will allow it, sir, I would like some of my men to conduct a search of the premises, specifically your study and your wife's bedchamber. With Mr. Masters in attendance, of course."

The very idea of watchmen and constables crawling over his house made David's heart stop. But he knew that Pinter's "request" was only a courtesy. The magistrate's office had the right to search where it would, especially in cases of a crime. Besides, they would find nothing to incriminate him, and it seemed best not to rouse the authorities' suspicions any further.

He turned to Giles. "Stay here. I'm sure I'll return shortly."

As he and Pinter headed off in the carriage, David was surprised to see how efficiently his men kept the crowds at bay. Even David knew how few men were assigned to the magistrate's office, yet they made do with the ones they had.

During the short trip, David apprised Pinter of George's disappearance and the significance of that. It galled him to make his private affairs known, but this was no time to be reticent.

David was so engrossed in laying out his theory about George and a possible connection to the moneylenders his wife had apparently frequented that he didn't realize they weren't headed to the magistrate's office until they turned down a familiar street.

His gaze shot to Pinter. "Where are we going?"

Pinter was watching him with that hawkish look of his. "To the office of Mr. Joseph Baines."

God help him. They had uncovered his connection to Baines. "Why are we going there?" he asked in a hollow voice.

"I believe you know why."

Of course he knew why. They'd probably traced the fake codicil back to Baines through his own solicitor. And now they wanted to know how that had come about and why.

Damn the man for being so good at uncovering all the wrong things. The man couldn't find Sarah's killer, but he could bloody well turn David's life upside down.

They entered the building in silence, with David wondering how much Baines had told Pinter. The solicitor was loyal to him, but this was an unusual circumstance, and Baines couldn't afford to find himself accused of having any part in Sarah's death.

It was only when they passed a runner posted in the hall outside Baines's office that David started to feel truly uneasy. And once they entered and he spotted Mr. Keel, the night clerk, David realized that Pinter had brought him here for another reason entirely.

As David groaned, Baines hurried forward. "I'm sorry, my lord. When Mr. Keel saw your name in the paper this morning, he felt he'd best come forward. He went to the authorities without my knowledge. I'd been trying to reach you, but—"

"Lord Kirkwood?" came a new voice from behind David.

He froze. No, it couldn't be. What was *she* doing here?

"What's this all about?" Charlotte continued as he whirled to face her. Her face showed clear bewilderment. "A clerk sent me a note saying that Mr. Baines had something to discuss with me, so I hurried here, but—"

"*I* sent you that note," Pinter put in smoothly. "I wanted you both present to hear Mr. Keel's story."

"You bastard," David hissed. His carefully constructed house of cards was tumbling down about his ears. "She has nothing to do with this."

"I beg to differ, sir," Pinter said. "According to Mr. Keel, she has everything to do with this."

As Charlotte stared at him, he could see her withdrawing, rethinking things. Confound it all to hell. He was going to lose her. He could see it already.

The time had come for his reckoning.

And there wasn't a bloody thing he could do to stop it.

Chapter Twenty-three

❦

Charlotte could not breathe. The look of guilt on David's face gave her pause. And why would Mr. Pinter have wanted him here at Mr. Baines's office? She knew Mr. Keel in passing, but what possible story could he have to tell? Unless David *was* Cousin Michael . . .

No, how could he be? She had already dismissed the possibility for obvious reasons.

Mr. Pinter took over, bidding them to sit with a politeness that belied the cool calculation in his dark eyes. After everyone else took a seat, he sat down where he could see everyone.

"Mr. Keel," he then said to the night clerk, "I would be most obliged if you would repeat for our benefit what you told me earlier."

The clerk looked none too eager to speak. "Begging your pardon, Lord Kirkwood," Mr. Keel said as he worked his hat through his trembling hands, "but I didn't think it right that you should be accused of murder when you were here with me the night Lady Kirkwood died."

Charlotte's immediate relief that David was exonerated was very brief. Why was David so chummy with Cousin Michael's solicitor that he would come to his office at night? A painful knot formed in her belly. Especially since David would not even look at her, but stared blindly at the wall.

"And why was his lordship here with you?" Mr. Pinter prodded.

Though Charlotte now suspected what the man's answer would be, it still rocked her when he said, "He was delivering a letter for Mrs. Harris."

Only one person sent letters from Mr. Baines's office. She could feel Mr. Pinter's assessing gaze on her, but she did not care. All she could do was stare at David, hoping for him to deny it, to say this was a huge mistake and she had misunderstood.

But it explained too much—his sudden reappearance in her life, the codicil to the will, the way she kept sensing that he was holding something back from her. It explained why he had said his "alibi" involved protecting a "friend."

Because his so-called friend was his own alter ego.

"*You* are Cousin Michael," she whispered.

He squared his shoulders, then nodded tersely.

And her heart broke. All this time, he had been lying to her, deceiving her, *manipulating* her . . . While she had been too much a fool to see it. "I-I considered that it might be you, but it made no sense. Why would you do it? I deserve to know that, at least."

He met her gaze with one so haunted that it made a fist close around her heart. "Which part do you want to know?"

"All of it! Why you lied to me, when you knew how desperately I wanted to know the truth. Why you continued the role even after I . . ." As she saw Mr. Pinter's eyes narrow, she caught herself. "After I learned there was no bequest from Sarah. And why you started the cursed masquerade in the first place."

Why you made me fall in love with you all over again.

No, she did *not* love him. How could she love such a liar?

"When you approached me as my husband's 'cousin,'" she went on, "it was only four years after that stupid letter of mine went to the papers. I cannot imagine why you would have let me rent your valuable piece of property—"

"Ah, but the property doesn't belong to him, does it, my lord?" Mr. Pinter broke in.

She had almost forgotten that the Bow Street runner was there, but clearly he had learned everything about her association with Cousin Michael. "Of course it belongs to him," she told Pinter, then glanced at David. "Doesn't it?"

"Actually, Mrs. Harris," Mr. Baines put in with a pained expression, "the property belongs to Mr. Pritchard. His lordship won a lien on it in a card game and is allowed only the rents for a period of fifteen years."

She shot the solicitor a glare as she realized how very much the man had kept from her. Then his words sank in. Fifteen years. It had been nearly fourteen and a half years since . . .

God help her. She felt another blow to her heart.

She shot David an accusing glance. "Is that why you invented the codicil and approached me about moving the school? Because you knew you would no longer be my landlord?"

"Look here, Charlotte—"

"*Answer* me, curse you!"

He nodded, his eyes dark with guilt. "Pritchard has said he'll evict you when the fifteen years is up. I could think of no other way to—"

"How about telling me the truth?" she bit out. "Instead of all this folderol about finding another property? If you had told me I was about to be evicted, I would not have vacillated about moving the school."

"But you would not have taken my money either, would you?" he pointed out. "You would have been trapped, unable to get past your pride and unable to afford moving to another location. I couldn't risk that. I didn't want you to lose your school."

"Do not blame this on me," she said, unable to keep the hurt from her voice.

David threaded his fingers through his hair, distractedly. "I didn't mean to. I just . . . didn't want you to suffer." He released a shuddering breath. "And I didn't want to reveal why I started the masquerade. I didn't want you to know the truth."

"That you were a friend to me? That you gave me money to start the school all those years ago and helped me with the rents?" Charlotte said in bewilderment.

David flinched. Glancing at Mr. Pinter, he hesitated, as if considering what he should say.

But right now, Charlotte didn't care about Pinter or Sarah's death or any of it. "Tell me all of it, curse you," she bit out. "Why did you become Cousin Michael?"

"Because I wanted to revenge myself on you." He gave a bitter laugh. "Godwin was right, damn his eyes. He just got the timing wrong."

Revenge. The fist around her heart tightened painfully. "I don't understand."

"I know. Why do you think I didn't tell you?" He leaned forward, his eyes alight with remorse. "I was so angry at you back then. When I heard you were teaching in that expensive school in Chelsea, it infuriated me that you were on the road to pursuing your dream while my life was still in a shambles. So I thought . . ."

He dropped his gaze. "I thought I'd offer you a loan and

a cheap rent so you could establish your academy. Once you had it going, I'd intended to demand full payment on the loan and raise the rents beyond your ability to pay. Then I could watch you fail. Watch you suffer. The way you made me suffer with your letter to the papers."

"Why do you keep talking about a letter to the paper?" Mr. Pinter demanded.

Both Charlotte and David ignored him.

She reeled from the idea that he could have set out to destroy her in such a calculating manner. "You . . . you hated me that much?" she choked out. "You thought it acceptable to publicly humiliate me?"

"The way you did me? Yes!" As if realizing how heated his words were, David let out an exasperated sigh. "Remember, back then I didn't know the truth of what had happened that night at my estate, Charlotte."

"I can understand your wanting to strike at *me*," she said, tears clogging her throat. "But your plan would have hurt others, too. I had students, teachers, people who depended on me—"

"As my family depended on me, before you ruined my hopes of a decent marriage!" When she recoiled, he groaned. "Damn it, I am only explaining how I felt *then*. How I justified my stupid plan to myself. At the time it seemed . . . fair."

"When did it stop seeming fair?" she whispered in a hollow voice. "Or has the past month just been the culmination—"

"Don't be ridiculous," he said in a low, aching voice. "The last month was heaven for me. And hell. I wanted to tell you, especially after I realized—" He broke off with a frustrated glance at Mr. Pinter. "But I knew what you'd think."

"That I do not know you at all?" She couldn't hold back her tears any longer. As they trickled down her cheeks, she shot him an accusing glance. "That the man I thought was my friend was merely a figment of my fancy? Instead, I find he is exactly the sort of cruel and manipulative man my father was."

He recoiled. "No! I never carried out my plan."

"Why not, when you went to so much trouble?"

"Because of your letters. I wanted to hate you, but you just . . . wouldn't let me. From that very first letter, I saw the girl I'd once fallen in love with, and I couldn't stay angry. It took only a handful of them before I decided I could never go through with it. After that . . ."

"You pretended to be my friend."

"I *was* your friend, damn it! I still am. Nothing has changed, not for me."

And everything had changed for her. He had lied to her repeatedly, manipulated her, kept important information from her, and for what? So he could save the school? But why?

Mr. Pinter cleared his throat. "How exactly did your wife fit into this cozy arrangement, my lord?"

David turned a fulsome glare on Mr. Pinter. "She had nothing to do with it! I married Sarah for her fortune, and she married me for my title. It's a common arrangement, and one that I'm sure you already know or you wouldn't be hounding me like this."

The runner's eyes narrowed. "I am trying to get at the truth, my lord."

A harsh laugh escaped David. "By unveiling my secrets to a woman who had nothing to do with my wife's death?"

"Are you sure?" Mr. Pinter said coolly.

When the runner turned his hard gaze on Charlotte, a chill of horror passed through her. "What are you saying, sir?"

"You and his lordship have clearly been . . . friendly . . . for some years. How can I be sure that you did not conspire together to kill his wife?"

"I did not even know that the man I corresponded with was Lord Kirkwood!" she protested. "How could I possibly have 'conspired' with him? Besides, didn't you bring us here to establish that he has an alibi?"

"Yes. But I am talking about *you* now, not him. What is *your* alibi?" Mr. Pinter asked.

David shot to his feet. "You've lost your bloody mind if you think Mrs. Harris would ever hurt a fly. She sure as hell wouldn't have killed my wife!"

"Can you be certain of that?" Mr. Pinter cast her a cynical glance. "How do you know this isn't all an act? That she found out that this Cousin Michael fellow was you, and then set out to gain you for herself by eliminating your wife?"

"How dare you, sir!" Charlotte hissed. "Sarah was my pupil. I would never have hurt her. And believe me, if I had known Lord Kirkwood was Cousin Michael, I would never have accepted the fake legacy he offered me in the first place."

"Perhaps you saw the means to save your school," Mr. Pinter said, "and jumped at the chance to get a bit of your own back against him while gaining his wife's money."

Charlotte gaped at him. "That is the most appalling accusation I have ever heard!"

"And one that will instantly be refuted by her letters to me," David ground out. "If you want them—"

"What do you think my men are searching your home for, my lord?"

"They won't find them there." A muscle ticked in David's jaw. "Mr. Baines has them. I did not want to risk my wife's coming across them and revealing my secret to the world. He also has all of my original letters to Mrs. Harris, since I had the clerk copy them out for me to keep her from recognizing my handwriting."

Oddly enough, that little deception cut her to the heart. He had gone to that length to keep her from knowing the truth? What kind of decent, honest man wove such a web of deception?

"Mr. Baines," she said, wanting only to be done with this madness so she could leave here, "if you would give my letters to Mr. Pinter, I would be most grateful. Now, gentlemen, I ask that you excuse me. I need to get back to my school."

As she rose, Mr. Pinter rose, too. "I'm not done with you, Mrs. Harris. I still have not heard your alibi for that night."

"I was at the school!"

"And did anyone see you?"

She thought back to the night of Sarah's death, when her pupil Lucy had run off with Diego Montalvo. She had retired early. "Not after I went to bed."

"What time was that?" he asked in a hard voice. "And remember, I will speak to your servants to confirm whatever you tell me."

"Nine o'clock."

"So you had plenty of time to slip out, ride to London, accost Lady Kirkwood in her bedchamber, and make sure she did not pose a threat to your romance with Lord Kirkwood."

Charlotte could only gape at the man, astonished that he could manufacture such a devious character for her.

"That's enough!" David snapped. "I wish to speak to you in the hall, Mr. Pinter. Now!"

Though the runner raised one eyebrow at David's imperious tone, he gave a faint nod and headed for the door. He paused there to look back at Mr. Baines. "Gather those letters up for me, will you, sir? I'll send a man in to help you with it. We don't want any of them to go missing."

Mr. Baines bristled at the man's insinuation but wisely held his tongue until Mr. Pinter and David had left the room. Then he came to sit beside Mrs. Harris. "I am so sorry, madam. I never dreamed they would accuse *you* of anything."

"It is not your fault," she said stiffly. "It's your employer's."

Now that Mr. Pinter was gone, the full ramifications of his accusations hit her. It was even worse than she'd feared when she'd told David that the authorities might think they had conspired together. Back then, she hadn't known that there would be proof of a previous friendship.

Lord help her, what was she to do?

The other runner entered the room, but they both ignored him.

"His lordship has long regretted the plan he threw together in such anger, I assure you," Mr. Baines went on. "He has been going mad these past few weeks, trying to figure out a way to save your school without alerting you to his identity."

"It's the subterfuge I don't understand," she said. "If he had only told me—"

"He said that if he unveiled the truth, you would never take his money."

Well, that much was true. She would have been mortified to discover to whom she was indebted and why. She certainly would not have accepted his help.

But that didn't change the fact that he had lain in her arms and asked her to *marry* him while keeping such a secret from her.

"Since he'd created the intolerable situation with Pritchard in the first place," Mr. Baines went on, "he felt honor bound to set it right."

"Hah! The man has no honor in him."

"That's not true, madam! He has worked himself into a frenzy trying to resolve your difficulties. He was willing to give you thirty thousand pounds of his own money to make up for what he'd done."

"Is that why he wanted to give me the money?" she asked. "Or was it a way to control me, to have a say in what happened to my school?"

She simply did not know whom to believe and what to think. David had never once said he loved her. And now it was beginning to dawn on her why that might be. But until this madness was over and his wife's killer caught, until she could speak to David alone, she could never know for sure.

She shook her head. Could she *ever* know for sure? She now knew the kind of deception he was capable of. How could she ever trust him again?

Everything had changed between them—and she feared it could never be made right.

Chapter Twenty-four

❧

David had just finished explaining to Pinter what the situation was between him and Charlotte, about her letter to him years ago, and why he'd felt a need to revenge himself. He'd had no choice; Pinter had demanded to know it all.

He stared at the man as Pinter mulled over what David had told him. David wished he could bash the man's head against the nearest wall, after watching him systematically destroy the fragile relationship David had built with Charlotte. But that certainly wouldn't help either him or Charlotte.

"Now you understand that she has been entirely deceived by me for years," David said. "There is no way in hell that Mrs. Harris had anything to do with my wife's death."

"So you say," Pinter retorted.

David curled his fingers into his palms to keep from throttling the man. "Look at those letters, and you'll know she didn't. And it's madness to think that she and I would have conspired over it, for God's sake. I sent her a letter the very night of Sarah's death! Why would I have bothered?"

"Because it was a convenient way to establish your own alibi while your lover was insinuating herself into your wife's bedchamber?"

"Don't be an ass, Pinter. Charlotte is a highly respected

schoolmistress. She's incapable of killing anyone, either at my command or on her own. Her reputation ought to speak for itself." His eyes narrowed. "And you've got other perfectly legitimate suspects you're ignoring—my wife's footman, for one. So while you're pursuing this mad line of investigation, the real murderer is roaming free about the city. Has that not occurred to you?"

"Believe me, my lord, we are pursuing every possible scenario."

But the man's implacable expression filled David with a futility he had not felt before. "So what will it take for you to believe that neither I nor Mrs. Harris had anything to do with this?"

"We'll question her servants and yours, try to confirm your separate alibis. And we'll look at those letters. Not to mention anything else we might find in your wife's room, like her own letters or a diary or—"

David snorted. "My wife was not the letter-writing sort. She certainly wasn't introspective enough to keep a diary, unless it was to record her gambling losses."

And all of a sudden, it hit him. The idea was so perfect he wondered why he hadn't thought of it before. How better to exonerate both him and Charlotte? And to eliminate whatever suspects were not viable?

"Mr. Pinter, would you allow me to make a suggestion regarding your investigation into my wife's murder?"

"Depends on what sort of suggestion it is," the man said dryly.

"Whoever really killed my wife doesn't yet know how far your investigation has gone. Is that correct? Even Mrs. Harris knows nothing beyond what you've said today, and that is precious little. And you've already acknowledged that my alibi prevents me from having done the deed with my own hands."

Pinter eyed him warily. "True. What's your point?"

"The newspapers are already full of the fact that Sarah's death was a murder. What I propose is that you make an official statement today that your investigation has brought to light that my wife kept a diary. Tell the papers that you expect the diary, which went missing after her death, to reveal important information about who murdered her, and that anyone who might know the whereabouts of said diary should come forward. With any luck, the real murderer will panic and attempt to break into my house looking for the incriminating evidence."

"Unless the real murderers are you and Mrs. Harris."

David stiffened. "That is why this will only work if you keep Mrs. Harris as much in the dark about the supposed diary as the rest of your suspects."

"Oh?" Mr. Pinter said skeptically. "You think I can trust you not to inform her the minute you have a chance?"

"You needn't worry about that." He drew in a heavy breath. "When we leave here, you're going to arrest me and place me in the gaol. That will ensure that I have no contact with any of your suspects, including Mrs. Harris. Since only you and I know the truth, the trap will be secure."

Mr. Pinter's eyes narrowed. "You're willing to go to such a length to prove Mrs. Harris innocent."

"I'm willing to do *anything* to prove her innocent—and me. I will not have this hanging over my head any longer. I want to know who murdered my wife as much as you do." He glanced at the closed door to Mr. Baines's office. "As long as you continue to follow false leads, that will never happen."

"Why should you care about finding your wife's murderer? Her death cleared the way for you and your . . . friend."

"My wife deserved better than to be drowned in her bath, and I should have protected her from that. My curse is that I failed to keep her safe while she was alive. I don't intend to fail in bringing her killer to justice, now that she's dead."

Pinter stared at him a long moment, then gave an odd little smile. "It's a good plan, actually. I wish I'd thought of it myself. Assuming that our murderer is not clever enough to see the trap, it might even work."

"If it doesn't, you haven't lost anything," David pointed out, then added acidly, "And you'll already have me conveniently in the gaol."

"Surely you realize, my lord, that I cannot put you in the gaol."

"Why not?"

"You're a peer. With as little evidence as we have right now, there would be such an outcry among your friends and family that it would make my work even more difficult. You have powerful friends in the government, like the Duke of Foxmoor, the present secretary of war. I am not taking on the whole world to solve this murder. Besides, if I arrest *you* for the murder, what incentive does the 'real murderer' have to come looking for the diary?"

"Fine, do as you please then," David snapped, in frustration. "But remember that my powerful friends also happen to be Mrs. Harris's powerful friends. And if you mean to pursue *her* as a suspect—"

"Let me finish, my lord. I'm only suggesting that you

not be arrested or go into the gaol. Instead, I propose another arrangement—that you remain at your town house, where you'll be guarded by my men, but without anyone's knowledge. You will inform your family that you are retiring to a friend's house in the country to avoid the press, and you will take up your knocker, close up the town house, and handle your servants as if you were leaving town."

David released a breath. Pinter had decided to pursue his proposition. Thank God. "What about the skeleton staff that generally remains to watch the house?"

"Give them a holiday. My men will take on their roles. But it must look as if the house is virtually empty if this is to work. That is why the public will be told the same thing as your family. It does no good for us to set a trap if our villain will not walk into it."

"Thank you," David said. "Both for considering my proposition and for giving me and Mrs. Harris the benefit of a doubt."

Pinter's gaze hardened. "I'm willing to try this unorthodox approach, but I can't allow it to go on long. I can't afford to have my men tied up in something that may not get results."

"I understand. But I suspect that whoever killed Sarah was close enough to her to know where she tended to hide things, or she wouldn't have allowed him into her bedchamber. And he won't be able to resist the urge to check and make sure she didn't hide a diary."

"You'd best hope you're right," Pinter said dryly. "I may not have enough evidence now to arrest either of you, but if you are guilty, I will find it."

"I would expect no less of you, sir." David glanced toward the closed office door. "I do have two requests that I hope you will grant me in exchange for my cooperation in letting you take over my life."

Pinter scowled. "And what might those be?"

"Since I won't be able to act on the knowledge, I think the least you could do is tell me who brought this matter to your attention in the first place."

For the first time all morning, Pinter looked a bit flustered. "Actually, my lord, we don't know."

"What do you mean, you don't know?"

"We received an anonymous letter saying that we should take a closer look at your wife's suicide note. It enclosed the draper's bill, and it also gave the information that your wife had planned dinner with a friend the day after her death. When we spoke to the friend, she confirmed that, though she did not recall telling anyone of it."

"So it could have been anyone—my brother-in-law, the footman, even that blasted moneylender Timms, if he'd happened to see Sarah that day and she'd mentioned it."

"Your brother-in-law?"

David sighed. He didn't want to get Richard into trouble with the law unnecessarily, but neither did he want to see the man create havoc for everyone he loved.

"Sarah's brother, Richard Linley. He has blamed me for her death ever since it happened. A week ago he asked me for money, which I refused to give him because he's as inveterate a gambler as Sarah was. I wouldn't put it past him to stir up trouble in retaliation."

Pinter drew out his notepad and jotted down a few words. "Perhaps my men and I will have a little talk with

Mr. Linley. If he wrote the letter, we want to know about it. We can determine if he knows more than he's saying."

"That's a start. And another thing . . ."

David briefly sketched out the situation with Timms. Pinter wrote notes on that, promising to look into the moneylender as well, though he agreed it was unlikely that Timms could have entered Sarah's bedchamber late at night without being seen.

After tucking away his pad, Pinter said, "You mentioned two requests. What is the other?"

"I want a few more minutes to speak with Mrs. Harris before we leave."

"I can't let you talk to her alone or—"

"I know, it will defeat the purpose of the trap. You can witness it. But I have to make her understand why I did what I did."

Something that looked remarkably like pity flashed briefly in Pinter's eyes. "All right. But be quick about it."

They went back into the room to find Charlotte staring out the window while Baines piled fourteen years of letters into a box for Pinter's man.

"Charlotte," David said. "I have to go now."

She turned from the window in alarm. "Are they arresting you?"

"No." He dared not say more about that, not if he wanted to free her of any suspicion. But God, it killed him to keep silent, knowing what she would think when he disappeared from her life without a word.

"Are they . . . arresting *me*?"

"We're not arresting anyone at this time, Mrs. Harris," Pinter put in. "But his lordship and I have a few important matters to discuss. You're free to go, but I would advise you not to leave the area."

She paled at that, then came toward the door without looking at David.

He couldn't just let her go like this. Stepping into her path, he murmured, "I want you to know that I never meant to hurt you."

"Really?" she said caustically. "Not even when you were concocting your plan for revenge?"

He flinched. "As I told you, once we began writing each other, everything changed. And by the time I invented the legacy, I wanted only one thing: to make amends for what I'd done."

"I do not believe that is all you wanted," she said in a heart-wrenching voice. "Whether you admit it or not, you wanted to punish me for humiliating you and your family all those years ago."

"That's not true!"

"Isn't it?" Her gaze was surprisingly clear-eyed. "Earlier, when you told me why you did it, your anger over it seemed as fresh now as it must have been fourteen years ago. You may not realize it, but you still resent me for what I did. Your anger bubbles to the surface whenever you speak of it."

"It's not that simple."

"I think it is simpler than you will admit. The real reason you did not tell me the truth was you wanted to 'guide' me as Cousin Michael always did. I took away your control of your own life back then, and you figured that turnabout was fair play. So it was *your* turn to make sure that things went according to plan. To make *me* dance to *your* tune."

The possibility that she might be right only fueled his temper. "I did this because I *care* about you!"

"You did this because you could not stand to let me learn what you really are. Because if I did, I would no longer feel a need to hold on to my guilt. We would both be culpable for wronging each other. And that would put us on an equal plane, wouldn't it? You were not about to allow that."

"Have you forgotten that I asked you—" He shot Pinter a glance, but what was the point of hiding anything now? He couldn't make things any worse. "That I asked you to marry me a few days ago?"

"How could I forget that? You proposed the sort of marriage where you had all the control, and I had none." Her eyes darkened with pain. "You proposed closing the school. How tidy it would have been for you if I had accepted. You would never have had to admit to being Cousin Michael. You must have been very desperate to keep control of my life."

Now he could see just how deeply he'd hurt her, and it struck the death knell to all his hopes for them. The fact that some of her suppositions were true only made it worse. He *had* tried to avoid ever admitting the truth to her. He *had* tried to manipulate her.

"You're right," he said. "I was desperate. But not for the reasons you say. I didn't want to lose you, sweeting."

"Do not call me that anymore." Tears welled in her eyes. "I kept wondering why you would not say you loved me. You said you needed me, but you said nothing of love. And today I figured out why. You cannot forgive me for breaking your heart years ago. And I doubt you ever will."

As he stared at her, stunned by her words, she slipped from the room.

You cannot forgive me for breaking your heart years ago. And I doubt you ever will.

How could she even think it? It wasn't true, damn it!

"My lord," Pinter said beside him. "We should go. We have much to do."

David nodded numbly. Charlotte was never going to forgive him for his deceptions. And that meant he'd lost her for good.

Chapter Twenty-five

For the next few days Charlotte tried not to think about David. It didn't help that Bow Street runners swarmed over the school for two of those days, questioning the servants and staff. Thankfully, the fall term had ended last week, so there were no girls around to gossip and spread news to their parents about the school's being involved in the investigation. But the teachers were present, and according to Terence, had praised her and defended her honor most vigorously.

With the papers full of speculation about Sarah's murder, she was grateful for her staff's support. Not to mention their discretion, since so far her connection to the investigation had not been mentioned in any story. The press was too busy chewing over the official statement from the magistrate's office, something about a diary it was looking for. At least Mr. Pinter seemed to have moved the focus of his interest from David, for the papers said that David had gone off to the country.

Without a word to her, without trying to see her alone? She should not be hurt, given her final words to him, but she was. She had not expected when they parted that she would not see him again.

With the Bow Street men now gone from the school, she struggled to bury her hurt and avoid her staff's questions. She kept busy assessing the school's financial situation. Acknowledging that she could no longer hope to find a place near London, she began investigating moving the academy into a more remote area where she might afford to rent a large enough building to house her pupils. Buying was out of the question. She lacked the money.

David was willing to give you thirty thousand pounds to buy property. And you threw it back in his face.

Of course she did! He was arrogantly trying to manipulate things to his advantage, to cover up his crime.

She sank onto the settee in her private drawing room. Crime? Giving her low rents for fourteen years? Loaning her money? Advising her in areas where she couldn't possibly have had any expertise?

"He lied to me, curse him!" she shouted to the empty room.

Yes, and there had been no mistaking his remorse over *that*.

Tired of the incessant thoughts running through her mind, she laid her head back and closed her eyes, but that only made things worse. This was where David had first kissed her after their years apart. This was where he'd nearly ravished her. For all his manipulating and controlling, he had not planned *that,* she was almost certain. It had seemed to take him as much by surprise as her.

Was she being unfair to attribute darker motives to him? Perhaps he was no clearer about his own feelings than she was. And perhaps she had been a trifle hard on him that day in Mr. Baines's office.

Or perhaps he had recognized that she was right—that he could never forgive or forget what had happened between them in their youth. Why else had she not heard a single word from him in days?

Tears flowed down her cheeks, and she buried her face in her hands. Why had he not fought harder for her? Why had he run off to the country instead, without telling her where he was going or what was happening with the magistrate's office?

Lifting her head, she strove to quash her tears. She was a fool to even be wondering—had she not decided to put an end to their mad affair? To stop him from hurting her anymore? She had as much as told him that at their last meeting. So why was she crying because he had taken her at her word?

"Mrs. Winter and her children are here, madam," said Terence's voice from beyond the door.

She shot up from the settee. Good Lord, she had entirely forgotten that this was the day she and Amelia had arranged to meet. Before she could do more than draw out her handkerchief to wipe her eyes and nose, Amelia was bustling into the room, tugging along two adorable little girls.

"Mrs. Harris, it's so good to—" Amelia broke off as she caught Charlotte surreptitiously dashing away her tears. "Oh no, what has happened?" the young woman said as she rushed to Charlotte's side.

That only started Charlotte crying again, harder than before.

"Terence," Amelia said, "would you take the girls down to the river landing to see the ducks? They're very fond of ducks."

"No," Charlotte choked out, "I-I want to visit with your girls . . ."

"And you will. Later." After waving off Terence and the children, Amelia urged Charlotte to sit back on the settee. "For now, I think you and I should talk."

Charlotte needed no more invitation than that to throw herself into Amelia's arms and start sobbing again.

Amelia took it all in stride, stroking her back, soothing her with soft words. After Charlotte had finally gained control, Amelia murmured, "Dare I guess that this has something to do with my husband's cousin?"

Charlotte nodded. She considered how much to tell Amelia, then realized she need not hold back anything from her. What was there to hide? She had to tell *someone* about David. She needed a female confidante, and Amelia would understand better than anyone, since she knew David better than Charlotte's other friends.

The whole tale came out: what had happened between her and David years ago, how he had come back into her life, the supposed legacy from Sarah. She left out only the fact that she and David had shared a bed, saying he had been courting her while helping her look at properties.

But when she got to the part about David's being Cousin Michael, Amelia gazed at her in stunned amazement.

"Lord Kirkwood?" she queried. "*He's* Cousin Michael? Are you sure?"

Charlotte gave a mad laugh. "As sure as I can be." She told Amelia everything that had happened at Mr. Baines's office, including what she'd said to David at the end. When she was done, Charlotte asked, "Do you think I was wrong to say those things to him? Do you think I am wrong now to be so angry at him?"

"About his deceiving you? Absolutely not." Amelia scowled. "A plot for revenge indeed. Next time I see my husband's cousin, I shall give him quite the tongue-lashing. How dare he lie to you and plot against you, all because you wrote some silly letter!"

"You don't understand," Charlotte said. "Thanks to my 'silly letter,' he was publicly vilified for months and months. I heard that whenever he walked into a room, mothers hid their daughters. Imagine having to face that every time you went into society, yet never even knowing why I had humiliated him so. He had no clue that I had seen Giles with the maid. One moment, I was promising to consider marrying him, and the next I was mocking him in a most public forum."

"Yes, but to engineer a plot to set you up for failure! That is abominable!"

"I quite agree." She blew her nose. "Still, he did not go through with it. And to be honest, without his vile plot, this school would not exist. I would never have been able to save enough money to begin it on a teacher's salary. And it would have been years before anyone even considered making me a headmistress. Thanks to him, I realized my dream. It is hard to hate him for that."

"Ah, but you can hate him for lying to you about Mr. Pritchard. What would have happened if this had gone on until Mr. Pritchard evicted you?"

"David would not have let it go so far. I know it."

"How can you be sure of that? My goodness, the man invented a fake legacy just to keep from admitting the truth to you!"

"He invented a fake legacy because he knew I wouldn't take the money otherwise. And he was right about that. If he had come forward and told me he was Cousin Michael that very first day, I would have demanded to know everything. Once I heard he had done it out of revenge, I would have thrown him out and never spoken to him again."

She glanced up to find Amelia smiling ruefully at her.

"Do you hear yourself, my friend?" Amelia said. "You defend him at every turn. You must not be quite as angry at him as you think."

That was the trouble. Every time Charlotte summoned up her moral outrage, she thought of the stricken look he had worn in Mr. Baines's office. She remembered the many times he had said rather harsh things about Cousin Michael. Had he even then been feeling guilty about his deception?

Worst of all, she remembered how sweetly he had made love to her at Stoneville's property. He might not have said he loved her, but he had shown it in so many ways—trying to protect her from Pritchard, pushing her to move the school, offering her his own money . . .

"I do not know what I feel anymore," she admitted. Tears welled in her eyes again. "And now he has left town, and I cannot even see him to find out."

Amelia hugged her. "Oh, I think you *do* know what you feel. You just don't want to admit it. It sounds to me as if you've already forgiven him." Drawing back, she took Charlotte's hands in hers. "It sounds to me as if you're still in love with him."

Charlotte stared bleakly at her friend. *Was* she? It was quite possible. Why else was she so miserable without him? Why else did the thought of never seeing him again send a knife through her heart?

He might have deceived her and manipulated her all these years, but he had also been a friend to her. A good friend, if she were honest about it.

"What am I to do?" Charlotte whispered. "I don't know if he only pursued me out of some long-suppressed desire to revenge himself for what I did to him. Or if he really cares and just cannot admit it to himself. I need to know that."

"Of course you do." Amelia squeezed her hands. "Do you still have the letters he wrote to you as Cousin Michael?"

Charlotte nodded. "Mr. Baines gave the magistrate's office his originals, so I still have the copies that were delivered to me. I have kept every one."

"Perhaps you should look there for some sign of what Lord Kirkwood really feels for you. I know he was playing a role, but I doubt that even my husband's Machiavellian cousin could hide himself entirely from a woman he cared about."

"Or from a woman he secretly hated."

"Exactly. You said that his anger leaks out whenever he speaks of the past. It must have leaked out in his letters, too. Perhaps if you can read them in the cold light of day, you can determine if his anger is at you. Or at himself." Amelia arched one eyebrow. "And if you can read them without wanting to strangle him for deceiving you, then you'll know how *you* feel as well."

Charlotte managed a smile. "It is a good suggestion, thank you." .

"You're welcome. I owe a great deal to what you taught me here, so the least I can do is offer a bit of advice now and then."

Impulsively, Charlotte hugged Amelia. "Oh, you do more than that, my friend." When she drew back, she squared her shoulders. "Now, let us go see how your daughters are faring with Terence. I don't think he is used to dealing with girls quite that young."

As they headed out to the river landing, they spoke of the school and Amelia's children. But Charlotte was still aware enough of where they were going to tense up as they neared the river.

And Amelia was astute enough to notice. "Still uneasy around the water, are you?"

Charlotte sighed. "I keep thinking I will grow out of this silly fear, but I never have."

"Did you know that Lucas has a fear of closed places? He spent two days trapped in a tunnel at Dartmoor, and he gets very uneasy whenever we are belowdecks on a ship or confined somewhere in a small room. But he always manages to fight back his fear."

"I should dearly love to know how he manages that."

"Mostly he talks, to me or to whoever is near. He rattles on about whatever he can think of, and I do my best to help by saying outrageous things to make him laugh. He says keeping his mind on something other than his surroundings helps."

"I shall have to try that sometime," Charlotte said, though she doubted anything so pedestrian could ever make her feel easy on the water.

The girls spotted them just then and uttered a glad cry. Five-year-old Isabel, with chestnut curls and eyes as blue as her father's, broke into a run to meet her mother, while black-haired, three-year-old Emily toddled less swiftly toward them.

"Mama, Mama, Mr. Terence showed us the river wherries!" Isabel cried as she threw her arms about her mother's legs. "Can we ride in one? Please, please?"

"Not today, sweetie. Perhaps another time. We're going to have tea with Mrs. Harris instead."

Isabel gazed up at Charlotte with wide eyes. "Will there be plum cakes?"

"There will be lemon cakes," Charlotte said, charmed beyond words. "Will that do?"

After they all trooped inside, an ache settled deep in her chest as she watched the girls with their mother. Would it be so bad to marry David, even if he did not love her? Or could not *say* he loved her, at any rate? They might have children together. After all, she was not sure she was barren.

And he would expect you to give up the school to raise those children, and be Lady Kirkwood.

Yet even that might be worth it, if she thought he truly cared for her.

As soon as Amelia and her sweet girls left, Charlotte headed to her private drawing room and pulled out David's letters. For several hours, all she did was read. Now that it was too late, she saw David in every turn of phrase, every acerbic remark. But though his arrogance was blazoned upon every page, there were flashes of kindness, too. Like when he showed such concern for her staying alone at the school over the Christmas holidays. Or when he blamed himself for what had happened with Lucy.

That letter in particular arrested her. He had written it shortly after his wife's death. Despite his grief, despite everything he must have been dealing with, he had taken time to assuage her guilt over Lucy's disappearance and blame himself for it.

With her heart racing, she flipped back to the letter he had sent the night of Sarah's death, the one he had been delivering while his wife was being murdered. It was full of assurances that if Diego Montalvo proved a blackguard, David would make sure the man was packed off to Spain.

It was one offer of intervention among many, the offers of a friend to a woman who had started her enterprise with few connections and even fewer friends. David's scheme might have begun as revenge, but it very clearly had become something more.

His voice echoed in her mind: *I was your friend, damn it! I still am. Nothing has changed, not for me.*

Did she dare believe him? Did she dare to believe that he felt even more? That in time he could love her again?

That was the question that plagued her for the next couple of days. With the girls gone and the investigators no longer around, she could not concentrate on school business. She spent her time reading through David's letters and strolling about the school grounds, trying to sort out her confused feelings.

Late one afternoon, she found herself near the boathouse where she and David had made love, and something dawned on her. David had been right when he'd said, *You use your bloody school as an excuse for not taking risks in your private life, for not letting any man close enough to gain your heart.*

She was proud of what she'd done, building this wonderful institution, but now she began to realize that it was not enough for her anymore. She was lonely. *That* was why Cousin Michael's defection six months ago had struck her so cruelly. Because in many ways he had been her closest friend, and without him she had felt adrift, uncertain . . . alone. So very alone.

Her parents' example and her two unsatisfactory romances had left her cynical that there could ever be someone else for her. But then David had come back into her life and offered the promise of a future. Of an existence beyond the cozy—and stifling—society of the school.

And it had frightened her, just as he said. Because what if she risked everything for him and ended up disappointed again? Then she would no longer have the safety of her school to fall back on. It was easier to wall up her heart here.

But that was no way to live.

She turned from the boathouse to go back inside, now that dusk was falling. A man stepped in front of her, startling her. It took her a moment to recognize him.

"What are *you* doing here?" she asked.

Then she spotted his pistol. Before she could even scream, someone stepped up behind her and pulled a filthy rag between her teeth to gag her while another person tied her hands.

As they pushed her toward the river, she saw the wherry waiting at the landing. Then panic really set in. She kicked and struggled against the strong arms hauling her back toward hell. Her heart thundered in her chest, her fear making her throat raw. Screaming behind the gag, she dug her heels into the ground, and when that didn't work, dropped to her knees in hopes of delaying them.

But it was no use. Within moments they had lifted her bodily onto the boat. And she was out on the river.

Chapter Twenty-six

❦

$\mathscr{D}$avid sat at the kitchen table with a pack of cards and three of Pinter's men, who were dressed in David's livery. "This time, gentlemen, we should play for sixpence a point," he said as he dealt the cards.

"Oh, Mr. Pinter wouldn't approve of that at all," the man across from him said. "So I say we do it."

They all laughed. It hadn't taken long for David to figure out that Pinter's men found him as much an annoying enigma as David did. The man could freeze fog with his cold glances, and David had yet to see him crack a smile.

But David had to hand it to the runner—he was nothing if not thorough. He and his men had searched the house from top to bottom and found nothing that was any help, not even under the floorboards in George's room.

Lately, when the man wasn't at the magistrate's office interviewing witnesses, he spent his time going through the Cousin Michael letters. David sometimes fancied that Pinter had softened toward him since starting to read them. And though Pinter wasn't the sort to be easily swayed from his convictions, he *had* seemed impressed when Sarah's father had stepped forward to argue on David's behalf. Given that David had initially married Sarah for her money, Linley senior's defense of his son-in-law had gone a long way to lift Pinter's suspicion of David.

But unfortunately not Pinter's suspicion of Charlotte.

David stared blindly at his cards. He'd tried not to think of her, of what she'd said to him at the end, but it rang in his head at night and tormented him when he rose in the morning.

Now that his anger had worn off and he could consider her words more rationally, he wondered if she might have been right. Deep down, was he still nursing that ancient wound?

All this time, he'd seen himself as doing everything for *her*, to help *her*. Yet he'd been protecting himself with every step. He'd manipulated her and lied to her . . . and goaded her—whatever it had taken to gain his way.

To gain her.

No, not *her* exactly. The Charlotte of his youth. If he were honest with himself, part of him had wanted to force her back into that role. To relive their past so they could make it come out right the second time.

But one could never go back. He was not the same man, and she was certainly not the malleable innocent he'd hoped in his youth to initiate tenderly into lovemaking. She was a woman full-grown, capable of making important decisions and eager to conquer the world in her own way. He should have approached *that* Charlotte, told her the truth, and laid his cards on the table.

Yes, she would have been angry. She might even have refused his help and lost her school. On the other hand, they might have been able to build a friendship that could have blossomed into an honest, open affection. It wouldn't have been the same as in their youth, but it might have been better.

So why hadn't he done that?

Because he'd been too afraid to risk it.

David shook his head. He'd accused her of being a coward, but *he* was the coward, afraid to expose himself. Afraid he might discover that their years of correspondence and his fond memories of their youthful love were as nothing against the lies and manipulations of his masquerade.

Now he was paying for that. With every day that he and Pinter's men waited for Sarah's killer to enter their trap, Charlotte was out there rebuilding her walls against him, higher and firmer this time. She always learned from her mistakes—and he'd made sure that she would want nothing to do with him in the future.

How would he bear it? When he'd lost her the first time, he'd had his anger to sustain him, to drive out the love that had consumed him.

This time he had nothing but remorse and regret. He almost didn't care what happened now with Sarah's killer. Let them take him to gaol. Let the press foment scandal around him. Let his life be ruined. Without Charlotte, he had no life anyway. If he could not have the woman he loved . . .

Loved? He groaned. Yes. What a fool he had been not to see it. For all his attempts to change her, he loved the new Charlotte as much or more than the old. He loved that she didn't let him bully her, that she knew her own mind, that she believed fiercely in her school. Being with her was like racing at breakneck speed down an endless road of possibilities.

Not being with her was hell.

"That brother-in-law of yours came again today, demanding to know where you'd gone," said the man across from David. "He's a little bastard, that one, lording it over me because he thought I was one of your servants. I told him to be off before I boxed his ears."

"I doubt that would do any good," David replied. "Richard is desperate for money these days. Still, if he was the one who sent the letter to your office about Sarah's suicide note, he has some nerve coming to me for funds."

"Pinter doesn't think he's the one. His handwriting didn't match the letter. Pinter made sure to get a sample when questioning him at the office a few days ago."

"Trust me," David said dryly, "that means nothing." And David should know, since he'd sent Charlotte letters for years that were not in his own hand.

The door to the kitchen banged open. "What the hell is going on here?" Pinter demanded as he saw the small piles of money and the glasses of brandy on the table.

The other men flinched, but David just continued re-arranging his cards. "We're playing whist for sixpence a point. Care to join us, Pinter?"

Pinter scowled. "I see you're determined to corrupt my men, Kirkwood."

David shot him an irritable glance. "It's been six days. You've ransacked my house, questioned all my friends, and kept me a virtual prisoner. The least you can allow me is a little entertainment."

The men watched to see what their superior would say. When he let out a long breath and took a seat at the table, they relaxed.

Pinter poured himself a glass from the decanter David had produced earlier in the evening. "You may be interested to know that we found your footman."

That got David's attention. "George? I assumed he was halfway to the coast by now."

"So did I." Pinter drank deeply, then set down the glass.

"But he didn't make it so far as that. He was at his sister's house in Twickenham."

"What did he have to say for himself?"

"Well, now, that's interesting. It took me awhile—and a few idle threats—to get the truth out of him, but apparently you were right about his taking your wife to the moneylender to offer the man her jewels. What you probably don't know is that her brother went with them, too."

David cursed. "I'm not surprised. The little devil was always a bad influence on her."

Pinter's gaze locked with his. "That fits with something else your footman told me. It seems that some of the money you were paying out for your wife's gambling debts was going to Richard Linley's debts."

"What?"

"Your wife was coming to you for money she was giving to her brother." Pinter took a sip of brandy. "You said he only started asking for money after your wife died. That's because his source of funds dried up with her death."

"Damn the bastard," David hissed. "He let her risk my anger, just so he could feed his obsession? When I get my hands on him—"

"There's more." Pinter set down the glass, his expression now quite solemn. "According to George, your wife had decided a few days before her death to cut Mr. Linley off. Apparently, the visit to the moneylender upset her. I suppose asking for money from you was one thing; pawning your family's jewels was a bit too extreme for her comfort."

David went cold. "If she told Richard she wouldn't give him any more money—"

"Exactly," Pinter said. "It's certainly motive for murder."

"But he was her brother, her pet! Surely he wouldn't . . . he couldn't . . ."

"We won't know until we can question him."

"He was here only a few hours ago," David said.

"Well, he's nowhere to be found now. I have several men out looking for him." Pinter took up his glass again. "But don't you worry. He won't escape us for long."

The bell rang in the kitchen, startling them all.

"It's probably one of my men reporting," Pinter said, "but just in case . . ." He waved a fellow in livery toward the door.

When the man returned, he had Giles with him.

David shot to his feet. Since Giles was a suspect like everyone else, David had written him a note with the same tale he'd given the rest of his friends and family. David's heart lodged in his throat as he saw the suspicious gaze Pinter leveled on Giles.

"What the devil is going on?" Giles said when he spotted David. "I thought you were in the country with a friend!"

"Why are you here?" David countered.

Giles glanced from David to Pinter and back. "A stranger came by my lodgings a couple of hours ago. He demanded to know where you were. He wouldn't believe me when I said I didn't know, but when I held fast to my claim, he told me to make sure this got to you and no one else."

Giles threw a letter on the table. "I debated whether to open it, but decided I'd best make sure it was worth tracking you down for." His expression was grim. "After I read it, I headed over here, hoping to go through your desk looking for information about where you'd gone. You'd better read it."

David opened the letter. It's few lines struck a chill to his soul:

> *I have your "friend" Mrs. Harris. If you wish to see her again, go to your estate in Berkshire and get the jewels you keep in the safe. Then bring them to Saddle Island. She and I will await you there. Come alone and unarmed. If you have not arrived by dusk tomorrow, she will die, and her death will be on your head.*
>
> Richard Linley

Terror gripped his heart, squeezing it until he could hardly draw breath. Lifting his gaze to Pinter, he choked out, "Richard has Charlotte."

Pinter took the letter from his numb hands and scanned it swiftly. "Where is Saddle Island?"

David fought for calm. He had to keep his wits about him. Charlotte's safety depended on it. "It's in the portion of the Thames that runs past my estate. It's little more than a grassy mound with a gazebo on it." His gut clenched to think of Charlotte's being forced to cross the river.

"So there's nothing to obstruct the view from land?" Pinter asked. When David shook his head, Pinter scowled. "Clever fellow, your brother-in-law. By having you row out to the island, he'll be able to tell at once if anyone is with you. We won't even be able to come at him separately without his seeing us. No doubt he intends to leave the island by boat and come down the Thames to the coast. From there he can catch any packet boat to France."

And if David didn't reach them in time . . .

"I suppose he heard about the Kirkwood jewels from Sarah," Giles put in.

"I don't care about the bloody Kirkwood jewels!" David snapped. "He can have every one of them, as long as he doesn't hurt Charlotte."

He headed for the door, but Pinter stopped him.

"Be sensible about this, Kirkwood. Let me and my men help you. It's looking more and more likely that he killed your wife."

"Don't you think I realize that? But I don't want you getting Charlotte killed, too! You said yourself he'd be able to see anyone coming."

"Not at night. There's no moon tonight, and we can be in Berkshire in four hours, five at the most, long before dawn." Pinter stared him down. "He won't be expecting that. He thinks you're in the country, remember? He'll assume that it took time for his message to reach you. So if you show up at night, you'll have the advantage."

"How do you figure that? If he can't see us coming, we won't be able to see *him*, damn it."

"He'll have to light a fire, if only to keep warm. And even if he doesn't, you'll need a lantern to get to the island. So once you reach it, we'll be able to see you and him, but he won't be able to see us." When David scowled, Pinter added, "He may not be the only one in this, you know. If he has other men and he's armed, how will you fight them off alone? You need our help."

David tensed, but Pinter had a point. Richard was so volatile that David needed to be prepared for anything.

"Very well," he said at last. "But you do as *I* say. If you hadn't wasted your time pursuing her as a suspect instead of going after my bloody brother-in-law, she wouldn't even be in this danger. So I won't let you muck this up, too, understood?"

Pinter colored, but he nodded.

"Come on then. My phaeton will be the fastest. You can ride with me. The rest of them can come behind in the carriage."

God help Richard if he harmed one hair on Charlotte's head. Because if he did, David wouldn't rest until the bloody bastard was dead.

Charlotte couldn't breathe, and it had nothing to do with the gag in her mouth. Richard and two scoundrels were taking her up the Thames, for what reason she didn't know. She supposed it was related to Sarah's death, but right now, all she could think of was that she lay bound and helpless in the bottom of the boat, with her head inches from the river. The treacherous, awful river.

If the wherry were to tip over, she wouldn't be able to help herself. Trussed up as she was, she would sink like a stone. The black water would close over her head, seeping in through the gag, and she would not even be able to hold her breath . . .

She did not realize she was gasping and moaning beneath the gag until one of Richard's bullies nudged her shoulder with his foot.

"What's wrong with her?" he asked Richard. "Looks like she's choking."

Taking the lantern that hung on a hook at the head of the boat, Richard leaned down to peer at her. That made the wherry rock, which only worsened her breathing problem. She was already starting to see spots before her eyes.

Oh God, she could not pass out, not here, not now, with the water so close . . .

"If I take off the gag, do you promise not to scream?" Richard asked her.

Somehow she managed a nod.

He removed the gag, and she drew in several deep breaths. She was still tied, still traveling on the river, but at least she could breathe.

"You're not going to be sick, are you?" Richard asked.

"I do not think so," she whispered. "Do you think you might . . . untie my feet as well?"

He considered that a moment, then bent to cut the bonds on her ankles. "I don't suppose you can swim without your hands free."

Though she could not swim regardless, it still lessened her panic a little to have her legs free.

"I didn't expect you to be such a coward," he went on. "Sarah was always talking about what a fierce female you are."

Perversely, those snide words bolstered her courage. "Why are you doing this?" If she was going to die, she at least ought to know what purpose it served.

He glanced away. "I have to leave for France, and I need money. Your lover is going to give me jewels in exchange for getting you back. I figure those will be easier for him to put his hands on than the amount of blunt I need. Besides, they'll fetch a pretty penny in France."

Richard meant to ransom her to David? "You know he is not in the city right now," she said, fighting down a new alarm. "How will you reach him?"

"Giles will find him for me, if he knows what's good for him."

And if he did not? She tried to tell herself that Terence would soon realize she was missing and come after her. But how would he know where she went, or who had her?

"Why do you have to leave the country?" she asked, remembering what Amelia had said about how Lucas kept his mind off his fears. If she could just keep Richard talking . . .

"Why else? My debtors are hounding me. And it's all Kirkwood's fault. How dare he give *you* the money from Sarah's estate that he should have given to *me*! Sarah would never have left your little school any money. He invented that legacy—I know he did."

She blinked. "How did you know about the legacy?"

"I heard the two of you talking that night you were at his town house." Richard sneered at her. "You were quite the cozy couple, too. I wonder if my sister was aware that you and her husband were having an affair."

"We were not! Everything between me and David happened after her death."

He shot her a disbelieving glance.

"And that money was not from your sister's estate, anyway," she said. Perhaps if she could reassure him that David had done nothing to cheat him of his rightful inheritance, he would see sense and stop this madness. And let her out of this wretched boat. "It was David's own money. He pretended that Sarah left the school a legacy because he knew I would not take money from him otherwise."

"I suppose that's what he told *you*," Richard said sullenly.

"It's the truth," she countered. "As you said, Sarah would never have tried to help the school. Besides, she did not have a will." She softened her tone. "I am sure she would have left it all to you if she could have."

Inexplicably he blanched, then turned his face away.

Once he fell silent, she became aware once more of the water and the unsteadiness of the boat. Though she could not see the river from her vantage point, she could feel the rocking and hear the rush of it going past. Fear rose again in her chest. *Keep him talking or you'll never make it.*

"So where are we going?" she asked, her voice shaky.

"Berkshire. There's an island in the river adjoining David's estate—"

"Yes, I know it." A hysterical laugh bubbled up in her throat. She'd managed to avoid crossing the water to Saddle Island years ago, and now she was being dragged there against her will. If David really had taken up with her again to punish her for her letter, he would certainly find *that* fitting.

But she no longer believed that he had. Reading his letters had cured her of that fear. Lord help her, would she ever see David again?

"Why are we going to Saddle Island?" she asked, desperate to ignore the sound of the water rushing past the sides of the boat.

"Because my message to Kirkwood told him to meet us there with the jewels."

She ventured the question she had been too afraid to ask earlier. "And what if he does not get your message?"

"You'd better hope he does," Richard snapped. When she moaned, Richard looked annoyed. "He'll get it, don't you worry. Though why the authorities let him go trotting off to the country, I can't fathom. They should have arrested him and charged him with murder the minute they read my letter about the suicide note."

"*You* sent that letter?"

"Damned right I did. I don't know why they didn't arrest him at once."

"Because he did not kill her!"

"I suppose you believed he really *was* out on a walk that night," Richard said nastily.

As his words registered, Charlotte's blood ran cold. "How did you know that is where he was?"

A frightening stillness came over him. "The Bow Street runner must have told me."

"Mr. Pinter did not even mention it to *me*. I would be very surprised if he mentioned it to you. And I know that the newspapers did not say anything of it." Charlotte's heart was clamoring in her chest. "You could not have known that David was on a walk unless you were there."

"I must have heard—"

"You killed Sarah, didn't you?"

He glowered at her. "That is absurd."

She probably should not have voiced her suspicion aloud, but now that she had, she wanted to know the truth. "If you were there that night—"

"So what if I was?" A muscle worked in his jaw. "You think I would kill my own sister?"

"*That* is why you are leaving the country, is it not? Because you are afraid they will find Sarah's diary, and she will have written something to incriminate you?"

"Enough!" he snapped. "You don't know what you're talking about."

"I know that Sarah could be difficult sometimes. Trust me, there were times I wanted to kill her myself—"

"I did not kill her, damn it! I *loved* her!"

"I am sure you did not mean to," she said, determined

to ferret out the truth. "It must have been an accident. You would never purposely have hurt her."

"No, never."

"She pushed you to it, I am sure she did. She probably said something cutting, as she always did, and—"

"She wouldn't give me the money!" Then, as if realizing what he'd admitted, he slumped on the bench and buried his face in his hands. "She wouldn't give me any more damned money."

It took all her control not to react to his admission. "Tell me about it," she said, dredging up the soothing voice she used when one of her girls came to her burdened with guilt over some infraction. "You will feel better if you talk about it." And then at least she would know the truth.

For a moment, she thought he would not answer. Then he lifted his head to stare out at the river. "All I wanted was for her to wheedle a little more money out of Kirkwood. Just enough to pay off the rest of what I owed that damned Timms, before things got so bad that he sent his ruffians after me."

"And she refused," Charlotte prodded.

"She said she was tired of fighting with Kirkwood. Everything would be easier if she could come to some understanding with him. Which meant she couldn't give me any more money." He scowled into the night. "So we argued. And I shoved her into the tub. But she hit her head on the side and lost consciousness. It happened so fast. I couldn't believe it. She just slipped under the water, and I stood there . . . not sure what to do."

"So it was an accident," Charlotte said, fighting to contain her revulsion. "It could have happened to anyone. Surely if you explained it to the authorities—"

"Are you mad? They'll say I should have pulled her out and brought her to a doctor. I did nothing while she drowned! They'll claim I killed my only sister."

Because he *had,* but she was not fool enough to point that out. Merciful heavens, she was in the clutches of a murderer. He might not have held Sarah under, but he'd killed her as surely as if he had. How could Charlotte hope that he would ever let *her* go?

"Once you saw she was dead, you cut her wrists and forged that suicide note, I suppose," Charlotte said dully. "To make it look as if she killed herself."

"I had to do something, don't you understand? I couldn't . . . I knew I would hang. When we were children, we used to play pranks on each other by writing outrageous letters in each other's hands, so I could write in her hand fairly well."

"Clearly well enough to fool the authorities." She stared at him. "But if you did accidentally kill her, why did you write the letter that started the investigation?"

A harsh laugh escaped him. "For the same reason I took you—to get money from my tight-fisted brother-in-law. After Sarah died, he felt sorry for me, and he gave me whatever I asked for. But then everything changed. *You* came along, taking all the money with your damned legacy—"

"So you framed him for murder?"

"I knew the authorities would never take him to trial, not a lofty viscount like him," he said defensively. "He wasn't even in the house. But I figured if it looked bad enough for him, he would be desperate to clear his name."

He dragged in a heavy breath. "Then I could offer to clear him in exchange for a substantial sum. I could tell them he'd gone drinking with me or gambling or something. But instead of charging him, they started asking questions of the servants. Next thing I knew, they were talking about some diary . . . I never even realized that Sarah had a diary! And it would be just like her to write about my peccadilloes in it. Then they would come after me for sure."

Staring out over the water, he scowled. "Even so, I would have offered to clear him if I could have found him. But he was in the country somewhere, and they wouldn't tell me where, and Timms's men were breathing down my neck . . . He left me no choice, running off like that. I had to do something." A petulant look crossed his face. "Besides, he deserves to suffer. If not for him and his penny-pinching, Sarah would still be alive."

Charlotte said nothing, afraid she would let her anger show if she did. How could Richard not see that he had brought everything on himself? First, he had used his sister for his own purposes. Then when he was done with her, he had killed her and tried to set up an innocent man for the crime *he* had committed.

What would he do with *her,* once she was of no use to him anymore? She shuddered to think.

But one thing she knew for certain—she was not going down without a fight.

Chapter Twenty-seven

∽⧁∾

David stood on the bank of the river with the satchel of jewels in his hand, trying to see beyond his lantern. Thank God his mother was away visiting his sister. Explaining his sudden appearance to her would have been tricky.

Not as tricky as this, though. Richard had to be there somewhere. David held the lantern higher, relieved when its light reached to the edge of Saddle Island. He thought he could see a flickering on the island beyond the gazebo, but there was no sound, which alarmed him. All he could hear was the water lapping against the rowboat moored at the nearby landing.

Somewhere on the opposite bank of the Thames was Pinter, waiting for his men to arrive. He had wanted David to hold off until they came, but since David wasn't sure why they'd been delayed, he wasn't taking the chance of Richard's hurting Charlotte while he stood by twiddling his thumbs. He meant to get her back. Now.

"Richard!" he cried across the water. "Where are you, damn it? Come get your bloody jewels!"

At first he saw and heard nothing. Then something moved into the edge of the lantern light. Richard was pushing Charlotte ahead of him. She appeared to have her hands bound, and Richard had a pistol pressed to her temple.

David's heart stopped. One slip of the foot, one trip, and Charlotte would be dead. Damn the bastard to hell!

"I didn't expect you so soon," Richard called out, suspicion in his voice.

"I wasn't far outside of London," David lied. Then he turned his attention to Charlotte, wishing he could see her better. "Charlotte, are you all right?"

"She's unharmed," Richard called back, "but she'll only stay that way if you get those jewels to me."

"I want to hear her say it herself!" David snapped.

When Richard murmured to her, she called back, "I'm fine, David. He has not hurt me, I swear." Her voice sounded surprisingly calm, and that eased David's panic a little.

"Just row over here with the jewels," Richard ordered, "and she'll remain perfectly safe."

Grimly, David nodded. Tossing the satchel into the rowboat, he balanced the lantern on the spare seat, then climbed in and picked up the oars. He'd rowed across to Saddle Island a hundred times in his youth, but the distance had never felt so far. Every minute that hung in the balance made his pulse treble, and he'd broken into a cold sweat by the time he reached the other side.

He just wanted this done with, so he could hold Charlotte again. He would not feel safe until he had her out of Richard's clutches. After pulling the boat up on the bank and setting the lantern down beside it, he reached for the satchel.

"Not yet," Richard said. "Take off your coat and waistcoat and throw them into the boat." When David did so, he added, "Now turn in a circle."

Though David had considered carrying a pistol, Pinter had advised him against it, anticipating just such a move on Richard's part. But the knife tucked in his boot would suffice, if he could get close enough to use it.

Once Richard was satisfied that David had no weapons, he said, "Bring the satchel up and set it on that rock between us." When David had done so, Richard said, "Now, go back to the boat."

David didn't budge. "I want Charlotte."

"You'll get her. Just do as I say."

Reluctantly, David backed down the bank. To his surprise, Richard drew a knife from his pocket, still holding the pistol to Charlotte's head, and cut her bonds. "All right, Mrs. Harris, go get the satchel. And don't think to run to your lover, or I'll shoot you in the back."

"You would never do that," she said in a steady voice. "I know that deep down you are a good man, Richard. You do not want to hurt me. Let me just go to David—"

"Quiet!" Richard cried and cocked the pistol.

The sound struck terror to David's heart. "Do as he says, Charlotte," David said hoarsely.

Paling, she walked to the satchel.

"Open it and show me what's in it," Richard commanded.

As she knelt to do so, David said, "Do you think I'd cheat you? At the risk to her life?"

"You were tightfisted enough when it was my sister who wanted the money."

"That was hardly the same. I didn't know that Sarah's life depended on it," David choked out.

Richard's gaze shot to him. "What are you talking about?"

Pinter had said to keep Richard off-balance, that it would make it easier to gain control of the situation. But seeing Richard's pistol waver now made David rethink that advice. The last thing he wanted was a bullet going astray and hitting Charlotte. "Nothing."

"You think I killed Sarah, don't you?" Richard demanded.

David remained silent.

"Show me the damned jewels, Mrs. Harris!" Richard growled.

Charlotte held up the boxes, opening them one by one to show a ruby parure, an emerald necklace, three strings of pearls, several rings set with diamonds, emeralds, and more pearls—jewelry that had been in his family for generations.

"Well, well," Richard said, his eyes gleaming at the sight. "Sarah wasn't lying when she boasted she had quite the little collection to wear to dinner parties. Very good, Kirkwood." He motioned to Charlotte. "Bring the satchel over here."

When she picked it up, David said, "No. She stays."

As Charlotte froze, Richard glowered at him. "Have you forgotten who's holding the pistol?"

"You've got what you wanted," David countered. "Now let Charlotte come with me. By the time we can row back to land, you'll be long gone."

Richard shifted his aim to David. "Mrs. Harris, bring the satchel here unless you want to see your lover die before your eyes."

"Stay there, Charlotte," he growled. "He won't shoot me."

"I will not take the chance," she said as she hurried back up to Richard.

Looping his arm about her waist, Richard started backing away, keeping his pistol aimed at David.

"You agreed to let her go if I brought you the jewels," David said as he marched after them. "Are you not a man of your word?"

"Stay back!" Richard commanded. "I need her to get me to the coast. No one will dare approach me if I have her. Then I'll let her go."

"I'm not letting you leave with her," David said, moving inexorably forward. "You can have the jewels—I don't give a damn about them. You can walk away a free man. Just let her go!"

"Take one more step forward, and I'll kill her!" Richard cried, and to David's horror, he started to turn the pistol back on Charlotte.

A sudden noise came from the other side of the island, a shout and the sounds of oars slapping the water. Apparently Pinter had gone after Richard's companions, whoever they were. Startled, Richard turned his head in that direction.

Then everything happened at once. Charlotte brought the satchel up, knocking the pistol into the air where it discharged harmlessly into the sky. Cursing, Richard pulled out his blade and lunged for her, but David launched himself at the man, yelling at Charlotte to run.

They rolled to the ground, David pummeling the younger man with his fists as Richard slashed wildly. Fighting to keep the knife at bay kept David from being able to reach for his own blade. He managed a stiff uppercut that sent Richard's head snapping back, but just as David bent to grab the knife in his boot, Richard stuck his own blade deep in David's thigh. Acting on pure reflex, David brought his knife up and buried it in Richard's heart.

Richard's face contorted in pain. He stared up at David, shock sharpening his features. As blood seeped out over his white waistcoat, staining it crimson, Richard glanced down, then back at David.

"I want you to know . . . I didn't . . . mean . . . to kill her . . ." he gasped.

Then he fell back lifeless.

David pushed off Richard, reeling from the man's words . . . and from the blood pouring everywhere. He felt light-headed. Somewhere beyond him, he heard Charlotte scream. Then she was gathering him up in her arms, chanting over and over, "Oh God, oh God, David, oh God . . ."

That was the last thing he heard before he passed out.

Charlotte laid David down only long enough to fetch the lantern and examine his wound. When she saw his thigh soaked in blood, her heart nearly failed her. There was so much of it!

Tearing off her fichu, she tied it tightly around his leg above the wound. She had to stop the bleeding! Tears poured down her cheeks as she knotted the tourniquet as she'd learned to do when the girls were volunteering at the hospital. "Don't you dare die on me, David Masters," she cried. "Don't you dare leave me!"

She used his cravat to bandage the cut, hoping the pressure might slow the bleeding. She had to get him off this island—he needed a doctor badly. Besides, she wasn't sure if the shouting and the pistol shots behind her came from friend or foe. They were receding anyway, as if someone were giving chase down the river. She could see David's horse tethered on the opposite bank. If she could just get him that far . . .

It took all her strength to drag him down the bank to the rowboat. She pulled and pushed him into it, before shoving the boat off the bank and climbing into it herself. That's when it hit her. She was on the river again. In a boat. And this time she alone was in charge of keeping it afloat.

Oh God, she'd never rowed a boat. What if they capsized? She gazed at the black water around her and felt her throat close up. Panic rose in her chest, and her arms shook so badly she couldn't even grip the oars.

Then David moaned. She would *not* let him die because of some foolish fear, curse it. She would not!

Grabbing the oars, she began to row toward the bank. At first, the boat seemed to have a will of its own. It drifted farther and farther down the river, and she couldn't figure out how to make it stop.

"Dip the right . . . oar deeper . . ." David rasped.

Startled, she glanced at him. He was trying to struggle up onto the seat.

"Lie still!" she ordered, tears of relief streaming down her face to see him conscious at least. "You'll injure yourself worse."

"You have to pull . . . the oars together. But . . . harder with the right."

She did as he said, and the boat spun.

"Not that hard! Just a little. Enough to aim it upriver."

It took her several tries to get the hang of it, but soon she was making some headway.

"Good." He collapsed against the seat. "Good girl."

Some water sloshed over the top of the boat, and fear gripped her again. *Talk to him. Don't think about the river.*

"You may not have noticed, David Masters, but I haven't been a girl in some years."

He managed a weak smile. "Believe me . . . I noticed, my love."

Her gaze shot to him. "What did you say?"

"I've been so . . . stupid . . . sweeting." He shifted position, and a spasm of pain crossed his face.

"Don't talk," she cried in alarm. "Just lie still."

He shook his head. "I want you to know . . . just in case I . . ."

"Don't you dare say it! You are *not* going to die, curse you! I won't let you!"

A tender smile curved up his mouth. "That's what I . . . love about you, Charlotte. You're stubborn as the very . . . devil." He wet his lips. "You were right, you know. About my . . . lying to you. Some stupid part of me . . . still resented you for . . . our past nonsense. But whatever's left of that . . . is gone. My fear of losing you again . . . drove it out."

"Please, David, not now," she said hoarsely as she rowed. She could see what talking cost him. His eyes were glazed with pain, and the cravat she'd tied around his leg was already soaked with blood. "And you're not going to lose me. Ever."

"Do you swear it?" he choked out.

"I swear it. I shall never leave you again."

"Does that mean . . . you forgive me for my . . . masquerade?"

"I forgive you for everything," she said fervently. "You were right, too. I was afraid to let you too close. But I'm not afraid anymore."

"I was afraid . . . to admit I . . . still loved you. But I do. And I always will . . ."

"Oh God, David, I love you, too. Please, please don't die! I couldn't bear it!"

As she spoke, his head fell back against the seat, and his eyes slid shut again.

She pulled for all she was worth, until her hands were raw and bleeding. Then suddenly men appeared on the bank, shouting to other men. For a moment she panicked, fearing that it was Richard's scoundrels, until she spotted Mr. Pinter.

Within moments, the men were pulling the boat up to the landing and lifting David to carry him off to a waiting carriage.

"Are you all right?" Mr. Pinter asked as he helped her out of the boat.

She had never been so happy to feel something solid beneath her feet in all her life. "He needs a doctor right away. You have to save him!"

"We'll do our best," Mr. Pinter murmured, putting his arm about her and leading her along the landing. "I'm sorry you had to struggle alone. I went after the other fellows, thinking you might be on their boat. When I caught up to them and saw that you weren't, I headed this way. Fortunately, my men arrived at the same time."

"There's something you have to know," she said. "David did not kill Sarah. Richard did. He told me—"

"Yes, we guessed as much. Where is Linley now?"

"I think he's dead. He's still on the island. David stabbed him."

He had done it to save her. And now the only man she had ever loved might die.

Oh God, he must not! If he did, how would she ever go on living without him?

Chapter Twenty-eight

✦

𝒟avid awoke in a sun-drenched room with his leg throbbing like the devil. It took a second for him to realize that he was in his own bed at the estate, wearing only his shirt. How did he get here? All he could remember was staring up at the dark night sky as Charlotte rowed—

"Charlotte," he murmured through a mouth that felt dry as toast.

"Well, well, I see the patient is finally awake."

He swung his gaze toward the decidedly male voice and felt keen disappointment when he spotted Pinter lounging in an arm chair. Where was Charlotte? Had he dreamed that she'd said she would never leave him? And that last part . . . He could swear she'd said she loved him. Though he wasn't sure of that. Everything was fuzzy.

"You've given everyone quite a scare, my lord," Pinter went on. "But you're a very lucky man. If that knife had been an inch to the left, you would never have made it off the island. Mrs. Harris's deft doctoring helped, as well. Your brother-in-law was not so lucky."

"Is he . . ."

"Yes. Quite dead."

"So we'll never know if . . ."

"Actually, we know it all now. Not only did he confess everything to Mrs. Harris, but we caught up to his compatriots, and they confirmed what she said, since they heard the entire conversation. According to Mrs. Harris, Linley argued with your wife and pushed her into the tub, where she hit her head on the edge. When she lost consciousness and sank under, he just stood by and watched her drown."

Scowling, David struggled into a sitting position.

"Here now," Pinter said, leaning forward in alarm, "I don't know if you should be doing that."

"I'm fine," David gritted out, though he was careful to favor his leg as he settled himself. "I want to know everything."

Pinter told him the entire story. It sounded exactly like something Richard would do when cornered, even down to the forged note.

"If he hadn't been so greedy," Pinter finished, "I daresay we would never have known of his crime. But he just had to squeeze more money out of you. And that was his great mistake."

David shook his head, appalled. Such a waste of a life. Richard had always been an impulsive hothead, but to kill his sister and then try to profit from her death . . .

"So we can pronounce this case closed, my lord. And I hope you'll accept the profound apologies of the magistrate's office—" Pinter paused. "I hope you'll accept *my* sincerest apologies. I shouldn't have been so ready to accuse you."

David could afford to be generous, now that he was no longer living under a cloud of suspicion. "You were doing your job. I would have expected no less of the man who set out to find my wife's killer."

"There's a bit more to it than that—but I'll save that tale for another day."

The bedchamber door burst open, and Charlotte

walked in carrying a tray. "The doctor says if we can get him conscious long enough to swallow a little broth, he might—"

She dropped the tray with a cry of joy. "David, you're all right!" Running to the bed, she grabbed his head and showered kisses on his brow, his cheek . . . everywhere except where he wanted them.

"I'll have to get stabbed more often." He cupped her head and pulled her down for a long, lingering kiss that she returned with such enthusiasm that his heart soared.

She drew back blushing, her gaze flitting to Pinter.

Pinter rose. "I believe that's my signal to leave," he said with a chuckle. "Now that I'm sure you're going to live, my lord, I had best get back to London. If you ever need anything . . ."

"You'll be the first man I ask," David answered.

As Pinter slipped out, David gazed up at the woman he adored. Her beautiful eyes were bloodshot, her gown was decidedly indecent without its fichu, and her hair was a rat's nest. She'd never looked lovelier.

He patted the bed. "Sit with me, my love."

"I don't want to hurt you—" she began, but when he tugged her arm rather forcefully, she acquiesced.

As she stretched out beside him on the bed, he drew her against his shoulder. "It appears that you saved my life, looking after my wound and rowing me to land."

She laid her hand on his chest. "It was the least I could do, after you risked your life for me."

That comment made him frown. "And that was the only reason? Because you were grateful?"

"You know it was not," she murmured, lifting her face to his.

The adoration in her eyes made his breath catch in his throat. Even in their youth, she'd never looked at him with such sweet caring.

Perversely, it roused his guilt anew. "I've spent the past week in agony, wanting to explain everything to you better but not being able to because—"

"I know. Mr. Pinter told me about the trap you laid."

He cast her a rueful glance. "It didn't turn out quite how we'd planned."

"Fancy that," she teased, eyes twinkling. "A plan of yours going awry. Who would have thought?"

"It certainly wasn't my only plan that has gone awry of late." Though he was loath to bring it up, he had to know where they stood. "Last night you said you forgave me for the whole Cousin Michael masquerade. Did you mean that?" He held his breath for her answer.

She dropped her gaze. "You hurt me badly, you know."

"I know," he choked out.

"You should have told me the truth—if not right away, then once we were lovers."

"Yes. I have no excuse, and I wasn't fair to you. I was treating you like the girl of eighteen I knew in my youth, and not like the sensible, intelligent creature I knew from our letters."

Oddly enough, that blunt statement made her smile. "Do you know what I spent the past week doing?"

"Cursing my name?"

"Reading your letters."

He blinked. "All of them?"

"All 1,263 of them. Give or take a few."

He wasn't sure what to make of that. "And what did you determine from that?"

"Well, first of all, that I should have guessed who you were from the very first arrogant statement you made," she said dryly.

A chuckle escaped him. "Was I that transparent?"

"Now that I know the truth, yes." She toyed with the buttons on his shirt. "But I also realized how important you had been to the school all these years. And to me. I realized that no matter how your masquerade began, it became an act of true friendship."

He let out a breath. "So you did mean what you said last night about forgiving me," he rasped.

"Yes." Gently, she kissed his jaw, then his lips.

"And what you said about loving me."

"You heard that?" she said, surprise in her voice.

"As if in a dream. I thought I might have imagined it."

"No," she said, a tender smile gracing her lips. "I did say it. I love you, David."

He took his heart in his hands and risked everything. "Does that mean you'll marry me?" When she took a breath, he pressed a finger to her lips and said, "Before you answer, I want you to know that I will take you however I can get you. You can continue to run the school, and I will live there, too, if you'll let me. Mother or Giles can run the estate. Just marry me, sweeting. That's all I want."

A minxish laugh bubbled out of her. "The last thing I need is a school full of young ladies trailing after my husband with adoring looks. You'd have them all in love with you in under a week." When he scowled, she sobered. "You were right, you know. I *was* using the school to protect myself. From men, from life, from you."

She cupped his cheek. "But I don't need that protection anymore. I've discovered that I want to have something else in my life as well. *Someone* else. So as soon as you're well enough, I'll be hiring a headmistress."

Joy coursed through him. At last Charlotte was his! Not for a night or a month or the span of an illicit affair, but for all eternity. "Sweeting, if that means you're agreeing to marry me, I'm well enough right now to leap from this bed and do a jig."

"Don't you dare!" she said, trying not to laugh as she gave him a stern look. "After what I went through to get you to a doctor, I'll stab you myself if you open up your wound."

He laughed, giddy with the thought of finally belonging to Charlotte, of having her belong to him. "I'll refrain from the jig then, considering that you braved the great Thames itself to save me. However did you manage that?"

"By thinking of what I would lose if you didn't live," she said earnestly.

"And what is that?"

"My mind. My heart. My soul."

Overcome with emotion, he kissed her, this time with more leisure. And more heat. When he drew back, it was to ask, "How soon can we be married?"

She arched one eyebrow. "Not until your mourning period is up. I shall not have people thinking—"

His mouth blotted out the rest of her sentence. They kissed deeply, so deeply he was sure she could feel the thumping of his heart beneath her hand.

He tore his lips from hers. "Wrong answer, sweeting. Let's try that again. When can we be married?"

"Now, David—" she began with a frown, but this time when he tried to kiss her, she held back. "I mean it. We are going to do this right."

"You're just tormenting me to repay me for all my machinations," he grumbled. "You're going to spend the next few months driving me insane, parading your lovely self about town, tempting me to madness, and making me eat crow. By the time the wedding comes, I'll be like clay in your hands."

"What a lovely idea," she said smugly.

"Watch it, minx," he murmured as he drew down the sleeve of her bodice. "If you think I'll go six months without bedding you again, you have another think coming."

Her eyes gleamed. "Well, my lesson on that subject *has* always been 'wed him before you bed him.'"

"You already broke that rule." He pressed a kiss to the slope of her bosom, then eased her gown down more when her breathing quickened. "Besides, I like your other lesson better."

"What other lesson?"

"Love him before you wed him. As much as he loves you." He gazed into her eyes, his heart full. "Because that alone takes care of everything."

With a smile, she looped her arms about his neck. "I do believe you're right, my love."

Epilogue

❦

*I*n the end, David got his way, and they were married within two months. Not because of his powers of persuasion, or even his prowess in the bedchamber. Charlotte discovered she was carrying his child. *That* consideration trumped all others.

Nor could Charlotte regret the hasty ceremony, now that they were enjoying their wedding breakfast on the new grounds of the school, surrounded by family, friends, and students. She would never have survived six months living apart from David. Besides, whenever they were in a room together, the whole world could see they were in love. There hadn't seemed much point in delaying the inevitable. Especially since the papers had finally lost interest in the story of Sarah's murder and had gone on to other scandals.

Of course, the Linleys had been hurt by their haste. Coming on the heels of losing both a daughter and a son, they were reeling from their pain. They did not begrudge David his happiness, but they did not seem in any hurry to embrace it, either. Charlotte wasn't sure if that could ever change. She suspected it would be a long time before they came to terms with the fact that their son-in-law had killed their son, who had admitted to killing their daughter.

"So where are you going for your honeymoon trip?" David's friend Anthony Dalton, Lord Norcourt, asked.

Beside him was his wife, Madeline, a former teacher at the school. She held the couple's newborn son, Toby, in her arms, and Charlotte had already made a fool of herself talking baby talk to him while David teased her for it.

"We're going to Italy, actually." David tucked Charlotte's hand in the crook of his arm. "It was Charlotte's idea. She's always wanted to see Venice, and she claims she'll be all right if the ship is large enough. But I suspect we'll spend most of the voyage closeted in our cabin."

"Closeted in a cabin with your lovely wife," Anthony said. "Whatever will you do for entertainment?"

David and his friends laughed, while their wives rolled their eyes.

"We invited the newlyweds to visit us in the Highlands," said Lady Venetia, a former pupil of Charlotte's, "but we couldn't tempt them."

"And no wonder," David's friend Lord Stoneville quipped. "Winter in the Highlands is ghastly."

"It's not so bad," Lady Venetia's Highlander husband, Sir Lachlan Ross, put in. "You haven't lived until you've seen the Highlands covered in snow."

Major Winter strode up to the group with his wife in tow. He was scowling at Sir Lachlan. "Have we met before today, sir?" he asked. "Your brogue sounds very familiar."

A strange expression came over Sir Lachlan's face, and he shot his wife an oddly panicked glance.

"I can't imagine when you would have met," Venetia said hastily.

David's cousin frowned. "I could swear I heard that voice when I was in Scotland—"

"I daresay we Highlanders all sound alike," Sir Lachlan broke in.

Venetia glanced across the grounds. "If you'll excuse us, it looks as if our son Ian is heading for the road. Come, Lachlan, we'd best go catch him before he gets into trouble."

They hurried off, making Charlotte wonder what *that* was all about. The only Highlanders Major Winter had met in Scotland were the masked ones who'd kidnapped him and Amelia years ago. And they were all dead. Or so she'd heard.

"Mrs. Harris . . . beg pardon . . . Lady Kirkwood, is it true what I just heard about Samuel Pritchard?" asked another voice as two couples walked up to join the group.

The man who'd spoken was another of David's friends, the Duke of Foxmoor. He had his wife, Louisa, in tow, and walking beside them was his cousin Colin Hunt, the Earl of Monteith, and the earl's wife, Eliza, another former pupil of the school.

"Colin tells me," Foxmoor went on, "that Pritchard's scheme to sell Rockhurst fell through."

Charlotte laughed. "Indeed it did. The licensing board decided that it might not be in Richmond's best interest to have a racecourse so close to their lofty residents. Once Mr. Watson heard he wouldn't be able to get the license he needed, he backed out of their deal."

"So then Pritchard came crawling to me asking if I wanted to buy it," David added. "After months with no buyer and his prime deal falling through, he was growing a bit short of funds."

"David considered it," Charlotte said, "but we like Lord Stoneville's property so much better."

"You ought to," Stoneville grumbled. "Damned good piece of property. If not for my grandmother's nonsense,

I wouldn't even—" Realizing that every eye was on him, he scowled. "Kirkwood paid me a decent price, never you fear."

"Considering the sorts of activities that used to go on here," Foxmoor remarked, "the neighborhood must be thrilled to exchange Stoneville for a girl's school."

Everyone laughed. Stoneville rolled his eyes.

"I still don't understand why you had to leave the old property," Louisa said, "Surely Cousin Michael would have allowed you—"

"As it turns out, he did not own it," Charlotte said smoothly. "He only had a lien on it for the rents, and that was about to end. Mr. Pritchard owned it, and since it's entailed, we could never have bought the place." She cast David a teasing smile. "My husband felt it was time that the school had some permanency, so he didn't even countenance Mr. Pritchard's offer to continue renting it. And then with Cousin Michael dying, there seemed no point to it anyway."

"Cousin Michael died?" Eliza exclaimed, with the others joining in the shock.

"Yes. A few days ago." Charlotte ignored how Amelia and Major Winter smiled. "It was very sad. Mr. Baines was beside himself with grief over it."

Charlotte was glad she and David had decided to let Cousin Michael die a natural death. Telling everyone his true identity would have meant resurrecting their painful past together, and the last thing they needed was another scandal. Only Amelia and Major Winter knew the truth.

And Charles Godwin, who was noticeably absent from their wedding celebration. He had taken the news of her impending marriage harder than expected, so she could forgive him for not attending. She only hoped he would find someone else to love one day.

"So will we ever know who your cousin really was?" Foxmoor asked.

"I'm afraid it looks to remain a mystery. Mr. Baines still refuses to reveal it." Charlotte squeezed David's arm. "Though I shall always be grateful to him for his years of friendship and kindness."

A sudden ruckus near one of the tables caught everyone's attention. Terence was trying valiantly—and unsuccessfully—to subdue a group of squabbling children. The parents rushed over to pull their young ones away from each other and settle disputes. Stoneville took the opportunity to go refill his glass. That left Charlotte and David alone for the first time since the ceremony.

David gazed over at the melee. "See what we have to look forward to?" he murmured, nudging her belly meaningfully.

That was something else they hadn't told anyone about. It wasn't exactly the thing in either of their circles to marry with a babe in one's belly. Not to mention that the last thing her students needed was *that* sort of example. The new headmistress might be in place already, but her young ladies still regarded Charlotte as their true guide. She still ran the teas for heiresses, after all.

"After everything we have gone through, I think we can handle whatever our children throw at us," she answered.

David was silent a moment. "Do you ever wonder how our lives might have been different if your letter had never been published? If I'd received it and come to demand the truth from you, and thus had found out about Giles? Might we now have been married for eighteen years?"

"Perhaps. Or perhaps I would never really have trusted you, stung by that incident." She squeezed his arm. "Besides, I think I got to know you better because of your masquerade as Cousin Michael than I might have while playing the role of wife to a lord of the manor."

"Sounds to me as if you miss Cousin Michael," he said, an edge to his voice.

"I confess I will always have a soft spot for him." She grinned at him. "Why? Don't tell me you're jealous of yourself."

He looked pensive. "I was. That day when we looked at properties and you waxed eloquent about his virtues, I almost hated the man. Especially since I knew he didn't deserve the accolades you gave him."

"That's not true," she said gently. "Without him, I might never have realized my dream of a girl's school. And I would have lost something vital to who I am. I learned a great deal from our letters."

"So did I."

"Oh? And what did *you* learn, sir?"

"Why, how to seduce a prim and proper schoolmistress."

Tugging her into a nearby copse, David backed her against a tree. It had been nearly a week since they'd made love—and judging from the quickening of her husband's breath as he leaned in close, he was as aware of that as she.

He flashed her a decidedly wolfish smile. "I learned how to read between the lines. And what I read taught me how to make you burn."

"Well, then," she said as she pulled his head down to hers. "Thank God for Cousin Michael."

New York Times Bestselling Author

Sabrina Jeffries

QUEEN OF THE SEXY REGENCY ROMANCE

The Summer of the School for Heiresses

Parlor Games / Regency Trivia
Excerpts / Author Video

**Monthly Drawing for $50
National Department Store
Gift Card / April-Aug. 2009**
(One prize each month for 5 months
— a prize fit for an heiress!)

**Inside scoop on two new
Heiress books for 2009**

Summer 2009

Join the
fun at:
www.SabrinaJeffries.com

True love
is timeless with
historical romances from
Pocket Books!

A Malory novel

Johanna Lindsey

NO CHOICE BUT SEDUCTION

He'd stop at nothing to make her love him.
But should she surrender to his bold charms?

Liz Carlyle

Tempted All Night

When deception meets desire, even the most
careful lady can be swayed by a scoundrel....

Julia London

HIGHLAND SCANDAL

Which is a London rakehell more likely to survive—
a hanging, or a handfasting to a spirited Highland lass?

Jane Feather

A HUSBAND'S WICKED WAYS

When a spymaster proposes marriage as a cover,
a lovely young woman discovers the danger—and
delight—of risking everything for love.

Available wherever books are sold or at www.simonandschuster.com

POCKET BOOKS
A Division of Simon & Schuster
A CBS COMPANY

POCKET STAR BOOKS
A Division of Simon & Schuster
A CBS COMPANY